SO MUCH TO LEARN

They stared at each other in the moonlight. It seemed that neither of them was breathing—that perhaps even time itself had stopped. He stretched out a hand to her and she took it with no hesitation, accepting the gift and offering one in return.

He drew her slowly into his arms, against his big, hard body. She felt the heat of him, the power carefully contained. And as she arched against him, tilting her head back to look up at him, she knew that the world *was* spinning.

Everything about him was so very different from anything she'd ever known; it was all wholly new and wondrous. Instead of touching her lips, his mouth trailed lightly along her cheek. His tongue brushed her ear and then moved oh-so-slowly down the sensitive column of her neck. A soft, strangled sound poured from her, a plea for him to claim the lips that parted in anticipation.

And when he did, she met his hungry demands with her own, learning quickly to parry the thrusts of his tongue, shocked and amazed that there could be such pleasure in it. How could her body have kept this secret from her, and what other secrets might be laid bare by this sensual onslaught?

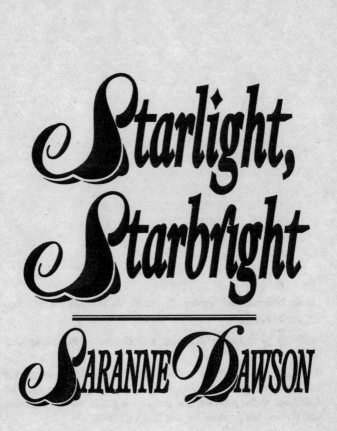

Starlight, Starbright

SARANNE DAWSON

LOVE SPELL BOOKS NEW YORK CITY

Leisure Entertainment Service Co., Inc. (LESCO Distribution Group)

A LESCO Edition

Published by special arrangement with Dorchester Publishing Co., Inc.

If you purchased this book without a cover you should be aware that this book is stolen property. It was reported as "unsold and destroyed" to the publisher and neither the author nor the publisher has received any payment for this "stripped book."

Copyright © 1999 by Saranne Hoover

All rights reserved. No part of this book may be reproduced or transmitted in any form or by any electronic or mechanical means, including photocopying, recording or by any information storage and retrieval system, without the written permission of the publisher, except where permitted by law.

Printed in the United States of America.

Prologue

He watched from behind a thick clump of berry-laden bushes, well hidden within the shadows of ancient trees. Their laughter was carried to him on a warm spring breeze that also brought the sweet fragrance of flowers from the gardens that ringed the play area.

Gardens were everywhere on this world: in play areas like this, along the winding cobblestoned streets, in window boxes on the tidy stone cottages, even in unexpected places deep in the woods that covered most of the land.

The large group of children were practicing ritual dances under the watchful eyes of several adults. There was a fey quality to them that intrigued him—at least in the case of the females. The males were another matter. He and his shipmates sneered at them in private and made coarse jokes. Even as adults, it was sometimes impossible to tell males from females. It was unnatural.

From time to time, his gaze strayed to encompass the others, but most of the time, he watched *her*. He'd been fascinated by that small, heart-shaped face and that pale golden hair from the first moment he'd seen the artist's rendering of her.

The children leapt and dipped and swayed and pirouetted, keeping perfect time with the rhythms of the drum and the flute. Perhaps it was only because he was concentrating on her, but it seemed to him that she was the best of all. Her slender body moved like a whirling dervish, then slowed to a sensuality far beyond her years—and probably beyond her understanding as well. Having now seen her, they all agreed that she was probably only ten or eleven, though with these people, it was hard to be sure.

He wondered if the commander would order them to take her. They'd never taken one so young before, and he knew that the High Priestess was opposed to the idea. Still, she had admitted that the girl possessed enormous talent despite her youth. She must have, or the Trezhellas would never have "heard" her.

Something about this place made him slightly uneasy, and he was sure he wasn't alone in his feeling. Until the High Priestess had informed them about the girl and then pointed the way, they hadn't even known that this world existed, even though it was in a sector they'd explored before.

The world they now called BB-G42 had probably escaped their notice because it lay hidden among its much larger neighbors, gas giants that were totally inhospitable to life. And in fact, there was some disagreement among them over whether or not it actually *was* a planet. Some thought it might be a moon that had been captured by all three of its giant neighbors, even though such an occurrence was unheard of.

It was a world of unparalleled beauty, that much was for certain. Furthermore, they had all felt, from the moment they set foot on it, that they had traveled back in time to a far simpler place. The inhabitants lived a primitive life, to be sure, but certainly not a life of hardship or deprivation, as had been the case centuries ago on his own world and on the others his people now ruled.

He thought—but hadn't said to the others—that there was something strangely appealing about that simplicity. Why he should think such a thing he couldn't begin to fathom—but there it was. However, being young and very ambitious, he kept those thoughts to himself.

Suddenly, he felt a small vibration against his wrist and glanced down to see that he was being summoned back to the landing spot. He cast one last glance at her, frowning. Had the commander reached a decision already? They'd intended to spend a few more days here, studying this world before deciding whether or not to take her.

He backed carefully away from the bushes and faded into the thick forest, where the leafy canopy overhead had created a world of permanent twilight. Then he switched on the homing signal and made his way back to the landing spot.

Chapter One

Serena sat down on the soft grass and lifted her face to the warm spring breeze. It was one of those teasing sorts of wind—there one moment and gone the next. Overhead, the sky was a soft, gentle blue, and the disc of Meiea a creamy white, streaked with black. Soon it would be invisible, as the sun reached its zenith.

Not far away, the children played their games, grateful for the respite from the rigors of their dance training. She smiled, remembering her own school days. They were not so very far in the past, and yet they now seemed very long ago.

The other teachers had gathered in the shade, at a table set amidst the fragrant blooms of the more delicate flowers that could not withstand the glare of the sun. She thought about joining them and had just started to rise to her feet when she saw Trenek come around the side of the school, pause, and then start toward her.

She sank down again and watched him as he made his way to her, pausing briefly to speak to the children and then toss a brightly colored ball high into the air for one of them to catch. And as always when she saw him, she felt that secret guilt, that certainty that something was wrong with her.

Why couldn't she love him with all her heart, as he did her? As others loved. She *did* love him, but it seemed that her love was a surface sort of thing, like the bright, gleaming top of a deep pond. But down inside, below that surface, there was nothing. She had dived deep into ponds and she knew there was much there, wondrous things. But beneath the surface of her love for Trenek, there was nothing.

She hated her thoughts and sometimes, as now, hated herself for thinking them. Love was all-important to her people: love for their blessed world and love for each other. And she *did* love it all. All but Trenek, her betrothed, who should be the most beloved of all to her—and he wasn't.

It wasn't as though there was someone else to lay claim to that love. If there had been, then she wouldn't have agreed to marry Trenek. No, the problem was clearly with her.

He had nearly reached her when suddenly everything faded to black. It lasted for no more than a second or two, as it always did, but in that brief time, she felt it again: a terrible vastness beyond her comprehension and voices whispering to her in a language she couldn't understand. Women's voices—she was sure of that, but of nothing else.

"Serena?"

The blackness vanished as quickly as it had come, and she saw that Trenek now stood before her, his lean face creased with worry.

"Have you had another spell?" he asked as he sank down beside her and took one of her hands in his.

She nodded, not wanting to talk about it. She'd talked about

11

the spells too many times, and all to no purpose. No one knew what caused them—not even their best healers. Nor did anyone know of such a thing happening to others.

"You heard the voices again, too?"

She nodded. She *always* heard the voices; that was nothing new. She'd been having these spells for years now, ever since she was ten years old, and they never varied: the sense of unimaginable distance and the soft murmur of voices.

"Maybe they *are* speaking our language," Trenek said carefully. "You said that you could barely hear them."

"Yes, but I know it's not our language. The sound is different. The . . . rhythm is different."

"It frightens people when you say that," Trenek said with faint reproof. "It makes some people worry that there could be others out there somewhere." He waved a hand toward the heavens.

"I know that, but would you have me *lie* about it?"

"No, of course not," he said hurriedly, squeezing her hand affectionately. "But it *is* troubling to think that there could be others out there."

"I've never understood why that should seem so troubling. What if it's true? They haven't bothered us. How could they, if they live on another world somewhere?"

"It's the Legend, love. Some people fear that they will come and take away our world."

"That's nonsense, and you know it, Trenek. I don't see how you can possibly believe such a thing. Even if they exist and they find some way to come here, how could they take away our whole world?"

"I don't know," he admitted.

"Then stop fretting about what can't happen. Besides, *I've* never claimed that those voices come from another world. That idea came from others. For all I know, I'm making them up and they exist only in my mind."

"But why would you do such a thing?"

"I *wouldn't* do it—not deliberately. Maybe I'm just . . . defective, like those who are born without sight or without hearing."

He merely nodded, but she could tell he didn't believe her. The truth was that she didn't believe it, either. The idea that the voices came from another world hadn't been hers originally, but once the suggestion was made, it had felt right to her.

That night, a lovely, soft spring night, Serena sat in the small garden behind her cottage. She'd moved there only weeks before from her family home, after the cottage was vacated by a woman grown too frail to live alone. In less than three weeks, Trenek would join her there, after their wedding. In the meantime, she was working hard to create a home for them. Trenek was, too. He came over every evening to work on the cottage—painting the interior walls and applying new mortar between some of the stones.

They were lucky to have drawn this place. Most newlyweds had to live in the new houses at the edge of town, houses that lacked the wonderful patina of age and the invisible glow of generations of happy families.

They'd worked hard on the garden, too. The old woman had been letting it go a bit as her health failed. No garden was ever truly abandoned, but still, it had required a lot of work.

Her mind still on the spell she'd had earlier, Serena studied the dark, star-studded heavens. Could there really be other people out there? Did they live on the stars? Her people believed the stars were nothing more than holes in the fabric of the universe that allowed the great light from beyond to leak through. So how could someone live on them?

Then she noticed something moving between the stars with a faint light of its own. She frowned as she followed it. In the Lesvarck Quarter to come, there were always showers of

13

stars—times when they seemed to burst apart and rain down on her world, though nothing was ever found. No one had an explanation for that—or at least none that made sense. But this wasn't the Lesvarck Quarter, and there was only that one faint light, still moving among the stars and seeming to grow brighter.

She wished that Trenek were still there to see it, though perhaps he was seeing it—or others were. Probably not many would be seeing it, though. Most people would be in bed, or at least inside, by now.

She took her eyes away from the object for long enough to glance at the homes of her nearest neighbors. Their houses were dark; they were mostly elderly and went to bed early.

Then she looked back at the heavens, and a startled cry escaped her lips. She'd thought that she might not be able to find the object again, but it was much brighter now, and still moving in a wide arc through the dark sky. She realized that if it continued on its present path, it would be lost to her view soon. The land was hilly here and her new home lay in a small, deep pocket between two hills.

She leapt to her feet and ran around the side of the cottage, then along the cobblestoned road that led up the hill and down into the next cluster of homes. The town sprawled over several miles because her people preferred to build in the low places and leave the hilltops as forest parks.

As she ran along the road, she tried to see the light, but the trees pressed too closely and it was lost to view. Finally, out of breath, she reached the summit, then cried out again as she saw it. It was even brighter now, and though it must be a trick of the night, it seemed to her to be coming down.

Then, abruptly, it vanished. She stood there, frowning. Even though she couldn't see them in the darkness, she knew the mountains were there: the tallest mountains on her world. It might have gone down beyond them.

It must have done that, she thought. She'd never heard of a star simply vanishing like that—not when it had been so brilliant. It was true that in the Lesvarck showers, they vanished, but they did it by simply growing fainter and fainter until they could no longer be seen.

Serena retraced her steps back to the cottage, walking slowly as she thought about what she'd seen. Perhaps someone would have an explanation. She would ask around tomorrow.

Commander Darian Vondrak's peripheral vision kept snagging on all that braid. He wasn't quite used to it yet, though most of those under his command would have said that he was born to it.

The thick, winding braids of pure gold crisscrossed his broad shoulders and covered most of his upper arms, contrasting sharply with his black uniform. The fabric had been specially created for the Space Fleet: a densely woven and matte-finished fabric that attempted to re-create the utter darkness of space.

He was seated at the very center of the control room, in a comfortable chair that swiveled in a complete circle to afford him an easy view of the large, circular "brain" of the spacecraft. All around him, men came and went or sat before display screens. Except for takeoffs and landings, the huge ship in fact required very little of its human cargo. If anything *did* go wrong—which was quite rare—Darian and everyone else would be notified immediately by the Voice, a computer-generated and preternaturally calm voice that would tell them where the problem lay. Darian thought privately that the Voice's creators might at least have put some emotion into it. However calm its tone, it was still announcing imminent danger.

But since none of them, including Darian himself, liked to be considered unnecessary, they remained in the control room most of their waking hours.

A sudden "bleep" from the fuel display drew his attention. They had now used up their second fuel pod. But there was no cause for concern. In point of fact, the cosmic winds had been kind to them; they would have fuel to spare on this journey.

He settled back in the chair, his mind turning to the mission itself. More than fifteen standard years had passed since he'd come this way. In fact, no one had been able to venture into this particular quadrant since that first, aborted mission.

Darian could still recall it quite clearly, perhaps because it had been his first long space journey—and also because of the world itself. He remembered that he'd been watching the girl when the signal had come to return to the landing spot. At the time, he'd wondered if the commander would decide to take her. She'd been very young, despite the apparent strength of her talent.

But that question had never been answered. When he reached the landing spot, he'd found a huge electromagnetic storm forming in the area. They had to leave at once, or risk not having sufficient fuel to return to base. Such storms were the bane of all space travelers, and even though technology had much improved over the past fifteen years, they were still a potent threat.

The commander had left a monitor at the outer rim of that system, and the experts had begun a long study of the pattern of the great storms. No one wanted to venture into this sector again without at least some degree of assurance that the storms could be predicted.

And curious though the one inhabited world in that system was, it held no real interest for Darian's people, the Ulatans. The inhabitants of that tiny, distant world were far too primitive to pose any threat to their plans.

And yet, here they were, heading back to that system at a time believed by the experts to be as storm-free as possible— and it was all because of one girl.

Not a girl any longer, he reminded himself—a woman now.

He still tended to think of her as the child he'd seen fifteen years ago.

The High Priestess said that the girl had unusual talent, that even without training she could reach out over greater distances than any Trezhella ever had.

That was why they needed her—and more like her, though none had as yet been found. Plans were being made to push deeper and deeper into unexplored space, but the lack of Trezhellas powerful enough to accompany them was one of the chief stumbling blocks.

The truth was that Darian, like all the other men who explored space, didn't like the Trezhellas, and he resented his dependency on them. The Trezhellas were unnatural—beyond scientific logic—and the men who had conquered space were, first and foremost, scientists.

He felt the vibration against his wrist and glanced down at the time display. His sleep period was approaching. He would have to cut it short because landing was mere hours away.

He turned over command to one of his lieutenants and went to his cabin, his thoughts already turning to the delicate task of finding and capturing the woman.

Nobody else appeared to have seen the bright, moving star. Serena wasn't really surprised, given the lateness of the hour and people's lack of interest in the heavens.

But her father had reminded her of a similar occurrence many years ago that had been witnessed by several people. She'd been only a child at the time and had paid it scant attention. No one had found any evidence that the star had fallen to the ground, but then, no one had really looked, either.

Because it was such a splendid day, the children were let out of school at midday, which meant that her work as their teacher also ended then. She wandered over to Trenek's home, where

17

she found him at work in the large building behind the house. Trenek's family were carpenters and furniture makers, and he was bent over what would become a table leg, carving the intricate design into the wood. The other three legs had already been completed.

She sat down on the floor to watch him. This one was for their home, and he had outdone himself, creating a table whose legs resembled twisted vines with tiny flowers: a beautiful replication of the shonza vines that grew on trees deep in the forest.

As he worked, she told him about the moving star. Since he was three years older than she was, he recalled that other time. But like the others she'd talked to, he showed little interest in trying to discover if the object had, in fact, landed somewhere.

"Why isn't anyone interested?" she complained. "If it did come down, it would be a wondrous thing."

"It would also mean that we've been wrong about the stars being nothing more than holes in the fabric of the heavens," he pointed out. "And people are comfortable with their beliefs."

"Are you?" she asked curiously.

He looked up from his work, studying her in silence for a moment. He often did that, and she had the feeling that he was trying to divine her thoughts so that he wouldn't say anything to displease her. He'd never actually said so, but Serena suspected that he found her as difficult as others did—or as different.

"I've never thought much about it," he said in that careful way he had. "But I guess that if we've been wrong, I would want to know that."

She doubted it, but didn't say so. She knew he was only trying to please her. "Then let's try to find it," she said, flinging the words out as a challenge. "I don't have to be back at school for three days."

said nothing as he looked around him. In other parts of

18

the large building, his father and two brothers were busy at work. Their skills were always in demand.

"All right," he said finally, smiling at her. "By the time you get some provisions together, I'll be finished with this. And Mother will be happy if we can bring back some herbs." His mother was a healer, and at this time of year, her supplies would be running low.

Serena thanked him and left, eager to be off on this adventure. She was glad that Trenek was going with her, although she'd been quite prepared to go alone. In fact, she'd often done so. Her mother complained that she liked her own company too much, and both her parents worried that she'd have an accident out there in the mountains. But she'd never felt frightened; she liked the vastness of the forest.

This time, however, they couldn't complain, since Trenek would be going with her. He'd never gone before, and it pleased her to know that he was willing to make such a sacrifice for her.

And just maybe they'd find a fallen star. She smiled at the thought, imagining a dazzling object just lying there in the dark forest.

"I hope that you don't really believe we're going to find something," Trenek said, turning in the saddle to face her. "Even if something *did* land, how can we hope to find it in all this?"

He waved an arm around them as they sat astride their horses on a hilltop. Beneath them was a narrow valley with a swift-running stream in its center, and beyond that lay the tall mountains. They had been following a trail carved out by the migratory herds of elk and deer, and she could see it winding its way from the little stream up into the mountains.

"It must be quite large," she pointed out, having given this matter considerable thought. "After all, it was very far away when I saw it. And since it has light, it must be fire of some sort. If it came down, it might have set fire to the forest."

Trenek shook his head in amusement. "You really believe in this, don't you?"

She bristled. "Well, if you don't, you should have stayed home."

"But then you would have gone alone," he pointed out as they started down the hillside.

By day's end, they were deep into the mountains, where darkness fell early. The trail more or less followed a small stream, and Trenek said they should soon find a campsite for the night. Serena nodded distractedly, her thoughts still on that star. Now that she was actually in the mountains, she was beginning to doubt their ability to find anything.

She tilted her head back and peered up through the tall trees. The sun was less than an hour from setting, she guessed, and already the sky was taking on that sunset glow. Trenek said something and she was about to lower her gaze when suddenly she saw movement just above the treetops.

She frowned. Whatever it was, it was gone as quickly as it had appeared. Logic told her it must have been a flock of birds, but the image burned into her brain denied that. Still, what else could move so swiftly and silently up there?

She said nothing to Trenek as they set up camp in the spot he had chosen. He would only tease her about her imagination, or maybe he'd suggest that her "star" was still up there, looking for a place to land.

It couldn't have been the star, of course; it was far too small for that. But she still could not reconcile what she'd seen with what her brain told her it must have been.

They ate their meal as the sky turned briefly to a fiery red, then darkened. By the time they had finished, the deep blackness in the forest had settled around them. Trenek insisted upon building up the fire. Serena smiled inwardly, knowing that he was uneasy. If she had been there alone, she wouldn't have bothered with a fire at all because she liked the darkness.

It was, she supposed, yet another indication of her strangeness. She'd always been fascinated by the all-encompassing blackness of nights in the mountains beneath the great trees that kept the silvered light of the stars from touching the land. She didn't know why this was so, but sometimes she thought it might have something to do with the vast blackness of her visions.

Though still quite comfortable, the night was definitely cooler in the mountains. Trenek sat down next to her and wrapped a blanket around their shoulders. They began to talk about their wedding, only weeks away. It would be a grand affair, with dancing and feasting and many gifts. Both their families had despaired of them ever marrying, so they were determined to make the wedding memorable.

Serena was twenty-six, well past the age at which most people married, and Trenek was three years older. He had made it plain years ago that she was the one for him, and then had waited patiently for her to agree. They'd known each other all their lives, having grown up in the same neighborhood.

After a while, their conversation was interrupted by kisses as they held each other and watched the sparks from the campfire spiral up into the night. Serena could feel his eagerness to make love to her, but of course they wouldn't do that until they were married. She was eager too, but she suspected it might be for a different reason. While Trenek seemed to have a need, she had only a growing curiosity. What would it be like to lie naked with him in their marriage bed? Was it really as pleasant as she'd heard?

In truth, what she'd heard was that it wasn't all that wonderful at first, but got much better with practice. No doubt they would quickly learn to please each other.

* * *

"We'll have to turn back tomorrow," Trenek said.

Serena nodded glumly. It was late afternoon, and they'd been riding through the mountains all day without seeing anything at all unusual. The narrow trail they'd been following rose ahead of them, climbing from a deep ravine toward the mountaintop. She had traveled this trail before and knew that it would climb to the very top of one of the highest mountains. She suggested that they camp there, and then begin the return journey in the morning.

"Did you really expect to find something?" Trenek asked curiously.

She shrugged, not quite willing to admit to her foolishness. And at this point, chasing after a fallen star *did* seem to be the height of foolishness.

After stopping to fill their water sacks from the stream, they began the long, slow climb up the mountainside. The trail was very narrow—so narrow that they were forced to ride single-file. Huge ancient trees, newly leafed, formed a canopy over the trail, casting the ground beneath them into deep shadow.

Though she loved this great forest, Serena was paying it little attention now as she wondered why she had insisted on making this journey. Somehow, in a way she couldn't begin to understand, it seemed to be connected to her visions: the blackness of the heavens and her sense during the vision of unimaginable vastness out there.

"Serena!" Trenek's voice was low and urgent—and frightened.

She was riding ahead of him and she turned quickly in the saddle, only to find Trenek staring up through the trees, his mouth agape. She too looked up—and caught one brief glimpse of something moving away rapidly, just above the treetops.

When she turned back to Trenek, he hadn't moved. Although

there was nothing to be seen now, he was still staring open-mouthed, as though in a trance.

"What did you see?" she asked, maneuvering her horse so that she faced him. Had he seen the same thing she'd seen yesterday?

He lowered his head slowly, then shook it vigorously. "I . . . nothing. It must have been a flock of birds."

"Are you certain?" she asked unnecessarily. The doubt was there in his voice.

"What else could it have been?" he demanded sharply.

Serena didn't take offense at his tone because she recognized in it the same feeling she'd had. "I saw the same thing yesterday. I didn't tell you because I thought you'd laugh at me."

"But what else could it be?" he asked again, though in a softer tone.

"I don't know—but I don't believe they were birds. I just tried to convince myself that was what it was."

"I think we should turn back now. We can camp down in the ravine."

Serena stared at him, realizing that he was badly frightened. Strangely enough, it hadn't occurred to her to be scared; instead, she'd been merely curious.

"Be sensible, Trenek. We both know there's nothing here that could harm us. I'm going on to the top of the mountain. Maybe we can see them again—if not today, then in the morning. We'll be able to see for miles in all directions up there."

For a moment, she thought he was going to argue with her, but then he gave her a slightly shamed look and nodded. They continued on their way, both of them scanning the treetops as they climbed higher.

The mountaintop was broad and flat, with only a few trees but many shrubs and berry bushes that were now covered with clusters of fragrant white blossoms. As soon as they emerged from beneath the forest canopy, they both stopped and studied the sky. The lowering sun was behind them now, and the color had leaked from the sky. The pale disc of Meiea hovered directly above them. A lone eagle floated in the sky, then vanished.

"It must have been the eagle," Trenek said, breaking the silence between them.

"What I saw was too big to have been a bird," she replied, still peering at the empty sky.

They found a patch of sweet grass amidst the shrubs and bushes and turned the tired horses loose to graze. Trenek began to set up their camp, staying close to the tree line. Serena walked through the bushes to the very edge of the mountaintop.

The last rays of the sun sparkled on a small lake far below to her left. She turned in that direction—and froze.

On the far side of the lake was a clearing—and in that clearing was something that didn't belong there. She stared, willing her eyes to bring it into focus. But the distance was too great. All she could see was a large object, dull gray in color, long and slender in shape—rather like the long boats used for fishing and sometimes for transportation from town to town. But unlike a boat, it appeared to be closed. And when she squinted and concentrated, she thought she could see movement all around it: tiny figures that were little more than dots.

She continued to stare, fascinated, question after question tumbling through her bedazzled brain. Could those figures be people? Was the object transportation of some sort? The only thing she was certain of at this point was that they couldn't be *her* people. No one lived out here in the mountains, and very few ever ventured this far from the towns. And even if they had, why would they bring a boat over the mountains? The color of the boat was wrong, too. Her people painted their boats in bright colors.

She heard a sound behind her, but said nothing as Trenek came to join her. Instead, she waited to hear what he would say when he saw it.

"What . . . ?" Trenek fell silent, and she turned to see him staring at the lake, his mouth once again hanging open in amazement.

He said nothing more, and so it was left to her to say it. "Those are not our people down there."

"How can you be sure they're even people?" he asked, still not taking his eyes off them. "They could be animals. It's too far to tell."

"Yes," she agreed, "they *could* be animals, but what about that *thing?* No animal made that."

They argued, neither of them able to take their eyes off it as the daylight faded. Trenek suggested that it could be nothing more than a huge, strangely shaped rock. Serena told him that she'd been here before—and had once even gone down to the lake. The object wasn't there then, and rocks didn't just appear suddenly.

It grew darker still, and then they could see a faint bluish glow near the object. The figures became mere shadows, clustered now around it. Was it some sort of strange campfire?

When night fell and the glow was extinguished, they retreated to their campsite. Trenek said that they'd better not light a fire, and Serena agreed. She still felt more curiosity than fear, but a small dose of caution had been added to the mix now.

"We need to get closer," she told Trenek, breaking a long silence. "The trail continues down the mountain, and there are several places where we should be able to see it better."

"I think we should go back and tell the others."

"They won't believe us," Serena stated firmly. "If *I* had come back with such a tale, you wouldn't have believed *me*."

"But there are two of us," he persisted. "They'd *have* to believe us."

"All right, let's suppose they do and a group comes back here. They could be gone by then."

"Gone where?" he asked nervously.

"Gone back to wherever they came from."

"But where could that be?" Trenek demanded, sounding, she thought, rather like a child in need of reassurance.

"I think they came here from another world," she stated, giving voice to the notion that had been hiding in her mind for some time.

"Another world?" he echoed disbelievingly.

"What other explanation is there? We know they aren't our people."

Serena awoke in the first pale light of early dawn, surprised to find that she'd slept at all. Then she wondered if it had all been nothing more than a particularly vivid dream. Trenek slept beside her, snoring softly.

She got up, wrapping a blanket around her to ward off the damp chill. She saw the fire that Trenek had built but never lit. It wasn't a dream. Leaving him there, she walked over to the edge of the cliff. The valley was filled with a thick fog. She went back to the campsite and gathered together a cold meal of bread and fruit and a bit of cheese, then returned to the cliff's edge to wait for the fog to lift. Trenek was still sleeping soundly.

The sun rose above a distant mountain. Slowly, the fog began to dissipate, revealing the valley floor directly below her. But it lingered by the lake, blocking her view of the spot where the strange object and the figures had been.

Serena wondered if it would still be there, then wondered if she *wanted* it to be there. And if it *was* there, should they risk being seen by going down there? And was there a connection between what was down there and what they'd both seen in the air? Certainly they hadn't seen that strange craft, which in any event couldn't possibly fly. But what was the likelihood that there was no connection? How could there possibly be *two* strange things out here?

26

Trenek awoke and joined her, his gaze going immediately to the fog-shrouded lake. Then they both watched and waited in silence as a breeze sprang up and the fog began to shift. Several times, they thought they could see something in the fog, but they couldn't be sure.

And then suddenly, they *did* see something. Three figures rose from the fog into the clear air, then moved away quickly to the southwest. Serena and Trenek stared at them and then at each other.

"They were *people!*" Serena cried. Before they vanished, they had come slightly closer, and she was certain she'd seen human forms—or nearly human. They seemed to have deformed backs.

Trenek swallowed hard before finally nodding. "They had arms and legs, at least," he said reluctantly.

"We have to go down there! Or at least get close enough to see them better. There were more than three, so some of them must have stayed behind."

She had turned to him, but now he took her arm and pointed behind her. "Look! Here come more of them!"

Three more figures rose through the rapidly dissipating fog, and this time they were coming straight toward them. Trenek pulled her to her feet and they both ran for the woods. Then, concealed beneath the trees, they watched. But the figures must have turned, because they saw nothing more.

"Were there more than six down there, do you think?" she asked, trying to recall how many figures they'd seen the day before.

"I don't know. Let's go back, Serena. We need to tell the others."

"We'll have more to tell them if we at least try to get closer," she pointed out.

Trenek was reluctant, but when Serena stated that she would go down there with or without him, he followed her to the trail that led down the mountainside.

27

Deep in the forest, they couldn't see any of the valley, but Serena remembered that there was a sort of lookout farther down the mountain—certainly close enough for them to get a better look at the object, and to see if any of the people remained.

Not people, she told herself. *They* can't *be people*. Instead, they must be creatures of some sort. But if they'd arrived in that craft, then who had built it? No creature was intelligent enough to have done that.

They weren't far from the lookout when they heard a strange, humming sort of sound that grew louder for several seconds and then died away to nothing. Both of them strained to see through the treetops, but saw nothing.

"It's gone!" Serena cried as they stared down from the lookout a short time later. "That was what made that sound. It must have flown away!"

Trenek started to argue again that they should leave, but Serena cut him off. "It will be back. We'll go down there and see what we can see, then find a place to hide and wait."

"How do you know it'll be back?" Trenek asked skeptically.

"Because it has to come back to get those . . . whatever they were."

"But they left on their own."

"Yes, but they probably can't fly that far. Remember when we saw them earlier? They were coming back to it then, and they will again."

Without waiting for Trenek's agreement, she urged her horse onward, down the path. Still complaining that it was dangerous and that their families would worry if they didn't return when they were expected, Trenek followed her.

There was no sign of anything at the lake, but it quickly became apparent that something had been there. The grass was flattened in a shape that corresponded with the object they'd

28

seen, and there were footprints in the soft ground next to the lake.

Serena crouched down, studying the prints. They were much larger than her own or Trenek's and consisted of wavy lines and small circles. But they certainly didn't look like any animal prints she'd ever seen. She decided they must have been made by shoes or boots with strange soles.

She straightened up and studied the area around the lake, seeking a good hiding place. It turned out that the best spot was a rocky outcropping where the trail they had taken reached the valley floor. They could easily conceal themselves, and yet would be close enough to see this spot quite clearly. And since they'd be near the trail, escape would be easier.

Trenek agreed with this, though he still wanted to leave. They let the horses graze for a time, then drink from the lake. In the meantime, they took turns keeping an eye on the sky for any sign of either the craft or the creatures returning. Serena didn't think the creatures would be back until the day's end, but she wasn't so sure about the craft.

"Where do you think they were going?" Trenek asked.

Serena stared at him, realizing that she'd given that no thought.

"I think they must have gone to spy on us," Trenek stated. "That's where they were headed, anyway."

She nodded. All of their towns and villages lay in that direction. Beyond these mountains was a great desert and beyond that the sea that covered much of their world. Her people all lived in a half-dozen towns and a few scattered villages to the west—and that was where the creatures had gone.

She was still thinking about that as they caught the horses and led them off into the woods at the base of the mountain near the trail. Then they returned to find a place to wait among the rocks.

We are spying on each other, she thought with some amusement. And they must find us as strange as we find them. She was more curious than ever to get a look at them.

And as it turned out, she didn't have to wait long. Less than half an hour after they had hidden themselves in the rocks, Serena, who'd been watching the sky, saw sunlight reflect off something. And before she could even point it out to Trenek, they both heard that humming sound.

Chapter Two

The strange gray flying boat hovered over the spot where it had previously landed, then settled gently to the ground. The humming sound stopped. In their hiding place, Serena and Trenek huddled together, holding their breaths to see what would happen next.

Serena could now see details of the craft that had been invisible before: a row of windows along the side, strange lettering toward the back, and the thin outline of what must be a door near the front. She watched it, waiting for one of the strange creatures to emerge. But minutes passed and nothing happened.

"Could it fly itself?" she whispered to Trenek, though they were certainly too far away to be heard.

"I don't know," he replied, not taking his eyes off it. "How can we know *anything?*"

Serena heard the fear in his voice and felt rather annoyed. It was obvious to her that she would have to be the strength for both of them. She wasn't afraid—at least not yet. She wanted very badly to see one of these creatures who could fly without wings.

"We know one thing," she whispered back. "They don't come from our world. We've been wrong about what's out there."

And even as she spoke those words, she was thinking about her visions: the vast blackness and the voices speaking another language. It *was* connected; she was sure of it now. But why was she alone in having the visions?

Trenek said nothing and she knew that he was trying to take it all in. It was, she thought, very fortunate that he had come with her. If she alone carried this story back to their people, no one would believe her. Either they'd believe she'd simply had another kind of vision, or they'd think she was making up the story to prove the visions they knew about.

She wanted to examine the craft up close and wondered how long they should wait before they could assume that nobody was inside. They couldn't wait too long, because the flying creatures might return.

Trenek began to whisper urgently again that they should leave. This would be a good time, he argued, since nothing had emerged from the craft. Besides, he added, they had already seen what they needed to see and should get back to tell everyone.

"We haven't seen everything," Serena reminded him. "We haven't see the flying creatures close up. We need to know what they are."

"It doesn't matter," Trenek replied. "We know they're trouble. We know they must be spying on us."

The sky remained empty as they carried on their whispered argument. Serena wanted more information, while Trenek wanted to get the word to their people as quickly as possible. She countered his argument by pointing out that there was nothing they could do in any event. How could they fight this invasion? There were the caves, Trenek suggested. They could hide.

In the end, she persuaded him to wait until the sun fell behind the mountains. By then, she hoped the flying creatures would have returned, and they would still have enough time to be away from this place before darkness came.

Darian's frustration showed in the grim set of his jaw. They had watched the marketplaces of the two towns closest to the one where he'd seen her all those years ago. But there was no sign of her. If the High Priestess hadn't said she was still reaching out to them, however innocently, he would have guessed that she'd died from some disease or accident.

He even considered that she'd met with some tragedy in the time they'd spent coming to this cosmic backwater, but that seemed unlikely. So he was forced to the conclusion that they simply hadn't searched in the right place yet.

As he watched the vendors close up their stalls and the last of the people drift away, he decided that tomorrow he would send everyone out separately, so they could cover more of the towns and villages. When they returned to the landing craft, the pilot would have a report from the ship that would dictate how much time they had. He'd gone up for more supplies, and while their ship hovered above this world's atmosphere, it had taken readings that would tell them if any of the dangerous electromagnetic storms were brewing.

He wished—not for the first time—that they'd brought a larger force. But they'd opted for speed over size, and he was stuck with what they had. Furthermore, the ship wasn't even carrying its full complement of men because of the necessity of carrying so much more fuel.

Darian heaved a sigh. He was proud of his people's surge into space, proud of the amazing technology that had made it possible. But he thought wryly that it was human nature always to want more. What he wanted now—what they all wanted—was a better source of energy to fuel their spacecraft. The synthetic fuel that had been developed was bulky and therefore limited their explorations. The last time he'd been to the Institute, he'd learned that there was considerable excitement over a type of crystal that had been brought back from one distant world. But it existed only there and in very limited quantities.

He put down his glasses and signaled to the others that it was time to leave, then pressed the button on his wrist-comm and ordered the other unit back to the landing craft as well. They retreated into the forest until they reached a clearing, then rose into the sky.

He wanted to be away from this world and its strange, seductive powers. The feeling was all the more troubling because in the past, he had been eager to explore new worlds. In fact, he hadn't been eager about this particular mission at all, since it wasn't intended for exploration purposes. He hadn't fought the assigment, though, because it was the first long journey for a newly designed ship, and because a part of him wanted to return to this place that had remained in his memory all these years.

And in any event, they *had* done some exploration. While he and his men were down there, the ship was sending out probes to gather data about this world, encoded information that would be sent to the Institute when they returned home.

Home, he thought. Now there was yet another source of frustration. After this mission, he was scheduled for his mandatory "home time" of six months. The Space Council, that irritating lot of planet-bound politicians, had some time ago decreed that no one could spend unrestricted time in space. They feared a loosening of ties to the mother-world, a loss of the proud Ulatan culture.

Others had also argued against the policy, but none had made as much noise about it as Darian. Given his family name and his own exploits, his complaints had been heard—but to no avail. He was sentenced to six months at home, time that would be spent doing research and teaching, which he considered to be the province of old men whose space days were behind them.

And, of course, his family would be after him again to find a wife and produce an heir. They would remind him that the pleasure houses were for younger men, that it was past time for him to settle down to one woman. He supposed that he'd have to do that, and perhaps this home time was as good as any. He'd find someone, marry her and get her pregnant, then return to the dark arms of his real love: space.

Throughout this strange journey, Serena had become more and more annoyed with Trenek. Why didn't he share her curiosity? Was the problem his or hers? And why had she never noticed before how timid he was?

They waited and watched the flying boat, but she could see nothing from their hiding place amidst the rocks at the base of the hill. Still, she held her breath in expectation.

And then they were there: three of them, gliding slowly toward the flying boat, human in every aspect except for their misshapen backs. They were dressed all in black.

They landed gracefully and began talking to each other, their unintelligible words carried to her on the breeze. And now she saw that they were men, after all, as they removed the square packs that had been strapped to their backs. With a soft whirring noise a door opened in the strange flying apparatus, and another man stepped out and joined the group.

Serena felt a sense of awe that she hadn't felt even when she first saw the flying boat. They were men—and they could fly! All they apparently needed were those backpacks. She was astounded.

She studied them. They were all big and bulky, but she saw now that there were some differences between them. One of them had thick hair of a ruddy hue, while another's hair was brown, not black. The brown-haired man was more slender than the others, though still quite large. And there were differences in their uniforms as well. Some had more of the gold braid on their shoulders than others, and one had none at all. But they all had the same strange symbol on their chests, an intricate design she couldn't make out from this distance.

Then, just as it occurred to her that there were more who had not returned, someone looked up and they all turned in her direction. For one brief moment, Serena feared that they had been discovered, but before that fear could quite take root, three more figures floated down from the sky.

Her gaze was drawn immediately to one man. He was very tall, though not quite as heavy as several of the others. His hair was thick and black, but with patches of silver along his temples. He was, she supposed, handsomer than the others, though still coarse-looking to her eyes.

But what had drawn her attention was the gold braid that not only crisscrossed his wide shoulders, but also covered most of his upper arms as well, hanging in braided loops.

"He must be their leader," Trenek whispered—unnecessarily, she thought.

That he was in command of this group was obvious by the way the others reacted to him—and by the man himself. She could not understand his words, of course, but as she watched him, she knew that this was a man accustomed to leading, to being obeyed implicitly.

Serena was fascinated. Her own people had no leaders, or at least no permanent leaders. The duties of running their society revolved among various families on a yearly basis, as it always had. But as she watched the man with all the gold braid, she guessed that he had *always* been a leader.

Then something else struck her: something she couldn't believe she hadn't noticed before. They were all men. There wasn't a woman among them. What did that mean? Certainly there had to be women somewhere. Why were none of them here?

Trenek began to whisper that they should leave. She whispered back that it would be better to wait for darkness. Then she turned her attention back to the leader, studying his every move and trying to pick out his voice from among the babble that reached her ears.

After a few moments, she was able to isolate his voice from the others as they all grew silent and listened to his commands. It was a deep, harsh-sounding voice, made even worse, she thought, by the unpleasant language he was speaking—a language that seemed to her to be filled with ugly, explosive sounds.

Serena thought he seemed angry or frustrated—or both. But his anger did not appear to be directed at the others because they all nodded and added their own comments from time to time.

She wondered what the source of his anger could be, but that, of course, begged the larger question: why were they here? Whatever their purpose, it appeared to her that they hadn't yet achieved it.

The men ate their meals, after which one of the two without gold braid gathered up the remains and the strange stove and carried them back to the flying boat, stowing them in the storage compartment. The others, including the leader, got up and started toward the lake.

They stripped off their clothing and waded into the water. Serena's eyes remained fixed upon the leader. She felt a vague sort of guilt over spying on their nakedness, but that was easily outweighed by her curiosity and her fascination with their very different bodies. Even as naked as he was now, the leader would have been easy to spot. It was in his stance, his carriage, his supreme self-confidence.

Three of them struck out across the lake, while the others gathered on the shore to watch them. Trenek started to insist that they leave, but she ignored him. She was determined to stay as long as she could, even though it seemed there was little else they were likely to learn.

"They're so ugly!" Trenek whispered, grimacing.

"Perhaps they would find us ugly as well," she replied, even though she agreed with him.

"I wish we knew why they're here and what they intend to do," he said, staring pensively at them.

"Maybe they're just curious," she suggested, though she didn't believe that. If only curiosity had brought them here, then why would the leader be angry and frustrated?

"They're up to something. I wonder if anyone else has seen them."

Serena thought about that, then shook her head. "I doubt it. It seems to me that they must have landed way out here so they wouldn't be seen. They're probably spying on us, but being careful about it."

Serena watched the leader walk slowly out of the water, running his hands through his thick black hair to smooth down the curls that had appeared when it got wet. Feeling a faint flush of embarrassment, she nevertheless studied him: the broad chest with its thatch of dark hair, the trim waist and hips, the dark patch between his legs that failed to hide his manhood.

Then, for one brief and very strange moment, she found herself wondering what it would be like to lie with such a man. The sudden thought brought heat to her face and she quickly looked away as the two men who wore no braid left the shore and walked back to the flying boat.

They went to the storage compartment and dragged out two large sacks of some shiny material. Then they walked off in opposite directions, with one of them headed toward their hiding place!

Serena felt Trenek stiffen beside her as the man came within thirty feet of them, then stopped. Seeing him up close, she realized that he was quite young—perhaps younger than she was. He reached into the sack and drew out a dull gray ball about the size of a large child's toy. After pressing against a darker patch that seemed to protrude a bit, he released it.

Serena gasped as the ball remained where it was, suspended in air about four feet off the ground. The man moved on and released another ball and yet another, making his way in a loose circle around their camp. And now she could see in the dim light that the other man was completing the circle on the far side, spacing the strange balls about thirty or so feet apart.

They returned the sacks to the flying boat, and now all the other men began to file into it. The door closed behind them.

"Good! They're going to sleep. Now we can leave." Trenek stood up.

Serena nodded and got up as well, but she was still staring at the closest of the balls. What were they, and how could they remain in the air like that?

Trenek started to make his way carefully through the rocks, heading back to the trail where they'd left their horses. Serena followed him, then stopped and turned once more. If she were to take one of those balls, they wouldn't miss it until morning, and then she and Trenek would have proof of what they'd seen.

Not wanting to risk calling out to him, she simply ran back across the rocks and grabbed the ball. It was very smooth and quite light. Then she turned and ran into the darkness.

Darian was the first to respond to the alarm, since he was in the sleeper seat nearest the door. He grabbed his stunner, then pressed the button to open the door, certain that the alarm had been triggered by an animal. They'd seen several herds of deer and elk, but nothing that appeared to be dangerous.

Still, he stepped cautiously into the open doorway, the stunner aimed. Several of his men had by now gathered behind him. His gaze swept the area. There were no shadows on the grass within the circle, but just as he was about to order that the lights be turned on, he caught a glimpse of something white, moving swiftly across the rocks near the base of the mountain. Then it was gone, vanished into the dense darkness beneath the trees.

He turned and told the others what he'd seen. "It was too light to have been a deer or an elk, and it didn't move like them."

They all poured out of the landing craft and headed toward the rocks. Darian ordered them to stay quiet and not to use the lights, even though twilight was rapidly approaching. But then he stopped as he reached the outer perimeter and saw that one of the motion spheres was missing. The chain of motion-detecting spheres was something they always used on strange worlds, though he'd had no reason to fear any intruders here.

At first, he thought it might have malfunctioned and fallen to the ground, then rolled away on the uneven terrain. But one of the men switched on his light, and it soon became clear that it was, in fact, gone.

"No animal could have done that," said Traynor, his lieutenant.

Darian nodded, thinking about that figure he'd glimpsed too briefly. "They've found us somehow," he said. "Or at least one of them has."

"There could be some of them living in the forest," Traynor said thoughtfully. "It's hard to see through those thick treetops. They could have small houses down there somewhere."

"Or they could be out hunting and just stumbled upon us," someone else suggested.

"But why would they take the sphere?" Traynor asked. "They must have known . . . "

"They *couldn't* know." Darian cut him off. "You forget how primitive these people are. They couldn't possibly know what it was. They probably took it as a souvenir—or maybe even to prove that they'd seen us."

He stared off into the trees, thinking. He'd seen only one figure, but there could be more; in fact, there probably were. He wondered briefly how long they'd been there, no doubt hiding in the rocks, watching. What must they be thinking? He'd never before encountered such primitive people, and he was annoyed that their presence had been discovered. He'd hoped that they could capture the woman and be gone without being seen by anyone else.

Now he had a decision to make. Should they pursue the intruders now, or should they wait for daylight? The truth was that they would probably be no easier to spot then than they were now, thanks to the tall, broad-leafed trees that predominated in the forests here.

"We'll go after them now," he decided aloud. "They can't have gotten far, and there might be a trail."

Trenek had stopped at the beginning of the trail to wait for her, and when he saw the ball in her arms, he stared in disbelief.

"I took it because it's proof of our story," she told him, though that was only part of the reason. Those strange men had so much magic that they surely wouldn't miss one small piece.

Trenek said nothing, but his look was disapproving.

"All right," she said angrily as they hurried along the trail, "So I stole it. It isn't like stealing from our own people. Besides, who knows what they plan to steal from us?" She considered it very likely that they would take something, though she had no idea what it could possibly be.

The horses had been left loosely tethered in a grassy clearing, and Trenek led them to a nearby stream for a drink before they set out.

Serena stared at her prize. She wanted to see if it would remain in the air if she let it go, but she was afraid to remove her hands, lest it fall to the ground and break. The material it was made of seemed so fragile—as thin as an eggshell. So she found a mossy cushion beneath a tree and crouched down, so that when she dropped it, it would fall only a few inches—which was just what it did, to her disappointment. But at least it didn't shatter.

Then she remembered how the man had touched the dark square before releasing it, and she tried that, still holding it only a few inches above the ground. She laughed with delight when it remained motionless, then raised it a bit more and let it go again, with the same results.

What a wonderful treasure, she thought. She would keep it for the children she and Trenek would have one day. She could almost envision the two of them telling their tale about it to their wide-eyed children.

Flying boats and magic balls and backpacks that allowed people to fly! What other wonders must they have? Was it magic—or did they simply have knowledge that her own people didn't have? Most of her people didn't really believe in magic, though they knew that there were events that defied explanation, and sometimes people among them "saw" things they couldn't have seen.

Trenek was still some distance away at the stream, and she was still off the path when suddenly it was bathed in a terrible bright light. Serena gasped, at first fearing that somehow the ball was responsible for the light. But then she could see that the beam traveled upward and ended somewhere above the trees. And she knew, with a terrified certainty, what had happened.

The men had discovered her theft and they were searching

for her! They were flying up there now, with their bright light. She huddled closer to the tree trunk, then turned to look toward the stream. It took a few seconds for her eyes to adjust after staring at that brilliant light, which was as bright as the sun but bluish-white in color. But she thought she could see Trenek there with the horses, his back to her as he let them drink.

The light moved on, following the path. She strained to see into the enveloping dusk, but could see nothing of the men. It was an awesome sight. The beam of light was very narrow, covering little more than the path as it moved upward through the forest, higher into the mountain.

She saw Trenek turn, and then stop as he apparently saw the light. Leaving the ball where it was, she leapt up and ran to him. He turned to her with a look of pure terror.

"It's them—the flying men. They must have discovered the ball was missing. I'm sorry, Trenek."

"But what is that light?" he asked in a thin, quavering voice.

"It's more of their magic, that's all—something they're carrying. We must stay away from the trail because they'll be back. They'll know we couldn't have gotten far. We need to find a place where they can't see us even if they shine the light down through the trees."

Trenek remained silent, still watching the light as it followed the curving path up the mountain.

"Come on!" she said, grabbing his arm. "I remember now that there's a place not far from here, just off the path. It's almost like a shallow cave, and it's big enough to hide us and the horses. I waited there once when a storm came up."

She took her mare's reins and began to run back toward the path, then stopped when she saw the dim outline of the ball. She wasn't about to give it up. Besides, if they were caught, perhaps the men would let them go if they gave it back.

She handed it to Trenek to hold for her until she'd mounted. He held it far away from him, as though it might bite him.

43

Then, holding the reins with one hand and curving the ball against her body with the other, she kicked her mare into action, followed by Trenek.

They both stopped at the same moment as the light suddenly came closer. And then she saw that the men were no longer just searching the trail—and that there were now three of the beams crisscrossing the forest. It was a strange and terrible sight that she knew would be forever burned into her memory.

Chapter Three

Darian stared in disbelief at the woman who sat astride a lovely dappled mare, carrying the motion sensor. He was aware of the man's presence, but it was the woman who drew his full attention. It was *her!* He could not believe his luck.

She brought the mare to a halt and stared at him, squinting at his light, as she struggled to hold on to the reins and the orb at the same time. But what struck him as he returned her stare was her lack of fear. In the brief glance that he spared for the man with her, he could see pure terror—but not coming from her.

"It's *her*, isn't it?" one of the cadets said in disbelief.

Darian nodded. "If the man makes a wrong move, use the stunner—but don't kill him."

The two cadets followed him as he walked slowly toward her. He saw her glance briefly at the man and then back the way they'd come. At first, he thought she would try to flee, but then it seemed she'd reached the very wise decision that flight would be useless. Instead, she sat there, clutching the orb, her deep blue eyes fixed on him with nothing more than a certain wariness.

Serena was terrified, but she knew that she could not let this man see her fear. He would not respect her if he knew she was frightened. She only wished that Trenek understood that, but it was obvious that he was frozen with terror.

He didn't seem angry, she thought as she studied the man. He was now close enough that she could see that his eyes were very black, like his hair. She'd never seen eyes so dark. He stopped about twenty feet away, and the two younger men without braid stopped beside him. Then, for one very long moment, no one moved.

Finally, Serena held out the ball to him. "I'm sorry," she said, even though she knew he couldn't possibly understand her.

Then suddenly—and so briefly that she couldn't even be certain she'd actually seen it—he seemed to smile at her. Could that mean that he understood why she'd stolen it and was accepting her apology?

She went very still as he closed the remaining space between them, flicking a brief glance at Trenek before returning his attention to her. She commanded her mare to be still and dropped the reins, then held out the ball with both hands.

He was so tall that his eyes were nearly level with hers even as she sat on the mare. He had a carved look to him, she thought, as though a chisel had been used to create that strange but compelling face. Or perhaps that thought came to her only because his skin was the color of lir-wood, a soft wood often used for carving precious objects.

He raised a hand, but instead of taking the ball from her, he rubbed the mare's brow beneath her fluffy white forelock. It was such a simple gesture, and yet one that gave her great hope. Despite his appearance, he could not be a bad man.

Then he took the ball from her outstretched hands, his fingertips brushing lightly against hers before he turned and handed it to one of the men with him.

After that, he made a gesture to both of them. It took Serena a few moments to realize that he was telling them to dismount. She glanced at Trenek, then did as ordered. Trenek hesitated, then followed her lead.

He turned and spoke rapidly to the two men, who merely nodded. Then he gestured again, this time clearly telling her and Trenek to follow him. Serena frowned. She understood the order, but she didn't understand why. He was leading them back to the spot where the men had left their magical backpacks.

She took a few steps, then stopped and turned to see if Trenek was following her. He was, though with obvious reluctance. But one of the other men was mounting Trenek's gelding, after which he gathered the reins of her mare and set off back toward the valley where they had been camped.

Serena whirled around to face the leader, suddenly certain she knew what he intended. Trenek must have guessed, too, because he cried out in fear.

"Run, Serena! They're going to make us fly with them. They'll *kill* us!" Even as he spoke, he took off, climbing the steep bank at the side of the trail.

The leader spoke sharply, and Serena saw the other man remove the small cylinder from his belt and aim it at Trenek.

"No!" she screamed. "Please don't kill him! He's just—"

But her words died abruptly as Trenek's whole body convulsed, then became inert as he tumbled back down the bank to the trail. Tears of rage sprang to her eyes as she faced the leader.

"How could you do that? He couldn't hurt you! He was just frightened."

The leader, who of course couldn't understand a word she'd said, merely stared at her impassively as the other man went over to Trenek and picked him up easily, then carried him to the spot where they'd left their magic backpacks. He lowered him to the ground and began to strap on his pack. Serena stared at Trenek's lifeless body, unable to believe what had happened—or how it had happened.

Then the leader's deep, quiet voice cut through her horror. He stepped closer to her and reached out to grasp her hand. But she pulled it away, then used all her strength to strike him, landing a loud blow to the side of his face that she knew instantly had hurt her more than him.

When he began to lift his hand, she thought he intended to strike her, but instead he brought it to the cheek she'd struck— and then did something very strange.

He brought up his other hand and pressed the palms together, and tilted his head slightly and closed his eyes. She frowned at him for a moment, uncomprehendingly. He opened his eyes, pointed to Trenek and repeated the gesture. And then she understood: he was telling her that Trenek wasn't dead; he was just asleep.

She gave him a doubtful look, then ran to Trenek and knelt down beside him to feel for the life-pulse at his throat. It was there—slower than it should be, but definitely there and seemingly steady.

The other man had finished strapping on his pack, and now he bent to pick up Trenek. Before she could do or say anything, he rose silently into the air, his arms locked around Trenek's chest. She heard the leader come up behind her, but she kept her eyes on the flying man until he vanished above the treetops.

Now the leader was strapping on the remaining pack. Serena rose slowly to her feet, fighting the volatile mixture of fear and anticipation that thrummed through her. She was going to *fly!* But would he put her to sleep first? Her gaze went involuntarily to the silver cylinder at his belt.

He saw her staring at it and shook his head. The movement startled her because it was the first indication that they could communicate at all. Then she bit her lip nervously. She wanted to fly—but she was frightened. Still, she knew she had no choice. If she tried to run away, he would surely use his weapon on her. And where could she go, with no horse and no food?

And of course there was always Trenek to consider. She couldn't leave him behind. If she somehow *did* manage to get away, they might kill him out of anger.

His pack now in place, the leader stepped toward her. His size and closeness were very intimidating, but Serena could not shake the thought that he was, for some reason, being very cautious. What possible threat could *she* represent to the likes of him?

She stood her ground and looked up at him. His wide mouth didn't move, but she could see the amusement in his eyes: tiny sparks of light against the blackness. It made her angry to know that he found her helplessness amusing.

Then she flinched slightly as he put his big hands on her shoulders and turned her away from him. His arms slid around her, holding her securely against his body. Instantly, her annoyance vanished beneath an onslaught of sensations: the hardness of the long body that was now pressed against hers, the sinewy forearms that pressed against the soft undersides of her breasts.

Her breath caught in her suddenly constricted throat. Nothing that had gone before prepared her for the heat that now suffused her entire body, or the inchoate longing that welled up in her—only to vanish as they began to rise slowly into the air!

She closed her eyes briefly, fighting the wave of dizziness she felt as they rose through the forest, then opened them again as the motion changed. They were now above the treetops, which spread out around them like an uneven green carpet in the twilight. Her legs dangled uselessly, and that sensation was probably the strangest of all.

They were moving slowly—much more slowly than the man

49

who had carried Trenek away. Was it because he thought she might be less frightened that way—or because he wanted to prolong her terror?

But after the confusion and disorientation subsided a bit, she discovered that she *wasn't* frightened. How very different the world looked from up here. With the aid of the man's strong light, she could see what had always been invisible down on the forest floor: an endless march of mountains off to the distant horizon, the ones closest to her standing out in sharp relief and the more distant ones becoming grayer and less distinct.

But it was that undulating carpet of green below her that fascinated her most. On the forest floor, she saw thick, ancient trunks, but up here, she saw a delicate beauty, almost like a variegated green cloud.

Serena forgot about her situation, about Trenek—about everything except the incomparable sensation of flying and the hard body of the man who held her. And when they began to descend slightly, following the contours of the forest below them, and she saw the stars reflecting off the distant lake, she could not prevent herself from making a small sound of disappointment that the end of their journey was already in sight. They had covered in mere minutes a distance that had taken her and Trenek many hours on horseback.

Their descent was slow as they left the moutaintop behind and glided over the valley. The flying boat was a tiny toy, with two even smaller figures moving about near it. For a moment, she thought one of them must be Trenek and was glad that he had recovered so quickly, but as they drifted lower, she realized that both figures were wearing black—and then she could see Trenek's body on the ground near them.

Guilt and fear coursed through her. What if he were dead now? He'd been alive when she touched him, but he could be dead by now. And all the while she'd been enjoying this incredible experience!

They were now directly over the two men, and she stared down at their upturned faces as the leader slowed even more, bringing them down with great gentleness. The tips of her boots scraped against the ground and she struggled to get her feet under her. But she wasn't fast enough and consequently fell back against him as they landed.

He took her weight easily, then held on to her until she managed to get her feet under her. Then he released her and removed the backpack. She stood there uncertainly for a moment, unable to believe how strange it seemed to be on her feet again. Then, once more, she remembered Trenek and went to him, kneeling beside his still body.

He was still alive. His pulse seemed much the same to her. One of the men had draped a cover of some strange fabric over him, even though the day was warm.

Behind her, she heard the three men conversing in their strange, unpleasant language. She turned and saw that the leader was talking into the band on his wrist.

They were all ignoring her for now, so she continued to sit there beside Trenek, wishing that he'd wake up so they could decide what to do. But did it really matter? How could he have anything to offer? She knew they couldn't escape.

The exhilaration she'd felt only moments ago in the air faded into a deep uneasiness that stopped short of outright terror only because the men hadn't really done them any harm so far. It occurred to her that they might simply intend to keep them there until they left, so that she and Trenek couldn't tell anyone about them.

She held tightly to that thought. After all, if they'd intended to kill them, wouldn't they have done so already? Perhaps that weapon they all carried couldn't kill, but they must surely have something that could.

A man emerged from the flying boat and began talking to the leader. The younger man without braid gathered up the back-

51

packs and put them into the cargo holder. Serena's hopes rose. Maybe they would leave as soon as the others returned: the ones who must have flown off somewhere and the man who was bringing their horses.

She shifted her position, still holding Trenek's hand, but now watching both the sky and the base of the mountain, even though she knew it would be hours before the man with the horses could get there. The leader walked past her, glancing at her briefly before he went into the flying boat. The others ignored her.

She grew tired of sitting there and thought that perhaps she should walk around a bit. So, after checking Trenek's pulse one more time and finding it just the same, she got to her feet and began to walk toward the lake. The leader was still in the flying boat and the other two men were sitting on the ground talking quietly. She walked past them and could feel their eyes on her, but neither one tried to stop her. Why should they? They knew she couldn't really go anywhere.

She reached the lake and began to walk along the shoreline, her thoughts vague and blurry from all that had happened and from lack of sleep. After a quiet life that had seen no real excitement and certainly no danger, she felt disoriented and longed to return to that peace.

But would she ever have it again, now that she knew there were people out there who could invade her world? Would everything change now for all of them, even if the men *did* leave? And what if they didn't? What if they were here for some other reason—perhaps to take her people captive? Could the ancient Legend come true?

Too tired to walk any farther, she sank down onto the grassy shore and stared unseeing at the lake. She might actually have dozed off for a time, because suddenly the leader was there, crouching down beside her before she'd even heard him.

"Darian," he said, pointing to himself.

She nodded, then said her own name as she too pointed. He repeated it, though it sounded different coming from his lips. Then she tried unsuccessfully to stifle a yawn. She must have dozed off. She could barely keep her eyes open now.

He stood up and extended a hand to help her to her feet. His hand was big and hard and engulfed hers completely. He released her and she followed him back to the campsite, where she saw that several others had arrived during the time she'd apparently slept. But they weren't all there yet, and the man with the horses hadn't arrived, either. She couldn't have slept long.

She walked past the cluster of men and stopped at Trenek's still-unconscious body. After reassuring herself that he was just the same, she looked around for a place to sleep a bit more. Her gaze had just fallen on the flying boat when the leader—Darian, she reminded herself—took her arm and pointed to it.

She realized that he knew how tired she was and was offering to let her rest inside. She hesitated for just a moment, thinking she should ask them to carry Trenek there as well. But he was unconscious, not sleeping, and they had covered him. She followed Darian to the flying boat.

She saw him watching her as she stepped inside, but she was too tired to be grateful. Instead, she simply fell into the first seat inside the door. It was wonderfully comfortable, and her eyes were already closed when she heard him moving about, and she was just barely awake when he tucked a blanket around her.

Darian stared at her for a moment. He found all the women on this world oddly appealing, but this woman—Serena—was beautiful. And not only beautiful, but possessed of a surprising strength and courage as well. Although it must have been an incredible experience for her to fly—truly unimaginable—she hadn't been frightened. He knew that her passivity now was the result of her tiredness, but it was also possible that she had

53

decided she would be released when they left. Even in her tiredness, she would surely have shown some of that fire he'd seen when she slapped him.

He didn't feel guilty about the deception—but he *did* feel a certain regret that she would become a Trezhella. His instincts told him that, wary as she was, she was still attracted to him.

He left her there, thankful that it had all been so easy. She would sleep for hours—and by then, they would be on their way back to the ship.

Outside, he paused to look down at the unconscious man. He must be her mate, though it was impossible for Darian to imagine her being attracted to him. The man was clearly a coward. He'd made no effort to protect her and had even tried to run away. Darian felt nothing but contempt for him.

Of course, he knew nothing of their customs. Perhaps she'd had no choice but to take him as her mate. Not so very long ago, that had been common among his own people and others as well. But then he thought about his observations of them and how it had actually seemed that there were no differences in the roles played by men and women. That argued against arranged marriages.

He continued to stare at the unconscious man, trying to decide what to do about him. If he killed him, then these people would never know that they'd been here. On the other hand, what did it matter if they *did* know? They certainly didn't represent a threat, now or in the foreseeable future. They were far too primitive.

In the end, Darian decided to let him live, though it was possible that his decision had as much to do with the woman, Serena, as it did with this poor excuse of a man.

In her dream, Serena was floating on a cloud, drifting high above the treetops, lulled by the susurrous sound of wind rushing past. Several times, she edged toward wakefulness, only to fall back again into bliss. But each time, the feeling that she should wake up grew stronger. There was something beckoning to her with increasing urgency: something was wrong. And finally, she opened her eyes.

Even as her brain began to register her surroundings, she already knew where she was: in the flying boat. The wonderful comfort of the cloud resolved itself into the deeply cushioned and contoured seat. But the sound persisted—a low whisper of wind, barely audible. Something was definitely wrong.

The seat had moved from an upright position, and she was now reclining, so that all she could see at first was the smooth ceiling of the craft. She tried to pull herself upright, but found that she couldn't move. An uneasiness stirred within her as she struggled to free her hands from beneath the blanket. Then, when she had finally accomplished this, her hands touched a wide band of some kind of smooth fabric that was holding her firmly in place.

Her uneasiness edged closer to outright panic. She tried to turn her head, to see anything other than the ceiling, but the seat was curved around her and she could see nothing. By raising her head the small distance she could manage, she could just glimpse the back of the similar seat in front of her, the one that was directly in front of the panel with all the strange devices.

Suddenly, a bell chimed once. Then a male voice spoke. She had no idea what he was saying, but she knew it wasn't the leader's—Darian's—voice. A moment later, she could hear other voices, low and indistinct, coming from behind her. That was accompanied by a series of whirring sounds, and then she could see the high back of the seat in front of her, rising now to an upright position. Her own seat remained where it was.

She wanted to cry out, to ask what was happening, but an innate caution kept her silent. What was the meaning of that bell? Why were the other men in the craft? Surely she hadn't slept through the night?

55

Then she remembered the windows and turned her head in that direction. But the window was too high now, with the seat reclining. Still, it seemed to be dark out there.

Why were they waking up now, when it was still night? And where was Trenek? Had he awakened yet? Could he be in here, too?

She was still looking up at the window when she sensed a presence. When she turned, Darian was leaning over her, his face very close to her as he apparently tried to see if she was awake. And in that first moment, when her eyes met his, she knew her instincts were right.

It was in his eyes: that wariness that people show when they have bad news to impart. Trenek, she thought as her throat suddenly constricted. *He's dead.*

Darian reached across her and touched something on the front of the armrest. She felt the band that had held her so securely vanish. Then he reached for something on the other side of the seat, down close to the floor on the aisle side, and the seat slowly carried her into a sitting position.

She kept watching his face, waiting for him to find some way to tell her about Trenek. But instead, he shifted his gaze to the window, and then pointed. The wariness was still in his eyes.

Serena turned to the window, fearing that she would see Trenek's body out there on the ground, now completely covered by the blanket to indicate that he was dead. But what she saw instead was so utterly incomprehensible that she blinked several times, then wondered if what she was seeing was some sort of picture that had been put up to cover the window.

It was the darkness of deepest night—the blackness of her visions. But there was a semi-circle of palest blue just visible at the bottom of the window. She moved closer, and the semi-circle became whole: a pale blue sphere with gossamer streaks across its surface.

She turned back to Darian, frowning. Then she faced the

window again and reached out to touch it, assuming that the glass had been covered with this strange picture. But it was still glass—or something like glass. And now, as she stared at the bluish sphere, she saw that it was receding, growing smaller.

Ignoring Darian, who was still watching her intently, she turned far enough to see the double row of seats and count the men who sat in them. They were all there. Some were talking quietly, a few were watching Darian and her curiously, and others were doing something with rectangular objects that rested on small tables in front of them. Trenek was not among them.

She returned her attention to the window. The sphere had grown even smaller. Panic welled up in her and she tried to force it down, unwilling to let Darian see it. What did it all mean? If what she saw wasn't a picture, then where was she?

As the sphere receded, the blackness around it drew her attention. And then something else moved into view, in the upper left corner of the window: a tiny corner of yet another sphere. She pressed her face against the glass at the opposite side, trying to see it better. And it was then that the knowledge began.

She neither understood nor accepted it quickly. Many moments passed before the new sphere came fully into view and then dominated the scene, nearly driving out the darkness. But she knew instantly what it was, even though more time passed before she understood its significance.

The new sphere was Traneed, one of three giant stars that alternated as the rulers of the heavens during the daylight hours. Traneed was easily identifiable. Her people had always felt the irony that this most beautiful of the Day Stars ruled the heavens during the worst season. It was the largest of the three, and its surface was covered by a series of dark bands that varied in width.

And so the knowledge settled into a mind that had to accept it very slowly. Traneed was huge now—so big that she could no longer see all of it even when she pressed her face to the window. And they were moving past it. She thought she could sense the motion of the flying boat now, where before she'd thought that the scene out there was moving.

The bell she'd heard before sounded, twice this time. The man in the seat ahead of her said something to Darian, who responded briefly, then reached across her and brought that belt around her again. After that, he lowered the seat until she was once more reclining. His gaze met hers briefly, but this time she could read nothing in it. And then he was gone from view, apparently back to his seat. She heard the whirring of the other seats being lowered as well.

She caught only a glimpse of Traneed, and then it was gone and the tiny portion of the window she could see was dark again. She understood now. She was in the heavens, rising up to the stars. That lovely bluish-white sphere she'd seen was her home.

Chapter Four

Serena snipped the dead blossoms from the brilliant purple and white lazenthas, then tilted her face up to the warm sun as she knelt in the garden. A laughing group of novices passed by, casting her the same strange looks she always received when anyone found her out here, working in the gardens.

She stared at the backs of their close-cropped heads and shuddered, remembering how she herself had barely escaped that fate four months ago when she arrived at the Trezhella compound. Her refusal to allow her head to be shorn was instinctive, though in retrospect it had become merely the first in a growing list of rebellions against the rules of the Sisterhood.

Of course, she hadn't known then just how much power she had. That knowledge hadn't come until much later, when she had mastered the Ulatan language and began to demand answers to her many questions. Shenzi, one of her few friends here, had told her that the High Priestess was overheard remarking that it was a pity they'd had to teach her the language. Serena had quickly become the bane of the High Priestess's existence, a designation she wore with considerable pride.

Lania, the special tutor who'd been brought in to teach her the Ulatan language, had been astounded at how quickly Serena had picked it up, a fact that Serena didn't dispute and which she ascribed to her determination to be in control of her fate in this world.

She stood up and moved on to the next section of the garden that needed some attention: the wonderfully sweet-smelling agapas that were overgrown and needed to be separated now that their first blooming was finished. As she dragged the little cart that held her tools behind her, she saw the Ulatan gardening crew in another area, giving her the same kind of looks she'd received from the novices. The Sisterhood employed a veritable army of servants to attend to the needs of both the Trezhellas and the large, walled compound, and everyone but her, it seemed, avoided doing any kind of work.

For Serena, these moments away from her studies that she spent in the garden served to maintain a tenuous link with her home, where gardening was about as close to a religion as her people came—religion being only one of many things she had learned about here, and which she still didn't fully understand.

What she *did* understand fully now was the Sisterhood and its role, as well as her own place in the scheme of things. Hence, her many small rebellions.

The Trezhellas—the word, she had learned, meant "long talkers"—had been founded to provide a means for Ulatan spaceships to communicate with each other and with their home base as they journeyed through space.

The Ulatans had struggled for decades to find a way to travel into space—that is, once they'd ceased their many centuries of war in their own world. They were clearly a people bent on conquest, and after nearly destroying their own world with their increasingly powerful weapons, they'd finally made peace and turned their attention to space.

Serena didn't understand the scientific discoveries that had resulted in their finally being able to venture into space, but what she did learn was that the method of propulsion they invented made it impossible for even their sophisticated means of communication to be carried into space with them. The source of energy interfered with normal methods of communications.

Apparently, there had always been among the Ulatans a few women who possessed the talent of Trezhella, their word for communicating through the mind over long distances. So, when all else failed, the men of the space agency reluctantly turned to them—and the Sisterhood came into existence. Then, as they discovered and conquered other worlds, they found a few more such women and brought them here, sometimes forcibly, but mostly with the women's consent.

How the Sisterhood had come to be what it was, Serena had learned over a period of time, beginning with her startling discovery of the status of women in Ulatan society—and in the other worlds that the Ulatans now controlled.

Her friends Shenzi and Lania told her earnestly that the situation of women was greatly improved, but Serena no more understood their reasoning than they understood the world she'd grown up in. They pointed out that women were no longer forced into marriage or stripped of their inheritances when they *did* marry. She, in turn, countered that women were still being denied the type of education needed to allow them to enter most professions, and that, as a consequence, men still ran everything.

Everything but the Sisterhood, that was. When the men who controlled the Space Agency reluctantly turned to the Trezhellas, the woman they chose to head what would become the Sisterhood was the daughter of a noble family. Mansia had been forced into marriage to a much older and apparently quite awful man, who—fortunately for her—had died only months before the Space Agency sought her help.

Serena always smiled when she thought of Mansia or passed her portrait, which hung in the Great Hall. She knew she would have liked this woman. Mansia had seen her opportunity—and she'd taken it. She organized the Trezhellas into a Sisterhood, demanded a luxurious home for them, and then moved them all there—even the ones who had been married. It didn't say much for the state of Ulatan marriages at the time that not one of the women protested.

Then Mansia decreed that Trezhellas must give up any relationships with men in order to focus on their essential task. And once again, she apparently encountered no opposition from the women, which was certainly a reflection on the state of Ulatan manhood, and later on the men of other worlds as well.

Fearing that the women who ventured into space would be mistreated by the men with whom they shared close quarters, Mansia had succeeded in getting a law passed that made death the penalty for any man who attempted to seduce a Trezhella.

Then she designed the beautiful but modest black gowns worn by all Trezhellas, as a way of guaranteeing that their identity would be known to all.

Succeeding High Priestesses had only embellished the mystique of the Sisterhood, creating a group of women who held more power than any woman ever had. And they made certain as well that novices were thoroughly imbued with the arrogance that powerful men always had. The result was that any woman on any world who showed talent for "long talking" was eager to join the Sisterhood, and it had been years since anyone had been brought here against her will.

Except, of course, for Serena herself.

For reasons no one understood, Serena possessed a greater talent than any of them. The Space Agency and the Sisterhood had discovered that there were limits to the distances over which a Trezhella could "talk." It worked well enough within the Ulatans' own star system, but none could communicate beyond that limit, which made it dangerous for the great spaceships to venture farther into space.

Serena had come to the attention of the Sisterhood when she was only ten years old: the very first time she'd had a "vision." Several of the more powerful Trezhellas had "heard" her incomprehensible thoughts and had even received a mental image of her. And as she grew older and was unknowingly communicating with them ever more strongly, they knew she possessed the talent they needed.

The High Priestess had been worried, because she'd been unable to find anyone capable of communicating over great distances, and the Space Agency had begun to talk about journeying into deep space without that capability. She very much feared that this would diminish the power of the Sisterhood as space exploration moved beyond them.

Upon learning all this, Serena had questioned how she alone could function. She would be able to speak to other Trezhellas, but they couldn't reach her. The High Priestess had told her that until they found another such person, they could at least receive the reports she could send back.

"But why is that important?" Serena had asked. "You could just wait and receive them when the ship returns."

"The ship might not return," the High Priestess had stated succinctly.

Then, when she saw understanding dawning on Serena's face, she had shown Serena her first sign of kindness. "I will not allow them to force you to go on any such voyage. There *is* danger, and I will tell them that we can't risk your life because we have much to learn from you—that perhaps you will be able, in time, to teach others to do what you can do."

So Serena understood that the decision to go on the first

deep-space voyage was hers to make. "But I've already made such a voyage," she reminded the High Priestess.

"So you have—but the next one will be even farther. I have been informed that as a result of that voyage, some design changes are being made to the ship, and it will be a year until the ship is ready."

That conversation had happened two months ago, so Serena now had less than ten months to decide if she would join it. In the meantime, she would be sent out on shorter voyages with an older Trezhella, but not in the servant role of the novice. That was the result of another of her rebellions. She already wore the gown of a Trezhella, despite the fact that her training wasn't quite complete.

She lifted her head from her gardening chores and stared into the heavens. A deep longing came over her. Space—and Darian. The two were now and forever entwined in her memory. But even as she stared into space, it was the memory of Darian that filled her and poured forth.

Her laughter had been the catalyst, the thing that had started it all. The attraction of male to female had already been there, of course—but it would have remained just that if she hadn't laughed. And Darian too would be haunted by that musical sound that had crumbled the already fragile wall of his resistance.

They'd stared at each other in the moonlight. They were nearing the end of their long journey to Ulata, though Serena hadn't known it at the time. Although they still shared no language, she had grown more comfortable with Darian and his crew. This respite on a lonely planet would soon be over, and after jumping and laughing in the planet's strange gravity fields, they stood, suddenly aware of the moment. It seemed that neither of them was breathing—that perhaps even time itself had stopped. And then he stretched out a hand to her and she took it with no hesitation, accepting the gift and offering one in return.

He drew her slowly into his arms, against his big, hard body. She felt the heat of him, the power carefully contained. And as she arched against him, tilting her head back to look up at him, she knew that the world *was* spinning.

Everything about him was so very different from Trenek that it was all wholly new and wondrous. Instead of touching her lips, his mouth trailed lightly along her cheek. His tongue brushed her ear and then moved oh-so-slowly down the sensitive column of her neck. A soft, strangled sound poured from her, a plea for him to claim the lips that parted in anticipation.

And when he did, she met his hungry demands with her own, learning quickly to parry the thrusts of his tongue, shocked and amazed that there could be such pleasure in it. How could her body have kept this secret from her, and what other secrets might be laid bare by this sensual onslaught?

She found out quickly when his hand slid down to cup her bottom and draw her more fully against him. The yearning that welled up from her female core was all-encompassing. She was certain that if it weren't for his arms around her, she would fall to the ground, her bones melted from the strange heat that suffused every fiber of her being.

Serena knew she was in danger of losing herself, but she was powerless to stop it from happening. Still, she might have struggled against it if she alone felt all this. But it was obvious that he too was a prisoner of these erotic forces. Unable to communicate with words, they seemed to feel each other's thoughts, and she knew that his own desire matched hers.

He drew her down onto the soft, mossy bank of the stream, his kisses heating her skin and warming her through the layers of clothing she no longer wanted. She moved away from him and he let her go, his expression surprised. And it became even more astonished as she stripped off her clothing. But just as she was beginning to wonder at his reaction, he smiled and began to remove his own clothing, his eyes never leaving her.

Their naked bodies collided in a rush for flesh to join flesh. She moaned with pleasure, and the sound was quickly drowned out by his low groan as they began to explore each other, hungry for knowledge, driven by desire that was rapidly reaching the flashpoint. His mouth closed first over one nipple and then the other, turning them into achingly sensitive nubs that craved his touch. Her hands and lips caressed his hard, hair-roughened body, glorying in the feel of his differentness, his uncompromising maleness.

And then he was kneeling over her, his dark eyes seeming to draw her into himself even as he thrust into her, shocking her at first with his size and hardness, then drawing from her a sigh of pleasure as her body accommodated itself to him and surrounded him and welcomed him.

Two bodies moved as one, slipping into the ancient rhythms that pulsed through them both and built quickly to a crescendo. Wrapped around him, Serena rode the crest of a wave into an explosion of pure sensation. Her body was no longer hers, but neither did his body belong to him. For one blinding moment, they merged into something far beyond themselves.

Reason returned slowly and in tiny pieces fitted between the aftershocks that quaked through them both. She lay claim once again to her own body—but a body that would never be quite the same. Every inch of her still bore his imprint. She thought that if she were to look at herself, she could somehow see the difference, even though her logical mind told her this couldn't be so.

But she wasn't looking at herself; instead, she was staring into a pair of dark eyes that captured a tiny bit of the giant star that still hung over them. She didn't need to ask if he felt what she felt. The fact that they couldn't speak to each other no longer mattered. She could see the answer in his eyes.

The memories continued to tumble forth: countless days and nights of love on other worlds as they made their way back to

Ulata—lovemaking made all the more eager because they knew
that this was the only time they would have. Serena didn't
know just how she had known that then, since they still couldn't
really communicate, except at the most basic level. But she
had, nonetheless, known.

Her comm unit beeped and she glanced at her wrist. It was
nearly time for her next training session, so she gathered up her
gardening tools and trundled the cart back to the potting shed,
then hurried to her quarters to clean up. Her thoughts turned, as
they frequently did, to the decision she had to make. Even
though her decision would have no effect on the departure, the
men who controlled the Space Agency were already pressing
the High Priestess for a decision, falsely believing that it was
hers to make, and not Serena's.

But there was one piece of information she needed in order
to make her decision, and Serena hadn't yet figured out how to
get it. So she temporized, waiting to see if she could learn who
would be commanding the mission. She wondered if it would
be Darian.

Serena had discovered early on that she didn't dare ask
questions about Darian, or show interest in him in any way.
And she also now understood the reason for Darian's caution
where she was concerned. She hadn't yet become a member
of the Sisterhood when they spent those glorious nights
together, but still, he had known that his behavior would, at
the very least, have resulted in some sort of disciplinary
action.

Or perhaps not. Serena *had* managed to learn a few things
about Darian Vondrak without even asking. It was no accident
or luck of the draw that he'd been chosen to command the long
and dangerous voyage to capture her. He was known to be a
risk-taker and a brilliant leader. He was also a son of the most
powerful of the old noble families of Ulata.

And he was not married. Lania, her friend and tutor, had

asked Serena about him as soon as they were able to communicate well enough. Serena suspected that Lania was in love with him. She herself was a member of the old nobility and had known Darian all her life. According to Lania, Darian's family was pressuring him to marry, now that he was "grounded" for the mandatory six months.

"But if he marries, then surely he won't go back to space," Serena had said. This was just after the High Priestess had told her about the decision she had to make.

"Of course he will," Lania had replied with a laugh. "He'll get his wife pregnant to keep his family happy, and then he'll go off again. Darian has the stars in his blood."

A short time later, Serena was back in one of the many small rooms used for training the Trezhellas. It was identical in every way to a room she'd seen on the ship—a room that she would never forget.

It was a very tiny room, and the walls were of a different substance. However, what immediately captured her attention was the object on a table in the center of the room. She frowned at it. Was it a carved telda? It rather resembled them, even though the color was slightly different. And if that was what it was, why was it here?

She glanced both ways, then walked into the room and sat down on the single chair that faced the object. Even though it was different from the teldas in the caves of her home, she felt a terrible wave of longing wash over her.

Her world was filled with caverns of varying sizes. It had often seemed to her that there must be miles of them, running under every town and village. And most of them had teldas, strange formations of smooth rock that hung from the ceilings or rose from the floors, in many cases making it impossible to pass through them.

It seemed very strange to her that such a thing would be here—and in a place of honor. Her people regarded the teldas as being nothing more than a nuisance, since they prevented further exploration of the caves.

Then she wondered how anyone had managed to carve this telda—if indeed it *was* one. Her people had tried to chop them down, but nothing would even make a dent in them: not even the tools used for cutting stone. "Hard as a telda" was a common expression among her people, used in exasperation about anything that had become very hard, such as food that had burned onto the bottom of a pan.

She reached out to touch the object, which had been carved into a sort of miniature pillar with six smooth, flat sides and a pointed top. It felt like a telda as well: much cooler than it should have been.

Her thoughts drifted as she stared at the telda. Suddenly, she recalled that the very first time she'd ever had the vision had been when she and several friends were exploring a cave not far from her home.

It was a cave well-known to all the children in town, one filled with teldas that protruded from the floor and hung from the ceiling. It made a wonderful maze, and generations of children had played in there, able to move between the teldas as their elders could not.

The vision had so terrified her that she'd run screaming from the cave as soon as it was over. She'd been teased quite a lot after that, so that, naturally, she'd forced herself to return. And it had happened every time she went in there, though she never admitted it to the others and continued to play among the teldas until she outgrew the game.

Then, as the years passed, the visions had begun to come in other places as well, so that she'd given up her original belief that the teldas had something to do with it.

Lost in her thoughts about the strange visions, Serena remembered the first time she had had a vision in one of these rooms—before she'd learned the Ulatan language. The room had gone dark—and then darker still, and this time the voices had been more distinct than on her homeland, filling her head with a cacophony that had made her unconsciously press her hands to her ears.

When that didn't work, she had stumbled blindly from the room, holding on to the door frame until the blackness went away. But the echoes of those voices had remained in her memory: women's voices, just like all the others, speaking over each other rather than carrying on normal conversations.

Then she'd realized something else: the voices were speaking the same language the men who had captured her spoke. She'd grown accustomed to the sounds and rhythms by then, and the voices in her vision had been much clearer this time.

Now, she stood quietly in the middle of the training room, thinking about what had happened that first time. Could there be some connection, after all, between the teldas and the visions? Or was it merely coincidence that she'd had the vision in here? But why was that carved telda there in the first place?

The foot-high carved obelisk was called a zhetla, she had learned. Zhetlas played no active role in the work of the Trezhellas. They were merely used to focus one's thoughts, as they had apparently been used for centuries before the Sisterhood came into existence. They were very rare, and therefore treasured. It amused Serena to think that something so very common on her own world could be treasured by these people, who had so much of everything. But she had kept her amusement to herself, because one of the first things she learned about the Ulatans was that they were an excessively proud people. So it seemed best not to belittle their "treasures."

She seated herself and focused her thoughts quickly, ignoring the zhetla and instead finding that calm, dark pool inside her. Immediately, the familiar cacophony of voices crowded her mind. But she had learned now to separate them.

Trezhellas repeated their given names at regular intervals, and by touching a button mounted just beneath the table where the zhetla stood, Serena could activate a screen on the wall that told her where each woman was now. She was sure that the button and the panel must have existed on the ship as well, but she simply hadn't noticed them. When the wall panel was inactive, it couldn't be distinguished from the rest of the wall.

She'd discovered that most Trezhellas heard their sisters' voices with varying degrees of clarity, depending on how far away they were. She, on the other hand, heard them all equally well. So she activated the screen and checked to see who was farthest away at the moment, then found that voice.

It belonged to Tesyava, a woman she'd encountered on her journey here. She knew by now that most of the others considered that Tesyava carried arrogance to new heights, which probably accounted for her cold behavior when Serena saw her. Shenzi said it was because Tesyava was of very low birth— something that was quite important to the Ulatans.

"She's just trying to mimic her betters," Shenzi had said with a toss of her luxurious black curls. Shenzi herself was from a wealthy merchant family—just a small step below the nobility.

Serena listened to Tesyava's report, which she was repeating in increasingly annoyed tones. Then she found Tesyava's partner, one of the recent graduates to Trezhella status. Tesyava was near the limits for all but Serena, and she considered entering into the conversation, to help out the new Trezhella. She was sure that Shara, the Trezhella receiving the report here, would welcome her assistance, but she wasn't sure which would annoy Tesyava more: to talk with her or to be forced to keep repeating her report.

Finally, out of pity for Shara, she broke in, identifying herself and offering to receive the report. Shara quickly thanked her and withdrew. Tesyava remained silent for a moment, waiting for Serena to tell her to proceed.

Serena touched the hidden panel on the table and the keyboard slid out from beneath. Then she told Tesyava to proceed and began to type in the report. She smiled at Tesyava's unpleasant tone, knowing that in all likelihood the other woman would receive her image as well. No one knew why it was that Serena's image followed her thoughts, but it did. She was the only one among them who didn't need to identify herself.

The report finished, Tesyava signed off, and they both waited for the report to be transmitted to Space Agency headquarters. There could be questions or messages to be passed back.

By now, Serena's withdrawal from the vision was as easy and unconscious as her entry into it. The temporary blackness gone, she waited for the wall screen to give her instructions. Then, when it did, she slipped effortlessly back into her trance and passed on the messages, which in this case were all personal messages for the crew.

Then she began to scan, listening to the other voices, seeking one whose report hadn't yet been picked up by one of the others who were working here. Trezhellas worked one-hour shifts because most of them were unable to sustain contact for any longer than that. Serena followed that routine as well, although she knew she could work much longer.

When her shift ended, she left the room and went to Central, where all communications were monitored by one of the Seniors: the oldest and most experienced of the Sisterhood. Since she was, at least in theory, still in training, she followed the routine of the novices.

Medri, the Sister who was monitoring this shift, smiled at her. "Shara asked me to thank you for your assistance. I'm sure Tesyava was grateful as well."

72

Serena doubted that, but she said nothing. Tesyava wasn't popular within the Sisterhood, but, at least in their public utterances, Trezhellas never spoke ill of another Sister.

She returned to her quarters on the upper floor, a large suite that had been given to her upon her arrival. She'd also been given a personal servant, but she'd soon persuaded the Residence Sister to limit the woman's chores to cleaning when Serena wasn't there. She just wasn't comfortable having someone else there all the time to tend to her every need.

When she stepped into the foyer, she saw that the message light was blinking on the wall-mounted comm. She could be reached at any time on her wrist-comm, but the Sisterhood reserved that for true emergencies, because it could interfere with their work.

She pressed the button and heard the voice of the Assignment Sister inform her that she would be leaving on her first voyage in two days' time: a five-day mission to Bultazar, one of the inner worlds. And Shenzi would be accompanying her, since it was her first voyage.

Serena smiled with pleasure. She had hoped she would get to go out with Shenzi. Then the next message played and it was Shenzi herself, passing on the same news and saying that she would see her at dinner.

The final message was from Lania—and it was also good news. Serena was to be allowed to leave the compound and join Lania at her home for an evening. Lania would pick her up early in the afternoon, so she could show her more of Ulata as well.

For more than a month now, Serena had been asking to see more of the world that was now her home, but so far, all she'd gotten were aerial views from Lania's hovercraft. The Trezhellas, it seemed, never left their elegant compound and were apparently quite content to stay within its walls when they weren't in space. But since most of them came from Ulata, they already knew what lay out there. Serena, on the other hand, had a great curiosity about this huge world.

She wondered why the High Priestess had finally given in to her requests—particularly her request to spend some time in a Ulatan home. Then it occurred to her that it might well be because she was under increasing pressure from the Space Agency to tell them if Serena would be going on Deep Space One. Granting her this request was undoubtedly the High Priestess's way of making a subtle request of her own.

What was she going to do? If the High Priestess was being pushed by the Space Agency for an answer, Serena would have to make her decision soon. She wondered if Lania would know whether or not Darian was going to be commanding the mission. It was possible that she would, since she knew him. But would she be suspicious if Serena asked?

The truth was that Serena didn't know what she would do with the information even if she could get it. She just wasn't sure she wanted to see Darian again.

During her first days and weeks here, Serena had thought of Darian constantly. Each night, as she lay in the big bed in her luxurious suite, she had relived their lovemaking. And during the days, when she was struggling to learn the difficult Ulatan language, helped by the patient Lania, she would remember Darian's patience as well. And she would try to forget her final moments with him, when he had delivered her to the compound, then walked away without so much as a backward glance.

Later, when she had mastered the language and learned about the Sisterhood, she understood their parting and his seeming coldness. But by that time, she had begun to learn as well how it was between men and women here—and slowly, despite her best efforts to convince herself that he was different, her feelings about Darian began to change.

She knew that if she were to tell anyone about what had happened between Darian and her, she would be told that he'd taken advantage of her and of her situation because that was what men did. They used women for their own pleasure, then ignored them the rest of the time. And she had heard many times that the men of the Space Command, those who were said to have the "stars in their blood" were the worst of all, no matter that they were regarded publicly as being the greatest of heroes.

Even his many kindnesses to her were brushed off by Shenzi, to whom she had once confided that. "Of course he was kind to you," Shenzi said. "He was under orders to treat you well and to see that you were made as comfortable as possible. He knew how valuable you are, to the Sisterhood and to the Space Agency."

And so, week by week and then month by month, her certainty that they had shared something rare and wondrous faded away, to be replaced by the belief that she had been used. Though she remained different from the other women in many ways, Serena had begun to adopt the prevailing attitudes of her Sisters.

So she was torn between the desire to see Darian again and confront him with this new knowledge, and an equally strong desire to forget about him and about that brief chapter in her life.

But still, sometimes at night when she was drifting slowly off to sleep, she remembered how he felt and how he smelled and how he could play her body like the finest of instruments.

"I think she decided to let me be the one to take you on your first voyage because she knows we're friends and she wants your answer soon," Shenzi told her at dinner, after Serena had expressed surprise and pleasure at the High Priestess's decision. Shenzi was only a few years older than Serena herself, and she'd told Serena that it wasn't likely they would go together into space. Novices were always sent out with older Trezhellas, and while Serena wasn't really a novice, Shenzi had been certain the same rules would apply.

"You're probably right," Serena replied, glancing briefly at the head table, where the High Priestess and her closest aides dined. Then she told Shenzi about Lania's call and the granting of her request to see more of Ulata.

"From what I hear," said Shenzi, who seemed to hear everything, "The men are demanding an answer now, though how it can matter, I don't know."

"The men," always spoken with undisguised disdain, referred to those in charge of the Space Agency and its military wing, the Space Command.

"I'll tell her that I'll give her my decision as soon as we return," Serena said. "She can tell them that she needs to see how I do on this outing."

"I hope you'll refuse to go," Shenzi said with feeling. "It's dangerous, Serena. Besides, no one really knows if you'll be able to reach us."

She made a sound of disgust. "I don't see the point to Deep Space One, to tell the truth. Who cares what's out there? It's so far away that it doesn't matter."

Serena felt a sudden, strange tug at her heart. Shenzi's words were near-echoes of statements she'd heard so many times from her family and friends back home. They didn't care what lay hidden in the vast forests or the far reaches of the ocean— because it was just too far away to matter.

"It *does* matter," she said firmly.

"Why?" Shenzi asked, frowning at her.

"Because it's *there*."

Shenzi rolled her dark eyes. "Maybe you *do* belong in space. It sounds as though you've got stars in your blood, too. Personally, I *hate* going out there, and so do the others. It means being constantly in the company of men—the very worst kind of men. And I hate knowing that my very life depends on them and their science."

The next day, as Serena awaited Lania's arrival, she thought again about her conversation with Shenzi. Was it true? *Did* she have stars in her blood? And with all the knowledge she possessed now, would she feel differently about going into space? It was probably a good thing that she would be making this brief journey before she gave the High Priestess her answer. The ship that had seemed so wondrous to her might now seem cramped and uncomfortable, and the fascination she'd felt might be gone, too.

She went up to the broad, flat roof of the main building at the appointed time, and found Lania just landing in her sleek little hovercraft. She smiled, recalling her first journey in it and how frightened she'd been to fly through the air in something so tiny and so naked. Hovercrafts like Lania's were made almost entirely of plastene, the same glass-like substance that was used in the windows on the spaceships and the landing craft she'd once called a "flying boats." And as a result, flying in one of them was almost like flying with an anti-grav pack, though much more comfortable.

She was in danger of losing herself in a memory of that flight with Darian, pressed against his hard body, when Lania opened the door and waved to her. Moments later, she was seated and they were taking off into the blue skies.

"Today, I'm going to show you Vondrak," Lania announced. "The High Priestess wouldn't let me take you that far away before."

Serena felt a ripple of eagerness at Darian's surname, then belatedly realized that Lania was referring to the place, not the name. Vondrak, which lay on the far side of the smaller of

Ulata's two oceans, was the largest city on the planet and its business and cultural center. Ul-tago was the capital, a smaller city that had been built expressly for that purpose. It lay only a short distance from the compound, and Serena had seen it on her last trip with Lania.

She wondered if Darian lived there. Vondrak was named for his family, of course. The present city had grown up around the site of his family's stronghold.

"It will take us longer in this," Lania went on, "but if we took the shuttle, you wouldn't be able to see much along the way."

Serena stared at the changing landscape beneath them. The gently rolling hills and wide valleys that surrounded the Sisterhood's compound gave way to steeper hills and then to dark, jagged mountains covered with fir trees. Lania flew close to the tops, where Serena could see snowcaps, even in midsummer.

Ulata's size still intimidated her. It was nearly ten times the size of her own small world, and with many thousand times the population as well. What that great size meant for her was too much sky and a feeling of vulnerability. The horizon was so much farther away that she often imagined she could feel the weight of the heavens pressing down on her.

At such times, Serena would find herself longing to be back in her familiar home, back among her own people, who seemed so much less complicated than these Ulatans. But truth be told, she didn't feel that way very often. Her previous life now felt to her like a long childhood, something to be treasured but not repeated. Despite all their complexities and their sometimes incomprehensible ways, Serena liked the Ulatans and liked her life here.

Now she could see beyond the jagged mountains to the great ocean, and as they approached it, she made a sound of surprise. Lania turned to her questioningly.

"Why is it such a strange color?" she asked. It was green, a strange sort of green that faded to muddy brown in places. And now that they drew closer, she could see that it was heaving madly, flinging itself against the rocky shore so hard that great fountains of water rose into the air.

"What color are the oceans on your world?" Lania asked.

"Blue—the color of the sky, or nearly that. And our sea isn't angry like this, either."

Lania laughed. "I guess 'angry' is a good word for it. It's at its worst right now because of the lunar cycles. But as to the color . . . " She paused. "I think it has to do with algae or some such thing. I'm not really sure. Both our oceans are this color. Blue would be very pretty."

Serena now remembered having read that Ulata's two moons affected the tides, but at the time, she hadn't really understood it, since the word "tide" was unfamiliar to her.

She had studied everything she could about this world and its people, and about the other worlds in this star system. Then she asked Lania and Shenzi endless questions, sometimes drawing exasperated looks. Slowly, she came to realize that in this highly complex society, no one person knew everything. That was a revelation to her, because in her own, far less complicated world, everyone had much the same level of knowledge.

Lania reached out to flip a switch on the console, then took the small steering wheel in her hands. The hovercraft dipped lower and skimmed along the edge of the land. Far below, Serena could see strange-looking houses, built out over the edge of the rocks and propped in place with long poles.

"I'm surprised that there aren't people out sailing today," Lania remarked. "This area is famous for rough-water sailing. One of those houses belongs to Darian Vondrak. He has a reputation for sailing in any kind of weather."

The sudden mention of Darian's name sent a thrill through Serena, making her question whether she could ever forget him. She peered down at the houses, wanting to ask which one belonged to him, but unwilling to show any interest, even to Lania.

Instead, she said that she was surprised that he lived in such a place. "I would have thought he'd live in Vondrak, since it's his family's home."

"Oh, he just uses that house when he goes sailing. Most of his family *does* live in Vondrak, and he keeps a place there as well, but he lives in Ul-tago most of the time—that is, when he isn't in space. He teaches and does research at the Space Academy."

Serena frowned, trying to imagine Darian as a teacher and then trying to understand how someone could have so many different homes.

Lania turned the hovercraft to the sea and flipped another switch, then took her hands away from the wheel. "I saw him at a party recently, by the way. He asked about you."

"He did?" Serena didn't have to fake her surprise, but she *did* hide her pleasure.

Lania nodded. "I told him that you were doing very well and that you were happy, and that we'd become friends."

She sighed. "Now *there* is a man I could marry—if he'd give up space, that is. But he won't, so I shouldn't waste my thoughts on him."

"Didn't you say that his family wants him to marry?" Serena asked, keeping her tone carefully neutral.

"Oh, they do. I'm sure the woman he was with is a candidate. I don't know her well, but she seems like the right type for him. Her family is old nobility, but they haven't much money, so she'd be happy to marry him and have him keep her in luxury while he's off in space."

Serena was shocked at the hot jealousy she felt toward this unknown woman. She decided to change the subject.

"What about you? Have you decided if you're going to

marry Trey?" Serena hadn't met him, of course, but she knew that Trey was pressing Lania for an answer and that Lania's family was pushing hard for the marriage.

"No, I mean I haven't decided—which, when you think about it, is a decision in itself, isn't it?"

Serena laughed. "I guess it is."

"What I wish is that I had your talent, so that I could join the Sisterhood and forget about men and marriage and children."

"It's hard for me to understand why women allow themselves to be pushed into marriage," Serena said. "It sounds as though things aren't so very different from the time of forced marriages."

"You're right. The only difference is that the pressures are more subtle now. Every time you talk like that, you make me wish I could live in your world."

She then began to ask questions about Serena's home and her life: questions she'd asked before. Serena suspected that Lania didn't quite believe her, but she understood that. If she weren't here to see it for herself, she wouldn't believe *this* world, either.

More than two hours passed as they talked and stared at the angry waters below them. Lania apologized for the low, whining noise and the slight vibrations of the hovercraft, explaining that she had switched it into high speed to get them to Vondrak quickly. Serena thought it was also Lania's way of letting her know that they were safe and not about to crash into the sea.

"There it is!" Lania said, just as Serena was squinting at the distant horizon, where she could see something looming up into the blue sky.

Seeing Ul-tago hadn't prepared her for her first glimpse of Ulata's greatest city. The sight was nearly beyond her comprehension. It filled a wide space along the coast, then spilled over several hills into the valleys beyond. All the buildings were made of a strange pearlized substance, unlike the starkly white buildings of Ul-tago. The underlying color was a creamy beige, but swirls of pastel shades moved like colorful shadows along their surfaces. She asked Lania about it.

"It's a type of stone. When modern Vondrak was built a century ago, they used every bit of it in existence. That's why Ul-tago isn't built of it. Wait until you see it at sunset."

"Sunset? I thought we were going to your home." She knew that Lania lived in Ul-tago and had assumed they were going there for dinner.

"Oh. Maybe I didn't make myself clear. We're going to my family's home here. They've been eager to meet you. Is that all right?"

"Of course." Serena smiled. "Will your terrible brother be there?" Lania had often spoken of her brother, with whom she had a stormy relationship.

Lania made a face. "He'll be there, but I'm sure he'll behave himself with you there."

They were now flying low over the great city, and suddenly Serena spotted a very unusual-looking building high atop a hill, surrounded by a park with trees and gardens. She asked about it, intrigued by its shape and air of great age.

"That's Vondrak Keep, the old family home. It's more than a thousand years old. We can go see it, if you like."

"Does the family live there?" Serena asked, her treacherous thoughts turning once again to Darian.

"Oh, no, they live over there." Lania waved an arm to the left. "In the same area my family lives in. The Keep is a museum." Then, when she saw Serena frown in confusion, she explained what a museum was.

"Yes, I'd very much like to see it," Serena told her.

"He *does* look like Darian, doesn't he? I'd forgotten about that portrait. I haven't been here for ages."

Both women were standing in the Great Hall of Vondrak Keep, staring at the huge oil painting over the marble mantel. Serena was stunned. Except for the clothing, it could have been Darian himself.

"Who is he?"

"That's Lord Teres. He's the one who ended all the wars. Of course, he did it by killing off every one of his enemies and even killing their women and children. He's always been a fascinating figure in our history. He was definitely not a nice person, but he *did* bring lasting peace. And his grandson, Dreyer, ended the rule of the nobility and created the government we have today."

They wandered through the vast rooms of the Keep, some of which contained a historical record of Ulata, while others attempted to re-create the styles and life of bygone centuries. Serena was fascinated. The Ulatans had gone from living much as her own people lived now to their present world in only two centuries. She could not believe her people would match that.

She was also very much aware of the fact that this was Darian's ancestral home. It seemed that after months of slowly forcing him from her thoughts, she was suddenly being confronted by him at every turn. And that evening was to provide yet another surprise.

"Welcome to our home, Serena! We're so happy to meet you." Lania's mother, who looked like an older version of her daughter, smiled as she greeted Serena. "Come join us on the terrace. The others are all there."

Even though she had become accustomed to the luxury of the compound, Serena was still startled by this grand house—and especially by its size. It seemed nearly as large as the compound, and yet it was home to far fewer people.

The wide marble terrace overlooked a formal garden with a big round pool that had a fountain in its center. Black-clad servants moved through a small crowd, dispensing crystal glasses of wine and finger foods. There were perhaps a dozen people there, which surprised Serena—and apparently Lania as well.

"I should have guessed that Mother would overdo it," Lania said in a low voice. "She just couldn't resist inviting people in to meet you. You're quite a celebrity, you know."

Serena *hadn't* known that, but she supposed that she must seem as exotic to them as Darian and his men once had to her. Then she saw that there were even more people than she'd at first thought, as several groups moved toward the terrace from the gardens at the side.

Remembering that day when she and Trenek had first seen Darian and his men, and how she'd found them repulsive, she wondered what these people must think about her. Did she look like a small, pale child dressed in her black, diamond-studded gown?

So many introductions were made that Serena couldn't begin to keep track of names. She met Lania's father, who, despite his daughter's complaints, seemed very pleasant. And then she met an assortment of other people, whose names drifted right through her mind and out again.

Shortly after that, three more people appeared from the gardens: an older man and woman and a young man about Lania's age. Something about the older man seemed vaguely familiar, but she had no time to think about it as Lania introduced her to the young man—her brother, Miken. Now that Serena turned her attention to him, she saw the resemblance.

"And this is Greyen and Tersia Vondrak—Darian's parents," Lania said.

"Darian has told us about you and your beautiful world, Serena," his mother said. "He found your world quite enchanting. I do hope you are happy here."

"Yes, thank you, I'm quite happy," Serena replied, trying to resist the temptation to stare past them into the garden. Could Darian himself be here? Did she want that? And had Darian really found her world to be "enchanting," or was this another of what she had privately come to call the "kind lies" practiced by Ulatans?

"And you are every bit as beautiful as he said you were," Darian's father added.

Serena smiled and thanked him for what she assumed was another of the kind lies. She doubted that Darian found her to be all that attractive; she'd just been available, that was all.

"He also said that you are a woman of great courage," Tersia Vondrak added. "And I have never heard my son speak of any woman that way. What a terrifying time that must have been for you, my dear."

"Darian was very kind," Serena said. "He was very patient, too, because I had so many questions and no way to ask them."

Greyen Vondrak chuckled. "I never expected to hear the word 'patience' and my son's name in the same breath. Perhaps it's best that you can't see him now, because he is impatient, to say the least. He wants to return to space."

She told them that she would be going on her first voyage as a Trezhella, and that she too was eager to return to space. She wanted desperately to ask if Darian would be commanding Deep Space One, but she kept silent.

The evening passed pleasantly, though Serena felt that she was being treated more like an exotic work of art than a person. And even though she knew he couldn't be coming, she kept expecting to see Darian walk in at any moment. Did he know she would be here, and if so, had he deliberately chosen to stay away? She thought that might be possible. He might very well have decided that it wasn't a good idea to see her now that she could actually speak to him.

"Guess who I met last night?"

Darian glanced over at Miken. His old friend was wearing a broad grin, and Darian suspected he knew what was coming.

"Who?"

"Serena. She came to dinner with Lania at my parents' house. Your parents were there as well, together with as many people as Mother could round up on short notice."

"How is she?" Darian asked as he untied the last line and leapt into the sailboat.

"She's incredibly beautiful, that's how she is. Did you really manage to keep your hands off her on that long journey? Because if you did, you're a better man than I would have been."

"She stayed in her cabin most of the time," Darian lied. "And you know I couldn't touch her. She's a Trezhella."

"But she wasn't then." He paused. "I'm not so sure she really is one now, either. At least, she's not as arrogant as they usually are. 'Self-contained' would describe her better, I think. And it couldn't have been easy to carry off, with everyone gawking at her."

Since he had his back to Miken at the moment, Darian permitted himself a smile. "Yes. She was that way from the beginning. Are you going to give me a hand with these sails, or are you just along for the ride?"

Miken quickly moved into action. "No decision yet, I take it?"

Darian watched as the mainsail billowed. "No, but it should be any day now."

"Do you still think your chances are good?"

"I think they're better than good. The only problem is convincing several of the older commanders that they should be passed over."

He grinned at Miken. "Just to help them along in their decision-making, I told them that I was going to quit if I don't get Deep Space One."

Chapter Five

Darian's long fingers were caressing her naked body as though it were the finest of instruments, drawing from it the voluptuous music of passion. She could feel his careful restraint and the hunger that matched her own. At first, it seemed as though they were floating on the gentle swells of the blue seas of her home. But then suddenly, they were being rocked by the huge waves of the green Ulatan ocean, clinging to each other as wave after wave of ecstasy broke over them.

The softly chiming bell of her bedside alarm woke Serena, and the lovespell shattered. She sat up and ran her fingers shakily through her sleep-tangled hair. Her body still felt heated and exquisitely sensitive from the dream.

It didn't require much thought to know why she'd begun to dream about him after all these weeks and months—or, for that matter, why she'd dreamed of oceans. She lay back against the soft pillows and thought about the evening just past.

The Ulatans never ceased to amaze her. She'd been quizzed

endlessly about her home. Nearly everyone present at that dinner had, at some point, made reference to the terror she must have felt and then asked if she were happy here. But not one of them had said a word about the circumstances under which she had come to be here. They all knew she'd been taken by force from her home as the result of policies put into place by people they had elected, and yet they'd pretended that she had come here of her own free will. Only in their mention of her terror had there been any indication at all that her journey here hadn't been her choice. Not even Lania and Shenzi ever referred to that.

Still, all things considered, she was glad that Lania had taken her to the party—and especially that she'd taken her to Vondrak. Even if she never saw that splendid city again, she would carry it in her memory—along with the man whose family had given the city its name.

She sighed heavily. Darian. Would he ever recede into the dim recesses of memory? Before last night, she had half-believed that would happen. Well, perhaps it still would. She knew that the High Priestess wasn't likely to permit her any more excursions into the outside world. The other women here saw their friends and families when they visited the compound, if at all, and most were happy to keep it that way.

Thoughts of the High Priestess made her frown. Tomorrow, she would be leaving on her voyage, and when she returned in five days, she had promised to give her answer. She *wanted* to go, despite the dangers, but there were dangers and there were dangers. If she could know for certain that Darian wouldn't be in command of Deep Space One, she would have said yes already.

And if he *was* named to command the mission? Well, she just didn't know. Perhaps during the upcoming voyage, she could think of a way to ask without casting suspicion on either of them.

She reached over to the bedside table, picked up the remote, and clicked on the vidcomm for the news. She'd been watching it carefully for any announcement about the mission, but so far, she'd seen nothing.

The business news, in which she had no interest at all, scrolled slowly across the screen, and then the general news began. Serena was only half paying attention, since none of it meant much to her. Then suddenly, she jerked herself upright and stared hard at the screen.

"The Space Command says that no decision has yet been reached regarding the command of Deep Space One. It is believed that the honor will go to one of the two senior Commanders, Marc Tongin or Vasik Wengor. But unidentified sources say that Commander Darian Vondrak has informed the Command that he will resign unless he is chosen.

"Commander Vondrak, though much younger than the other two men, is the most highly decorated officer in the Command's history, and it was he who commanded the longest voyage thus far, to bring back the Trezhella, Serena, whose talents are such that it is believed she could maintain contact with home base for Deep Space One.

"The High Priestess has not yet made a decision about sending Serena on this mission, claiming that she has yet to prove herself ready for the rigors of space."

Serena clicked off the vidcomm. She couldn't believe that Darian's superiors would take his threat seriously. They certainly would know what everyone else seemed to know: that Darian had stars in his blood.

On the other hand, in the devious manner of these Ulatans, Darian might well have been using the threat to remind them of his family's power. "Ignore my request at your own peril." She'd learned enough about the ways of the Ulatans to know that even though those in high elected or appointed positions had great power, the *true* power in this strange world was held by a handful of the old noble families—chief among them the Vondraks.

She climbed out of bed to face a busy day, to be followed by an early night. Before dawn tomorrow, she would be off to Tligid on her first voyage as a Trezhella.

"I don't understand what it is that you find so fascinating out there," Shenzi said as they stood in front of the big window of the spacecraft. "There's nothing to see."

Serena smiled. "That's what fascinates me: all that 'nothingness.' When I stare up into the heavens at night, it seems filled with stars—and yet, out here, we can see that it isn't. It helps me to understand the size of it all."

"I think you're just trying to avoid what is *really* important," Shenzi stated, turning her back to the window.

"Shenzi, he didn't *do* anything."

"You don't understand. If we let him get away with staring at you like that, it will only encourage him and others. He should be reported and disciplined."

"What would happen to him?"

"The rules are very strict. He'd be grounded for a year and be demoted as well."

"All for *staring* at me? That's too harsh."

"No, it isn't. Don't you see how vulnerable we are—out here with all these men? If we let them get away with anything at all, we'll soon be in serious trouble."

"When I was brought here, Darian assigned Sevec to help me, and he stared at me all the time. His interest in me was plain to see. But even if I'd been able to speak your language then, I wouldn't have reported him because he never *did* anything—and I knew that he wouldn't."

"You weren't a Trezhella then."

"True, but he knew I would soon be one, and as you know, they were all under orders to treat me well. What you don't seem to understand is that *everyone* stares at me because I look different. I stared at them a lot, too, in the beginning. We fascinated each other."

"Did that include Darian?" Shenzi asked, her tone changing to one of teasing.

"Of course. From the first time I saw him, I knew he had to be their leader and it was important for me to understand him as best I could."

"And did *he* stare at you?"

"If you mean in the same way that the cadet or this man stared at me, the answer is no." But she was thinking how glibly she could lie now. Was she in danger of becoming a Ulatan?

"Darian *watched* me. He was concerned for my well-being. And as I told you before, he was very kind."

Shenzi waved a beringed hand in dismissal of the subject. "That young man is obviously making a point of being where we are as often as he can. At the very least, he should be told to stay away from you."

Serena sighed. "Oh, very well: a warning then. But speak directly to *him*, not to his superiors."

Shenzi nodded and left. Serena was glad to be alone for a time. She hadn't expected Shenzi to insist that they stay together whenever they left their cabins, but Shenzi said those were the rules. Serena had pointed out that she'd spent more time than this wandering about a ship by herself. Now it appeared that her friend was willing to break one rule while insisting on keeping another. But at least the cadet wouldn't suffer anything more than a tongue-lashing.

She turned back to the window. Tomorrow, they would reach Tligid. The mysteries of space travel never failed to amaze her. Distance, she'd discovered, did not determine the length of the voyage. In some complex way she couldn't begin to understand, the ships made use of planets' gravitational fields and of the powerful electromagnetic storms in space to move from one world to the next. So, while Tligid was Ulata's nearest neighbor, it took longer to reach it than it did to get to more distant worlds.

She heard voices behind her and turned to see a group of men coming into the lounge. They all stared at her, no doubt shocked to find her there, let alone without Shenzi, who had insisted that they stay in their cabins when they weren't working.

Then suddenly, she saw a familiar face among the group of Ulatans. It was Sevec, the young cadet she'd just told Shenzi about. She smiled at him, and got a shy smile in return. He hesitated, then left the group and came over to her. His friends stared at him in shock.

"Good day, Trezhella Serena," he said with the slight bow that all the spacemen used to acknowledge members of the Sisterhood.

"And good day to you, Sevec. How nice to see you again— and to be able to talk to you as well." She really was glad to see him. If she hadn't been so besotted by Darian, she might have tried to get to know him better.

He laughed, drawing looks of consternation from his comrades, who had gathered nearby and were pretending to look at the view beyond the window. "You speak our language very well now," he said, then laughed again.

He continued, "I felt so frustrated, trying to communicate with you—but you must have been frustrated with me at first as well. I'm surprised to find you here alone."

"I'm not alone. My Sister has gone to tend to something. I know we're supposed to stay in our cabins, but I need exercise and I like coming up here."

He smiled. "Yes, I remember how you were always roaming around the ship. I used to follow you, but then Commander Vondrak said I should just let you wander."

"Speaking of Commander Vondrak, I saw on the news just before we left that he wants to command Deep Space One."

Sevec nodded vigorously. "He sure does. He's even threatening to resign if he doesn't get it."

"Do you think he will?"

He nodded. "Most everyone is betting that he'll get it. And if he does, I sure hope he'll take me along—but then, so does every other cadet. Has the High Priestess decided whether or not she'll let you go?"

"No, not yet, but I think she'll decide soon—maybe when I get back from this voyage."

"Do you want to go? Everyone says that the Trezhellas really hate to go into space."

"Maybe that's true of the others, but it isn't true for me. And yes, I very much want to go, even if it *is* dangerous."

"I didn't think a woman could have stars in her blood, but maybe you're the exception," Sevec said admiringly.

By now, the other men had given up all pretense of keeping their distance from her, and one of them spoke up, saying that he hoped the High Priestess would permit her to go.

"It would mean a lot to the men to be able to keep in touch with their families on that mission," he explained. "They'll be gone for two years, after all."

"Two years?" Serena echoed. "But I was told that the mission would last a little over six months."

"It will—in ship time," another man explained. "But they'll really be gone for two years."

Serena shook her head. "I spend much of my free time trying to understand space travel, but I can see that it hasn't helped."

One of the men began to try to explain it to her, with the intermittent assistance of Sevec and the others. But before they'd gotten very far, Serena saw them staring at something behind her, and she turned to see Shenzi standing at the entrance to the room, wearing a deep frown.

"Thank you for trying to explain it," Serena said to the men. "I will study some more. And it was nice to see you again, Sevec. I hope you're chosen."

"How dare they bother you like that!" Shenzi proclaimed as Serena joined her. "I was terrified when I came in here and found them crowded around you like that."

"Terrified? Shenzi, we were just talking. And it was *I* who initiated the conversation."

That wasn't strictly true, but she would have, if Sevec hadn't approached her first. "And as for them 'crowding around me,' that isn't true. I didn't feel threatened in any way. We were just talking about space travel."

"Serena, you just can't do things like this! It's dangerous!"

"Shenzi, I think you must try to understand that I don't hate or fear men the way all of you do. I grew up in a very different world."

"But you're in *our* world now—and this is where *they* grew up."

"That's true, and I understand that many of the Sisters have suffered at the hands of men, but it's wrong to think they're all the same. They respect the Sisterhood. They were asking if I'm going on Deep Space One, and saying how important it would be for the men to be able to communicate with their families because it's such a long voyage."

Shenzi threw up her hands. "I give up! You'll just have to learn for yourself. I only hope that the lesson won't be too harsh. Have you decided yet about Deep Space One?"

"No, not yet."

"Why? There's nothing to see. It's an ugly place."

"I don't understand you, Shenzi. Don't you have any curiosity about *anything?*"

"No. I hate these trips. I'd much rather be at home."

"All right, then, I'll see if I can find Sevec. He offered to show me Tligid."

Shenzi threw her an exasperated look, and Serena knew that her lie must have worked. Sevec *hadn't* made the offer, but she thought he would if she asked. Still, since she worried about getting him into trouble, she probably wouldn't have asked.

Shenzi called the hotel desk and requested a hovercraft and a driver, but it was clear that she wasn't happy about it. A short time later, they were seated in a larger version of the craft that Lania had, flying low over the strange terrain of Tligid.

"Is it all like this?" Serena asked, staring down at the raw, reddish land. There was almost no vegetation, except for some scrawny grayish shrubs.

"I don't know. I suppose so."

"You mean you've never even seen it?"

"No."

Serena leaned forward. Their driver was Tligidian, but he spoke Ulatan. She asked him the question she'd asked Shenzi.

"It's not all flat like this," the man replied. "There are big, deep canyons on the other side. I could take you there."

"Yes, please do. Show us the places you like best."

The man turned to her with a surprised expression that slowly transformed itself into a smile when she smiled at him. "Yes," he said eagerly. "I can do that."

Serena settled back again, wondering if all Ulatans were as uninterested in this world as Shenzi was. Her first impression had been that Tligid was a truly ugly place, but as they skimmed over the red, wrinkled land, it began to take on a strange sort of beauty—for her, at least.

And over the course of the next few hours, she became quite intrigued with this small world. The canyons were spectacular: deep cuts in the red rock, several of them so deep that their pilot flew down into them and they were completely surrounded by the ruddy walls.

Then he showed them a place where great geysers of steam poured from cracks in the soil, creating a mist that somehow softened the rawness of the land. And he took them to small villages where the houses were carved out of the faces of mountains, layered one on top of another. By the time they started back to the Ulatan base, even Shenzi reluctantly admitted to having enjoyed the trip.

As they got out of the hovercraft, Serena dug into her small purse and gave the pilot several gold coins as she thanked him. He beamed at her and bowed several times, while Shenzi looked on disapprovingly.

"He's paid well enough," Shenzi said as they walked back into the hotel.

"Maybe so, but this looks like a poor world. Perhaps the money can help someone else, then."

Shenzi rolled her dark eyes. "Next, I suppose you'll want to buy some of the awful things they make here."

"What do you mean?"

Shenzi took her arm. "Oh, come on. I'll show you. There's a small shop here in the hotel."

"I think this would look lovely on my wall," Serena said the moment she spotted the weaving.

"If you want something for your walls, you have only to ask. We can have anything we want."

"This is what I want. I'm going to start a collection of art from different worlds."

She stared at the rough weaving and the muted colors, knowing that by Ulatan standards, it wasn't attractive. But it reminded her of the weavings her own people did, using natural plants and dyes. The Ulatans, it seemed, disdained anything natural. If they wanted something different, they simply invented it.

"Well, we leave for home tomorrow," Shenzi said as they left the shop. "Have you made your decision yet?"

Serena nodded. "I'm going to go."

"I was afraid of that. I can see how you really enjoy going into space. I hoped you wouldn't go. It's so dangerous, Serena. You could die out there."

"I know it's risky—but what a wonderful opportunity it will be to see new and strange places."

"Well, at least I know you'll be treated well. The men will be so glad to have you along that they'll surely behave themselves."

Later, as she sat in her room, staring out at the setting sun that turned the entire world gold and red, Serena thought about Shenzi's final words. Her lips twisted wryly. No doubt the men *would* "behave themselves"—including Darian, if he were the Commander. Her power would now be nearly as great as his—perhaps even equal to his.

But in truth, Darian's presence or absence had little to do with her decision. After tormenting herself about it all this time, she realized that he had little to do with it. She would go because she *wanted* to go. She was as curious as any of the men about what was out there, and the fact that two years would pass on Ulata didn't trouble her. She would miss Shenzi and Lania, but that was all, and they would be there when she returned.

And if Darian Vondrak didn't get his way, she would surely be able to forget him and would, in any event, probably come home to find him long since married and a father.

Still, if she was totally honest with herself, she knew that she wanted him to come with her. There were things left unfinished between them, things she needed to know.

* * *

"Are you truly certain of this, Serena?" The High Priestess asked, studying her intently with her large, dark-brown eyes.

"Yes, I'm sure, Your Excellency. I've given it much thought."

"Why do you want to go?"

The question caught Serena off guard, but she decided to answer it honestly. She shrugged and smiled. "I fear that I have stars in my blood, Your Excellency."

The High Priestess merely nodded, as though Serena's words had confirmed what she already knew. "Well, I suppose I should be grateful for that, since your talents are well-suited to the longest journeys. Is it because you don't really feel at home here?"

That question too surprised her, but once more, she tried to be honest. "I think I feel as much at home as it is possible for me to feel. I will always be different from the rest of you, though."

The High Priestess stared at her in silence for a moment, then got up to walk over to the big windows that looked out over the gardens. "Perhaps what you are is what all of us will be in the future."

"What do you mean?"

The High Priestess turned to her with a smile. "Our world is changing, Serena. I can see it with our young novices. Many of them do not hold men in contempt as most of us older Sisters do. There is even talk of permitting women to be educated for certain professions."

"Really? I'm very happy to hear that. It should have happened long ago. I find it so hard to understand a world that is so far ahead of my own world, yet treats women like children."

"Well, as I said, that may be changing. I've heard that Lessa Vondrak has persuaded her father to fund a sort of experiment—a special academy to try to train women for various professions in the sciences."

98

"Who is Lessa Vondrak?" Serena asked. She was sure that wasn't Darian's mother's name.

"I forget that you wouldn't know the name. The Vondraks are the wealthiest and most powerful of the old nobility. Lessa is Greyen Vondrak's daughter." The High Priestess smiled. "Some would call her a troublemaker."

"I met Greyen and Tersia Vondrak that evening at Lania's home."

"Oh? I hadn't realized that. It's a pity you didn't meet Lessa as well. I think you would like her."

"Because I'm a troublemaker, too?" Serena said with a smile.

To her amazement, the austere woman laughed aloud. "So you are, but I rather enjoy you for it. It wasn't always so, of course, but I've come to realize that this place needs trouble-makers from time to time." Then she grew solemn again.

"Serena, you *do* realize that two years will pass here, although you will be gone only about six months?"

"Yes, I know that. I will miss all of you, but it may be easier for me than it would be for many others." She hesitated. "Do you know yet who will be commanding the mission?"

The High Priestess frowned. "Why should that matter? Oh yes, I see. Darian Vondrak is the one who brought you here. If he is chosen, will that be a problem? I thought you said that he had treated you well."

"He did." Serena affected a casual shrug. "It really doesn't matter. It's just that I know Commander Vondrak and I know I can trust him."

"Well, I think we shall know soon."

Serena paused outside the closed door to the High Priestess's office and rubbed her perspiring palms against the rich black fabric of her gown. She decided that it was probably for the best that she hadn't known about this meeting until just a few hours ago. She took a deep breath, let it out slowly, and then pressed the doorplate to announce herself.

Darian was already there, seated in one of the ornate chairs in front of the High Priestess's desk. She forced herself to meet the High Priestess's gaze first, but out of the corner of her eye, she saw him rise from the chair.

The two women greeted each other formally, and the High Priestess gestured to Darian. "You know each other, of course."

It seemed to take Serena forever to turn her gaze to Darian, and in that long moment that was actually less than a second, she heard the High Priestess's words echo with a meaning the woman had never intended. They knew each other, all right, and in a way that would undoubtedly have shocked the High Priestess.

Darian nodded and bowed slightly. She acknowledged him with a similar gesture. She realized that she had somehow been expecting him to seem different. But how could he, when she had carried a clear image of him in her mind and in her dreams all this time? She tore her gaze away from his quickly, but not before she saw that glitter of amusement in his dark eyes that was also part of her memories, and to which she had ascribed many different meanings this past year. Why was it there now? Was he too thinking about the double meaning of the High Priestess's words?

She took the other chair and he resumed his seat. The chairs were positioned at an angle to each other and to the desk, so that she wasn't exactly facing him, but he wasn't out of her line of sight, either. He hadn't said a word to her, and she wondered why.

"I have already told Commander Vondrak that you were quite pleased to learn that he will be commanding Deep Space One, because you know him and trust him." The High Priestess's gaze went from one to the other of them.

Serena forced herself to turn to Darian. "Yes, that is true. Congratulations on your selection, Commander." She thought of adding something about her gratitude for his many kindnesses to her on her journey here, but she was afraid she might choke on the words.

"I'm very grateful for your trust in me, Trezhella," Darian responded, and she saw that the twinkle was still in his eyes. She could only hope that the High Priestess hadn't seen it.

"And I'm also very grateful that you are willing to undertake this journey," he added.

"Commander Vondrak requested this meeting so that he could assure us personally that every effort will be made to see that you are both comfortable and safe, Serena."

"I appreciate that," she said, flicking a glance at him before turning her attention back to the High Priestess. "Have you told him yet about our problem?"

"No. He arrived only moments before you did." She turned to Darian. "As you know, Commander, it is our rule that Trezhellas are accompanied at all times either by other sisters or by novices. But I'm afraid that in this case, that presents a problem.

"Let me be candid with you, Commander. The decision to make this journey was Serena's alone. Had she chosen not to go, I would have made suitable excuses. But as it happens, she *wants* to go. After she made her decision, I asked for a volunteer to accompany her. But no one else is willing to undertake such a long and dangerous mission, and I cannot bring myself to force anyone to go." She paused briefly and glanced at Serena, who kept her eyes on the High Priestess.

"Serena has told me that she is comfortable with this arrangement, though I'll admit that I'm not. I do not like to think of her being alone for so long a period of time with several dozen men."

"I can understand your concern, Your Excellency," Darian

said. "The only comfort I can offer you is that I have hand-picked the crew for this mission, and most of them were also on the ship that brought Trezhella Serena here."

He paused and Serena could feel his gaze upon her. She turned to him, fearing now that her failure to do so would seem strange to the High Priestess. In fact, with each passing second, she grew more fearful that the High Priestess would somehow detect the truth in their careful, formal behavior. She thought that if *she* were in the older woman's position, she would have guessed it before this.

Darian's dark eyes met hers only briefly, then turned to the High Priestess. "Perhaps you are unaware of this, but Trezhella Serena spent most of that journey roaming about the ship on her own. I was reluctant to confine her to her cabin for such a long period, and I didn't want her to feel that she was a prisoner. So I let her wander about, but assigned one of my cadets to keep an eye on her and provide assistance if she required it.

"I tell you this now as a way of pointing out that she was quite safe then—as she will be on this mission."

"Do I have your word, then, Commander, that if Serena raises any concerns about your men's behavior, you will take appropriate action?"

"You have my word, Your Excellency."

The High Priestess rested her head against the ornately carved high back of her chair and regarded Darian solemnly. "I have spoken with my Trezhellas who have traveled on ships under your command, Commander Vondrak, and your record is excellent. On two occasions when problems arose, you dealt with them immediately—unlike some other commanders. So I accept your word that Serena will be safe with you."

"Thank you, Your Excellency."

Serena felt a bubble of laughter welling up in her throat and coughed discreetly. She could feel Darian's eyes on her again, but she didn't dare look at him now. She hoped this interview would be over soon. She'd never before been in a situation so fraught with tension and unspoken words and double meanings.

Still, she knew that the High Priestess was correct to trust Darian to protect her from the men, should that problem arise. But who would protect her from *him?* And who could protect her from her own feelings?

The High Priestess stood, indicating that the meeting was over. Serena rose as well, taking care to stay away from Darian as he too got up.

"Serena, perhaps you could escort Commander Vondrak back to his hovercraft."

No! cried her brain. But she merely nodded. "Of course, Your Excellency."

Hovercraft parking was on the roof of the main building. Serena started down the hallway to the elevator without bothering to see if he was following her. She knew it wasn't likely that anyone else would be going up there at this moment, but she pressed the button and hoped that when the doors opened, someone would be there. She didn't want to spend even a few seconds alone with him at this point.

The doors opened and the car was empty. She could feel Darian's presence behind her as she stepped onto it. When she turned, he was standing beside her—unnecessarily close, given the fact that there was no one else in the car.

The doors slid shut, and Serena waited for him to say something. She had thought endlessly about this meeting ever since the announcement was made that he would be commanding the mission. But now she found that she had nothing to say to him—or too much to say. So she waited.

The car moved upward swiftly, and the doors opened onto the roof enclosure, and still he had said nothing. She scanned the flat expanse of roof beyond the small plex enclosure. Only one hovercraft was there, and no one else was in sight.

"Somehow, I thought that you might have quite a lot to say to me," he said in a tone of dry amusement.

She turned to face him and found him leaning against the wall of the car, his arms folded across his broad chest as he stared at her.

"Oh?" She arched a brow. "And exactly what did you imagine that I would say, Commander?"

"What I *hoped* to hear was that you've missed me, but what I *expected* to hear is more along the lines of what a cad I was to have taken advantage of you. My guess is that you *did* miss me—at least until your sisters convinced you that all men are animals."

She said nothing, since she couldn't think of a response. In fact, she could scarcely breathe. She moved out of the car into the enclosure and he followed.

"Will you at least satisfy my curiosity about one thing?" he asked.

She gave him a sidelong glance. "What one thing?"

"The High Priestess said that the decision to go on Deep Space One was yours alone. Why did you decide to go? I know you must be aware of the dangers."

"The decision had nothing to do with you, Darian."

"I'm aware of that. My appointment wasn't announced until much later."

She paused in the middle of the roof and raised her face to the warm breeze. The sky was a pale blue, and one of Ulata's two moons was visible as a faint, milky sphere.

"I think I have stars in my blood," she said, lowering her gaze until she met his. "My people paid scant attention to the heavens, and they believed that the stars were merely holes in the fabric of the world. Looking back now, I think that even then, I had a problem with that explanation.

"I was always fascinated by the heavens—especially at night. I annoyed people with my questions. They never understood my curiosity. I started to have my visions when I was only ten, and I think I made the connection right away: that the blackness and great distances I felt were somehow connected to the heavens.

"Even though I know much more now, I am still amazed by the great distances up there. When the stars are out, it seems that they fill all the space, but of course they don't."

As she spoke, she had lifted her face to the sky, but now she looked at him again. He was staring at her intently and was utterly still. She shrugged.

"You asked, and I have told you."

"What did your people think about your visions?"

"They didn't know what to think. Most of them probably thought—as I did myself—that it was some sort of affliction, like being born blind or deaf or subject to seizures."

He was silent for a moment, and then, just when the silence began to fill up again with tension, he spoke. "The man who was with you—what was he to you? He couldn't have been your husband."

"How could you have known he wasn't my husband?" she asked, thinking that he was probably referring to Trenek's failure to try to protect her. She felt an angry need to come to Trenek's defense.

He smiled at her. "If he *was* your husband, your people must have very strange marriage customs."

"What . . . ? Oh!" She stopped, finally realizing what he meant. She turned away from him and pretended to be studying the hovercraft. She could feel her face growing warm and hated herself for it. Memories crowded her mind, and she pushed them away.

"We were to be married." Then, thinking about Trenek and the last time she'd seen him, she turned to Darian again.

"Tell me the truth, Darian. Did he live?" She knew by now what the weapon had been, and that stunners could either kill or render the person unconscious.

105

"He lived. I had no intention of killing him. I'll admit that I considered it, but it seemed pointless. Killing him would have meant that no one would ever know we'd been there, but I decided that it didn't matter. Your people pose no threat to us."

He paused, and when he spoke again, his voice was low, reminding her of the then incomprehensible words he'd spoken to her when they made love. She'd tried so hard to remember those words, but she couldn't.

"You couldn't have loved him, Serena. Was it an arranged marriage?"

"No!" she replied with more force than she intended. "Such a terrible thing could never happen among my people. Men and women are equal and always have been."

"But you didn't love him," Darian persisted.

Instead of answering, Serena took a few steps away from him, as though by doing so, she could remove herself from those memories of his lovemaking. She understood his reasoning. If she'd loved Trenek, then she couldn't have made love with *him*.

"I was very fond of Trenek," she said. "We had known each other all our lives. He loved me, and so he waited patiently until I finally agreed to marry him."

Darian's expression became one of disgust. "He loved you—and yet he tried to run away, rather than protecting you from us."

Anger flared up in her. "You don't understand, Darian! I told you that men and women are equal in my world. Women don't need to be 'protected.' Furthermore, until you came there, there had never been any need for protection of any kind. My people have never known anything but peace, and violence is so rare as to be nearly nonexistent."

"Nevertheless, I have sworn to the High Priestess that *I* will protect you."

"Oh, indeed!" She tossed her head angrily, her long blond

hair floating in the breeze. "I have no doubt that you will, Darian—but who is to protect me from *you?*"

He stared at her in silence for a long moment, then smiled crookedly. "You no more need protection from me, Serena, than I require protection from *you.* The ways of your people may be strange to me, but I find it even stranger that you have permitted yourself to become a Ulatan. I will see you in two weeks."

Before she could even begin to think of a response to that, he had climbed into his hovercraft. She didn't move, even when the wind created by its takeoff whipped around her. Then she stared at it until it had become a rapidly vanishing speck in the sky.

She clenched her fists in helpless anger, but the anger was directed at herself as much as at him. He had spoken the truth— or at least partly so. His words mirrored her own earlier thoughts about them. But she had *not* become Ulatan, however much she might have sounded like a Ulatan woman.

And what did he mean, anyway? How could he criticize her for behaving like a Ulatan when he himself was one?

She glared at the now empty sky, thinking that she had liked him much better when they couldn't talk to each other—when words hadn't mattered. And now, words were all they had left: words and memories.

Chapter Six

Serena stepped out of the hovercraft. Her hand was immediately engulfed in Darian's much larger one. She met his eyes briefly, then stared in shock at the assemblage of people. No, not people, she told herself as she scanned the crowd. Men. It was the great and powerful who were gathered here today, and they were all men.

When she had descended the steps, Darian released her hand and tucked it into the crook of his arm instead, taking the opportunity to lean toward her for a moment. "Don't worry, it'll be a quick."

She resisted the urge to smile as they walked toward a line of men, some in uniform and others in formal civilian clothes. She guessed that he disliked this ceremony as much as she did.

Darian introduced her to them, one after the other—names and titles she'd heard on the news, faces she'd seen on the vidscreen. And she assumed that the objects being held by other men who hovered around them were recording the event for the rest of Ulata.

It was late in the day—nearly sunset. The clear sky was streaked with red and gold, and even the great ship reflected those colors. It looked bulky and awkward now, surrounded as it was on both sides by the small, powerful vessels that would boost it gently into the air and then up beyond the heavy atmosphere. The black-uniformed crew were lined up beside it.

At last, the formalities were over—not as quickly as Darian had said—and they walked to the ship. The crew had by now disappeared up the steps and through the big open door. When they reached the top, Darian paused and turned to look back at the sea of faces in the distance, faces that included his family. She wondered if this was even more difficult for him than it was for her. She'd given that no thought before, because everyone said that he was unhappy at home and wanted only to be in space.

Lania had told her that his family was urging him to marry before he left, and then to impregnate his wife so that he would leave behind an heir. But Darian had refused. According to Lania, that was rather shocking, given the fact that he was an only son and if he failed to return, the line would end with him.

But strangely enough, even that reminder of the dangers they faced did not make her rethink her decision, though she was sure that was the reason Lania had told her about it. She did not deny the dangers—but neither did she dwell upon them.

Darian's situation, however, was very different. He had a family to come home to, while she didn't even have a home in the true sense of the word. Her own world was part of a different lifetime and one she couldn't imagine returning to now, and Ulata was still too big and too strange to be her home.

She was still thinking about this hours later as she stood in the lounge, staring out into the blackness of space. She was alone because the crew were all busy with their duties or sleeping in order to assume those duties later.

She didn't hear Darian come up behind her and was surprised when he suddenly appeared at her side. She'd thought he would be busy in the control room.

"I was surprised to see that you were up here," he said. "I expected you to be sleeping by now."

His phraseology made her frown. It suggested that he knew she was here even before he came here himself. But before she could say anything, he gestured to the wristband she'd been given earlier.

"I can find you through this."

Her frown deepened. "I'm not sure I like that, Darian."

"It's just a precaution. I'll give you my code and show you how to find me. Will that make it fair?"

She heard the amusement in his voice and found herself smiling. "As fair as anything is in your world, I suppose."

"Would you like some wine?" he asked, gesturing to the refreshment center in one corner.

"Yes, thank you—just a small glass." She walked over to sit down on one of the sofas facing the window, thinking that she should get herself out of here now. But how she was drawn to this man, no matter how much he sometimes angered her—or made her angry with herself.

He brought her the glass of wine, then sat down beside her. She wondered just how unconscious her choice of the sofa, rather than a chair, had been. She sipped the wine and stared out into space.

"I was thinking how I belong to space even more than you do, Darian."

"What do you mean?" he asked in surprise.

"You have a home and family: people you love who love

you. But I don't have that." Then she cast him a quick glance, realizing that she sounded self-pitying.

"Don't misunderstand me. I'm not unhappy and I don't want to go back to my home world. I wouldn't belong there any more than I belong to your world. That's why I belong to space."

"What about the Sisterhood?"

"Oh, I enjoy my work and I have friends there, but their rigid rules and their attitudes annoy me. That isn't my world, either. I'll probably spend as much time in space as I can. The others all hate it, you know."

"So I've heard."

Darian stared at her. The low lighting in the lounge reflected off the tiny diamonds in her elegant black gown. Her pale hair and creamy skin glowed. Her beauty took his breath away—and did other things to him as well.

Memories flickered through his mind—the memories that had been tormenting him for more than a year now: her soft, luminous body entangled with his, her small cries of pleasure, and her uninhibited enjoyment of their lovemaking.

Darian was a man of his world, and he felt that fierce possessiveness of knowing that he had been her first lover—and the only one. She belonged to him—or so he'd thought until he listened to her soft voice with its faint, charming accent.

Now he was uneasy. In her words, in the tone of her voice, he heard what he thought no one else felt—and certainly not any woman. She had said not that she belonged *in* space, but that she belonged *to* space, and he didn't think it was a misuse of words because it was exactly the way he'd always expressed it to himself.

Darian supposed that he should be pleased that she felt as he did, but that was definitely not the case. If he refused to accept that he had lost her to the Sisterhood, he certainly couldn't accept that he'd lost her to space. He wanted her to want him. He *needed* her to want him, though it was difficult for him to admit that, even to himself.

"Have I shocked you, Darian?" she asked, turning away from the window to look at him with that level gaze he'd never seen on another woman—except, perhaps, for his troublesome sister, who specialized in shocking him.

He attempted to avoid her question with a chuckle. "Right now, you remind me of my sister, Lessa. That is the question she puts to me regularly—just after she's said something outrageous."

She smiled. "Lania has spoken of her. I hope to meet her sometime. But you didn't answer my question."

"I doubt there is anything you could do or say that would shock me, Serena," he said honestly. "After all, I've seen the world you came from, and I've seen what an extraordinary woman you are."

He managed to hold her gaze as she studied him, no doubt trying to determine if he was speaking the truth or merely attempting to flatter her. It occurred to him that it would not be in his best interests to flatter this woman. She'd see right through him.

He was surprised when she set down her glass and got to her feet, then turned to face him as he rose hastily, wondering if he'd somehow insulted her.

"Very well, then, let me say this. I have not forgotten how it felt to make love with you, Darian Vondrak. But I also have not decided whether I want it to happen again."

Darian stood there, stunned into silence, as she walked out of the room, her black gown swirling around her slim figure. He felt as though she'd first caressed him—and then slapped his face.

As his shock wore off, he started to go after her, then

stopped, knowing he couldn't risk a scene that others might see. He wasn't shocked to hear her say that she'd liked making love with him, even though no other woman he'd known would have spoken so forthrightly. Instead, it was her final words that echoed through his mind.

He wondered if he had misinterpreted them, if perhaps her command of the language was at fault. If she'd said that it *couldn't* happen again because she was now a Trezhella, he would have accepted that—maybe. But he was left instead with the very strong impression that that was not what she'd meant.

His friend Miken, whose sister Lania was Serena's tutor and friend, had passed on bits and pieces of gossip about her. So Darian knew that she had taken full advantage of her unique position in the Sisterhood. And he'd also heard about her unusual behavior on the other voyages she'd made, when she'd roamed about the ships, talking to the crew, and then went sightseeing on other worlds. So he'd had every reason to believe that she would break any rule she chose to break.

Darian Vondrak was not accustomed to rejection. Women always did his bidding, and the list of those wanting to become his wife was very long indeed.

But Serena hadn't "decided" if she wanted him again, and he knew this wasn't some female game.

Serena returned to her cabin with a triumphant smile on her face. She hadn't really intended to shock Darian—or so she told herself—but it was clear that she had. Still, she'd only spoken the truth. Despite the truly astounding things that happened to her body in his presence—or maybe even partly *because* of that—she really didn't know that she wanted to resume their affair.

And it had little to do with the rules of the Sisterhood. She wasn't inclined to pay them much attention. They needed her far more than she needed them. Besides, she knew that Darian could be trusted to be discreet; after all, his future depended on it.

Her thoughts turned for the first time in a long while to Trenek. He had loved her selflessly, demanding nothing in return. But Darian Vondrak was another matter altogether. She doubted very much that he loved her, and in fact, she didn't much care, either. She'd learned with Trenek that being loved could be a terrible burden.

But Darian was another kind of burden. With him, she felt as though she were in danger of losing herself, of giving so much that there would be nothing left.

She was still puzzling out this strangeness when her door chimed. As if she required any further proof of just how much power Darian had over her, her treacherous body grew heated just thinking about him standing out there. But it was not Darian who stood before her when she opened the door.

"Sevec!" she cried. "You were chosen! I'm so glad for you." And she was—truly glad. The young cadet had taken pity on her during that first voyage, and they'd managed a quiet friendship.

He grinned at her. "We're all really glad that you're here, too, Trezhella Serena. Everyone feared that you'd change your mind."

He introduced her to the two men with him, men she recognized from the other voyage. Then he seemed to grow slightly embarrassed. "We—uh, have a gift for you. If you like, we can show it to you now."

"A gift?" Serena frowned. None of them was carrying anything.

Sevec nodded. "We paid for it ourselves because we wanted to show you how much we appreciate your being here."

"How very nice. Of course I'd like to see it."

He gestured to the door next to hers, which she assumed must be another cabin. "It's right in here."

She joined them in the hallway as one of the men opened the

door, then stood back so she could enter. She walked into the room and frowned. It was nearly twice the size of her own cabin, but it was completely empty. The walls were covered with mirrored panels, and both the ceiling and the floor were made of a springy, padded material. In each corner, from floor to ceiling, there were what appeared to be handles of some sort, and near the door, there was a large panel whose purpose she couldn't begin to guess.

"We remembered how much you liked dancing on Gara—the grass planet—because of its low gravity. So we had this room fixed up for you to be like that. See, the whole ship has to maintain an artificial gravity, or else we'd all be floating. So the engineers just came up with a way of decreasing the artificial gravity in here."

He showed her the panel. "You just turn this dial—after you've closed the door, of course. That red mark is the setting that will make it just like Gara, but you can experiment a bit if you want."

He pointed to the handles mounted in the corners. "In case you reduce the gravity too much and start to float, you can pull yourself back down by grabbing the handles." Then he turned back to the panel. "And this controls the music. We didn't know what you'd like, so there's a good selection of different kinds. And we thought you might enjoy the mirrors, too."

Serena was rendered temporarily speechless. She wondered what the High Priestess would think of this wonderful gift. Surely she would be forced to reconsider her beliefs about men if she saw this.

Impulsively, she seized Sevec's hands and squeezed them, then did the same with the other men. "I don't know what to say. This is *wonderful*! Now I can exercise just as the rest of you do. Dancing is very important to my people, though of course, we never had anything like this."

One of the other men, an officer of some rank, to judge from his braid, spoke up. "We also want you to know that you will be safe, and you can wander around the ship as much as you like. We know how the Sisterhood views us, but they're wrong—at least about the men on *this* mission. It means a lot to us that we'll be able to communicate with our families and friends at home—at least for a while."

Serena nodded. She was greatly tempted to tell them that it might be possible for the entire journey, but she decided not to raise their hopes too much. Not even Darian knew about the work she'd been doing these past months with Shenzi, and only time would tell if they were successful.

"My wife is pregnant," the other man told her, "and I'm hoping she'll give birth before we're out of range."

"I hope so, too," Serena said. "But even if I can't receive any messages, at least your wife and others will be able to know that everything is going well."

At that moment, another figure appeared in the open doorway: Darian. Serena saw him, but the men all had their backs to him. He paused for a moment, his dark eyes boring into her, then vanished. She wondered if his own cabin was nearby.

Sevec and the others left, after he reminded her that she should be sure to wear her wrist-comm, in case she needed it to summon help. "If you decrease the gravity too much and can't get to the handholds, someone will have to come and peel you off the ceiling," he said with a parting grin.

After they had gone, Serena considered trying out her present, but then decided to wait until morning. She was truly touched by the men's thoughtfulness and by their assurances as well. More and more, she became convinced that the Sisterhood was clinging to a past that, however awful it had been for women, was no longer the reality. Perhaps her experience on this mission would help to change their attitudes.

Days passed as the great ship edged closer to the limits of the known universe. The Ulatan star system was left behind by the end of the fourth day—much more quickly than had been expected, thanks to the ship's ability to take advantage of the cosmic storms. Serena was no closer than before to understanding any of this, but she had come to think of it as being much like sailing, with the cosmic storms providing an unpredictable wind that could either slow down or greatly increase their speed.

She quickly established a routine. First thing in the morning, she would dress in the old, comfortable trousers and blouse that were the only things she had left from her old life, and then go to her dance room. She was glad that the men had chosen a room next to her cabin, since that meant nobody would see her in anything other than her official uniform. Or so she thought. But on her second morning, as she stepped out of her cabin, Darian was just emerging from his own cabin next door.

He ran his gaze over her, and she immediately felt compelled to explain that she was going to dance and her uniform was far too cumbersome. It sounded even to her as though she were babbling, but she couldn't help it. Only moments earlier, she'd been dreaming about him.

"I'm relieved to hear that," he said with a smile. "For a moment there, I thought perhaps we'd gone through a time warp during the night."

"Time warp?" she echoed, having never heard that phrase before.

He nodded. "There are those who believe that a particularly powerful cosmic storm could push the ship to such speeds that time would move backward."

Her mouth dropped open in amazement. "B-but how would you know if such a thing happened?"

"We have a device that would tell us if it happened."

"Would *we* change—grow younger or older, I mean?"

"No."

117

"But if it happened, then when we return, it could be to a very different Ulata?"

He nodded. "Of course we'd know that well before we returned, thanks to your ability to communicate. But it isn't likely."

"Still, it means that all of you are taking an even greater risk than I'd thought."

"But not *you*, since, as you said, you belong to space."

She heard the slight change in his tone, though she couldn't be sure what it meant. Then he wished her a good day and walked off down the hall.

Serena went on to her dance room, pushing aside thoughts of Darian. After going through her warm-up routine, she tried the various music settings until she found something quite similar to the music her own people had, then set the dial to the gravity of the grass world.

For the next hour, she lost herself in the dances, both amazed and amused as she watched herself in the mirrored walls. It was fortunate indeed that the men had installed padding on the ceiling, because several times she leapt too energetically and crashed into it.

After that, she returned to her cabin and showered, then changed into her uniform and went to the dining area, which was empty at the moment. She had been asked for her food preferences some time ago, and was pleased to find everything she wanted. Ulatan food had proved to be a delight for her: much more varied than the fare of her home world, and no expense had been spared to provide the crew of Deep Space One with every amenity.

Then she went to her communication room, where she quickly got down to business. Many technical reports awaited her on the vidscreen, and as soon as she made contact with one of her sisters, she began to read them off, having no knowledge at all of what she was sending.

118

After that, she was free to do as she pleased until her next reporting time. She could walk around the ship or watch a film in the recreation room or return to her cabin, where she could read one of the many books available on the ship. They weren't actually books, but were instead objects that were shaped like books and could be programmed to print out whatever she chose from the ship's computer.

Once a day, she also passed messages to and from the ship's crew. The men would leave their messages on the vidscreen for her to send, and she would type into the comm any incoming messages, then send them on to the units in the men's private quarters.

She was busy—but not busy enough that she didn't have entirely too much time to think about Darian. Even though they were on the same schedule, she rarely saw him. She assumed that he spent most of his waking hours in the control room, and so she avoided that part of the ship. But at night, as she lay in her bed awaiting sleep, she was achingly aware of his presence beyond the wall that separated them.

Twelve days into space, now far beyond the Ulatan star system, Serena was startled in the midst of her dance routine by the sudden stopping of her music, which was followed instantly by three chimes. She sank to the padded floor as a shiver ran through her. Three chimes meant an emergency. Then she heard Darian's voice, so clear that he might have been in the room with her.

"Deep Space One has now reached an historic moment. Just moments ago, we reached the farthest point any ship has gone. We are now entering the unknown, gentlemen—and Trezhella Serena."

The music returned, but Serena stayed on the floor, trying to ignore the feelings his use of her name summoned. The unknown. She knew that she should be fearful—but she wasn't.

119

So much had already happened to her that she felt prepared for anything.

Then too, perhaps her lack of fear was the result of her work. It seemed that the farther they'd gotten from Ulata, the more she could actually *feel* those great distances, and the less frightened she was of them. More than a year ago, on her journey to Ulata, she had imagined herself cut off from everything and everyone, floating forever in that all-encompassing blackness. Then, the sensation had been terrifying, but now she welcomed it each time she went into her trance.

She knew too that she was the only one who felt that way. The other Sisters claimed to have no awareness of the distances—or of anything else. They simply went into a trance and reached out to other Sisters' voices.

She cut her dancing short and returned to her cabin. Then, after showering and changing, she skipped breakfast and instead went to her communications room. It was too early to make her first report, but she was eager to try to make contact. Already, she had surpassed the greatest distance at which such contact had been achieved, yet she had managed to both send and receive quite easily.

The test would come soon, she thought—perhaps even this day. She knew they must have picked up a particularly powerful cosmic "wind" while she slept, because one of the men had told her that it would probably be another three days at least before they reached what Darian just called "the unknown."

From the moment months before when Serena had decided to come on this mission, she had been spending as much time as possible with Shenzi, in an experiment that was designed to enhance their abilities to reach out to each other. The idea had been hers. It seemed to her that she should concentrate on reaching one person in particular, and Shenzi was the most likely candidate, both because she herself was quite powerful and because they were close friends.

But they were quite literally working in the dark. No one knew how the Trezhellas managed to do what they did. Over the years, the men of the Space Agency had from time to time tried to persuade the High Priestesses to permit scientific experiments to determine how their talents worked. But the requests had always been denied, because the High Priestesses had known that such experiments, if successful, could one day lead to the end of the Sisterhood. So they claimed to fear that the Trezhellas could be "damaged" by such experiments.

Still, as Serena walked into the communications room, she was hopeful. What gave her hope was that shortly before she left the compound to come on this journey, she and Shenzi had begun to pick up on each other's thoughts—not just when they were attempting to communicate, but at other times as well. But by mutual agreement, they had kept this discovery to themselves, since neither of them wanted to raise false hopes.

She sat down before the zhetla and willed herself into a trance, welcoming the blackness as it swarmed around her and enfolded her. Immediately, she heard the voices of her Sisters, but they were much fainter than they had been only ten hours before, and some were so faint as to be unintelligible.

She sent her name out into the darkness, then listened. There were no breaks in the reports of the others, no indication that they had heard her. She was surprised at that. She had assumed that she would be heard, even if she couldn't hear the others. Now it seemed it was the opposite. She tried again, but still there was no indication that she'd been heard.

She pulled herself from the trance and checked the time. It was still too early for Shenzi to be trying to contact her. Then she slipped back into the trance and tried again to make contact, but nothing happened. The voices droned on, sending and receiving reports. She was about to give up and go to get some breakfast while she waited for Shenzi to come on at the

121

appointed time, when suddenly her friend's voice came through the babble, loud and clear.

"Shenzi calling Serena. Shenzi calling Serena."

"I'm here, Shenzi!" Serena said excitedly. "You're early."

"Thanks to you. You woke me up."

"I did?" Serena knew they were breaking every rule with this personal conversation, but she could not have cared less. All their work had not been in vain!

"Yes. I wonder if sleep works as effectively as a trance. Do you think that's possible?"

Serena said that it made sense to her, then went on to tell Shenzi that the ship had left the known universe some hours ago. Shenzi didn't reply, and for a moment, Serena feared that the connection had been broken. Then, just as she was about to call her name again, her friend finally spoke.

"It's really worked, hasn't it? I can hear you as clearly as if you were right beside me."

"I hear you that well, too. I think we can tell the others now."

Then, with a nod to the rules, they began to work. The only real training Serena had required was to develop the ability to remain in her trance while still seeing the information on the vidscreen that she had to transmit. It appeared in bright green letters in the midst of the blackness, as though the words themselves were hanging in space.

When she had finished, Shenzi sent back some data for Darian and the ship's Chief Engineer, and then they lapsed into personal conversation again. Shenzi asked if everything was going well for her, by which Serena knew she meant whether she'd had any problems with the men. So she told Shenzi about their gift to her. Once again, there was silence, during which the faint voices of the other women droned on.

"Sometimes, I'm almost willing to believe that not all men are bad," Shenzi said finally. "But we've had two incidents since you left, and in one of them, someone tried to break into Gezheena's quarters."

Serena's heart sank. She knew it was no use telling Shenzi that such incidents were very rare; her friend already knew that. And Gezheena couldn't have been in any real danger. She would have had both a stunner and her wrist-comm to summon help.

"Maltus Konrav was the commander," Shenzi went on, "and he's the worst of them. He just doesn't control his men. They have no respect for him. At least you don't have that problem."

"No." *My problem is very different*, she thought privately. *My problem is the commander—and myself*,

"What are you saying?" Shenzi asked. "I didn't quite catch that."

Serena made a sound of surprise. "Nothing," she said hurriedly. "I was just thinking about something. I didn't realize you would hear it.

"Shenzi, I know it isn't the time for personal messages, but do you happen to know if there's one for Sergeant Daven Roslev? His wife is expecting a child any time now, and he's been very anxious."

"Hold on. I'll have to leave to check on it."

Serena waited and thought about her "slip." Fortunately, Shenzi hadn't been able to understand what she'd thought, but she would have to be very careful in the future. Still, she was excited that their experiment had worked.

She supposed that protocol dictated that she would have to tell Darian first. She would go to the control room as soon as she finished here.

"Serena?"

"I'm here. Do you have anything?"

"Yes. Sergeant Roslev has a son. That should make him happy."

"It will," Serena said, ignoring Shenzi's sarcasm. "They already have a daughter."

They signed off and Serena withdrew from the trance. She was about to type the message for Sergeant Roslev when she decided that she would enjoy delivering that news in person. She keyed in the ship's roster to get his code, so she could find out where he was.

"He's on duty in the control room," said a familiar voice behind her. "I hate to pull rank on Sergeant Roslev, but shouldn't you be calling *me* first?"

Serena swiveled the chair around to face Darian, surprised that he'd managed to open the door without her knowledge. He was leaning casually against the wall, giving every indication that he'd been there for some time.

"I intended to see you first, but I have wonderful news for Sergeant Roslev—one I wanted to deliver in person."

"Do you suppose the news of his fatherhood could wait long enough for you to explain to me how you've managed to receive it—not to mention the other reports?"

"I can't really explain it, Darian. Shenzi and I began to work together as soon as I decided to make this voyage. We thought that perhaps since she is also powerful and we're close friends, it might work—and it has."

Darian shook his head as he walked over to touch the zhetla. "I know you can't understand just how important this is, but what it means to me is that I can have the benefit of all sorts of expertise that we don't have on the ship."

"I'm glad about that," she replied, staring at his long fingers as he stroked the zhetla. There was something strangely intimate about it. Could he be deliberately tormenting her? Perhaps she shouldn't have told him how much she'd enjoyed their lovemaking. But then, he knew that. She hadn't needed to tell him.

"My fondest hope for this journey is that we might find a

world that could provide us with these—but of better quality. It would revolutionize space travel."

"These?" She echoed. "You mean zhetlas?"

He dropped his hand and nodded. "Didn't you know that we use them to power the ship? They're very rare, and we haven't been able to replicate them." He gestured to the obelisk. "The ones that are now powering this ship are different. They're almost transparent. But there are so few of them that unless we can find more or manage to replicate them, we'll never be able to make another voyage like this one. The ones like this aren't quite so rare, and they're used for most space travel."

"No, I didn't know that." Serena kept her expression neutral with considerable effort. She had to see those zhetlas. She'd never bothered to go into the power room of the ship. Was it possible?

She got up. "I'm going to tell Sergeant Roslev about his son."

Darian's hand closed around her arm. "How much longer do we play this game, Serena? When are you going to admit that you want me as much as I want you?"

Her breath caught in her throat. The heat from his touch filled every part of her. She throbbed with desire, ached from a hunger that only he could satisfy.

"I've already admitted that, Darian," she said huskily.

"Then why are we still making love only in our dreams?"

"You wouldn't understand."

"Try me. It can't be because you've decided to obey this one rule of the Sisterhood."

"No," she admitted as she pulled her arm from his grasp. "It isn't that."

She raised her eyes to meet his. "You make me lose myself, Darian—and I don't like that."

Then, without waiting for his response to that, she left the room.

* * *

Darian waited a few moments, then followed her, knowing she would be headed to the control room with her news for Roslev. Something was bothering him—beyond the usual frustrations of an encounter with her. It seemed to him that her reaction upon learning that the ship was powered by zhetlas had been out of proportion. He supposed it could be because she'd believed that the zhetlas were the sole province of the Sisterhood, but it nagged at him nonetheless.

In what he was beginning to believe was an act of masochism despite telling himself that he was justified because he was responsible for her, Darian had made it a habit to check regularly on her whereabouts. And when he'd checked a short time ago and discovered that she was in the comm room, he'd decided to go there.

Until he'd entered the room to find her in a trance and receiving data, he hadn't believed that it would be possible. They were well beyond the limits of any previous Trezhella communication. Given what he knew of Serena's talents, he had hoped she would at least be able to transmit for a while yet, but he'd had no hopes that she would also be able to receive.

Her talents were proving to be invaluable to this mission, and yet he remained troubled by them because he could not and never would understand such a thing.

He thought about what she'd said about "losing herself" with him. They were strange words to be coming from a woman, but then, they weren't the first strange words he'd heard from her. Neither were they likely to be the last.

And like her earlier statement about "belonging to space," they were a challenge—one that drew him as powerfully as the challenge of space itself. She couldn't know that, of course, though any other woman might have. Serena was incapable of the kind of dissembling practiced by other women, just as she was incapable of making a man the focal point of her existence—which was what she'd meant when she'd said she feared "losing herself."

He stepped off the elevator into the control room to find himself totally ignored. Normally, the lieutenant commander he'd left in charge would immediately have announced his presence, but he, like all the others, was crowded around Serena and Sergeant Roslev, who had taken both her hands and looked as though he were about to start dancing.

Darian thought wryly that it was a damned good thing the ship could run itself because not one man was at his assigned station. It was one of those moments that separated a by-the-book commander from a true leader of men.

Serena was apparently the first to see Darian step off the elevator. Their eyes met, and she knew that he had every reason to be angry with them all—and especially her—for disrupting the routine of the control room.

Her sudden silence in the midst of the noisy happiness over Sergeant Roslev's new baby and the news that she could still communicate with the Sisterhood finally caused at least a few men to turn and see Darian standing there. A sudden silence fell, broken only by the faint hum of the machines.

And then she understood what made a great leader of men, as Darian strode toward them, smiling, and offered his congratulations to the flustered Sergeant Roslev. Darian understood that there was no need to chastize; they all knew that they had broken the rules.

The men quickly returned to their posts, leaving her alone momentarily with Darian. "Thank you," she murmured in a low voice. "I know I shouldn't have come here. It won't happen again."

She felt his dark eyes piercing the armor of polite formality she'd erected around herself, shattering it with a frightening ease. She felt naked and vulnerable and so very needy, as

127

though she could not even so much as draw a breath on her own. His only response was a slight nod, but it was enough to break the spell. She turned and walked quickly to the elevator.

When she pressed the button, she saw that her fingers were trembling. How could one human being have so much power over another? It was beyond her understanding.

It will *happen again*, she told herself. No matter how much she tried to prevent it, the moment would come and she would be in his arms again, ignoring the rules of the Sisterhood and forgetting the warnings of her brain.

She went to the dining area, where she was grateful to find herself alone. As she ate, her thoughts turned to Darian's stunning revelation in the communications room. She certainly hadn't forgotten it, but it had managed to get itself buried beneath her pleasure at delivering the news to Sergeant Roslev and the others—and then Darian's reappearance.

She had to see the zhetlas that powered this ship. The description Darian had given her made them sound very much like the teldas in the caves at home. Her now-full stomach churned uneasily. What if it were true—and they were the same? She hadn't told Darian or anyone else about them, though she probably would have during her voyage to Ulata if she'd been able to communicate. Since then, she'd kept quiet about them only because she'd discovered that the Ulatans placed such a high value on them, and she hadn't wanted to insult them by saying that at home, they were considered to be nothing more than nuisances that prevented exploration of the caves, or at best, play-objects for children.

She left the dining area just as some men were coming in for lunch. They told her they'd just heard how she was still able to communicate with home and repeated the expressions of happiness she'd heard from the men in the control room. And once more, she thought about their eagerness to stay in contact and how ironic it was that she should be the one to make that possible, though it mattered so much less to her.

After taking the elevator down to the lowest level, Serena turned right, to the ship's stern. She hadn't actually seen the power room aboard this ship, but she had studied the diagram on the wall in the dining area and knew it should be down here.

This level of the ship was used primarily for storage, so no one was around, for which she was very grateful. She could always claim that she was merely curious, but it would be much easier if she didn't have to lie.

The closed doors were all marked, and she was just beginning to think she might have misunderstood the diagram when she suddenly came to the end of the curved hallway. Ahead of her was a closed door—the one she sought. She paused, thinking beyond the moment. If she found teldas in there . . .

To forestall pointless thoughts, she pressed her hand to the doorplate. Nothing happened. She frowned and pressed harder. This had not happened before. As far as she knew, the only doors to which she would be refused entrance were the private quarters of the crew.

Darian swiveled his chair toward the display where the buzzer had sounded. It took him a second or two to realize that someone must have attempted to enter the power room, and by the time the verbal report came, he knew who it must be. A moment later, his suspicion was confirmed.

"It's Trezhella Serena, sir." The man smiled. "She's apparently decided to do some exploring. Shall I contact her and explain why she can't go in there?"

At that moment, the lieutenant commander got off the elevator and Darian realized it was time for his lunch break. "No, I'll go down there on my break. I just explained to her earlier that the ship is powered by zhetlas. No doubt she wants to see them."

Serena finally gave up and started back toward the elevator, wondering if Darian would find it strange if she requested to see the power room. She decided that was unlikely. Since he undoubtedly believed she revered the zhetlas like the other Trezhellas did, he wasn't likely to question her interest. He didn't know that she had no use for them, and hadn't, really, since that first time she'd unwittingly transmitted all those years ago in the cave.

Still, she wished that she could get in there without his knowledge. That first long journey with Darian, before she'd learned his language, had left her half-believing that he could often read her mind. Maybe she should wait and approach Sevec about taking her there. If Darian found out and questioned her, she could always say that she hadn't wanted to trouble him with such a minor request.

She reached the elevator and was about to press the button when it opened—and revealed Darian standing within.

Chapter Seven

He *can* read my mind! Serena thought with a horror she couldn't keep from her face as Darian stepped out of the elevator.

"The power room is restricted to those who have a need to go in there, and who understand the procedure," he said, his eyes glittering with amusement. "When you tried to gain entry, an alarm went off in the control room."

"Oh." Having failed to hide her shock at his supposed mind-reading, she now tried to hide her relief. But apparently she wasn't entirely successful.

"Could it be that you were thinking of me?" he asked in a dry tone.

"Umm—I was, actually. But then I decided to ask Sevec to show it to me." She affected a casual shrug. "I'm just curious about the zhetlas in there. You said they were different."

"If the reason you're curious is that you think they might work better for your purposes, they don't. Experiments were done on that years ago. In fact, everyone other than the

Sisterhood thinks that the zhetlas aren't really important for communicating. Through the centuries, Trezhellas have traditionally used them, so they continue to use them. It's merely a way of focusing the mind. Any other object would do as well."

He frowned thoughtfully. "Now that I think about it, you never told me how you managed to communicate from your home world."

A chill swept through her, but this time she managed to keep her expression neutral. She told him about the exercises taught to her as a child to prepare her for the rigors of the dance.

"We never used any object. Instead, we were taught to reach into ourselves and find that quiet center of our being. My teacher described it as being a deep, dark pool, so that's how I always think of it, too."

"Does the Sisterhood know that?" he asked curiously.

She shook her head. "Shenzi knows—the Sister I worked with before I left. The one I'm communicating with now. I told her because I thought it might improve her skills, and perhaps it has. But I didn't tell the others because I knew they revere the zhetlas and I didn't want to insult them by letting them know that they're useless for me."

And as she finished, she realized her mistake. If they were useless to her, why should she be so curious about them? Her mind raced, seeking an answer to the question she was sure must be coming. But instead, Darian led her back down the hallway toward the power room.

"The reason that not everyone is allowed in there is that the room must be kept perfectly clean. Any foreign matter can affect the efficiency of the zhetlas. So there is a procedure that has to be followed before you enter."

Serena only half heard him because she was busy being surprised and then relieved that he hadn't questioned her interest. Perhaps he was merely enjoying his role as instructor. As a former teacher herself, she could understand that, though she wouldn't have guessed that Darian would enjoy such a role.

Her relief was short-lived, though. As he pressed his hand to the doorplate, she was already thinking ahead. If the zhetlas in there were in fact the teldas of the caves at home . . .

The door slid open to reveal a small room with yet another door in the opposite wall. On one side of the room was a long bench, and on the other side was a rack holding strange-looking clothing made of a thin, shimmery fabric. Darian began sorting through them.

"We'll have to put on these suits. There won't be anything small enough for you, but I think we can make do."

His back was to her as she stared at him suspiciously. She had to admit that she hadn't yet seen any trace of deviousness in his behavior, but now she wondered if his willingness to show her the zhetlas could have anything to do with this procedure. Did he actually believe that she would be willing to remove her clothing?

In her mind, she envisioned him arching a dark brow challengingly and remarking that he'd already seen her naked. Beneath her modest uniform, Serena could feel her body growing warm, remembering the imprint of his hands and lips, remembering how he had felt against her and inside her.

He pulled one of the suits from the rack and handed it to her. "This is the smallest one here. It should fit easily over your gown, but if you want to take the gown off, I'll wait outside."

His words were matter-of-fact, laden with no more meaning than if he'd been describing various dining alternatives, but she saw—or imagined that she saw—the challenge in his eyes.

"Thank you," she said politely. "But I'm sure I can manage."

He turned away to select a suit for himself, and she began to struggle into the oversized one-piece suit, carefully folding the skirt of her uniform so that she could fit her legs into the garment. The result was anything but comfortable, but at least it avoided the necessity of insisting that he leave.

"Why is this necessary?" she asked when they had both gotten into the white suits.

Darian lifted two of the unwieldy-looking headpieces from the shelf above the garment rack and handed one to her. Then he gestured to the door. "Through there is a decontamination chamber. This fabric is designed to work with the gases used in there. They're not harmful to breathe, but they can destroy or discolor other fabrics."

She lifted the headpiece and placed it over her head. The front part was clear, made of some substance that she'd never seen before. They were both now totally unrecognizable, covered from head to toe in the shimmery white suits, which included boots and gloves. The fabric was somewhat stiff and they both rustled when they moved toward the door.

The decontamination chamber was about the same size as the changing room, and the moment the door slid shut, an eerie blue light filled the room, along with a faintly sweet odor. After only a few seconds, a bell chimed and another door slid open.

Serena had been hoping she was wrong, but the moment she saw the long rows of carved zhetlas, that hope vanished. The room was smaller than she'd imagined, though at least three times the size of the outer rooms. The zhetlas were about three feet high and set into upright rows, held in place by a clear rack that might or might not be the same plas of which the ship's windows were made. They were all carved similarly into obelisks—like the zhetla in her communication room, but with many more facets.

And they were the exact translucent creamy-white shade as the teldas at home.

"I thought there would be more of them," she said, knowing that he would expect some comment from her.

"What you see here is just about all there are," Darian told her, his voice muffled by the mask. "The only place they exist is in some caves on Darseen. And the only others we have are being used for study purposes."

Darseen was a small, lifeless world that was Ulata's nearest neighbor, and Darian explained that if they hadn't found the zhetlas and then discovered how they could be used, any further space exploration would have been useless because there were limits imposed by the use of liquid fuels.

"Eventually, we found the kind that you use—or don't use—on several other worlds and discovered that they'll suffice for shorter journeys. They're also more durable than these are."

"More durable?" she repeated. "What do you mean?"

"Come. I'll show you."

They walked over to the closest row and he began to examine them closely. "We don't use all of them at all times, and we've learned that the way they're carved can improve their durability, but eventually, they begin to break down and develop cracks. See this one?"

He pointed to one of the obelisks and she moved closer to peer at it. There were fine cracks along several of the facets. She asked why that happened. She'd seen broken teldas, but could not recall seeing tiny cracks like this. But then, she'd never paid them that much attention.

"It happens because of the vibrations. We can't feel those vibrations, but as the zhetlas react to the electromagnetic storms, they begin to vibrate. The storm we harnessed last night caused this one to begin to crack. I saw the report a short while ago."

Serena continued to peer closely at the carved zhetla, glad for the opportunity to study it without arousing his curiosity. Were they the same as teldas? Outwardly, they certainly seemed the same, but there was just no way she could be sure.

"It's strange that you found them on only one world," she remarked.

"Not really," he replied as he walked along the rows, bending to study the obelisks. "We know that they grow under very specific conditions, and so far, Darseen is the only place we've found where those conditions exist. Apart from general exploration, our biggest hope for this mission is that we'll find more of them."

One thing both puzzled her and gave rise to the hope that she was mistaken. If finding those zhetlas was so important to them, wouldn't Darian's crew have looked for them on her world? Since they apparently knew the conditions that produced them . . .

Then she remembered what she'd been told after she had arrived on Ulata. If they hadn't found her when they did, they would have been forced to leave without her. The mission was cut short because the ship, hovering high above her world, had come under bombardment from radiation produced by a certain type of very dangerous cosmic storm.

Was that all that had saved her world from being taken over by the Ulatans in their quest for the teldas? That made sense to her—but only up to a point. Surely they must have made some studies of her world during their brief stay. Wouldn't they have found at least some indication that the teldas existed there, then planned a return mission?

She had many questions she wanted to ask Darian, but none that she could ask without arousing his suspicions. There was, however, another way to gain that knowledge, and now she had enough free time to pursue it. She would simply have to begin educating herself about zhetlas and see if she could access whatever information they had gained about her world.

Back in the changing room, she thanked him for taking the time to bring her here. He responded by asking her to join him for lunch in the dining area. There was a casualness to the invitation, and she replied that she would enjoy that.

It's a game, she thought—for both of us. Lurking just

beneath the surface of what seemed to be shipboard friendliness was that dark, powerful hunger they had for each other, a restive force that could surface at any time. But the dining area, at least, was safe.

"You never really told me what you thought of my world, Darian," she said as they sat at a small table in a secluded corner of the large dining area. She was hoping that he might reveal any information they'd gathered about it. It would certainly be easier to learn it from him than to try to find her way through the complicated data bases.

"Did you know that I was there twice?" he asked in response.

She was surprised. "No, I didn't know that. You mean you were on the first mission—when I was just a child?"

He nodded. "It was my first long voyage. I was only a cadet then and lucky to have been chosen. I was the one who identified you from the sketch that was done by one of the Sisters. I found you on a playground at the school."

"You must be older than I thought," she commented before she could stop herself.

He chuckled. "I'm twelve years older than you are, but the difference isn't really as great as you might think. My people undoubtedly live longer than yours do."

That was true. She had been very surprised to discover the ages of some of the Sisters. They had seemed much younger to her.

"Your world is the most beautiful place I've ever seen," he went on. "There are places on other worlds that are just as lovely, but taken as a whole, yours is by far the most beautiful. And also one of the most intriguing."

"What do you mean?" she asked, hiding her nervousness.

"I'm not even sure that it's actually a planet. It might be closer to one of our moons. Unfortunately, we couldn't stay long enough to study it closely. It's in a dangerous system."

She busied herself with eating to conceal her relief. So they apparently hadn't learned enough to suspect the presence of the teldas. "Will you ever go back?"

"I doubt it—at least not in the foreseeable future. There's too much risk involved." He paused for a moment. "There's also another reason not to return—at least for me. If we were to return and make our presence known, it would almost certainly change your world forever."

She frowned at him. "That doesn't seem to have stopped you Ulatans from going to other worlds."

If he heard the note of disapproval in her voice, he didn't comment on it. "It's our destiny to rule our star system. We're by far the most advanced. But the other worlds you referred to were far more advanced than yours. Most of them were already beginning to venture into space. If we hadn't conquered them, they would have tried to conquer us."

Ulatan arrogance, she thought but didn't say. "I doubt that my people will ever venture into space. They simply lack the curiosity."

"Even if they had it, they'd find it difficult—for the same reason we find it dangerous there. But I think you're right. It takes bold men to venture into space, and the men on your world lack that."

She bristled. "My people have never known war or conquest—and they never will."

"Yes, I know. I've read the report on your society that you wrote for the Space Agency at their request. I was asked to confirm it."

"And?"

He shrugged. "And I did—to the extent that I could."

"Does that mean that they didn't believe me?" she demanded.

He chuckled. "Let's just say that they were a bit skeptical about a society where men and women are truly equal."

"I hope it gave them all some sleepless nights," she grumbled. "And perhaps it'll keep them from wanting to return, lest it prove to be contagious."

Darian laughed, drawing the attention of several nearby tables. "I don't think there's much danger of that, but I have to confess to feeling a certain . . . affection for your world. I found the men to be faintly repellant, frankly, but beyond that, the place had an almost enchanted quality to it. Like a children's story."

She glared at him, feeling not at all "enchanted." "Would you like to know what I thought of you and your men?"

"I have a feeling I'm going to be told whether or not I want to hear it, so let me guess. You thought we were huge, hairy creatures with loud voices and a manner that seemed crude. A lower life form."

She was annoyed that he had guessed it so easily, and her annoyance must have showed because he laughed again.

"But obviously you stopped believing that rather quickly," he said in a low voice.

She felt that treacherous heat sliding through her again, but said nothing.

"Or was it only the attraction of opposites?" he asked in that same soft tone. "And what will happen if I come to your door some night?"

She cut off the fantasy that his words summoned. "Nothing—unless you can enter against my will."

"I can—but I won't. And you know that. It wasn't against your will when it happened before, and it won't be when it happens again."

His eyes caught hers and held them just long enough for that restive hunger inside her to begin to stir and threaten to sweep all reason before it.

Serena's eyes snapped open as the dream receded. But at least this time, she didn't sit up and her heart wasn't thudding noisily. For three nights now—ever since her conversation with Darian over lunch—she had awakened at some point in the night, certain that she'd heard the door chime.

Ever since she'd learned the Ulatan language, Serena had been studying in her spare time, and no field intrigued her more than psychology. So she understood that where she might once have believed her dream of the door chiming to be a portent of some kind, it was in fact the product of her own subconscious desire.

It was strange, though, that the interrupted dream hadn't even been about Darian. Instead, it had been a troubling dream about Ulatans swarming over her world, blasting into the caves. Darian hadn't even figured into it.

She frowned, glancing at the bedside clock. It was halfway through her sleeping period and his as well—an unlikely time for him to be out there. She'd actually opened the door the first time—the night following their conversation. No one was there, but of course he could easily have returned to his own cabin in the time it took her to shake off sleep and open the door.

Except that he wouldn't do that. He would wait to see if she opened it, and he couldn't know that unless he stood there. The cabins were amazingly soundproofed. She knew that because she'd lain awake many nights, knowing he was just beyond the wall, listening for any sounds.

She thought back to that conversation and, not for the first time, decided that she had liked him much better when they couldn't communicate and she was unable to hear his Ulatan arrogance.

On the other hand, had he really said anything that she herself hadn't thought, especially once she was away from her people?

Her mind began to drift back toward sleep and she thought

again about her dream. Then her eyes snapped open again. The Legend! How could she have forgotten about it?

There was an ancient myth among her people, rarely mentioned in recent times, that one day their beautiful world would be taken away from them. How this was to be accomplished was never stated, though, which was why few people spoke of it anymore. But she realized that what she'd seen in her dream was just that: her lovely world being destroyed by the Ulatans' machines to provide them with the precious teldas.

"It won't happen," she whispered. "No one knows about the teldas."

But sleep was still a long time coming.

The next morning, she awoke late and was forced to forgo her dancing in order to keep her morning appointment with Shenzi. Serena had kept her own shipboard schedule the same as daytime at the compound, so it was morning for them both.

The reports were lengthy and boring—at least to Serena and Shenzi since they were filled with incomprehensible words that sometimes had to be spelled and long series of numbers that also meant nothing to either of them. But she was careful to get it right. The ship's Chief Engineer had already praised her for the accuracy of her reports and acknowledged their difficulty.

Then Shenzi began to tell her about the goings-on at the compound. Some of the older Sisters weren't very happy with the latest group of novices. It seemed that while they certainly were talented, they chafed at some of the rules and a few had even gone so far as to suggest that the Sisterhood was falling behind the times.

"I think you'll get along with them very well," Shenzi said in a dry tone. "Oh, and by the way, you might want to pass on to Commander Vondrak the news that the Institute for Women will be opening its doors later this year."

"Oh? You mean the school his sister wanted, to provide better education for women?"

"The very one. Perhaps she'll send him a message about it. And in any event, it will certainly be on the general news later today." Shenzi transmitted important news of a general nature in the afternoon, to be read from the computer by all the crew.

"Only a Vondrak could get away with it," Shenzi went on. "And even so, there are threats from some in Parliament to ban it, though there isn't really much they can do since the family is financing it themselves."

Serena thought that she'd enjoy delivering this news to Darian. She'd never spoken to him about his sister. But since she was doing her best to avoid him at the moment, she decided to let him find out for himself.

"I thought you liked him," Shenzi's voice said in her mind.

Serena drew in a sharp breath, realizing that once again, she'd allowed Shenzi to catch her thoughts. "I *do* like him—as much as I like any Ulatan man. But I can't believe he'd be pleased with this news."

"I doubt that it would be happening without his approval, since family money is being used and Darian is the eldest son."

Later, as she danced to a newly discovered piece of music, Serena could not quite let go of her thoughts of Darian, which became obvious as she watched herself in the mirrors. She thought Shenzi must be wrong. Darian either hadn't been consulted, or he'd agreed because he didn't much care, since the family had more money than they could ever spend and he was away in space most of the time.

She pushed Darian unceremoniously from her mind and concentrated on the dance. She had by now invented all sorts of variations that were possible only in low-grav. She was pleased with them and sometimes wished that she had an audience.

When she finished the dance, she returned to her cabin next

door to shower and change, then went to the dining area, where she grabbed some food to carry with her to the ship's "library."

The library was in fact nothing more than a series of small cubicles with computer workstations that allowed her to tap into vast scientific data bases. She had been spending as much time as possible here ever since her visit to the power room.

It was, however, very rough going. The information she sought was for scientists rather than for the general public, since every man on the ship was well-trained in the sciences. Fortunately, however, there was also a good dictionary available online. Still, it was taking her even longer than she'd thought to learn about the conditions under which the zhetlas grew.

Unfortunately, not even that information, once she understood it, proved to be of much value without a scientific survey of her own world. Still, she thought she was making slow progress—and she was erasing all doubt that the teldas on her home world weren't the same as those in the power room.

Darian studied the record with a frown. Could she possibly understand what she was studying? He couldn't bring himself to believe that, though she was certainly spending a great deal of time at it.

Yesterday, one of his officers had mentioned in passing that Serena was spending quite a lot of time in the ship's library. That had struck Darian as being rather odd, since he would have expected her to be interested only in the arts, which she could easily access on her personal vidscreen, or in works of fiction for which she could use the vidbook.

But the information that now appeared on the screen showed that she was studying the research into zhetlas. It seemed strange to him, since she hadn't asked many questions when he showed her the power room, and if she had questions now, the logical thing to do would be to ask him.

He stared at the screen some more and saw that she was accessing all the information about conditions on Darseen, where they came from. Then he recalled her surprise when she'd learned that the ship was powered by them.

None of it made any sense, unless . . . Darian's fingers drummed restlessly on the tabletop. Her interest in zhetlas went all the way back to her first voyage—before she could have known that they had any meaning for Trezhellas. He could remember trying to explain without words what its purpose was when she'd discovered the communications room.

He ran his mind over their various conversations, trying to recall if she'd said anything that would indicate she'd seen them on her own world. But all he could recall was that she'd said she didn't use them to enter into her trance.

He began to think how he could get her to talk about it. If he let her know that he could find out what she was studying, she'd probably accuse him of spying—which, of course, was just what he was doing. She wasn't likely to know that each time she recorded her name to gain access, that information went into the record. It wasn't kept for purposes of spying on private research, but rather as a way of permitting any of them easy access to information they'd accessed before. Darian was impressed with her skills, but he doubted she would know this or if she did, she didn't realize that he too could find out what she was studying.

Was it possible that zhetlas existed in her home world—that the one world they'd visited but not studied could hold the key to the future of space travel?

It was, he knew, a logical explanation for her behavior. Thanks to him, she'd seen the zhetlas and knew their importance and their scarceness. But her studies would seem to indicate that she wasn't sure they were the same as the formations she knew existed on her home world. And perhaps they weren't. But if they were . . .

Darian knew he was in a very difficult situation. If he let her know he was aware of her studies and then demanded an explanation, he would destroy any chance he had of getting closer to her.

The dilemma forced him to confront his obsession with her—and to admit that it was, in fact, an obsession. He clenched his fists in helpless anger. If only they could manage without the accursed Trezhellas. Then she wouldn't be here and he would have long since put her from his mind.

Right, he told himself sarcastically. You did a great job of that for the past year. You probably didn't think about her more than once or twice a day.

He was saved from further contemplation of his foolishness by the approach of the Chief Navigator. They were about to enter the targeted star system—well ahead of schedule. The problem of Serena and the zhetlas could wait.

"I didn't come on this voyage to stay in the ship while the rest of you go exploring, Darian."

"I promised the High Priestess that I would keep you safe. Besides, you have to keep to your communications schedule."

"I can change it. And I don't care what you promised the High Priestess. I want to go down there. If you won't let me, I may develop a severe headache that could last for days and prevent me from communicating. It's happened to others."

"But it hasn't happened to *you*."

"Not yet."

"You're a *professional*, Serena—*Trezhella* Serena."

"That's right—but this is personal, *Commander Vondrak*."

"What do you mean?"

"You have no professional reason for refusing to permit me to go down there. I won't be in any danger. If we encounter wild animals or hostile people, I can use a stunner as easily as any of the men." She paused and fixed him with a steady glare.

"You won't let me go because I refuse to go to bed with you."

Serena regretted her outburst the moment it was too late to hold it back. And the proof of her foolishness was his grin.

"Perhaps you'd like to report an 'incident,' Trezhella Serena?" He challenged softly.

Under the circumstances, Serena could think of nothing to do but to turn on her heels and walk away. She couldn't believe that she'd been so stupid as to make that accusation. The fact that it was probably true didn't matter. She had just handed him a victory in the game they were playing. He knew perfectly well that she would never report an incident. Incident reports were about unwanted advances, and Darian could claim quite truthfully that he'd never made such an advance.

He didn't *have* to make an advance, she thought disgustedly. All he had to do was to *exist*. And worst of all, he *knew* it.

She went up to the lounge, where she stood before the windows and watched as the first of the landing craft moved out of the ship and began a slow descent to the planet's surface. She hadn't expected to be allowed on the first expedition. Much as she wanted to see this world, she knew that the crew in this craft were all specialists, who would take readings and determine the conditions on this unknown world. But if they proved to be safe, she wanted to go later.

When the craft was finally lost to view below the clouds, she turned away, her thoughts now going to the results of her studies. She had exhausted all the research on the subject of zhetlas and the conditions on Darseen, and she was nearly certain now that they were identical to the teldas in the caves at home.

The final piece of information that had convinced her had to do with the effects of thunderstorms on their growth. Research on the caves of Darseen showed that zhetlas that grew near the mouths of the caves were both smaller and not as hard, the result of their being affected by the energy released by storms.

146

That was true of the teldas as well. Although even the smallest ones could not be broken by any of the crude tools her people had, they often found them cracked and broken near the cave's entrance after the great storms of the Traneed Season.

The decision to hold on to her secret should have been easy for her, and it shocked her to realize that it wasn't. Had she forsaken her heritage and become a Ulatan in the space of one year? She thought of the child who had stared up in wonder at the distant stars—the same child who had often played among the very means by which those stars could be reached.

She wanted to live her dream—and yet she could not bring herself to betray her people and watch as her beautiful world was destroyed.

The discordant note sounded a second time before Serena realized that it wasn't part of her dance music, but was instead the door chime. She dropped to the padded floor in a crouch, then switched off the low-grav mechanism and the music just as it sounded again. Was there some sort of emergency? No one had ever bothered her in here before, though she wasn't usually here at this time of day.

She opened the door to find Darian standing there. It was the first time she'd seen him since their argument two days before. Since that time, the landing craft had come and gone many times, and she'd learned from the crew that no life had been found on the world they were exploring—all the more reason, she thought, why Darian's refusal to let her go down there made no sense.

His dark gaze swept over her and then her dance room. "I'd like to see you dance sometime."

"And *I'd* like to go down there," she replied.

"Does that mean that if I take you, you'll invite me in to watch you dance?"

"Yes." She saw no harm in that, though the thought of being alone with him *did* give rise to some doubts.

147

"We'll leave as soon as you're ready. Meet me in the cargo bay."

He started to walk away—and too late, she realized that he'd won again. "You were going to take me anyway. That's why you came here."

He merely nodded without turning back.

Serena made a sound of disgust, but then she hurried back to her cabin. Deciding that her uniform would be too cumbersome for exploration, she stuffed her old clothes into the cleaner while she showered, then put them on again and hurried down to the cargo bay. One of the landing craft had just returned, and Darian was busy examining the soil and rock samples that had been brought back.

The other men in the big bay stared at her in surprise, but when Darian finally turned her way, he nodded his approval. "Much more sensible than your gown, but I doubt the High Priestess would approve."

"I wouldn't know, because I didn't ask for her approval," she replied to laughter all around.

She had assumed that others would be going with them, but Darian motioned her to the second pilot's chair, then took the controls himself. They edged forward through the series of chambers—and then out into space, where they immediately began to drop toward the reddish-orange world that filled the windows.

"Why did you change you mind?" she asked curiously.

"We found no life of any kind—but we *did* find something today that I thought you might want to see."

"What is it?" she asked excitedly. "Did you find zhetlas?" She hoped that was the case, because then she could easily keep her secret.

Darian turned to her and studied her in silence for a moment. "No. It's nothing like that. But I think you'll find it interesting."

Serena stared at the world that seemed to be rushing up at

148

them with great speed. The sensation was strange, but it wasn't what was making her uneasy. Instead, it was that look on Darian's face when she'd asked if they'd found zhetlas.

He can't know, she told herself, then repeated the thought again and again, like a chant. *He can't read your mind and you've said nothing that could give it away.*

They dropped below the streaky clouds, and now the color of this world was even more striking. It reminded her in some ways of Tligid, the first world she'd visited as a Trezhella, but here the colors were deeper and darker: reds, oranges, browns. She told him of its similarity to Tligid and he nodded.

"They *are* similar—in many ways. I'd forgotten that you explored Tligid."

She searched her memory, certain that she hadn't told him. And that made her uneasy again. What else might she have forgotten?

"I don't remember telling you that I'd been to Tligid," she ventured, hiding her uneasiness.

"You didn't. I heard about it elsewhere. Trezhellas rarely leave the hotel, let alone go exploring."

"Do you disapprove of me, Darian?" she asked, even though she hadn't detected any disapproval in his voice.

He turned briefly to her and there were silver lights dancing in his dark eyes. "I feel many things where you're concerned, Serena—but disapproval isn't one of them. Not that it would do any good if I did," he added after a brief pause.

She turned her attention back to the world below them. She was not about to pursue *that* remark, even though she wanted very much to know just what those "many things" were.

They were now close enough so that she could see individual features of the landscape. Just like Tligid, this world had raw, jagged ridges and what appeared to be deep canyons. "Is all of it like this?" she asked, recalling that Tligid had a fringe of green along the shores of its ocean.

"Yes. The only water on the planet comes from deep springs in some of the canyons."

They skimmed the surface of the planet, passing over another landing craft where she could see men busy at work collecting rocks and soil. And that meant she and Shenzi would be kept busy, because all the information would be sent back to Ulata for further analysis.

Serena wished that she could find such things exciting, as so many of the crew did. But in truth, she had no interest at all in what a world was made of and what that said about its origins. What she had hoped for was that they would discover some inhabited worlds—or at least some with interesting animal and plant life.

"Do you think we'll find any inhabited worlds?" she asked Darian.

"Yes," he said succinctly—and rather strangely, she thought. She was about to ask him why when he banked the craft sharply and dropped altitude.

"Ohh!" Serena gasped, any questions forgotten. He had brought them into a canyon, much as the pilot on Tligid had done. But there the similarity ended.

The canyon was very deep—much deeper than the one she'd seen on Tligid. But the real difference was the walls. She felt dizzy and disoriented as she stared at them. The bold striations ranged from deep red to pale orange to browns and creams, wavy patterns that filled the windows.

She dragged her eyes from them and turned to Darian, suddenly worried that he too might become dizzy.

"Don't worry. It's on auto, and there's a collision avoidance system," he said as he continued to stare at the scene. "We photoed this earlier, so it can be turned into a holo."

"It's incredible!" she said, mesmerized by the swirling colors that seemed to be moving past them.

"There are some others, but this is the best one."

"So this is what you wanted me to see. Thank you, Darian."

He glanced briefly at her. "This is part of what I wanted you to see. The rest of it is up ahead."

She peered into the distance. It was difficult to focus as the colors continued to streak past, but it looked as though the canyon ended not far ahead of them. And then, as they drew closer to that point and Darian slowed the craft, she saw that it didn't end, after all. Instead, it made a sharp turn, then widened out beyond that.

He slowed the craft still more, then began to drop to the canyon floor. When he landed, she looked around, wondering what it was that he wanted her to see. The only thing she saw was that the canyon was wider and the colors weren't quite so bold.

Darian popped both doors open, and by the time she climbed out, he had come around to her side. "What am I supposed to see?" she asked as she peered at the rock-strewn canyon floor.

"Up there," he said, pointing to the high wall to their right.

When she followed his pointing finger, she thought at first that what she was seeing was only a different pattern in the colors. Then she squinted and studied them more closely.

"They're *houses*—like the ones on Tligid! But you said there was no life here!"

"There isn't, and there hasn't been for a long time. But there was once."

"Can we go up there?" she asked excitedly.

"Of course." He opened the cargo hold of the craft and produced two of the backpacks she hadn't seen since she first saw them on her own world.

He helped her strap it on as she stared up at the tiny houses carved from the rock: row upon row of them, piled one on top of the other, with wide ledges in front of them.

"How do I make this work?" she asked, eager to get up there.

He reached out to touch the square pad that partially covered her chest, and for one brief moment, she forgot about the houses—but only for a moment.

"Just press this. I've set it for a slow ascent. When you reach a ledge, press it again and draw up your legs so you land in a crouch—unlike the last time."

She laughed. "Do you know that when I first saw you in these anti-grav packs, I thought you weren't men at all, but some sort of strange flying creatures?"

Darian chuckled. "What I remember is how unafraid you were when I flew off with you. It seemed impossible to me then that such a small, fragile woman could be so brave."

Hearing the slight huskiness in his voice she met his gaze—and felt dizzy all over again. But this time, it had nothing to do with the striped walls of the canyon.

He held out his hand. "Stay with me. I don't want you deciding to pour on the speed."

She took his hand, then, with her other hand, she pressed the button. They began to rise slowly from the canyon floor. She tilted her head back to see the little houses gradually becoming more defined. Darian's leg brushed against hers, and she could feel the heat of him through the light fabric that separated them.

Rising slowly into the warm, dry air with Darian at her side as they passed layer after layer of color, Serena felt a rush of emotion. There was, quite simply, nowhere else in the universe she wanted to be at this moment. This was where she belonged—where she had *always* belonged, even if the dreamer who'd once stared up in wonder at the stars could never have imagined this.

They approached the first level of houses, and now she could see the rotted remains of wooden ladders that had once connected them, and great stone urns that had probably been intended to catch rainwater.

"Bend your legs," Darian reminded her—just in time. She

pressed the button and did as she was told, and they landed on the ledge.

"Is there anything in the houses?" she asked, rising quickly from her crouch and starting toward the nearest doorway.

"Serena, wait!"

But by the time he spoke, she had already reached the open doorway and was peering into the dim interior. She saw a crude wooden table and several chairs and stepped inside, waiting for her eyes to adjust so that she could make out the other objects. Then her foot struck something and she stopped to see what it was.

Her scream shattered the great silence just as Darian reached her. She staggered backward and collided with him. His arm slid around her waist to steady her.

"Dammit, why didn't you wait so I could warn you?"

She stared at the skull—and the rest of the bones nearby. When her foot had struck the skull, it had separated from the rest of the body. And now, as her eyes adjusted to the gloom, she saw two more, including one that must have been a small child, lying next to what had probably been its mother.

Darian began to drag her backward out of the house, then continued to hold her when they were back in the bright sunlight of the ledge.

"I'm sorry," he said gently. "I wanted to surprise you, but I should have warned you about them."

She shook her head and moved away from him. "I'm all right now. I just didn't expect to find *that*. Did you see that one in the corner? It was a child."

She studied the other houses. "Are there skeletons in all of them?"

"Nearly all," he said. "And a few on the upper ledges as well. Are you all right now?"

"I'm fine. I'd just never seen a real skeleton before." She

walked back to the doorway, then went in again, this time maneuvering carefully around the bones.

On the table was a crudely made pitcher. She picked it up, studying the designs painted on it. They were crude as well, the sort of thing a child might draw. But they were also oddly compelling: the legacy of a vanished people.

"Take it if you like," Darian told her. "We've already gathered up samples of their work."

She carried it with her as they made their way through other houses, all of them containing at least two or three skeletons. Serena's fascination turned slowly to sadness as she thought about the people who had lived their lives in this strange place.

"What happened to them?" she asked finally, as they stood once more on the ledge.

"Think like an explorer," he replied. "What do you know from what you've seen here?"

She frowned. "They died in their homes. It must have been a disease of some sort."

Darian shook his head. "If a plague struck them, they wouldn't have all died at once, and those remaining would have buried their dead. There's a burial ground on top of the mesa."

"Then what killed them?"

"The answer isn't 'what'—but 'who'?"

She stared at him, aghast. "You mean they were all *murdered?*"

"It looks that way. On one of the upper ledges, we found some crude spears and bows and arrows next to the skeletons. But only a few. Whoever killed them struck quickly—and left no trace of their weapons. Some of the skeletons are better preserved than others, and we couldn't find any evidence of trauma on any of them."

"I don't understand."

"What I mean is they were killed with weapons that worked quickly and cleanly."

Her fingers brushed against the stunner in her pocket. "Like a stunner?"

"Or a laser or some weapon like that."

"And you found no sign of any more advanced people?"

He shook his head. "I think we weren't the first visitors to this world, and however bad you think we Ulatans are, those who got here before us are far worse. These people could not have posed any threat to them, and as far as we can tell, there was nothing here they could have wanted. They came and killed and left."

Serena had studied the history of the Ulatans' conquest of their star system, and though she neither understood nor accepted their determination to reign supreme, she also knew that they had never killed simply for the sake of killing.

Darian had turned away from her and stood staring up at the milky sky, his hands braced against the wall at the edge of the terrace. "We have to assume at this point that they came from this star system—unless, of course, they can travel as far as we can. Our astronomers and physicists are convinced that there are no other systems nearby that could support life."

"What do we do now?" she asked.

"We move on to the next world in this system—but we move cautiously."

Serena said nothing. She would soon be transmitting all of this information back to Ulata—to the Space Command. She could only hope that Darian's superiors would order them to end their explorations and return home. But she knew her hopes were about as substantial as the morning mist. The proud Ulatans would not be likely to turn tail and run.

Chapter Eight

"Oh, Serena, you could be in such terrible danger!"

"Yes," Serena acknowledged. "But I placed myself in danger the moment I agreed to come on this mission."

"Not *this* kind of danger," Shenzi's voice said in her mind. "I wish you were back here now."

Serena said nothing. Strangely enough, she didn't wish that she was back in the stifling, rule-bound life of the compound—however dangerous her future in space now appeared.

"I'll never understand you," Shenzi said as Serena belatedly realized that she'd once again permitted her friend to read her thoughts. "You might dislike our rules, but at least you're safe here."

"I was safe in my own world, Shenzi—but I don't want to return there, either." She smiled to herself. She could pick up on Shenzi's thoughts as well, and while her friend spoke the truth when she said she didn't understand, she also admired Serena for her courage.

They had just completed a very lengthy report about the vanished world of the cliff-dwellers. It ended with Darian's strong recommendation that they proceed, but with extreme caution. Shenzi had ventured the opinion that the Space Command would accept that recommendation—especially since it came from Commander Darian Vondrak.

"We'd better sign off now," Serena said. "I'm actually beginning to get a headache. That's never happened before."

"I have one as well," Shenzi confirmed. "But it makes me feel that you are safe as long as I can talk to you."

They signed off, after setting up a special time in three hours that Darian had requested because of the urgency of receiving his orders. Until they came, the great spaceship sat motionless in space, hovering just above the world of the cliff-dwellers.

She typed a message to Darian, confirming the next transmission, then returned to her cabin to rest. She didn't like to admit it, even to herself, but these last few transmissions had begun to take a toll on her. Could that mean that she would soon be unable to communicate?

Shenzi had told her that she had begun to work with Clea, another of the sisters and a good friend of Shenzi's, in the hope that the two of them might be able to link up somehow and increase the power of their transmissions. Serena was pleased and surprised at Shenzi's initiative, though she had no way of knowing if it would work.

A little less than three hours later, when Serena returned to the communications room, she found Darian there waiting for her. "Will it disturb you if I'm present?" he inquired.

She hid her smile. His presence disturb her? No, of course not. It only threatened to melt her very bones. She shook her head.

"If they decide to bring us home, I want to lodge a protest," he told her.

"Do you think they will?" she asked curiously, still ambivalent about the matter herself.

"No, I think they'll see it as I do." He hesitated, and Serena was shocked to sense a certain awkwardness in him.

"It's important that we find out who these people are, Serena, and where they come from. I want to be sure you understand that."

"Why is it important that *I* understand?" she asked, thinking that perhaps he believed she would somehow alter the transmission, something no Trezhella would ever do.

Annoyance flashed in his eyes. "Do I have to spell it out for you? Sometimes it seems to me that we understood each other better *before* we could actually talk to each other."

And then, of course, she *did* understand. She was also surprised to hear him echo her own thoughts. "I *do* understand, and I appreciate your concern for my safety, Darian. But I knew the risks when I decided to come along on Deep Space One."

His expression didn't change, but before he could say anything else, she announced that it was time for her to make contact with Shenzi. He remained standing just inside the door while she took the chair. He was now out of her sight, but certainly not out of her mind.

Still, she had no difficulty putting herself into the trance, but when Shenzi's voice slipped into her mind, she could tell right away that something was wrong. Before she could ask, however, Shenzi answered her question.

"Supreme Commander Valens is here with me, Serena, and he asks that you summon Commander Vondrak."

No wonder poor Shenzi was nervous. Serena was amazed that she was able to transmit at all, under the circumstances. "Commander Vondrak is already here," she told Shenzi.

What followed was an hour-long discussion unparalleled in

the annals of Trezhella communications. In order for the two men to have their discussion, the women had to receive a transmission, come out of the trance to relay it, then go back into the trance to send the reply—over and over again, and in the presence of two men impatient to get their points across.

There was no disagreement about the actual decision. The Supreme Commander agreed with Darian's recommendation that they continue the mission. Instead, they wanted to talk—endlessly, it seemed—about the possible confrontation with a people who might possess all the technology of the Ulatans.

Serena's head throbbed and she began to feel light-headed, but she suspected it was even worse for Shenzi, whose voice was slowly getting weaker and weaker. She guessed that her friend was unwilling to tell the Supreme Commander that she could not continue much longer. So, after she had relayed his latest remarks to Darian, she interrupted his quick response.

"This will have to end soon, Darian. Shenzi's voice is getting weaker, and even I am having difficulty keeping it up."

Darian gave her a startled look. "I'm sorry. I didn't realize. Tell Valens that I need some time to think things over and set up another appointment in . . . six hours. Will that be sufficient time?"

"I think so. Thank you." She turned back to the zhetla and slipped into the trance again, then passed on Darian's words. She could feel Shenzi's gratitude even before her whispered "thanks."

"Will that be enough time for you to recover?" Serena asked her.

"Yes, I think so. I'd try using Clea to help me, but it won't work in this case. She'd be too terrified of the Supreme Commander, I think."

They signed off and Serena came out of her trance slowly. Even under normal circumstances, when she came out of that

159

blackness, the softened light of the communications room still came as a shock at first. But this time, when the room came into focus, it felt as though needles had been plunged into her eyes.

I must sit here for a few moments, she told herself through the pain. *Then I will go to my cabin and rest until the next transmission.*

Suddenly, two hands curved about her shoulders and she jumped and cried out. For the first time since she'd met him, Serena had managed to forget about Darian's presence.

"Why did you wait so long to tell me?" he asked gently.

"I knew how important it was that you discuss this with him," she replied, nearly sighing with pleasure at his touch. "I'm going back to my cabin now to rest until the next transmission."

She got up slowly, bracing her hands against the table. Her legs trembled and she wondered if they could carry her back to her cabin. But she would never know, because in the next instant, Darian picked her up and strode from the room.

"You can't carry me all the way back there," she protested weakly, recalling that she'd seen litters in the ship's infirmary.

But he did, and seemingly without effort. She was only barely aware of the looks of consternation on the faces of the crew they encountered, and of Darian's terse words to the effect that she just required rest. But she must have missed some of what happened, because when they reached the hall-way where her cabin was located, the ship's medical specialist was waiting outside her door.

"There's nothing wrong with me that rest won't cure," she protested as Darian opened the door and carried her in to deposit her gently onto her bed.

"I think she's right, Commander," the medical specialist said. "I could give her something, but that's always risky with Trezhellas."

"No! I don't want anything," Serena cried. "I just want to

rest. Wake me in five hours, so I can have something to eat and clear my head before the next transmission."

Darian studied her for a moment, then removed her low boots and drew a blanket over her. The last thing she remembered was his hand grazing her cheek in a soft caress.

"Serena."

She opened her eyes to find Darian bent over her, his face only inches away. For one giddy moment, she was back in that hotel, waking up beside him after their lovemaking. She smiled at the memory even as it began to fade under the weight of the reality that was now rushing at her.

But then she made a startled sound as his lips brushed lightly against hers—a soft, feathery touch that was gone almost before she could register it. The imprint lingered, however, and the warmth traveled all the way through her.

He straightened up and looked down at her with an endearingly crooked smile. "I suppose we could tell Supreme Commander Valens that we have more important things to do than talk to him."

She laughed. "That wouldn't do much to help either of our careers. How much time do we have?"

"Not enough," he replied, still grinning. "A little less than an hour."

She felt the heat creep into her face, only now realizing that he'd misinterpreted her question—or had pretended to. Or maybe he hadn't. In that moment when he kissed her, she had felt poised on the very brink of madness, ready to give up all of herself to this man.

"How do you feel?" he asked, studying her closely.

"I'm fine—but hungry."

He gestured to the small table in the corner. "I brought food for both of us."

* * *

This time, she found it somewhat harder to slip into the trance with him there. It was that kiss. Her lips still felt his imprint, and her mind refused to stop carrying it far beyond a mere kiss. But she managed it, and was delighted to hear Shenzi's voice sounding normal again.

They continued as before, but after only twenty minutes, Shenzi informed her that the Supreme Commander was ready to sign off. Then she told Serena that the High Priestess had given him a tongue-lashing for his "abuse" of the Trezhellas' talents. Serena smiled. She'd met the Supreme Commander before they set off on this journey, and she could just imagine a confrontation between those two.

She relayed this information to Darian, after which she rescheduled their next transmission and signed off. She was tired, but not nearly as tired as last time, and her headache was no more than a minor nuisance.

She got up from her chair. Darian started to move toward her, but she waved him off. "I'm fine this time—just a little bit tired again. Are you satisfied with the discussion?"

He nodded. "We think alike on most things. The only thing I was worried about was that the High Priestess would demand that we return, for your sake."

"Could she do that—overrule the Supreme Commander?" Serena knew that there were volumes of rules regarding the relationship between the Trezhellas and the Space Command, but she'd never bothered to read them.

"According to the rules, no, she couldn't. But the Space Command does not care to start a war with the Sisterhood. Besides, they're brother and sister."

"They are?" Serena was shocked. She'd never known the High Priestess's name.

Darian nodded. "And she's never forgiven him for his failure to take her side when she refused to marry the man her family had chosen for her—who just happens to have been my uncle. I can't blame the High Priestess for her feelings. He's not one of my favorite relatives."

"So that's how she came to join the Sisterhood?" Serena asked as they started back to her quarters.

"Yes. She'd kept her talent a secret until then. At that time, the Sisterhood didn't have quite the same prestige it does now—at least among the old nobility. But when her father wouldn't relent, she demanded to be tested. He refused, so she ran away and got to the compound herself."

Darian chuckled. "Old Valens is terrified of her. He thinks that she's going to find some way to exact revenge on him for his failure to stand up for her. He was the eldest son, you see, so he might have persuaded their father to back off."

"Speaking of family," she said as they waited for the elevator, "I assume you know by now that your sister has opened an Institute for Women."

Darian smiled. "I know more about it than I want to, believe me. Fortunately for Lessa, both my father and I are more enlightened."

"Are you saying that you *approve?*" she asked in surprise.

He shrugged, stepping aside to let her enter the elevator first. "I'm neutral. If Lessa proves that women are capable of working in science, I'll support that, I suppose. But those who oppose it *do* have a point. It will inevitably mean many other changes."

"They'll understand it," Serena stated firmly, thinking of how she, with so much less education than most Ulatan women, had managed to understand the research she'd studied. "If I can understand it, with the limited time I've spent, then so can they."

"Oh? And what have *you* been studying?" he asked as they left the elevator and started down the hallway to their cabins.

"Oh, many things," she replied as her mind raced to find a

way out of her stupid blunder. "I had a lot of catching up to do."
Could he possibly know what she'd been studying? "And I was
curious about the zhetlas, after I found out they provide the
power for the ship, so I studied them, too."

They stopped in front of her door. Darian was silent for a
moment, then quickly bade her good night and went to his own
cabin. She entered her room, feeling slightly uneasy. The
abruptness of his departure troubled her. Had he believed her?
Was there any way he could have made the connection between
her study of the zhetlas and her secret?

The ship moved on toward the next planet in the system. Serena
could feel the change in the atmosphere. The initial excitement
of making history and discovering new worlds had lessened,
though it was still very much there. Talk among the men was
quieter and more sober, with much discussion of the ship's
weaponry.

Serena was shocked to learn that the ship, which had previously seemed to her more like a flying hotel, albeit one with
rather cramped quarters, was in fact a warship with incredible
firepower. It was Sevec and one of his friends who explained to
her that the weaponry was kept concealed because the Space
Command didn't want to frighten any people they encountered.
The same was true of the harmless-looking landing craft,
which, according to Sevec and his friend, were quite capable of
wreaking great destruction on their own.

All of this did not sit easily on her mind. The voyage of discovery she had anticipated began to sound more and more like
a journey into battle.

Nor did her communications with Shenzi do much to soothe
her fears. The reports grew longer and longer, most of them
now filled with details of the ship's weaponry that neither
woman could begin to understand. And while Shenzi said noth-

ing more about her fears for Serena, Serena could all too easily tune in to her friend's thoughts and find them there.

She saw little of Darian, but that didn't surprise her. It was obvious that he was preoccupied with what might lie ahead. In the face of all this, she forgot about her secret—and her fear that he might have guessed it.

There were shipboard drills, times when the crew were summoned to battle stations, and even a few test firings that she didn't learn about until afterward, when the men talked excitedly about them. Somehow, it troubled her even more to know that the ship could fire its lethal weapons so silently.

And then, not quite a week after they left the world of the vanished cliff-dwellers, they reached the next world. Serena left her communications room to find men rushing toward the lounge, and followed along after them. This was after her morning report, so she'd had no opportunity to hear any news before that. Her reports were prepared several hours before transmission, so the news that they had reached the next world hadn't been included.

At first glance, the distant sphere reminded her of her home: a softly glowing blue color, partially covered by gauzy white clouds.

"Do we know anything about it yet?" she asked a young cadet next to her as they stared out the window.

"Only that it's far more hospitable to life than the last one," he replied. "The probe was fired only an hour ago, so it'll be another couple of hours before we learn anything more. There—see it? It's catching the sun now."

She followed his pointing finger and saw a slender object reflecting the sunlight as it seemed to be falling into the planet. That was only an illusion, she knew. Darian had explained to her that the small probes sent back information, then burned up in the planet's atmosphere.

"Then this could be where we'll find them," she said, referring to the killers of the cliff-dwellers.

"Not likely," said another crew member. "Unless they're too dumb to have a warning system and a defense."

"What do you mean?" she asked.

And then she learned that the Ulatans had long ago erected an elaborate satellite system that would provide ample warning if any alien craft entered their star system, together with a series of space and planet-based weapons that could destroy invaders.

Two hours later, the probe sent back the news: this world had an atmosphere and gravity almost identical to that of Ulata, and a plentiful water supply as well. But there were no indications of intelligent life, which was measured by the presence or absence of radio transmissions or other electronic pulses that could be picked up by the probe.

Serena and the others waited and watched as the first landing craft approached the new world, carrying the ship's specialists at initial forays onto new planets. Communication over short distances such as this were carried out through normal means, and the men in the landing craft reported back to the ship regularly as they flew low over the planet.

Serena was once again in the lounge. As she listened to the report that was coming back from the landing craft, which was being played over the ship's general comm units, she found herself thinking about her home. The world that filled the space beyond the window looked more like it than anything else she'd seen, and the men's report seemed to confirm that impression. They spoke of vast forests and a great ocean—and then, suddenly, of seeing a large town in the distance, on the shoreline.

"This can't be their home," the officer in charge of the crew stated. "It's far too primitive. We're going to set down outside town and have a look."

Then she heard Darian's voice, reminding them to stay out of sight for the time being. After that, there was no communication for a while, until finally, the men had apparently found a spot from which to spy upon the town. Serena was once again reminded of her home and how Darian and his men had once spied on them.

"Something's wrong, Commander!" The officer's voice was low and urgent. "We've been watching the town for some time now. It's the middle of the day and the weather's fine—but there's no one around. We've seen a few animals, but that's all."

The reports continued sporadically, but they were all the same: no sign of the inhabitants. Darian told them to stay until dark, and then return to the ship. By the time they did—still without seeing any sign of life—everyone was convinced that when they entered the town, they would find exactly what they'd found on the world of the cliff-dwellers.

But it was different this time. The next day, three landing craft went down. They found other towns and villages, all of them scattered along the coast—and all of them empty. But there were no skeletons.

Over the next two days, they searched all the towns and villages, but turned up no evidence of the fate of their inhabitants. By now, Serena had heard the descriptions of the small stone houses and the pleasant towns and villages, and she was reminded even more of her own distant home.

She also wanted to see the place for herself, and since it was clear that there was no danger, she went to Darian in the control room and requested permission to see the abandoned world.

"It sounds so much like home, Darian. I want to see it."

"It *is* very much like your world," he admitted. "I'll take you. You can help us by telling me how it compares to your world. The sociologists at home will want to know that, and you're in a better position than I am to give them that information."

167

She was both pleased and surprised, since she'd expected him to refuse her. On the few occasions when she'd actually spoken to him over the past week, he'd been polite but distant: the commander and not the man. In fact, it would have been very easy for her to convince herself that the tender, concerned man who'd carried her back to her cabin was a figment of her imagination. Except, of course, that she remembered the lover as well. *That* Darian Vondrak still haunted her dreams, even if she was able to banish him from her waking hours.

From the first moment she saw the abandoned world, Serena felt as though she'd stepped back in time. At any moment, she expected to encounter the old Serena—the woman who had been busy planning her wedding and fixing up their new home, or to hear the soft, musical voices of her people.

The similarities to her home world stunned her, but there were differences as well—and it was these small differences that she concentrated on. The stone houses were much the same, but the stone itself was different: a soft, weathered gray instead of the golden hue of her home. And while these people too had filled nearly every space with gardens, the flowers themselves were different.

She and Darian were alone as they walked through the streets of a town that was slightly larger than her own hometown and was built up the hills too, instead of just occupying the flat land near the sea.

She stopped in front of one cottage, trying to summon up the courage to go inside. She knew she wouldn't be tripping over any skeletons this time, but she felt closer to these people than she had to the cliff-dwellers, and therefore more reluctant to invade their private lives, even though they were gone.

She studied the little house, thinking that the roof was in need of rethatching, then turned to look at neighboring roofs. Some were in quite good condition, while others would soon require attention.

"Whatever happened here could not have happened very long ago," she said, as much to herself as to Darian, who stood silently beside her.

"What do you mean?" he asked, following her gaze with a frown.

"The roofs. Some of them have been rethatched quite recently." It then dawned on her that neither Darian nor any of his men were likely to think about that. They knew nothing of thatched roofs.

"How recently?" Darian asked sharply.

"Well, I can't be sure because I don't know what the weather is like here, but . . . "

"Assume that it's much the same as your own world."

"Then whatever happened happened within the past year, I would say. Certainly no more than two years." She waved an arm toward the large garden that separated the houses. "And this garden doesn't appear to be too badly overgrown, as it surely would be if much time had passed."

She went into the nearest house, uneasy in spite of the fact that she knew it would be empty. It was painful to see the furniture and the wooden toys and the colorful quilts and all the other objects that made up good, simple lives. Surreptitiously, she brushed away the tears that sprang to her eyes. She didn't want Darian to see her crying—certainly not the Darian who was with her now.

In the tiny kitchen, she picked up one of the small, colorful jars she knew would hold herbs. When she removed the lid, the pungent aroma of letisi poured forth. It was a favorite cooking herb among her people, too—and one that lost its flavor very quickly, even in a closed jar. She explained this to Darian.

"At home, we grow it on windowsills during the winter, because unlike most other herbs, it doesn't last all that well when it's dried."

She scanned the shallow sills and saw no pots. "Apparently,

169

they didn't do that here—or at least this family didn't—so that confirms my belief that it happened within the past year, perhaps even less."

Suddenly, she wanted to leave this place and the memories of her home—go back to the ship and the world she knew now. She knew that her home world was far away in another star system, but it was far too easy to imagine such a thing happening there.

She walked hurriedly out of the house, then turned to see Darian following her, carrying the little painted jar of herbs. He held it out to her. "You could add it to your collection."

She was touched by his thoughtfulness and by the fact that he'd even remembered her penchant for collecting, but she shook her head. "I can't, Darian. These people remind me too much of my own. It would feel like stealing."

He studied her silently for a moment, then took the jar back inside, surprising her again. When he reappeared, she was staring at the empty streets and gardens. Knowing what she knew now of the Ulatans' hideous weaponry, she understood that Darian and his men could have easily killed all of her people as well. It was nothing more than fate that had spared her people—and destroyed these equally primitive folk.

But what had happened to them? Where were the bodies? She felt his presence behind her and asked the questions without turning.

"I think it comes down to one of two things," he said in that Commander voice she disliked. "Either they were rounded up and blasted with neutro-guns or something like them—or they were carried off."

Serena felt as though he had thrown icy water over her. "What are neutro-guns?" she asked, even though she knew she didn't want to hear the answer.

"They're weapons that totally obliterate all carbon-based lifeforms like people, but leave buildings or ships intact. We have them because it would be a way of destroying an enemy while still allowing us to study their ships or weapons or anything else they've created."

She clenched her fists in cold rage at his matter-of-fact tone. "Darian, did you hear yourself? Did you *really* hear what you just said? How can you describe such a thing so coldly?"

He actually took a few steps backward as she leaned toward him in her anger. "I didn't mean to sound cold," he insisted. "You asked for an explanation."

Then he seemed to recover from his surprise. "Is it necessary for me to remind you again of the difference between us and them? We had those weapons when we came to *your* world—but we didn't use them. In fact, we've *never* used them."

She forced herself to relax. He was right. She was overwrought, just as she'd promised herself she wouldn't be. "I'm sorry. Seeing this has affected me more than I'd expected. You said there was another explanation—that the people might have been carried off. What did you mean?"

"Maybe they wanted slaves for some reason."

"Slaves?" She echoed the unfamiliar word. "What does that mean?"   .

"It means forcing people to work without pay—worse than that, actually. It happened occasionally in my people's history, usually to a defeated army."

"I read Ulatan history and I never heard that mentioned."

He shrugged. "My people have a tendency to ignore the worst parts of our history. And it didn't happen often. But it *is* another explanation for what happened to these people. The only problem I have with that theory is that a people as advanced as they must be shouldn't have any need of slaves. Slavery was practiced only when there was a great need for human labor to harvest crops or work in mines, for example."

Her mind was still caught in the comparisons of these people

171

to her own. What would her own people have done to try to save themselves if invaders came?

"Caves," she murmured, not even realizing that she'd been thinking aloud. They would hide in the caves. Could these people have done the same? Might they still be here, hiding now because they couldn't know that the Ulatans weren't their enemies?

"Caves, you said? We hadn't given any thought to that." He activated his wrist-comm and spoke into it, ordering someone to commence a search for caves.

"What made you think of caves?" he asked. "Is that where your people would hide?"

"Possibly," she said with an affected casualness. "We never even considered that we might need to hide."

"Are there many caves on your world?" he asked, and she thought his casual tone sounded as false as hers had.

"Yes—miles and miles of them. But no one pays them much attention, except that children play in them sometimes, and the men use them for shelter when they're hunting."

Darian merely nodded. The silence hung heavily between them. *He knows something*, she thought, *but he's waiting for me to tell him*. She hated this wedge that her knowledge had driven between them, but she knew she couldn't trust him enough to tell him about the teldas. He might have thought her world to be lovely, but he wouldn't hesitate to tear it up to get the teldas. And even if they were careful, the mere presence of Ulatans would change her people forever.

They found caves, but still no people. They also found a broad, flat plain large enough to land the ship, and a nearby supply of fresh water as well. And when they explored the plain more closely with their sensitive instruments, they discovered that another ship had landed there. Grasses and soil samples were analyzed, and they further confirmed what Serena had said. The

172

other ship could not have been there more than six months before. As Darian said in his report to the crew, the trail was getting warmer.

Seeing that his crew needed some time on land again, Darian declared that they would spend two days on this world while they checked out the ship's systems thoroughly, took on fresh water and replaced the ship's recirculated air with the fresh air of this world. He knew that tensions had been running high ever since the discovery of the cliff-dwellers' world, and in the long run, a few days wouldn't make any difference to their schedule.

But Darian had a different source of tension. Serena had been avoiding him ever since their conversation about the vanished people of this world. He knew that she disliked hearing about the weaponry his people possessed, but he doubted that was responsible for her behavior. It was that slip she'd made: the comment about her people hiding in caves. He was nearly certain now that there were zhetlas on her world—and perhaps a great many of them, since she had said there were many caves.

A confrontation between them was inevitable, and Darian had never been one to postpone such a thing. But this time, with this woman, he wanted very much to avoid it.

"Do you find it difficult to be here, Trezhella Serena?"

Serena nodded. "But only because I find myself putting my own people into their place. Like my people, they seem never to have known war, though even if they had, it couldn't have prepared them for what must have happened here."

They stood on a hillside, looking down at the town. Sever Tronning was the ship's historian. Although he held the rank of Lieutenant Commander, he had told her that he was actually a civilian. The Ulatans were very much interested in learning of the history of any people they encountered, and sifting through ruins or attempting to communicate if they actually met other people was his job. He was somewhat older than the rest of the crew, a pleasant and courtly gentleman she quite liked.

When he invited her to join him in this expedition to the town she'd visited previously, she had accepted quickly. Not only did it mean she could be away from Darian, whose dark gaze was on her all too often now, but it was also an opportunity to be of some assistance on this mission beyond her regular duties.

He had spent most of their time together asking her for more detailed information about the lives of her people, after telling her that he had, of course, read the report she'd written for the Space Agency. Now the two of them were seeking evidence of more similarities or differences between her society and this one.

"It seems likely to me," he said as they started down the hill, "that they even had a political structure such as your people have. At least I've uncovered nothing that would suggest a permanent sort of government."

"What would be evidence of that?" she asked curiously.

"Buildings, written laws, a palace of some sort for a leader. I've seen none of that. I think I will go next to the buildings at the harbor, to study their commerce."

"Then perhaps I'll take this opportunity to go for a ride—if I can catch a horse, that is." She'd seen some horses grazing in a meadow at the edge of town and she knew where the town stable was.

He looked faintly alarmed. "Will that be safe?"

She smiled. "I've ridden horses for far more years of my life than I've ridden in spacecraft, Lieutenant Commander."

He chuckled. "So you have. But won't they have gotten wild?"

"Some might have, but not all of them. I'll be careful."

They parted company as they reached the main street, and

Serena went first to the stable, where she found numerous saddles and bridles. Taking a bridle and lead with her, she went to the meadow where she'd seen some horses.

The first few animals she approached snorted and rolled their eyes and shied away from her, but before long, she had persuaded a pretty little chestnut mare to come to her. She led the docile mare back to the stable and saddled her, then set off, happy to be riding again. There were horses on Ulata, kept purely for pleasure, but since there were none at the compound, she hadn't ridden since she'd left her own world.

She rode out into the hills beyond town, where the forest closed quickly around a narrow path. The day was warm and pleasant, and the air was filled with the sweet scent of some purple flowers that grew in abundance along the borders of the path.

The hills became steeper and the ravines deeper. Ancient trees reached high into the sky, forming a thick canopy beneath which very little grew. Looking down at her old clothes, she thought that she might easily be back in her own world. Then she realized that she'd forgotten to put on her wrist-comm this morning and didn't have her stunner with her, either. So she had well and truly gone back to her old self.

Though she was still deeply saddened by the terrible fate of the people who had called this lovely world home, Serena was happy to be here, swaying gently with the rhythm of the horse, breathing in the old, familiar scents of pine and rich, damp soil.

On and on she rode, following the twisting trail as it snaked around the base of ever steeper hills, then climbed zigzag fashion over others. Without her wrist-comm to remind her of the time, and with the sky visible in only tiny patches, she gave no thought at all to anything other than the forgotten pleasure of being alone in a familiar place.

Finally, though, as the shadows grew darker, she realized that it was time to turn around and get back to the town.

Lieutenant Commander Tronning might already have been trying to contact her, unaware that she'd left her wrist-comm in her cabin on the ship.

She urged the mare down a steep bank to a swift-running stream where they could both drink. The bank of the little stream was covered with a thick cushion of moss. Serena let the mare drink, then tied her to a tree, where she began to munch contentedly on some nearby bushes. Then she knelt on the moss and drank water herself from her cupped hands.

The sharp, damp smell of the moss and its spongy texture pulled her back to another time, another world—and Darian. How simple the act of love had seemed then, before language could get in the way. Then, she had wanted nothing more than to follow her heart. Now she feared losing herself—and yielding up her secret.

It was so quiet here deep in the forest, and so peaceful. No spaceships, no fearsome weaponry, no complex man she might love but couldn't trust.

She sat there, staring at the sparkling little stream, knowing she must return to her new life. She *wanted* to return to that life—just not now. Tomorrow they would be in space again, away from everything that was lovely and alive and green, seeking yet more worlds—and perhaps an enemy.

She tilted back her head and stared up at the small patch of sky she could see, thinking that she felt like two people, not one. There was Serena, the woman who was content to ride through ancient forests and sit beside a mountain stream. And there was the Trezhella, the highly skilled professional who was part of a space crew, making history for a people who were not her own.

Had it reached the point where she could make even herself sound complicated? she thought in disgust as she got to her feet and turned away from the stream.

She started toward the mare, then stopped abruptly as she

saw movement high up in the trees. When she raised her head, she saw something moving away, just above the treetops. Tronning! He must be out looking for her.

Without giving it any thought, she put her fingers into her mouth and whistled: the shrill, piercing whistle every child on her world learned at an early age. The figure had vanished, but now she saw it returning, following the trail above her. She knew she couldn't get up there in time, so she whistled again, then waved her arms, feeling guilty that she had put the kind historian to such trouble.

The black-clad figure reappeared on the trail above her. And then she saw that it was not Lieutenant Commander Tronning.

Chapter Nine

Darian! She stood there, frozen in place as he unstrapped his pack and came down the bank. At first, she was sure she must be wrong, that it was merely one of the crew. But even as she thought that, her body was telling her differently. Only Darian could make her body throb with memory. Something in her recognized him even when her mind wavered.

"What are *you* doing here?" she asked, too flustered to hear the foolishness of her question.

"Reliving my past, apparently," he said dryly as he came to a stop before her. "On a world very much like this one, I once hunted for a golden-haired woman in a forest."

He glanced at her bare wrist and arched a dark brow. "That woman wasn't wearing a wrist-comm, either."

She laughed. He'd been so serious and so grim lately that she'd almost forgotten how much she enjoyed his occasional flashes of humor. "I'm sorry. I forgot to put it on this morning. Did Lieutenant Commander Tronning call you?"

Darian nodded. "Let me call off the search party."

He spoke into his wrist-comm, then gave her a quizzical look. "No Ulatan woman could whistle like that."

She shrugged. "Every woman on my world can. Even the men can do it."

Then it was his turn to laugh. "I hope someday we can go back to your world, even though it will surely be a humbling experience."

"Humbling? What could possibly be there to humble a Ulatan?"

"Thousands of women like you," he replied with a smile. "I'm not sure I could take that. I seem to have quite enough trouble dealing with only one."

A flock of birds flew through the trees, chattering noisily. But between the two humans, the silence lengthened, stretching taut, keeping them both immobile as they stared at each other. Serena knew what would happen, but still she clung to the moment, pretending that she had a choice. But she had made her choice long ago. She had chosen this man, whom she could not keep and from whom she *must* keep her secret.

Neither knew who moved first, but suddenly they were in each other's arms, pressed against each other, grasping greedily as their lips met and they swallowed each other's cries of a need too long denied.

It was a wild coming together, a hot and fierce rush of discarded clothing and mouths and fingers laying claim once again. They tumbled naked to the mossy cushion as the little stream gurgled its musical approval and the birds chattered on, unaware of the sensuous writhings of the two strange wild creatures below them.

Darian's mouth traced a hot, damp trail down across her throat to one dusky nipple and then the other, then on, as she arched to him, begging for more and still more as her hands groped blindly for him and closed around his hard shaft.

179

She urged him to her when he needed no urging at all to plunge himself into her and fill the space that had felt empty for so long. And still she wanted and urged him deeper and moved with him in a pounding rhythm that welded them together with its heat.

Darian's mouth sought hers again and his tongue prodded hers, setting up an erotic counterpoint to the other, more powerful rhythm. Then he rolled them over until it was he who was pressed against the fragrant moss and she was the one touched by the sunlight that streamed down through the trees.

She shook her head to rid herself of the hair that had fallen across her face and Darian saw it catch the light and become a pale golden fire around her, cascading over her shoulders and curling toward her breasts. What he felt in that moment, before he drew her down to claim a taut nipple once again, was something far too deep and powerful to have a name.

Her hair fell forward again as Darian drew first one nipple and then the other into his mouth. She grasped his face between her hands and held it within the shimmery curtain of her hair as she stared at him and saw her own passion reflected back from the depths of his dark eyes.

Then, with a cry that was a demand for release, she arched back and let her hair fall against his bent legs as she rode him and he bucked beneath her and they surged into another dimension, their bodies shattering and melting and quaking with the force they had created.

She sprawled atop him, too weak to move, too satisfied to want to. And gradually, she began to feel him as something separate from herself again: a hard, bristly body breathing in a ragged rhythm as his hand stroked her hair and caressed her still-heated flesh. She knew it was impossible, but how she wanted to hold on to that oneness, that thing that was *them*, and not just Serena and Darian, Commander and Trezhella.

"Why did we wait so long?" he asked in a low, husky voice that she felt as well as heard.

When she didn't answer, he lifted her away from him and laid her on the moss, then propped himself up on one arm and stared at her. "Why, Serena?"

She struggled to find an answer. It seemed foolish now to protest that she didn't want to lose herself, when only moments ago, she had done just that—willingly, eagerly. Was it because they had no future, and she feared that each time would be the last?

"Is it because of who we are?" he asked, his dark eyes still boring into her.

She smiled and reached up to trace the outline of his lips with one finger. "You were right when you said that things were simpler when we couldn't talk."

He sat up and nodded as he ran a hand through the thick black hair with its wings of silver. Then he looked up through the trees at the darkening heavens.

"Somehow, when you spend as much time in space as I have, time itself loses all meaning, and you don't think about the future. I don't want to think about it now, either, because I refuse to believe in a future where we can't be together."

He lowered his gaze slowly as his words seeped into her, bringing forth an echo that came from her very soul. "I love you, Serena," he said simply.

"And I love *you*, Darian." The words came so easily, despite all the fear that lurked behind them. Then she too stared up at the heavens, thinking about that girl who had once done the same thing, thinking too about the woman who'd said that she belonged to space: to space and to Darian.

This time, the discussion between Supreme Commander Valens and Darian, carried on through Serena and Shenzi with the addition of Clea, was much briefer. Shenzi told her that the

181

High Priestess had demanded that it not exceed one hour, which left little time, given the fact that everything had to be repeated.

Furthermore, Shenzi said that the High Priestess insisted that Serena end it any time before that if she felt stressed, since unlike Shenzi, she was working alone. Serena told her that Darian had already issued just such an order to her, though she didn't say that the "order" had come as they lay naked in each other's arms in the forest of a strange world—and she was very careful to mask her thoughts.

Much of the discussion centered on speculation about the capabilities of the unknown killers, based on the readings taken at the site where they had landed. Serena understood none of it, and she was therefore eager to have Darian explain it to her.

As he had done the last time, Darian stayed behind her, this time seated in a chair he'd brought in and pushed against the wall. There was no time when she was not aware of his presence, even in her trance. She could feel him there even though she couldn't see him, but the sensation was pleasant—even comforting in a strange sort of way.

Then the discussion shifted to less technical matters. Valens expressed some concern about the members of the crew, like the historian, Tronning, and Serena herself, who were not military personnel and who had come on what they believed to be a peaceful mission of exploration.

Given what she knew of the forbidding Supreme Commander, Serena was surprised to hear such concern from him, and said as much to Shenzi.

"It's not what you think. Valens is just unhappy about the presence of civilians and the problems they could cause."

The words in her mind came not from Shenzi—but from Darian! Shocked and thoroughly confused, Serena was suddenly jerked from her trance even before Shenzi had finished.

She turned to Darian—and saw her own confusion mirrored in his expression.

"Did you speak?" she asked, certain that he must have, even though he knew to wait until she had left her trance to report Valens's words. And then, as though her present state of confusion was not enough, she was suddenly faced with the question of just how he knew what Valens had said, since she hadn't yet told him.

Darian shook his head, and for the first time, she saw before her a vulnerable and even frightened man.

"Darian, what happened?" she asked, her voice shrill with her own fears. "I heard you reply when you couldn't have known what he said."

"I don't know what happened. But I didn't hear Valens. I heard *you*. You said you were surprised at his concern."

Could she have spoken aloud? That was the logical explanation, and yet she'd never done that before—or at least not that she knew of.

"They must wonder what's happened to us," Serena said. "I'll have to ask Shenzi to repeat her last transmission. I didn't catch all of it."

Finding that calm, dark pool inside her was far more difficult this time, but finally she slipped back into the trance, to hear Shenzi calling her with great urgency.

"I'm here," Serena said. "I don't know what happened. Could you please repeat that last transmission?"

There was a brief pause, during which Serena heard the faint murmurings of other Trezhellas. She hoped fervently that Shenzi wasn't going to question her about the break, and perhaps that thought transmitted itself to her friend because after a moment, Shenzi began to repeat the communication.

Serena left her trance and turned to Darian, who still looked rather shaken. When she repeated it all to him, he told her to say that *all* of the crew were in agreement that these killers must be found because all had witnessed their cruel and wanton destruction.

She transmitted Darian's words to Shenzi, and then, after a few more matters were discussed, they signed off. Serena came out of her trance with a sigh of relief. At least she had some time now to come up with an explanation before her next transmission. She had no doubt at all that Shenzi would not let the matter rest. The best she could hope for was that she'd keep it to herself in the meantime, though that would be difficult for her, given that both Clea and the Supreme Commander undoubtedly knew something had gone awry.

She turned to Darian, who was still sitting in his chair, staring at her with a stunned expression. "I must have spoken aloud," she told him, wanting to ease his mind as well as her own.

"You haven't done that before—at least not when I've been here," he stated doubtfully.

"What you heard wasn't part of the regular transmission. It was just a remark to Shenzi. Maybe that made a difference." She tried desperately to think if she had made such off-the-record statements before when he'd been here. She didn't think she had.

Darian continued to stare at her. "I can't swear that you didn't speak aloud—but I know that *I* didn't."

A chill slithered through her. What was going on here? She wanted to believe that he was wrong—that he *had* spoken aloud—but that still didn't explain everything, unless she too had spoken aloud. Confusion swarmed over her like a dark, threatening cloud. She put a hand to her head.

"I think I'd better go and rest now. Shenzi is certain to demand an explanation for the break, and I've got to come up with something that will satisfy her without involving you."

They both got to their feet and Darian drew her into his arms.

"We'll be getting under way in about an hour. After your next transmission, I'll have a surprise for you."

"Oh?" She tilted her head back and smiled at him, only too glad to forget about the strangeness. "And what will that be?"

"A solution to a minor problem," he replied as he seemed to shake off his own confusion.

"What happened, Serena?"

Any hope she'd had that Shenzi would forget about the incident vanished with her friend's very first words after they had made contact again.

"I'm not really sure," Serena said honestly, then began her careful lie. "I was tired. Our sleeping schedules changed because of our explorations, and seeing this world was difficult for me because it reminded me of my home. I must have simply lost my concentration for a moment, that's all. I'm fine now."

"You've been leaving the ship?" Shenzi asked, and Serena could feel her astonishment, as well as hear it in her voice.

"Yes," she admitted. "But only after Dar—Commander Vondrak has determined that it's safe."

"You're not telling me all the truth, are you?"

Serena wondered just how good Shenzi was at reading her thoughts. "What I've told you is what you must tell the others. I'm sure they want an explanation—particularly the High Priestess."

In the brief silence that followed, Serena could feel her friend's thoughts center on Darian, but she couldn't sense anything more.

"Have you had any . . . problems?" Shenzi asked.

"If you mean with the men, the answer is no. They've been unfailingly kind and polite to me."

"I can understand that you might not trust me enough to tell me the truth," Shenzi said, and despite her words, Serena could feel her disappointment. "But will you tell me the truth when you come home?"

"I *have* told you the truth," Serena lied.

Shenzi accepted that, though with obvious reluctance, and they turned to business. After that, Serena signed off quickly, claiming that she was still tired. Then she came out of the trance and sat there, staring at the zhetla.

She hated lying to Shenzi, but not only was it necessary to protect Darian, it was also necessary to protect their friendship. Shenzi had joined the Sisterhood when she was only eighteen, and she believed in all its rules. Serena was certain that Shenzi forgave her for the other rules she'd broken, but she was even more certain that if Shenzi knew what had happened with Darian, she could not forgive that.

She recalled Shenzi's question about whether she would learn the truth when Serena came home. The compound wasn't her home, and Serena could no more imagine returning to its stifling, if luxurious, life than she could imagine going back to her own world.

Oh, there were certainly times when she thought about the comforts of her life in the Sisterhood, and times as well when she thought of the pleasures of life in her own world. But she belonged to neither.

She left the communications room and went to the nearby lounge, which was thankfully empty at the moment. Beyond the window was the unrelieved blackness of space—the great space between the stars that had once seemed so small. Somewhere out there were worlds where people lived out their lives not knowing what she knew—not even able to imagine that she could be here.

And out there as well was Evil—a cruelty beyond her understanding.

She turned away from the window and started back to her cabin, remembering only as she emerged from the elevator that

Darian had a "surprise" for her: something, he'd said, that would take care of a "minor problem."

She was very tired, but not so tired that she couldn't smile at the irony of those words. Whatever problems they had were certainly not "minor." He'd said that he could not imagine a future when they wouldn't be together, but that was only because Darian Vondrak had always gotten what he'd wanted—and that now included her.

The door to her cabin had barely closed behind her when her wrist-comm buzzed. She stared at it in surprise. No one communicated that way aboard ship; they all used the ship's system. She pressed the button and Darian's voice came through immediately.

"Remove anything you have in your closet, then stay away from it for a few minutes."

"What?" she asked in confusion.

"Just do as I say. I'm about to take care of our problem."

She started to demand an explanation, but the tiny click told her that he'd cut off his own wrist-comm. The closet? She stared at it, then approached it cautiously, as though half expecting to find something there other than her few items of clothing.

She flung it open and took out everything, tossing it all onto her bed nearby. Then, remembering that he'd also said to stay away from the closet, she closed the doors and retreated to her chair in the opposite corner. Was he in his cabin? It was next door, and the wall that separated them was the wall that held the closet.

Suddenly, she heard a faint whining sound emanating from the closet. Then she gasped as she saw a strange bluish light outlining the doors. She was nearly out of her chair when she recalled again his admonition to stay away from the closet. So instead, she sat there gripping the armrests and staring through the semi-darkness of her cabin at that light.

Then, abruptly, both the sound and the light were gone. She heard a faint "thunk"—and then a rapping sound from inside the closet! Still mesmerized by the unknown goings-on in her own closet, she rose slowly to her feet.

"You'll have to open the door. I can't open it from this side."

Darian's voice was clearly coming from inside her closet, but until she opened it to find him standing there, she couldn't quite believe it. Behind him was a gaping hole where the back of the closet had been, and an acrid odor preceded him as he stepped out into her cabin with a decidedly smug grin on his face.

Her mouth agape in her astonishment, Serena stared through the hole to his cabin, which, she noted, was considerably larger than her own. His closet backed up against hers, and the wall separating them was gone.

"What happened to it?" she asked, meaning the missing wall.

"I cut it out. I think it will fit beneath my bed. If not, I'll have to find another place to hide it."

She turned back to him. "You cut a *hole* in the *ship?*"

"Only an interior wall. I got the idea when I remembered the crew had cut out a wall for your dance room. Now we don't need to worry about being seen by anyone."

Serena started to laugh. "You have a devious turn of mind, Darian Vondrak. But won't it be discovered at some point?"

"I'm not devious—just determined," he protested. "And it can be put back almost as easily as it was taken out. It's not like anyone's likely to notice the seams in a closet. Just don't open the closet doors when anyone is here."

"I'm not in the habit of inviting men into my cabin."

"Present company excepted, I presume?"

"I don't recall issuing *you* an invitation, either," she replied dryly. She turned back to the closet. "If there was ever an 'incident' that needed to be reported, this must surely be it.

'Commander Vondrak cut a hole in the wall to invade my cabin, Your Excellency.' Now *that* would make history."

Darian chuckled. "It's likely that it would be the end of the High Priestess *and* the Supreme Commander. And speaking of that esteemed lady, were you questioned about the *other* incident—the break in transmission?"

She nodded, her smile giving way reluctantly. "I told Shenzi that I must have slipped out of my trance because I was tired and because our visit to a world so much like my own had upset me."

"Will they believe that?"

"I think so—though I don't think Shenzi believed me. In fact, I think she suspected that you had something to do with it. She can sometimes pick up on my thoughts. But she won't tell anyone."

"That's what happened to *us*, isn't it?" Darian asked quietly. "We read each other's thoughts."

"I don't know," she admitted. "When you were bringing me to Ulata, there were times when I thought you'd done that—and of course I tried my best to read your mind as well. After all, my life was in your hands and I didn't know anything about you." She paused, then added softly, "And there have been times since then that I've thought you were reading my mind."

Darian stared at her in silence for a long moment, and she could feel him waiting and wanting to say something. He *does* know about the teldas, she thought—or else he's simply guessed somehow. She turned away from him and began to replace her clothes in the closet.

"Would that be so bad?" he asked. "We love each other, Serena. We shouldn't be keeping secrets from each other."

"As far as I know, we're not," she replied, glad that her back was to him at the moment. Lying to him was very difficult. Lying to his face would be impossible.

When she turned back to him, he put his arms around her. "We're both tired. Let's get some sleep."

They chose his bed because it was much larger. Serena felt strangely vulnerable, but she knew it had nothing to do with her being in his cabin. Instead, it was the intimacy of going about their routines to prepare for bed. Before, they'd seized opportunities. Before, there'd been spontaneity rather than a willful decision.

And as they lay in bed, their bodies curved about each other, she smiled sleepily. She liked this warmth between them, this desire on both their parts to be together even if they were too tired to make love.

Her last thought, before she floated off to sleep, was that they *were* making love—just in a different way.

Serena first heard the voices as she listened to Shenzi's reports. They were very faint, nearly submerged beneath the only slightly more audible murmurings of other Trezhellas. But they were definitely male.

"Shenzi," she said, interrupting her friend, "Do you hear male voices?"

"What?" Shenzi was shocked.

"Male voices. They're very faint, but I can hear them. I just can't hear the words."

Both women were silent for a moment, listening. Even without Shenzi's clear voice, Serena could not hear them any better. She tried to concentrate on them, the way Trezhellas did when they were seeking one voice among many of their sisters, but still it made no difference.

"I don't hear anything," Shenzi said finally.

Not wanting to alarm her friend, Serena said that perhaps she was mistaken, that she could no longer hear the voices of other Trezhellas very well, so it might only be some of them. But after they had completed their transmission and Shenzi had signed off, Serena remained in her trance, listening. Despite what she'd told Shenzi, she knew that the voices weren't those of her sisters. They were definitely there—and they were definitely male.

She finally withdrew from her trance and frowned. Was it possible that, for some unknown reason, she was picking up shipboard communications? That had never happened before, but after that episode two days ago with Darian, she was more willing to accept the possibility of changes.

She was reluctant to say anything to Darian or anyone else at this point, so she returned to her cabin, then changed into her old clothes and went to her dance room. She hadn't danced this morning because Darian had pointed out that there were other forms of "exercise" that could satisfy them both.

She smiled as she began her stretching exercises. He was right. There was scarcely a muscle in her body that didn't feel well-used. Then, after she had turned on the music and lowered the gravity in the room, she watched her contortions in the mirrored walls and wondered idly what it would be like to make love under these conditions.

Here in her dance room, she had started out, as Sevec had suggested, using gravity comparable to that of the grass world. But then she'd begun to decrease the gravity slowly, until she had now reached the point where she began to float as soon as she pressed the switch.

The feeling was wonderful. She felt as light as a feather, and the slowness of her movements added a whole new dimension to her dancing. The rapid movements associated with the dances were impossible in gravity this low.

She smiled. Darian made her even more aware of her body, which seemed to argue against her contention that he would rob her of herself: a fact he'd pointed out to her just this morning. Perhaps he was right. The body that she'd taken for granted all her life now seemed a wondrous thing indeed.

"You are beauty to me now," he'd said softly as his gaze traveled slowly along the naked length of her. "I think you were from the very beginning."

"That didn't stop you from seeking out the pleasure house on Mandwa," she had replied archly. She still became angry when she thought about such places—and embarrassed as well, when she recalled her naivete that time.

Darian's laughter had filled the cabin. "I was merely following *you*. I walked into the hotel and saw you going out into the gardens, so I followed you. Then, when I saw where you were headed, I thought I'd better intervene."

"Those women were very beautiful," she said, not quite mollified.

"Of course. That's their business, but as I said, my tastes have been changed."

Serena would have liked to pursue that topic, to let him know just what she thought of such things, but there'd been no time. It was only now, as she continued to dance, that she reminded herself of the differences between his world and the one she'd grown up in.

Don't think about it, she counseled herself. You're both in the same world now, and that's all that matters.

After she finished her dancing, she went to the dining area, where she was quickly invited to join Sevec and another cadet. When she had first come aboard, Serena had always eaten alone—except for the few times she'd eaten with Darian. But now she was always invited to share a table with whoever happened to be there. This pleased her, because she knew it meant that the men had accepted her completely as being one of them.

One of them had remarked that she now knew all their secrets, since it was through her that they could communicate with their families back home. The messages themselves were scarcely dark secrets, but they had given her a glimpse into the men's lives that they probably didn't even share with their shipmates. Men were like that—or at least Ulatan men were. The longer she lived among them and observed them, the more she realized how strange the men of her own world must have seemed to those who'd been there.

"I hear that the Commander has been making you work hard," Sevec said with a grin.

Serena hoped that her brief moment of shock hadn't showed. "Work" wasn't exactly the right word for what she and Darian had been doing only hours before. Fortunately, she quickly realized that he was referring to the dialogue between Darian and Supreme Commander Valens.

"It's gotten easier," she said with a shrug. "And apparently the High Priestess told Supreme Commander Valens to keep it brief."

"He must have loved that," Sevec chortled. "And probably she liked telling him, too. They're brother and sister, you know, but she really hates him."

"Yes, I know that. From what I heard, she has good reason to be angry with him."

Sevec nodded. "Yeah. If I'd been in her shoes, I'd have felt the same way. But the problem with the High Priestess and the other, older Sisters is that they don't understand that things have changed."

"The Sisterhood changes very slowly," Serena said carefully, not wanting to criticize it in front of these men.

"My cousin's a novice," the other cadet said, "And I talked to her just before we left. We're the same age and we've always been close. She says that none of them can stand the older Sisters' attitude toward men. They took a secret poll among the novices, and nearly all of them thought that Sisters ought to be able to get married and to live wherever they want to live."

"Really?" Serena was surprised, even though Shenzi had hinted that the older Sisters were having some problems with

193

the novices. She herself had had little to do with the latest group because she'd been busy with her own studies.

"What do *you* think about that?" Sevec asked.

"I agree with them. Given a choice, I wouldn't live there, either, even though it's very luxurious."

"I bet if you demanded to live elsewhere, you could," Sevec said. "Tormy's cousin said you can get away with anything because they need you so much."

"Does she resent me for that?" Serena asked Tormy.

"No—at least I don't think so. Lieta said that they all wish *you* were the High Priestess, because then things *would* change."

Serena laughed. "She makes me sound like an old woman. Many years would have to pass before I could be considered, and even then I might not be, since I'm not Ulatan. Besides, I wouldn't want to be High Priestess. I like being in space."

"Lieta said that she and the other novices can hardly wait to go into space—unlike the rest of them."

After they had gone, Serena continued to think about the Sisterhood. It seemed to her that it would probably be a very long time before the attitudes of the novices would prevail, but both the Sisterhood and the world beyond the compound *were* changing. It would be interesting to see those changes happen. Their ability to change was one of the most fascinating things about Ulatans—especially when she compared it to her own people's lack of interest in change.

Even though it was several hours until her next scheduled transmission, Serena returned to the communications room. Those faint voices were still very much on her mind, and she wanted to see if it might have been merely some sort of fluke that she'd heard them before.

Her question was answered quickly when she entered her trance. They were still there, and it was possible that they were slightly louder, though she still couldn't make out what they were saying. She listened for a time and learned that, as before, they came at irregular intervals. She couldn't hear individual voices well enough to know if they were speaking to each other, but the pauses seemed to suggest a transmission of some sort.

She withdrew from her trance and thought about it some more. She had no real idea of how much shipboard communication there was, and it could simply be general announcements over the ship's system or individual conversations through comm units or even wrist-comms that she was hearing. What else could it be?

Then a chill settled into her. Was it possible that she could be hearing the killers—that they were somewhere nearby? She didn't know at what point the ship's sensors would discover them, but that thought was enough to send her to Darian.

She found him in the control room, seated in his chair that was at the moment swiveled away from her as he talked to one of the crew. The other man must have alerted him to her presence because he swung around to her, then stood quickly.

It was a strange moment. In this room more than any other, Darian was the Commander rather than the man. The black uniform with its heavy gold braid that she scarcely noticed anymore seemed to mask the man who wore it. And yet, that man had made love to her only hours before.

"What is it, Trezhella?" he asked. Even his voice, which had been so low and husky, was now louder and filled with authority.

"Commander, something has happened that I think you should know about." And then she told him: how she had first heard the voices during her normal transmission, while Shenzi had heard nothing, and then how she'd returned to listen again and now thought they seemed somewhat louder.

"But I can't begin to make out what they're saying. All I know is that they're male." She shrugged. "I suppose it could be that I'm somehow picking up shipboard communications, but that's never happened before."

"Can you make contact with the Sisterhood now?" he asked.

"Yes—at least I think so. Shenzi heard me one other time when it wasn't our regular schedule. She was asleep then, though, and she wouldn't be now. Why do you want me to contact them?"

"I want you to find out if any other sister has ever had such a thing happen. It's possible that it has and they never reported it to *us*. But I'm sure they would have reported it to the High Priestess. Then call me as soon as you receive an answer. And be sure to stress the importance of this information. I don't care if the Sisterhood failed to tell us in the past—I just want to know now."

She nodded, then even bowed slightly, a subtle way of letting him know that he was overdoing things a bit with his sharp commands. He didn't smile with his lips, but she saw the gleam in his eyes just as she turned away.

Contacting Shenzi proved to be easy, and when Serena put the question to her, Shenzi's reply was quick. "I'm sure that's never happened before, but I'll speak to the High Priestess immediately. Will you be waiting?"

"Yes. And Shenzi, please tell her that it's really important that she's honest about this. Dar—Commander Vondrak doesn't care if the Sisterhood withheld information in the past—but they can't do it now."

There was a slight hesitation and then Shenzi said she would pass on that message. Serena wondered if she should find a way to tell Shenzi that things aboard ship were less formal and that both she and Darian had fallen into the habit of using only their names and not their titles. This was the second time she'd slipped—and it might not be the last.

While she waited, she remained in her trance and listened again to those men's voices. If only she could isolate them better. But they were barely more than faint, low murmurs beneath the higher and clearer voices of her sisters.

Shenzi was back quickly. "The High Priestess says that no one has ever reported hearing anything other than the voices of other sisters. She would also like a full report on this *before* Commander Vondrak contacts the Space Command."

"Tell her I'll do that, as soon as possible. Commander Vondrak has asked me to bring her response to him immediately."

They signed off and Serena slipped out of her trance, then punched out the code for the control room. "Commander Vondrak, this is Trezhella Serena. I've received a report from the High Priestess. She—"

Darian's voice cut in quickly, coming out of the speaker in the vidcomm on the wall. "Come right away to the conference room. It's just off the control room—the door next to the elevator."

"Right, Commander. Right away, sir!" Serena muttered as soon as he'd clicked off, mimicking the crew's usual response to him. Still, she understood the reason for his behavior. Not only was he trying to protect the two of them, but he was also obviously concerned. His thoughts were undoubtedly the same as hers: the voices she'd heard could be those of the killers.

When she reached the conference room, Serena found all the senior officers gathered there with Darian. All eyes turned to her as she walked in. She felt slightly uncomfortable, since she didn't really know these men as well as she knew the younger, more junior crew. She thought wryly that while she'd never been invited to join any of them when she'd found them in the dining area, they certainly wanted her here now.

The room was rather small, with a round table and chairs taking up most of the space. The one long wall was filled with big screens that were blank at the moment. The lighting was rather too bright, and it reflected off far too much gold braid as the men stood when she entered.

Darian waved them to their seats, then gestured for her to take one of the two empty chairs. She noticed that there was no gleam in his eyes now, though she might not have seen it anyway, with all that gold flashing at her. Still, whether or not he acknowledged it, she certainly felt a secret thrill as she thought about what all these somber-looking men would say if they knew what their commander was doing in the privacy of their now-joined cabins.

"I've already told them what you told me, Trezhella," Darian said crisply. "What did you learn from the Sisterhood?"

"The High Priestess herself has assured me that nothing like this has ever happened before." She paused. "I should also tell you that I have been ordered to give her a full report before this is reported to the Space Command."

"Perhaps the High Priestess hasn't read the rule book lately," Darian responded dryly. "But since I have no control over what you say when you're transmitting, she must know that you're free to obey her orders."

In spite of herself, Serena laughed, drawing startled looks from the other men. "That's true enough. Any report I send can easily be given to Her Excellency before it's transmitted to Space Command."

Darian nodded, and she now saw that gleam in his eyes. But she was also aware of the other men looking from Darian to her and back again. Were those glances speculative? She didn't know, but she knew they had to be careful. It was one thing for her to engage in light banter with the younger crew members, but quite another for her to treat the Commander in the same manner.

Darian folded his hands on the table and gazed steadily at her. She tried her best not to think about those hands and what they'd been doing this morning.

"Would you care to speculate about the origins of those

voices?" he asked, drawing some surprised looks from the others.

"Well, it seems to me that they can come from only two sources. Either I'm picking up shipboard communications for some unknown reason, or what I'm hearing is coming from another ship—or even a planet somewhere.

"It does seem to me that they're growing slightly more audible, but I still can't begin to make out words. And there are pauses at irregular intervals, which suggests transmissions rather than ordinary conversation." She saw puzzled looks on the men's faces and explained.

"It may not be apparent to any of you, but since this is my field, I find it easy to distinguish formal over-the-air transmissions from mere private conversation. A single transmission will be longer, for example, and then the pause after it will be slightly longer too."

She saw nods of understanding—and maybe even a grudging respect. What Darian thought, she couldn't say, because she avoided meeting his gaze. One of the men turned to Darian. "Well, there's a way to find out if it's just shipboard communications."

Darian nodded. "We'll just shut down all communications for a while. Do it now, Toban. Serena can use my office."

The startled looks on the men's faces was difficult for her to decipher. She chose to assume it was because they would have expected her to go to the communications room, which was some considerable distance away. She didn't know where Darian's office was, but she assumed it was close by—perhaps even behind the door opposite where she sat.

She stood up. "Commander Vondrak knows that unlike my sisters, I don't require the presence of a zhetla to go into a trance. Any quiet place will do."

The men all stood when she did, an annoying habit she'd

finally gotten used to. One Lieutenant Commander left to return to the control room, and Darian walked over to the door she'd noticed. "My office is through here," he said as he pressed the doorplate. "I suggest that you wait a few minutes, until the order reaches everyone."

She walked past him, trying not to think about the big, hard body beneath his loose-fitting uniform. It seemed to her that since they were actually spending more time together in private, she shouldn't be feeling this way about him—but the opposite seemed to be true.

The door closed behind her, and she found herself in a small, neatly organized office with many screens and several keyboards. She sat down in the big, comfortable chair and, despite Darian's suggestion, immediately went into a trance. If she heard the voices and then they were abruptly cut off in a moment or two, she would know that they were coming from the ship. And she hoped fervently that that would happen, despite the problems that might pose.

The voices were there—perhaps a little louder, but perhaps not. Certainly she was no closer to being able to decipher their words. She waited and listened, straining her talents to try to hear them better, expecting them to vanish at any moment. Each time there was an interval of silence, she thought it would be the end. But then they were back.

She came out of her trance to check the time, and discovered that she'd been listening for nearly eight minutes—certainly long enough for all shipboard communications to have ceased. A cold knot of dread formed in her stomach as she got up from the chair.

When she opened the door into the conference room, all conversation ceased and five pairs of eyes turned to her expectantly as they all stood. She focused on Darian as she returned to her seat. "The voices are still there."

A heavy silence fell over the room that was broken, finally, by Darian. "Then we have to assume that you are picking up transmissions from the enemy—either from their ship or from their world. It seems more likely to be a ship. If you were hearing planetary transmissions, there would be many more voices—overlapping voices."

"Yes, that's true. But I know of no way to figure where they're coming from."

Chapter Ten

"Explain to me what I've just said," Serena demanded as she massaged her throbbing temples.

Then she saw the expression on the face of the ship's Chief Communications Specialist and instantly realized that her tone—or perhaps even her question—was inappropriate. But it was too late now, and in any event, she was almost beyond caring.

For the past hour, she had been working with Shenzi and Clea, whose voices were becoming fainter and fainter as they tried to facilitate a discussion between Darian and the Communications Chief on Serena's end and the Supreme Commander and a communications specialist back on Ulata.

If Darian noticed his officer's shock, he chose to ignore it. "What it comes down to is this," he said. "We still know next to nothing about how Trezhellas communicate, but we think it likely that you've been picking up communications between ships, rather than merely shipboard communications. It's a

202

matter of both frequency and power—plus the fact that you now know you're hearing only two voices."

Serena nodded. Now, in addition to her headache, she had that tight knot of dread in her stomach again. "So they have more than one ship."

"Yes. It looks that way, although it could be ship-to-ground."

"Which means that we could be nearing their home world."

"Possibly," Darian replied. "Or maybe the world of their next victims."

Serena thought about the dead worlds they'd already seen and knew she didn't want to see another. "We have to stop them," she stated firmly.

"We will if we can," Darian told her.

Something in his tone made her raise her head to stare at him. It was a measure of her tiredness that it took her a few seconds to realize that what she was hearing was a grudging admission on his part that the all-powerful Ulatans might have some doubts about the extent of their power.

Throughout this exchange, the Communications Chief had remained silent, his gaze going from Darian to her and back again. Serena thought there were likely to be some whispered conversations among the officers later. It was obvious to her that he, like the other officers, regarded her as being little more than another piece of equipment on the ship, and he couldn't understand why his commander was wasting his time explaining all this to her.

"I don't know how much longer I'll be able to reach Ulata," she told him. "Their voices are getting harder to hear, and to judge by the number of times I've had to repeat myself, I think it's even worse for Shenzi and Clea. I can no longer hear the others at all."

"But the men's voices are getting clearer?"

She nodded. "Of course, that's partly because the other Trezhellas' voices are gone."

She got slowly to her feet and reached out to steady herself against the table. Darian stepped forward, reaching out to her—oblivious to the staring officer.

"I'm all right," she said, waving him off.

"No, you're not," Darian replied as he picked her up, still ignoring the other man.

Serena awoke to the soft chime of the bedside alarm and the pleasant heaviness of Darian's arm curved around her and one leg across hers. She felt his lips against her hair, and his hand began to trace a soft, warm line down across her stomach.

Their lovemaking began with slow caresses and soft kisses as they each awoke to the pleasures of the other. They lingered, toying with each other, even as their joint passion urged them on. And when that shattering moment of ecstasy came, it seemed to startle them both, as though neither of them had known what lay at the end of this sensuous journey.

Afterward, Darian continued to stroke her absently, his body pressed warmly against hers. But the moment was slowly passing and reality was asserting itself. Then suddenly he sat up, and a moment later leapt from the bed.

"What is it?" she asked in alarm as he headed toward the wall comm.

"We've just fired a probe," he said as he keyed in the control room.

Confirmation came quickly from one of his lieutenant commanders. They were now close to the next world in the system, and a probe had just been released. The officer wanted to know if he should awaken her.

"Yes. Ask her to listen for voices immediately."

By the time Darian had switched off his comm, Serena was hurrying through the closet to her own cabin—just in time to respond to the officer's request.

Darian followed her, but she ignored him as she sank down

into a chair and willed herself into a trance. Only silence greeted her: silence and the blackness of space. It was unnerving, and she left the trance quickly.

"Nothing," she said to Darian. "Somehow, that's even more frightening than hearing their voices."

Darian ran a hand through his thick black hair, smoothing back the silver that was sticking out like small wings from his temples. "Try again," he ordered in his commander's voice.

She nodded. By now, she was coming to accept this duality in him: the tender lover one moment and the authoritarian commander the next.

Silence. It seemed to fill her, expand inside her until she felt as though she were hollow. But this time, she forced herself to remain in the trance, listening, pleading silently for voices to break that utter stillness.

When she came out of the trance, Darian was sitting nearby, on her bed, the question in his eyes. She shook her head.

"Perhaps the probe will give us answers," she said hopefully. Then she remembered how he'd suddenly sat up in bed and announced that one had been fired, even before the officer had contacted him.

"How did you know it had been fired?" she asked him.

"I felt it," was his distracted reply.

She frowned. She had felt nothing—not this time or the other times when they'd released probes or test-fired the weapons. She supposed that he understood the ship in much the same way she understood how to communicate across space: an instinctive reaction.

He got up. "I'm going to the control room. Keep trying."

Then, when he was about to step into the closet, he paused and turned back. She was still frowning at him questioningly when his lips touched hers in a soft, warm reminder of his earlier kisses. The commander had let the man come through for a moment.

205

* * *

Over the next hour, Serena tried several times to find the voices again, but found only that profound and frightening silence. Then, realizing that it was time for her first transmission of the day to Shenzi, she went to the communications room. There were no reports yet from the probe. She learned from one of the cadets who was in the dining area gathering up food for the control room crew that it would be at least another hour before they could expect anything.

In the communications room, she switched on the vidcomm and saw what appeared to be a lengthy report waiting to be transmitted, and at the appointed time, she went into her trance and called out to Shenzi, hoping against hope to hear her friend's voice. Five minutes passed, and then ten, and she heard nothing.

She slipped out of the trance as she felt her concentration wavering. Shenzi had never been late. Their long experiment was over. She hadn't expected to feel so . . . alone. How wrong she'd been to believe that she was the one who would be least affected if communications ended. It wasn't just that she missed hearing Shenzi's voice; there was far more to it than that. It was the utter emptiness she felt inside now. Even out of the trance she could feel it. And after a time, she realized that what she was feeling was her own failure—and her uselessness.

It startled her to realize just how much of her sense of herself had been bound up in her work as a Trezhella. The Sisterhood encouraged that, of course, but Serena had thought herself immune to their self-serving teachings.

It's possible that she can still hear me, she thought. After all, that was what they'd expected all along. Neither she nor Shenzi had ever believed that Shenzi could transmit over such great distances.

So she returned to her trance and began to send the report. And then, when she had finished, she sent a message of her own.

"Shenzi, you probably know by now that I can no longer hear you. I'm not hearing anything now—not even those voices I heard before. And of course I have no way of knowing if this is reaching you.

"I'll continue to keep to our schedule, though. We've just launched a probe toward the next world in the system. I can't recall its code. There is a chance that this is the home world of the killers. I should have more information when I transmit in four hours."

She signed off, feeling somewhat better even though she had no way of knowing if she'd been heard.

Then she went to the control room. It was important to let Darian know that she could no longer receive transmissions, and it was also possible that by now, the probe might have sent back some information. If Darian didn't want her there, he would have to say so.

But she entered the control room to find Darian's chair occupied by his chief lieutenant, a man she barely knew. He stood up as she approached him. She thought he was the coldest man on the ship. Never once had she seen him smile—or even appear to relax.

"I need to see Commander Vondrak," she explained.

"He's in a briefing with the others who are going down," came the clipped response.

Going down? "Then the probe has sent back information?" she asked.

The man hesitated, then nodded. It was clear that he had no desire to give her any information. "Thank you. Would you please ask Commander Vondrak to contact me after they leave?"

She had turned and was heading back to the elevator when she heard his reply—and froze.

"He's going with them, Trezhella. Whatever you had to say to him should be said to *me*."

"He's going with them?" she asked without turning. "But he's never done that before."

As she spoke her final words, she turned back to him and saw something flicker in his eyes. She just wasn't certain what it was.

"Was it about the voices?" he asked, and his voice seemed slightly less harsh, though she could have imagined that, distracted as she was.

"No. I still haven't heard them again. What I wanted to tell Commander Vondrak is that I haven't received any transmission from my Sister."

"Nothing at all? This was at your appointed time?" Now his tone was sharp again, reminding her of Darian.

"Yes. And she's never been late before. I waited, and then went ahead and transmitted my report, but I have no way of knowing if it was received."

He nodded. "Thank you, Trezhella. Please continue to keep to your schedule."

He gave her a slight bow that signaled dismissal. She stared at the conference room's closed door. Darian was probably in there, but she knew she couldn't just barge in, however much she wanted to. Did he intend to leave without seeing her?

Then, just as she was about to turn toward the elevator, the door to the conference room opened and some men came out. Darian was the last one and his eyes locked onto hers immediately. In that instant, she became very sure that he hadn't intended to tell her he was going. In fact, it was even likely that he'd planned his departure for now, knowing that she would still be busy—which she would have been if Shenzi had been able to reach her.

Angry and hurt, she turned again to the elevator, but by now it was filled with the crew and the doors were closing. Behind her, she heard Darian's voice as he spoke to his chief lieutenant. She headed for the lighted door that led to the stairwell, unwilling to wait for the elevator's return.

She was just starting around the first bend in the narrow stairwell when the door above her opened and Darian appeared. She paused long enough to acknowledge his presence, then started down again. But before she'd gotten more than three steps, he caught her arm and brought her to a halt.

"Let me go, Darian! Your men are undoubtedly waiting for you."

"Serena . . ."

"You timed this so you could leave without speaking to me—so leave! I have nothing to say to you. I made my report to Lieutenant Commander Trollon."

"You're right. I *did* plan to leave without telling you. I apologize. I didn't want you to worry."

"Why are you going this time, Darian? You never went before."

He looked surprised. "Didn't Trollon tell you?"

"He told me nothing. He doesn't like me, though I suppose I shouldn't take that personally. I don't think he likes anyone."

"That's not true," Darian protested. "He's as grateful as the rest of the crew are for your presence here. He'll be in charge while I'm gone, and I've just told him that you are to be treated as a senior officer."

"Thank you," she said formally. "What didn't he tell me?"

"The reason I'm going is that something is down there—possibly their ship. The probe picked up some low-level electrical noise."

She felt as though shards of ice had suddenly encased her spine. "But that doesn't explain why *you're* going," she protested.

"I have to see it for myself."

She was standing one step lower than him, and now she

raised her head and glared at him. "I remember hearing that you're known as a risk-taker. Is this what they meant, Darian?"

"I won't send my men into any situation that could be dangerous without my being there as well."

She turned and walked the remaining steps to the next level, where the door opened onto the hallway that led to her cabin. She could think of nothing to say to that, but as she pushed open the door, she hoped that he would follow her. He didn't. The last she saw of him was his broad shoulders with the twisted gold braid as he hurried down the next set of stairs.

She went to her cabin, telling herself that she wouldn't go to the lounge to watch him leave. She was still angry, but a cold dread was rapidly overtaking that pain. She didn't understand him—and that meant she didn't really *know* him.

She lost her resolve within moments and left her cabin to hurry to the lounge. A half-dozen men were already gathered there, standing before the big window. She saw Sevec among them and joined him.

"Wish I were going with them," he said after greeting her.

How can you? she asked silently, even as she gave him a sympathetic smile. How could any sane person *want* to walk into danger?

And yet, in the next moment, she realized that she too had done just that when she'd agreed to come on this mission. It was, after all, only a matter of degree. Shenzi and the others and even the High Priestess had thought she was insane.

Below the window, the ship disgorged the landing craft, which immediately began to drop toward the cloud-covered sphere that filled their view. Tears sprang to her eyes. Why hadn't she understood all this earlier?

"Commander Vondrak is with them," Sevec said. "That's why the men all want to serve with him. He wouldn't send anyone into something he wouldn't go into himself."

She merely nodded as she tried to brush the tears from her

eyes. But she knew Sevec had seen them. She could feel him watching her as she stared at the landing craft. Already, it was little more than a dark spot against the white clouds, and a moment later, it was gone, enveloped by them.

The others who'd been watching left, but Sevec remained at her side. "I guess I know why you're crying," he said in a low, hesitant voice.

Startled, she looked up at him and saw a faint flush creep through his bronzed skin. "I mean, it's Commander Vondrak, isn't it?"

"How . . . how did you know?" she asked, even though she should be denying it.

He shrugged awkwardly. "I just guessed, that's all. But I don't think anyone else knows and I wouldn't say anything."

She thanked him, but she wondered just what it was that he knew. Perhaps he thought only that she was in love with Darian. Darian might have done a better job of hiding his feelings for her. At least she hoped that was the case. Let Sevec—and any others who might have guessed—believe it was a case of unrequited love.

After she had completed her next transmission—still without hearing Shenzi—Serena looked into the lounge and then, finding it empty, went to the staff dining area. Sevec was just leaving, carrying a heavily laden tray that was probably intended for the men in the control room.

Nearly five hours had passed since the landing craft left. By now, it would have reached the surface. Sevec had explained to her earlier that this time there would be no transmissions from it, because they feared being overheard if there *was* a ship down there. But if they ascertained that nothing was there, they would break silence.

"I've been transmitting for the past hour," she told Sevec. "Is there any news?"

He shook his head. "Lieutenant Commander Trollon thinks they must have found something. Otherwise, we'd have heard by now."

"Would you please tell him that I've just sent another report and that I've still heard nothing?" She didn't want to speak to Trollon again. She was certain his attitude toward her wouldn't change, regardless of what Darian had said to him.

"Will do," Sevec assured her, then gave her an encouraging smile.

She went into the dining area, where several crew members immediately leapt to their feet and invited her to join them. For once, she regretted their friendliness toward her. She would have preferred to be alone. But she smiled and thanked them and joined them; then, in response to their questions, she told them that she'd still not been able to contact her Sister.

They were clearly disappointed at that, but she could also feel their excitement. They were all eager to take on this unknown enemy, and being Ulatans, were still confident of victory. She only wished she could share their excitement, and she tried hard to pretend that she did.

No day had ever been so long. Again and again, Serena went to the lounge to stare at the cloud-shrouded planet, hoping that at any moment she would see a tiny dark dot that would turn into the returning landing craft.

And as the interminable day wore on, the crew's excitement drained away bit by bit. She could see it in the solemn faces, hear it in quiet conversations. No matter what the conditions were on the unseen world, more than enough time had long since lapsed for Darian and his crew to have conducted the standard preliminary search and returned. They had found something down there, and the conversations that Serena tried not to overhear all centered on what actions they might be taking.

Serena made her scheduled evening transmission, by now no

longer expecting to hear Shenzi's voice—or any other voices. Lieutenant Commander Trollon had prepared a detailed report of the launch of the landing craft with Darian in command, including the opinion that something had indeed been found and that their failure to return indicated that they were engaged in "studying the situation."

She finished the transmission, trying to envision Shenzi sitting in one of the little rooms at the compound, feeling as frustrated as she herself was as she received the transmission, then trying over and over again to contact Serena.

"Oh, Shenzi," she said, lapsing into personal conversation that her friend might or might not be hearing, "I've seen the faces of the crew and I've heard their conversations. Everyone is worried that something has happened to them. Lieutenant Commander Trollon is putting the best face on things, but the truth is on the faces of the crew. I . . . " She stopped herself just as she was about to pour out her heart to her friend and tell her that she loved Darian and he loved her and they had parted badly, thanks to her stupidity.

She signed off abruptly, then withdrew from the trance and went immediately to the lounge a short distance away, knowing that at this time of evening, at least a few of the crew would be there. It was a favorite place for relaxation and conversation and games before the "day" crew went to bed.

"I've been transmitting for the past hour and a half," she told the first man she saw. "Is there any news?" But she knew, even before he shook his head, what the answer would be. As she'd just told Shenzi, it was in their faces.

"How long will we wait before something is done?" she asked a junior officer who'd always been pleasant to her.

"That's hard to say," the officer replied. "Commander Vondrak left orders to wait as long as possible before sending another craft. He said he didn't want to risk more lives."

"That might not be long," said another junior officer who

had come over to join them. "We're keeping a close eye on a Force Five storm that seems to be headed this way."

Serena felt that ever-present knot in her stomach clench itself a bit tighter. "What does Force Five mean?" she asked, not having heard the term before.

"Our instruments rate them from one to five, with five being the most dangerous—for us, at least. But they're unpredictable, just like their planetary counterparts. It could break up, or it could change direction."

"But if it doesn't, it means we have to leave, doesn't it?" she asked.

He nodded. "At least until it passes."

"I don't envy Trollon," the other officer said. "It'll be a tough call."

"You can count on him to do just what Commander Vondrak would do," said the officer who'd told them about the storm. "He'll put the safety of the crew first."

"But *which* crew?" Serena blurted out.

"The crew up here, Trezhella. There are more of us."

There would be no sleep for her this night. Serena knew that, and didn't even bother trying. She tried for a time to interest herself in a classic Ulatan story about war and intrigue in that world's bloody past. Then she clicked through the various entertainments available on the ship's vid-library: guided tours through the great art of the Ulatans, classical dance, numerous sporting events. But not even the dances could hold her attention for long.

She got up and walked through her closet into Darian's cabin, keeping her eyes away from the big bed. He had a few personal items here: holos of his family, one of his first command, and one of himself with the entire crew of "Operation Trezhella," posed in front of the ship that had carried her to Ulata.

She picked up the cube that held the holo of Darian with his family, wondering if they knew yet what had transpired. She supposed that if her transmissions had been received, they would have been informed—especially given who they were.

The holo showed Darian with his parents and his two sisters. He had no brothers. She recalled Lenia's having said that his family wanted him to get married and impregnate his wife before this mission. They knew how dangerous it was—but Darian had flown into danger before.

She studied the faces of his two sisters, guessing right away which one was the rebellious Lessa. She was striking rather than beautiful, and the defiance that had marked her life was there in the upward tilt of her chin. The other sister had a more docile look, much like Darian's mother.

Darian himself looked slightly younger, though not by much, and the silver hairs at his temples weren't quite so numerous. She smiled, recalling how they looked like silver wings when he got up in the morning.

"He'll be back!" She spoke aloud, as though saying those words would guarantee their truth. She had little understanding of violent death because it was so rare on her world. People did sometimes die before their time in accidents or from illness, but it didn't happen often.

The only real evidence she had of sudden, violent death were those ancient skeletons on the world of the cliff-dwellers and the emptiness of that world that was so much like her own. Those worlds had certainly left an indelible memory in her mind, but they lacked immediacy.

So the truth was that while Serena knew at some deep level that Darian *could* be dead, she didn't truly believe it. And while she was often secretly amused by the Ulatans' pride and arrogance, she could not help sharing some of that. Surely these killers, whoever or whatever they might be, could not triumph over the dazzling technology of her adopted world.

She forced herself to leave his cabin when she found herself staring at the bed, remembering their slow, delicious lovemaking. And by the time she had returned to her own cabin, she was once again berating herself for her behavior before he left—never mind the fact that *his* behavior didn't bear close scrutiny, either.

She returned to the lounge, grateful to find it empty. The world that had swallowed up Darian and his crew was unchanged, still hidden behind the thick cloud cover that revealed nothing of its surface. The probe had reported a gravity similar to Ulata's and a climate that was, at least presently, cold and damp, with vast bodies of water and abundant plant life.

Serena shivered, even though the temperature on the ship never varied. She wanted to ask about the latest reports on that storm, but she was reluctant to contact Trollon. She knew that the Lieutenant Commander must have many good qualities or Darian would not have chosen him as his second in command, but she still didn't like him, and she sensed that he felt the same about her.

After pacing for a time, she poured herself a small glass of wine and settled down on one of the sofas, still staring at the sphere that filled the windows, willing a dark dot to appear that would signal the return of the landing craft.

She grew sleepy, but resisted it, unwilling to let herself relax while he was down there, facing who-knew-what kind of danger. But at some point, she fell into a light doze, with images of Darian drifting through her tired brain.

"Serena . . . captured . . . ship."

She bolted to wakefulness and swiveled around sharply, her heart swelling with happiness. He was back! But her welcoming smile turned slowly to a puzzled frown as she scanned the empty lounge.

216

After shaking her head to clear away the cobwebs of sleep, she concentrated on his words. There was no doubt in her mind that she'd heard Darian's voice. It was a dream. It *had* to be, and yet . . . She thought about that incident in the communications room that they had, by mutual unspoken agreement, not mentioned again.

Her heart thudded noisily. Was it possible? Had Darian actually made contact with her? When she had reached Shenzi that time while her friend was sleeping, they had both speculated that sleep wasn't so very different from their trances.

It took her several minutes to find that calm, deep pool that allowed her to enter her trance, but when she finally reached it, there was nothing. She started to withdraw, then stopped herself. He might not understand the necessity of repeating himself over and over. So she waited and listened through the vast darkness—and then, just when she was about to give up, it came again, the very same words.

She came out of the trance, both terrified and exhilarated. Darian was alive—but he was in trouble. If only he'd told her more: the location of the ship, for example. Was it down there, or somewhere in space? But she understood that it would be far more difficult for him, and that he'd undoubtedly decided to concentrate on the essentials.

She started to get up, to hurry to the control room to tell Trollon or whoever was there now—but then she stopped and sank down onto the sofa again. Would he believe her? And if he did, would Darian's talent cause problems for him? The talents of the Trezhellas were accepted because they were essential—but she knew that the men who ventured into space, as well as their leaders back on Ulata, were very suspicious and even contemptuous of those talents. Furthermore, they were talents never before seen in a man.

She was still trying to decide how to handle the situation

217

when she heard footsteps behind her and turned to see Lieutenant Commander Trollon come to a brief stop at the top of the stairs as he saw her.

He nodded and bowed slightly, keeping his distance from her as he walked toward the window, where he stopped, his back to her as he stared out at the cloud world. Serena took a deep breath, stood up, and approached him. When she addressed him, he turned toward her slightly, barely acknowledging her.

"Lieutenant Commander, I've had a vision," she began carefully.

That certainly captured his attention, though his expression indicated that he was only humoring her.

"Commander Vondrak has been captured and is being held aboard a ship," she said quickly. "I saw him."

Trollon's dark brows knitted together as he stared at her. "You had a *vision*, Trezhella? I've never heard of Trezhellas having visions."

"As far as I know, they don't," she replied. "And I've had none since I came to Ulata. But I had them occasionally as a child—including a vision once that I would one day fly through the heavens."

She told herself that it wasn't a *complete* lie. She'd often daydreamed about it, at any rate. "I believe it's accurate," she told him.

He continued to peer at her intently. "But you saw only Darian? What about the rest of the crew?"

"I saw only Dar—Commander Vondrak."

He seemed to ignore her slip of the tongue. "What about the ship? What did you see of it?"

"Only enough to guess that it must be a spaceship—curved white walls, a large space like the cargo hold on this ship," she added, embellishing on her lie.

218

"Are you aware of the fact that a Force Five storm is approaching us?" He asked.

"Yes," she replied. "At least I heard something about it from one of the officers." She didn't understand that sudden change in topic. "Do you mean that we must leave?"

"It's possible," he said, still studying her. He was silent for a moment.

"Let me be candid with you, Trezhella. I need to know if what you've just told me is the truth—or if it's nothing more than your personal hope. I can't send more men down there to their possible deaths just because you want Darian back."

Serena stared at him. He knew! Either Sevec had talked after all, or this man and others knew from their own observations. She lowered her face, but not before she felt a faint flush creep through her skin.

"I'm telling you the truth, Lieutenant Commander," she stated softly but firmly.

"Darian told me, Trezhella—not in so many words, but he told me. When a man is about to embark on a highly dangerous mission and his final words to me are about the safety and welfare of one woman, it's easy to fill in the gaps. And what I just found in his office confirms that."

"What do you mean?" she asked uneasily.

He turned away from her to stare out the window again. "As you may or may not know, written communications aboard ship are very rare. For everything, we use the comms. But when I went into his office a short time ago, I discovered a sealed letter, addressed to me, with instructions to hand it over to his father in the event that he didn't return.

"Since we have no way of knowing his fate at this point, I opened it. It's a will, and in it, he leaves a considerable portion of his personal fortune to you, designating his father as trustee."

The coldness settled through her, numbing her to the reality of what he'd said. She had, in any event, only the most rudimentary understanding of such things.

"Then . . . then he didn't expect to return?" she asked, having trouble getting the words out through her constricted throat.

"No, that's not necessarily true," Trollon said, his voice slightly softer as he turned back to her. "We all have wills, and because Darian is a very wealthy man, it's even more important for him to have one. Any space voyage is dangerous. What is interesting to me is not that he had a will—but that he felt the need to *change* it, to see that you are provided for."

"It doesn't matter, Lieutenant Commander. He's *alive*, and we have to go down there to bring him back. I don't know about the other men."

"We?" He asked with a grim sort of amusement. "Are you volunteering for the rescue mission, Trezhella? I was instructed to keep you safe and that hardly qualifies as being safe."

But Serena ignored his sarcasm because her mind was racing on, thinking things through more clearly. When Darian was in the communications room with her, she'd heard him quite easily. If she *did* go down there, it meant that she might be able to get more information from him that would help them rescue him. But to do that, she had to tell Trollon the truth.

She took a deep breath, then did just that: telling him about the incident in the communications room and her certainty that he had somehow managed to reach her just a short time ago.

"I lied to you because I wanted to protect him," she admitted to the silent man. "I know how all of you feel about us and our talents, and I was afraid that it could cause problems for Darian if anyone knew he possessed such a talent."

"And you're being honest with me now because you want to be part of any rescue party, since you might be able to make contact with him again."

"Yes. If I can, he might be able to help us find him and rescue him."

Trollon abruptly turned away from her again to stare out the window. "I've served as Darian's second in command for three years now, and I've gotten to know him well. I consider myself to be very fortunate indeed to have served under such a man. You have created a dilemma for me, Trezhella. I believe what you've told me, but I also know that Darian asked me to keep you safe.

"If we had the luxury of time, I would send down another crew to try to find this ship, which shouldn't be difficult. But we may not have much time—and you are, of course, correct. Your presence might enable us to find him and rescue him more easily."

He turned back to her, and she was shocked to see an ironic smile appear on his normally taciturn face. "It's probably just as well that we've lost contact with home. If I had to run this one past the Supreme Commander . . ."

"Then you'll let me go?" she asked eagerly.

"Yes, because neither of us could rest unless we knew we'd done everything possible to save him—and the others, if they're still alive."

"Why wouldn't they be? If Darian . . ."

"It would be obvious that Darian is the leader. They may have kept him alive in the hope of learning something. It's far easier to hold one man than to hold six."

She suppressed a shudder. His brief lapse into humanity was gone; what she heard now was his own version of a commander's voice.

Barely more than an hour later, Serena entered the landing craft, followed by five grim but very determined men. Trollon had had no choice but to tell them the truth: that Darian had made contact with her. What they truly thought about it wasn't evident as she'd sat in the conference room watching them. Several of them were men she'd spent time with in the dining area or the lounge, but their expressions gave away nothing. They were warriors now—a team, she'd learned, that had trained for just such a mission. Like the weaponry on the ship and landing craft, it was one more thing she hadn't known about.

Everyone but the pilot was silent as the landing craft eased its way through the locks and then surged forward into space, falling slowly toward the cloud world. Soon they were completely enveloped in the thick white mists.

It seemed to Serena that a lifetime passed before they broke through the cloud cover and saw at last the surface of the world. What they could see as they continued their descent was a vast gray-green ocean, much like the one on Ulata, with scattered patches of dark land that were too small to be called continents. She was just beginning to wonder where there could be enough land to put down a spaceship, when the crew's leader spoke up from the co-pilot's seat.

"We're going to stay high and take a look at the other side. Unless we're dealing with a technology very different from ours, they couldn't have landed a ship anywhere down there."

There were murmurs of agreement from the other men as the craft leveled off, then turned. But as the rest of the world came slowly into view, they still saw no great land masses. Even the largest of the islands had no open space that would permit anything much larger than their own craft to land.

"Maybe they're in space, after all," Captain Honek, the crew leader, said in disgust as they all stared at the heaving sea below them. Then he turned to Serena. "Do you think you could contact Commander Vondrak again?"

"I'll try," she said as all eyes fixed on her. "But it could take some time."

Given the circumstances, it was surprising that she could go into her trance so quickly. But what greeted her was total silence. She called to Darian and waited impatiently, then called again.

"I'm here," came the reply, much clearer now.

"We're on our way, Darian, but we can't find you. Where are you?"

"*You're* coming down? I told Trollon . . . "

"Stop it, Darian! There's no time to argue about it. The storm is getting closer. Where are you?"

"In their ship—the cargo hold, I think. But I don't know where it is. They sneaked up on us and used stunners. When I came to, I was here. We never saw their ship, and I don't know where the others are."

She could feel his voice growing weaker and knew that he wouldn't be able to manage it much longer. Holding the trance was always difficult for novices, which was what Darian was.

"It doesn't seem likely that I was out long enough for them to have gotten me back to a ship in space—at least one far enough away that we wouldn't have spotted it. But there's no open land. Try looking for calm waters. I can't feel any movement, but the ship could have landed on water. We could do it if we had to."

"All right. Rest, Darian—if you can. I may need to reach you later."

" . . . love you. Sorry . . . "

"Yes. I love you and I'm sorry, too. Rest for an hour, and then try to contact me again."

Serena broke the trance, warmed by his words but fearful because he might not be able to make contact again. Five pairs of eyes met hers. She repeated Darian's words—except, of course, for his final ones.

They all turned to the windows and stared down at the angry, heaving sea below them. There certainly didn't appear to be any calm waters down there.

223

"He's right," said one man. "We *could* land on water if we had to—but not on *that*."

"Let's go back and have another look at the other side," the Captain suggested. "And we might have to drop altitude, so prepare the shields." This last was spoken to the pilot.

They circled the watery world until Serena recognized a strangely shaped island that had been among the first things she'd seen. Then, as they all stared at the foaming sea, the pilot brought the craft lower.

Serena cried out as a strange sensation swept over her: a prickling of her skin that came and went quickly.

"It's just the shield," the man next to her said. "Sorry. We should have warned you."

"What does it do?" she asked.

"It should protect us if they spot us and try to knock us down. It could be the first indication that we've found them."

And a half hour later, he proved to be correct. They had just begun to notice a calming in the waters below them when suddenly their view was obscured by a bright green light. An alarm went off at the same time, and the pilot immediately put the craft into a steep climb that had them all plastered to the backs of their seats.

"No damage," the Captain reported. "But we've got a lock on the ship. It's down there, all right. Now we just have to figure out a way to get to it."

Chapter Eleven

"Can you swim?"

Serena nodded, wondering about the strange-looking items one of the crew was removing from the craft's storage compartment.

"Does that mean you've been in a pool a few times—or that you're actually comfortable in the water?" the Captain asked.

Serena turned to him. She wasn't certain if she'd really heard a hint of humor in his voice, though she'd heard it a few times on the ship. He was well liked by everyone.

"I've been swimming all my life—and we don't have pools on my world. We swim in the ocean." She didn't add, though, that the sea on her world wasn't the angry sea of Ulata—or of this world. They hadn't actually seen the sea in this area close up yet, but from the bird's-eye view they *had* gotten, it appeared as placid as the ocean of her world.

He seemed to be hesitating. "It could be very helpful to have you with us when we go out there. We'll be going at night, so we won't be able to get a good look at the ship, at least not in great detail. And it's possible that if Darian *is* being held in the cargo bay, that spot will be below the water line and we won't be able to see the door.

"So if you can contact him once we're out there, it could help us find him. But it's dangerous, Serena, and you've had no training for this kind of thing."

She noticed tha he had dropped her title, as had the others. In any other situation, she might have spent some time savoring this small victory. Obviously, she had become just one more member of the crew.

"I know it's dangerous, Captain," she said. "But you're right—it's certainly possible that I can contact Darian and enlist his help. I'm willing to go."

The Captain nodded and turned away to tend to other matters. One of the crew grinned at her. "So we're going to turn you into a fish? I'll bet the High Priestess will love hearing *that* report. Come on. I'll show you how it works."

He led her over to the gear that had been unloaded and picked up a thing that in fact looked very much like the anti-grav packs that enabled them to fly. Then she saw the difference as he pulled out a hose with a sort of mask at one end.

"You strap this on. It'll seem heavy until you're in the water. The mask goes over your face like this." He demonstrated on himself, going on to show her how to use it. "It also helps to propel you through the water. With it, you can cover the same amount of space in about half the time as you would if you were swimming. And there's nothing in it that will show up on any scanners they have."

"But how will we get him out?"

"We'll just carve a hole in their ship," he said with grim satisfaction. "And we'll take along an extra one of these for Commander Vondrak."

Over the next hour, as she listened to them go over and over their plan, Serena thought that it sounded quite simple. They had landed in a small clearing on one of the larger islands, as close to the ship as possible. Then they'd moved the craft itself into the shelter of the trees, where it couldn't be seen by the killers if they sent out any similar craft.

And before long, they had done just that. They all crouched beneath the thick-leafed trees and watched as a craft quite similar to their own passed over several times, flying just above the treetops, especially in the vicinity of the clearing. But the Captain had wisely anticipated this, and they had pulled and pushed their own craft uphill some distance away from the clearing, reasoning that if the enemy came looking for it, they would concentrate their search in the immediate vicinity of the clearing, or on the downhill slope to the other side.

Furthermore, the craft itself was covered with a fabric that reflected the colors of the surrounding forest, which would make it nearly invisible from above. The Ulatans, it seemed, had thought of everything.

Serena saw that the crew's old confidence was returning. Though she didn't understand the technical talk, she knew that it had to do with what they'd learned from the weapon that had been fired at them earlier. One crew member had referred to it as a "toy."

Still, she reminded herself that these people had managed to capture Darian and perhaps had killed his crew, and after listening to the talk for a time, the Captain had said much the same thing, which sobered them all quickly.

Finally, the shadows began to lengthen and they all set out for the shore, leaving behind only one heavily armed man to guard the landing craft. Even though one of the other men was carrying her "fish" gear, Serena still had trouble keeping up with them as they made their way through the forest. The Captain finally noticed this and ordered them to slow down. She apologized.

"Not necessary," he said in a clipped tone. "What you lack in strength, you more than make up for in talent. We might not have found him at all if it hadn't been for you."

The others all nodded, and one of them even jokingly suggested that when they got back to the ship, they should get her to work out in the exercise room to strengthen her leg muscles.

By the time they reached the shore, darkness had fallen. Some fifty feet below them, down a rocky slope, the water lapped gently at the land. Overhead, the sky was murky, with no stars showing through the ever-present clouds. And far away, perhaps several miles off shore, was a faint white dot.

"That must be it," the Captain said with satisfaction, then turned to Serena. "See if you can raise him now."

She walked a short distance away from the others and sat down on the pebble-strewn ground. The trance came quickly, and she began to call out to him. The last time she had reached him was while they were still circling, looking for a landing spot, and she'd kept it brief, simply reassuring him that they were on their way. His voice had been faint and broken—but still there.

This time, however, there was no response. Fighting off the panic that threatened to pull her out of the trance, Serena called again. The response came—but in a form she couldn't have imagined. Instead of words, there were visual images—some of them very clear and others she could barely make out. And they were all of her.

She saw herself naked, sitting astride him, her hair cascading down over her face. She saw herself asleep, an intimate view that could only have been his. And she saw herself as he first saw her, sitting defiantly on her pretty mare the day she'd encountered him on the trail.

There was more, and they all fascinated her. She understood that she was seeing herself through his eyes. But why? Why was he sending these images? She called to him again, but the only response was still more images and repeats of ones she'd already seen. Badly shaken now, she lost her grip on the trance.

So intriguing were these images that she wanted to go back, to see them again. But she knew that she had to make sense of them, so she resisted that temptation.

The images were those of a man in a deep sleep. But why would he sleep when he knew they were near? "Drugs," she murmured, finally understanding. He'd been drugged and the images she'd seen were his dreams, no doubt prodded by her voice calling to him.

She gave in to the desire to return to her trance, but this time she made no attempt to contact him because she realized that amidst the images he'd sent were some very hazy ones she hadn't recognized. Nothing came to her, so she called him again, and once more the same images began to flow rapidly through her mind.

But this time, despite her fascination with his memories of her, she summoned up her training, the part of it that was designed to focus still more sharply within a trance. It was the most detailed and difficult part of a Trezhella's training. She soon found out that focusing in order to hear one voice out of many was one thing; focusing to pluck certain images out of a rapid flow of highly personal and intimate memories was quite another.

Twice, the flow of images stopped, but they started again quickly when she called his name. And finally, she had what she wanted. She withdrew from the trance, albeit reluctantly, and got up to go back to the waiting men.

"He's been drugged. I'm reaching him, but his only response is a series of images: his dreams. But I also saw him. He's lying on a padded floor, and I could see what looked like bars of some sort nearby, as though he might be in a cage."

"You mean that he's sending images of himself?" The Captain asked with a frown. "But if he's drugged, how . . . ?"

She shook her head. "I don't think he's actually sending those images. I think that somehow I'm just able to see them. I can't explain it, but it might mean that when we're closer to the ship, I can locate him."

The Captain nodded doubtfully, then began to issue their instructions. A short time later, they all scrambled down the rocky slope and walked into the water.

If she had not been on a mission to rescue Darian from an unknown enemy, Serena would certainly have enjoyed herself. The ocean, at least in this area, was pleasantly warm—a great stroke of luck, the Captain had said, because they had no thermal skinsuit that would have fit her. And she adapted quickly to the breathing apparatus, as well as to the propulsion system that let her glide smoothly through the water with only a minimal effort.

But this was no pleasure outing, and Serena wanted only to rescue Darian and return to the ship without harm coming to any of them. They had made an attempt to find the other landing craft, in the hope of also finding Darian's crew, but as the Captain had pointed out, the first thing that crew would have done is what they themselves had done: camouflage the craft beneath the trees. And since they would also have shut down all systems on the craft, the locater device would also have been deactivated.

The pack that was strapped to her back contained a comm, but they'd all been instructed not to use them, for fear that they might be overheard by the enemy. Instead, they stayed close together, so that even in the murky water, Serena could see the dark shapes of the men surrounding her.

They were swimming just below the surface to prevent anyone on board the enemy's ship from seeing them, with only the Captain surfacing from time to time to judge their distance from the ship. Then, when it seemed to her that they couldn't possibly have been in the water long enough to have reached the ship, she felt a tug on her right ankle—the signal to stop. Quickly, she pressed the button on her mask that switched off the propulsion system.

She wanted to surface so she could see how close they were to the ship, but their orders were to stay submerged, so she floated, staying within the tight circle of men. Then the Captain, who was just ahead of her, turned in the water and tapped her head. It was the prearranged signal for her to try to contact Darian again.

The trance came easily, and she called to him urgently. For a long, heart-stopping moment, there was no response. And then his drug-induced dreams began to flow once more. The sensation was powerfully erotic, its impact perhaps enhanced by her floating in the warm water. A part of her "watched" with a sort of detached amusement, wondering why certain of those images had remained with him.

She saw herself looking up at him, desire darkening her eyes. She saw herself as he had seen her that day on the grass world, as she leapt high into the air and pirouetted. She saw images she had seen before of their lovemaking, images that made her ache with wanting to make them real again.

Then, improbably, she saw herself sitting in the communications room, her face lifted as she spoke soundlessly while he stood there, his hand on the telda. And she suddenly remembered the secret she was keeping from him.

That disturbing thought nearly broke the trance, so she banished it quickly even as more images flowed from his slumbering brain to hers. And then, without realizing what she was doing, she began to swim, propelled now not by the pack on her back, but by an overwhelming urge to find him.

She was still in a trance, completely unaware of the dark waters around her and of the men following her. When the images began to fade, she called his name again and they were back, guiding her to their source as surely as a beacon could have done.

Suddenly, her head bumped into something solid, and immediately the trance was broken. Before her lay the smooth white hull of the enemy ship—and beyond that, she knew, was Darian. Frustrated in her attempt to get to him, she suddenly remembered the others and started to turn just as someone grasped her ankles and began to haul her backward in the water.

For one brief, irrational moment, Serena thought they were trying to keep her from Darian, and she began to fight the man who now held her. By now, he had gripped her firmly around her waist and she could do little more than kick out. Somehow, he managed to turn her so that she was facing him. He pressed his face mask close to hers and she heard her name echoing strangely. She stopped fighting, embarrassed now that she hadn't understood.

He let her go, and she turned to face the ship again. One of the men was now aiming a gun at the hull, and as she watched, a bright green beam split the dark waters.

The next moments were confused. She saw a small hole appear in the hull, just large enough for the two men who quickly swam through it, one of them carrying the spare pack. In the next instant, she heard a distant clanging of alarm bells. The Captain had hoped they might not have sensors all over the ship, but apparently they did.

Serena watched helplessly, floating in the water with the other men, waiting for the reappearance of the two who'd gone inside. And then, just when she was about to try to rush in there herself, the first man appeared at the hole, slipped through, and then turned to reach back inside. Serena breathed a sigh of relief as she saw another figure emerge—and then another. They had the mask on Darian, who floated lifelessly between them while they each attached a tether to him and began to propel him through the water between them.

They all switched on their propulsion systems and dived beneath the ship, as prearranged. Then, still staying well beneath the surface, they headed for shore. The Captain had cleverly chosen to land their craft not on the closest island, which he reasoned would be where the enemy would focus its attention, but rather on one much farther away.

Serena maneuvered herself into position just behind Darian as he floated between the two men. In the darkness, she could just barely make out his dangling feet—but it was enough. Now they had only to get back to the landing craft and then to the ship.

She realized that they had reached shore when Darian's dangling feet began to churn up the pale sand. She switched off the propulsion system and got her own feet beneath her, then staggered out onto the shore with the men. There was no time to rejoice. The two men who were with Darian paused only long enough to remove his mask before lifting him between them and hurrying up the rocky slope to the protection of the woods.

It was very dark in the woods, and Serena wondered how they could find their way back to the camouflaged landing craft, but before she could ask that question, she had her answer. The Captain, who was in the lead, began to sweep the ground with a small device, and she saw a tiny, bright dot on the ground.

After that, they moved quickly through the darkness, following the trail of dots until at last they reached the disguised craft. She knelt beside Darian as the men tore off the cover, and it was only then that she saw the ugly red wound in his upper arm. The gold braid had been burned away, together with the fabric of his uniform.

"He's wounded!" she cried as the Captain approached.

"I know. We'll take care of it as soon as we get out of here."

"They're coming!" someone else cried, pointing to a bright light in the sky that was moving steadily toward them.

The Captain and another man lifted Darian again, and they all ran for the landing craft, which was hastily covered again. Two men, armed with heavy weapons they'd taken from the cargo hold, remained outside, while Darian, Serena, and the others huddled in the covered craft, unable to see anything.

Suddenly, there was a loud "whump!" and the men around her began to cheer. "Got them!" one cried gleefully as he slid the door open and pushed the cover out of the way. The others piled out after him, and Serena reluctantly left Darian to see what had happened.

A short distance away, the woods were on fire. Bright orange flames split the darkness, and an acrid odor blew toward her on the evening breeze. The men were thumping each other on the back and laughing and talking about the type of fuel the downed craft had been using. Serena didn't much care for their obvious pleasure at having killed, but it was difficult for her to summon up any sympathy for those who'd lost their lives either.

The Captain didn't give them much time to celebrate. They still had to drag the craft, with the unconscious Darian inside, back to the clearing for take-off, and he reminded them that more of the enemy were likely to appear quickly—and this time without lights.

They had just reached the clearing when they all heard a sort of whirring sound. By the time Serena turned toward it, one of the men was already raising the big weapon. A moment later, a huge fireball appeared in the night sky, and flaming debris fell to the woods, setting off yet another fire.

The moment they were all inside the landing craft, the pilot took off. Below them, the forest glowed in two places as the flames began to devour the underbrush.

"LC2 to base. We're coming home!" The Captain's voice

broke through the self-congratulatory clamor of the crew. "We've got him!"

"It's best to let him sleep it off. The blood tests showed what they used, and he'll be fine. The wound was only a flesh wound, and the patch will heal it in a few days."

The ship's medical specialist was addressing himself to both Serena and Lieutenant Commander Trollon as they stood in the corridor outside Darian's cabin.

"Just to be on the safe side, I've put a monitor on him. So if there's any reaction to the drug, I'll know it. But I don't anticipate any problems."

Then, since he'd been interrupted in the middle of his sleep period, he left them and returned to his own cabin just a short distance down the corridor.

"You saved his life, Trezhella Serena, and we're all very grateful for that," Trollon said. "If you hadn't led the crew to the exact spot on the ship where he was being held, we could never have rescued him."

She merely nodded, too tired now to think of a reply. As they stood there, the ship was moving away from the water world, taking them out of the path of the cosmic storm.

Trollon cleared his throat and looked decidedly uncomfortable. "After you've had some sleep, I'd like you to resume your transmissions. I realize we have no way of knowing that they're being received, but I'd prefer to continue."

She nodded, wondering why he was so uncomfortable. Surely he knew that she would continue to send the reports.

"I will prepare a report on this incident," he went on, "But I'm—uh, uncertain as to exactly what I should say."

Now she understood. "You don't want to tell the truth."

He looked even more uncomfortable. "You have a way of speaking bluntly, Trezhella."

"I will leave that to your judgment, Lieutenant Commander,

since you know far better than I do what sort of reception the truth would get."

"Yes, well, there are *two* issues here. First, there is the matter of Commander Vondrak's—uh, talents, and then there is also the question of what you want the High Priestess to know of your own activities."

"What you're saying is that the High Priestess might use 'my activities' in her ongoing battle with her brother, the Supreme Commander."

"Ahh, so you *do* know about them. I wasn't sure."

Serena thought that he'd almost smiled. "Yes, I know about it. Perhaps between you and the Captain, you can come up with an appropriate story, which I will then confirm with my own report to the Sisterhood."

He nodded. "Im sure we can manage that."

"What about the other men, Lieutenant Commander—Darian's crew?"

"I think we have to assume that they're dead, but I'm sure that Commander Vondrak will want to return after we ride out the storm. Perhaps he'll be able to help us locate them."

She nodded. She knew by now that the men who had gone into the ship for Darian had found other cages like the one in which he was being held—but they'd all been empty.

"Uh—there's one other thing," Trollon said as his gaze went from her to Darian's closed door. "If you like, I can code his door so that you can look in on him."

Serena was too surprised at his kind offer to hide it. "Yes, I would like that. Thank you." Of course she didn't need it, but he couldn't know that.

Saying that he would take care of it immediately, he gave her a slight bow and left her there. She went into her own cabin and stripped off her old clothes, which were still slightly damp from the swim. Then, after showering and putting on her uniform, she stepped through the closet and into Darian's cabin.

She dragged his big, comfortable chair over to his bedside and settled into it. Within moments, she was fast asleep.

Serena awoke groggily, certain that she'd heard something. But Darian slept on. It didn't look as though he'd moved at all. Then she caught movement in her peripheral vision and turned sharply—to see Trollon standing in front of the closet door she'd forgotten to close. By the time he turned to her, she had awakened enough to feel embarrassment heating her face.

"I guess you didn't need my help, after all," he said, and even in the dim light, she was sure this time that he was smiling.

"I just stopped by to check on him," he explained. "He should be waking soon."

Then his gaze went to the bed, just as Serena heard Darian stir. By the time she had turned to him, he was already sitting up and staring blearily at the two of them—and then at the open closet with its missing wall.

"Welcome back, Commander," Trollon said as he closed the closet door.

Darian stretched and yawned and glanced briefly at the patch on his arm, then got out of bed, paying no attention at all to the fact that he was wearing only a pair of briefs. He said nothing as he walked rather unsteadily into the bathroom, then came out a few minutes later with a glass of water.

He sat down on the edge of the bed, stared at her for a moment, then turned his attention to Trollon. "For now, just give me the short version," he said hoarsely.

The Lieutenant Commander did just that, omitting the details of his rescue.

"How soon can we go back?" Darian asked.

"We're not sure yet. Do you think there's a chance the others could still be alive?"

"I don't know. The details are still a little hazy. What did they give me?"

"Tharzon—or something similar."

Darian nodded. "Then I should be all right soon. What about their ship?"

"We didn't wait around to see if they took off. The storm was getting too close."

Serena sat there, listening to the exchange and trying to keep her eyes off Darian. She couldn't decide if he didn't realize he was nearly naked, or if he knew, but didn't care. She was sure that he'd seen the open closet door, but perhaps it hadn't registered.

"Have you written up the report yet?" Darian asked, his gaze sliding briefly to her.

"I just finished it," Trollon replied, glancing at Serena as well.

"Don't enter it into the permanent log until I see it," Darian ordered, then addressed her for the first time.

"Have you made contact with your Sister?"

"No, but it's nearly time for me to make my morning transmission."

"Let it go. I want to see that report before it's sent."

"I'll put it on your comm as soon as I get back to the control room," Trollon said before he left.

"You were there, weren't you?" he asked as soon as the door had closed behind Trollon.

"Yes. I had to go, Darian, because I was the only one who could find you."

"Trollon was under orders to keep you safe on the ship."

Her anger flared. "If I'd stayed on the ship, we wouldn't be having this discussion because you'd be *dead!* Surely you expected Trollon to use his best judgment—which he did. Besides, I volunteered."

Darian smoothed back the silver wings that were sticking out from his temples, then got up and stretched his long, lean body.

Even as angry as she was now, Serena still felt herself responding. How could she not, when she knew that body so very well?

"I seem to recall that our last conversation turned into an argument," he said in a cool voice. "Are we just picking up from there?"

She had rather hoped that that particular memory was as hazy as he claimed others were at the moment. "I'm sorry about that, Darian. There were things I didn't understand then—but I do now. And I'm sorry about leaving the closet door open. I was tired and I wasn't thinking." I was also worried about *you*, she added silently, unwilling to admit that now.

"I trust Trollon's discretion," he replied in the same tone. "I'll talk to you later."

He disappeared into the bathroom, leaving her sitting there too stunned to protest. This was definitely not what she'd had in mind for their reunion! She wanted the *man*, not the commander!

When Serena went to the communications room to send her evening report, the first thing she did was to switch on the comm and check to see if the report on the rescue mission was among the reports. Neither Darian nor Lieutenant Commander Trollon had spoken to her again.

She scrolled through the routine reports and found both Darian's report on his mission and the report on the rescue. She read Darian's report first, annoyed that she should have to learn about it in this manner, instead of hearing about it firsthand from him.

Darian and his crew had circled the cloud world several times, but had not spotted the enemy ship. He was unable to explain this, since they had searched carefully—including the area where the ship was subsequently found by the rescue crew. Nor had they picked up any electrical signals, as the probe had done.

Finally, they'd chosen a spot at random and landed not far from the one spot where they thought a large spaceship might be capable of settling down. Darian assumed that they'd managed to camouflage the ship in much the same way that his men disguised their landing craft. So, rather than risk a low fly-over of the area that could have put their landing craft at risk from the weaponry on the larger ship, they'd decided to search on the ground.

The six men then split up into teams of two and spread out to conduct their search, avoiding any radio contact that might be overheard by the enemy. But he and his partner had gotten only a short distance into the forest surrounding the grassy plain where they guessed the ship might be hidden, when he'd been struck by a stunner.

Darian theorized that either the stunner was defective or at the very limits of its range because he wasn't rendered unconscious. His partner was behind him and off to one side at the time. Darian spun around, drawing his laser weapon at the same time, and saw his partner on the ground, not moving.

He never saw his opponent or opponents, though he thought they might have been up in the trees or perhaps flying. He was struck a glancing blow by a laser, and almost immediately after that was struck again by the stunner and rendered unconscious.

When he came to, he was in a small cage in what appeared to be the cargo hold of the ship. He could see that there were other cages nearby, but was unable to see into them. After calling out repeatedly to see if the other men might be there and receiving no answers, he gave up.

The pain in his shoulder from the laser attack was severe and he was also suffering from the stunner attack, so he slipped in and out of consciousness for an indeterminate period of time. At some point, his captors must have given him an injection, but he never saw them. He couldn't judge the time or signal for help because his wrist-comm had been confiscated.

Serena winced at his brief mention of the pain he'd endured. She'd heard about the wracking pain in the aftermath of a stunner attack, and he had suffered not only that, but the laser as well. It amazed her that he could still have contacted her. She'd described to him once how she herself went into a trance, but she knew she could never do that under such conditions.

Then she read the report of the rescue mission. Lieutenant Commander Trollon had signed it, together with Captain Honek. The two men had been very inventive. She wondered if Darian had helped them.

According to the report, they were able to locate the ship and Darian because of his wrist-comm, which Darian had managed to switch to the "on" position while he tried to fight off his attackers. She went back to Darian's report and saw now that he'd mentioned that, though she'd not noticed it when she read his report—probably because she'd been too busy envisioning the rest of it.

Trollon and Honek speculated that the wrist-comm had been taken aboard the ship as well, though at the time Honek had, of course, assumed that Darian was still wearing it.

All in all, she thought, it was a masterful job of lying. Darian was protected, and so was she. But how could they believe that lie would hold up once they returned to Ulata? By now, the entire ship's crew knew the truth, and it seemed unlikely, to say the least, that they would keep such a tale quiet when they returned home.

The fact that the truth about *her* activities might get out didn't really trouble Serena. The High Priestess would be appalled—but what could she really do? Serena would make it clear that *she* was the one who had volunteered, that no pressure had been put on her.

She realized now that the full burden of blame—if blame was to be cast—would fall onto the shoulders of Lieutenant Commander Trollon. She'd overheard the men talking about

241

him. They all respected him, even if they didn't like him very much. And she'd heard more than one man refer to his ambition. After this mission, he was in line for a command of his own.

Serena promised herself that she would do everything in her power to protect him and keep him from losing his career because of a decision he'd been forced to make to save Darian's life. She still wasn't sure she liked him very much herself, but she now understood why the men respected him.

She went into a trance and called Shenzi, then began to transmit her report. As before, she tried to envision her friend, sitting in one of the little rooms at the compound, hearing her but unable to respond. It comforted her to believe that, even though she knew it might not be true. Her words might actually be getting lost forever in the blackness of space.

She added a personal message to Shenzi at the end, saying that she was well, she was glad Commander Vondrak had been rescued, and she hoped they might find the others alive when they returned to the cloud world after the storm had passed.

"Shenzi, I know that after hearing this report, you must be terrified for me. But I am safe and happy, and if I had stars in my blood before this mission, I have even more now. This is where I belong."

She came out of her trance and sat there staring at the zhetla. It was true. For all the danger she'd faced—and all that she might yet encounter—she was happy to be here.

But as she stared at the carved obelisk, her thoughts turned to the problems ahead—not in space, but here on the ship. With all that had happened, she had pushed from her mind the secret she was keeping about the teldas. But she was now certain that Darian knew about them. Several of the images she'd caught from his drug-induced dream had been of times when she'd talked to him about the zhetlas, and she'd also caught his doubts about her truthfulness.

She might have been able to convince herself that she'd only imagined those doubts, except for the images themselves. The scenes she'd drawn from his mind were all scenes of a highly charged eroticism—except for those images of their conversations about zhetlas.

She hated the fact that her secret stood between them—but then, it wasn't the only thing standing between them at the moment. She might now understand why he'd felt compelled to go on that disastrous mission, but she still wasn't inclined to forgive him for planning to leave without speaking to her.

Nor was she about to forgive his behavior since his return, though she'd had enough time to think about it that she now understood why he was behaving this way. It was that accursed Ulatan pride: *male* Ulatan pride. He was embarrassed at having been rescued by *her*.

But understanding it did not mean that she had to accept it. If he wasn't prepared to accept her as his equal, that was *his* problem, not hers. The crew had certainly accepted her as an equal. That was evident in their behavior toward her now.

She left the communications room and went to the lounge, where a half-dozen men were gathered, their games ignored this night as they all sat around rehashing the events of the past two days.

Captain Honek was there, together with one of his crew members from the rescue mission. As soon as he saw her, he waved her over to join them. She noted with satisfaction that none of them stood as she entered the lounge. No longer did they regard her as being a woman and a Trezhella; now she was one of them.

Honek got her a glass of wine, then proposed a toast to her. Every man in the lounge stood as he extolled her bravery, then Honek added with a smile that they all thought she should be given a commendation by the Space Command.

She thanked them graciously and replied that that might be rather difficult to do, since she hadn't even been there.

"Ahh," Honek said with a grin. "So you've seen the report. Of course. You just transmitted it."

She smiled. "You and Lieutenant Commander Trollon were very clever, and I thank you for it."

"Well, much as I'd like to take the credit, as I'm sure Trollon would as well, it was Commander Vondrak who came up with it. Did you read his report as well?"

She acknowledged that she had, and he went on.

"What I don't understand is how he could possibly have been able to go into a trance and then contact you in the condition he was in. I'll admit that I don't know a lot about that kind of thing, but it probably isn't all that much different from the kra-toza training that I've had."

"What is kra-toza?" Serena asked. She'd never heard the term before.

"It's a very ancient form of fighting—one that was used before we got smart and let weapons do the fighting for us. Basically, you train to think of your whole body as being a weapon, and then use it that way—arms, legs, head, every part of you."

He frowned. "It isn't quite like going into a trance because you have to be fully aware of your surroundings in order to fight your opponent. Once weapons took over actual fighting, kra-toza became highly ritualized. We fight in a large ring, and before you go into that ring, you try to focus all your thoughts on one thing and one thing only: using your entire body to defeat your opponent. That's what I meant about maybe understanding to some extent what it's like to go into a trance."

Serena was intrigued. "Are all of you trained in it?"

Honek shook his head to the accompaniment of loud groans from the others. "No. It's just a game that some of us keep up. The only other man on the ship who's trained in it is Commander Vondrak. He and I hold regular sessions down in the cargo hold, where we set up a ring. Ask him if you can come to watch us sometime."

"I'll do that," she replied, wondering if she and Darian would ever even speak to each other again. So that was how he did it, she mused. Darian hadn't mentioned this skill to her.

"Yeah, but I still don't see how he could have managed it in that much pain. I took a light stunner blow once, and believe me, I couldn't have focused on anything but that pain."

Another man spoke up, saying that *he'd* taken a "laser hit," a glancing blow like Darian's, and it was much worse than a stunner. After that, they all began to argue about which was worse, playing a game of one-upmanship the way Ulatan men so often did. But it was clear to Serena that far from being diminished in their eyes by his newly discovered talents, Darian was even more respected for his ability to withstand pain.

She sighed inwardly, longing for the simplicity of her home and the men there. At times like this, Ulatan males seemed to her to be an alien species and not simply the other half of the population. What else could you call beings who respected a man for his talent to deny pain, rather than his goodness and kindness?

Back in her cabin, Serena stared at the closed closet door and wondered if he was in his cabin. Earlier in the day, she had both closed and latched the door, knowing that he couldn't get through with the latch in place. It was intended to be a statement, but she had no way of knowing if he'd even tried to come through to her cabin.

She undressed and got into a bed that felt very lonely. Serena lay in bed, fighting the urge to go to him until sleep finally carried her off—only to torment her with the sensual images she'd stolen from his own dreams.

Chapter Twelve

The ship rode out the storm and then turned back toward the cloud world. Few on board believed that they would find the missing crew members alive, but everyone agreed that they had to search for them.

There was general agreement as well that their killers must be made to pay. Though she deplored the probable loss of life, not to mention their treatment of Darian, Serena failed to understand how risking more lives and killing the killers could be justified. In this, as in so many things, she didn't understand Ulatans.

She knew they were a people who believed strongly in fairness. They were understandably proud of their justice system and had imposed it upon the other worlds they'd conquered, though in all other ways they did not interfere in the affairs of those people.

"This is war," Sevec told her when she complained to him about their determination to kill the enemy. "This is different."

She was spending more time with Sevec these past few days. His duties as a cadet were minimal, since cadets were there to learn by observing. Darian continued to avoid her, and if it weren't for the reports he wrote that she transmitted, she might not have known he was on the ship. The closest she came to actually seeing him was once when she opened the door to leave her cabin and saw his back as he entered his own cabin.

She had waited in the doorway to see if he would try to come through the closet, but he didn't. Every night, she lay in bed waiting for him to try to come into her room, but the closet latch remained silent. Still, he hadn't gone so far as to replace the wall he'd taken out.

Furthermore, the longer he avoided her, the angrier she became with him. She was beginning to think that she'd never really known him—or that she'd known his body, but not his mind.

Five days after their hasty departure from the cloud world, they were back to it again. The great storm had passed on into deep space, beyond this star system. Sevec told her that unlike ordinary storms, these cosmic giants never died out. They simply moved off, following an erratic path of their own.

Shipboard news was posted on the comm, so when Serena awoke one morning, she learned that they were now in high orbit around the cloud world once more, and a probe had been launched to determine if the enemy ship was still there.

By the time she finished her transmission, the probe had reported back that there were no indications that the ship was still there, though of course it might be lying in wait with all its systems shut off. Captain Honek had told her several days ago that it would probably have taken them a day or two to get the water out of their ship and repair the hole in the cargo bay. Apparently they'd done that and then taken off.

Serena returned to her cabin—and found Darian there, pacing restlessly around the cramped space. All the anger she'd been holding vanished, lost beneath a surge of hunger for him. She stopped in the doorway and her gaze went automatically to the closed closet door.

"I came in through that door," he said, gesturing to the door where she stood. She'd forgotten that he could do that, and she decided not to remind him that he'd once said he wouldn't.

"I came to tell you that I'm going down there again—to search for my crew."

She nodded, having already assumed that he would be leading the search.

He ran a hand through his hair distractedly. "We don't have much time. There's another storm headed this way—not as big a one, but still big enough to cause problems."

"How much time do you have?" she asked. It was a large world, as big as Ulata itself.

"Five hours, maybe more. We're taking two crews, but we can't risk using our comm units because they could still be down there. Even if the enemy ship itself left, they could have left some men behind."

"That will complicate things, won't it—if you can't communicate with each other?" An idea was beginning to form, but she was reluctant to ask.

He nodded. "But I can't risk losing more men—especially when I doubt that they're alive anyway."

"Wouldn't they stay near the landing craft?"

"Maybe, but maybe not. The enemy could have discovered it, and in that case, they'd get as far away from it as possible. They'd have fish gear, so they could go anywhere they wanted."

"In that case, I don't see how you can possibly hope to find them in such a short time, unless . . . " She stopped as his eyes locked on hers.

"No!" he said sharply, cutting her off.

"It could mean the difference between finding those men and

leaving them there to die. And if they're already dead, you still want to bring back their bodies."

Sevec had told her that it was a matter of pride among spacemen that no one be left to spend eternity in a place other than his own world. Great risks had been taken in the past to retrieve the bodies of men who'd died in space.

Darian remained silent, so she pressed on.

"How can you justify not using every means available to you to rescue them or bring back their bodies? I know that you dislike my form of communication and you must hate the fact that you have that talent as well. But it saved your life, Darian—and it could save those men."

He still said nothing. Her anger grew. "Don't you understand, Darian? *I* didn't save your life. You saved it yourself with your talent."

"It isn't that," he said dismissively. "I don't want to put you at risk—again."

"Forget the promise you made to the High Priestess! I'm perfectly capable of being responsible for my own safety."

"It isn't the promise, either."

"Then what is it?" she demanded in an exasperated tone. "Why can't you Ulatans ever say what you mean?"

"What I mean is . . . " He stopped abruptly and gestured to her closet. "Forget it. I don't have time for this. Get changed and meet me in the cargo bay in ten minutes."

He brushed past her and was out the door before she could manage to get out another word. She glared at the space he'd occupied, thinking that if he'd stayed one minute longer, even *she* might have been tempted to violence.

When she arrived in the cargo bay, the men were all assembled and receiving their last-minute instructions from Darian and Captain Honek. She was glad to see Honek there because that meant he would be commanding the crew that she would be with. She liked him and respected his abilities.

"It may not work," Darian was saying. "But if it does, it means we can stay in contact."

He glanced her way, and the eyes of the other men followed him. Serena suddenly wondered if Darian even knew how he'd managed to contact her the other time.

"Commander," she said, trying hard to keep the sarcasm out of her voice, "we haven't had a chance to discuss that. But Captain Honek told me about your skills at kra-toza, and I think that's how you acquired this talent. In fact," she said, turning to Honek, "it's possible that you and I could communicate as well."

Honek looked startled, but then nodded. "And if we can, then we could take a third crew." He glanced at Darian. "I think it's worth a try, Commander."

Darian nodded, though he looked anything but pleased. "All right. You two go somewhere and try it, and I'll round up another crew."

"I'll stay here," Serena told Honek, "because it's probably easier for me to go into a trance. You go somewhere else in the ship and try to contact me. Just focus your thoughts as you do for kra-toza and then think my name."

"Give me five minutes or so," he said. "I'll go all the way to the control room. That's as far away as I can get."

He was gone before she could explain to him that if he could do it, distance wouldn't matter—at least, not the distances they were facing down there.

"If this works," said one of the crew with a grimace, "we're all going to be forced to study kra-toza."

Serena laughed with the rest of them, but it suddenly occurred to her that if it *did* work with Honek, then her belief that her intimacy and shared love with Darian was responsible would be disproved.

And a moment later, a stunning realization hit her: if it worked, this could also spell the end for the Sisterhood!

That thought shook her so badly that she had some difficulty willing herself into a trance. But when she finally succeeded, Honek's voice was calling her name.

"I'm here, Captain. Congratulations."

"I can't believe it can be this easy!" he exulted.

"Don't get over-confident," she warned. "You could slip out of the trance."

A brief silence followed, and then he called her voice again.

"I lost it there for a minute. I guess it's not as easy as I thought."

"The important thing is to avoid any strong emotion that will distract you, and that could pose a problem on this mission."

"Right. I guess I don't have Commander Vondrak's skill, since he was able to manage it when he was in pain."

"Everyone has different levels of skill, Captain."

"Right. Over and out, then."

Serena came out of her trance and walked back to the group of men who were waiting eagerly for the news. She nodded and cheers erupted just as Darian reappeared.

"It worked," she told him.

He looked so relieved that she knew now he hadn't spoken the truth earlier when he'd claimed not to be troubled by his talent. Now he could accept it because it sprang from something he could understand.

Captain Honek returned, grinning broadly, though Serena was certain that his reaction would have been the same as Darian's if he couldn't ascribe it to his beloved kra-toza.

"This is *great!*" he told her as the rest of the men began to prepare the landing craft. "It almost makes the beatings I've been taking the past week worthwhile."

"What beatings?" she asked, frowning.

"Maybe you haven't noticed, but our Commander's been a

bit out of sorts since we rescued him. And he's been taking it out on me when we practice down here." He glanced at Darian, who was talking to another captain, the leader of the new crew.

"Most of the time, it's easy enough to forget who he is, but he *is* a Vondrak, and let's just say that they've got more than their share of pride. It was bad enough that he had to be rescued—but it was even worse that he was rescued by a *woman*, and a very capable one at that.

"I take it from your comment earlier that he's been avoiding you?" he asked, his dark eyes glittering with amusement.

Serena didn't know how much the Captain knew about them, but she nodded.

"Don't take it personally. He didn't get around to thanking *me* for a couple of days. But he's a good man—the best."

Serena was tempted to say that she was tired of hearing the men sing his praises, but she wisely kept her mouth shut. The men saw him as a commander and were willing to forgive his faults. She, on the other hand, wasn't inclined to be so charitable. After all, unlike Honek and the others, she hadn't grown up in a world that was impressed by family names and great wealth and power.

Darian had been unable to pinpoint the exact landing spot of his ill-fated crew, but he knew the general area. So the three craft on the second rescue mission set down at points that formed a rough triangle around that area. Darian had ruled out low-altitude fly-overs of the cloud world to check for any signs of their enemy. To do so would only alert them to their return.

The area to be covered was still considerable, and Darian had also decided against the use of anti-grav packs, which would have made the search much easier, but would also expose them to far too much enemy fire from the ground. Nevertheless, they all wore the lightweight packs, in case they should become necessary.

By prearrangement, they spread out and began their search. The captain of the third crew, which Serena had joined, ordered her to remain with him. It meant one less pair of eyes and ears for the search, but she didn't protest, certain that his orders had come from Darian.

Darian had also ordered that he and Honek and Serena check in with each other every fifteen minutes. Serena was very curious to see if the two men could communicate with each other—something she knew they would try. And she got her answer at the first check-in, after she and Captain Mendig had stopped long enough for her to go into a trance.

"I can't reach Commander Vondrak," Honek's voice said in her mind. "We've spotted nothing so far."

"Neither have we," Serena responded. "I'll contact him now."

She hoped that Honek hadn't heard the relief in her voice. She was rapidly becoming very concerned about the future of the Sisterhood if the men could learn to communicate without them.

The crews were all covering the difficult terrain in an intricate crisscross pattern that the Captain told her had been invented long ago for just such occasions. At designated intervals, one man's path would intersect another's, then those two would meet up with still others, and in that way, word would be passed to the crew leader.

Still in her trance, Serena waited a moment to see if Darian would contact her. And just when she was about to give up and reach out to him, his familiar voice spoke to her mind: definitely the commander's voice and not the one that she wanted to hear.

"Nothing so far," he said in clipped tones. "Honek and I tried to reach each other, but it didn't work."

She thought she heard a faintly accusatory note there, as though he suspected her of somehow having prevented that.

She might have tried to soothe him by saying that they probably just needed more training, but she was in no mood to calm Darian's ruffled pride.

"Captain Honek just reported to me that they've found nothing," she replied. "And neither have we."

Then she withdrew from the trance without waiting for any further statements from him. After relaying this to Captain Mendig, she set out again.

This scenario was repeated many times over the next few hours as they made their way through the forest. From time to time, as they reached the top of a hill, they would see the restless sea lapping at a rocky coastline; the island they were searching was not large.

Captain Mendig paused at one hilltop to study the scene, then suddenly pointed. "There's Honek's crew, down in the valley. We should be seeing Commander Vondrak's crew soon, too."

By the time they reached the valley floor, Darian and his crew were making their way down the opposite hillside toward them.

"We found the spot where we landed," he announced without preamble. "And we found where the landing craft had been hidden. They must have tried to steal it," he said with a faint smile Serena couldn't interpret, but which didn't look at all pleasant.

One of his men produced a folded packet that she belatedly realized was the reflective cover they used to camouflage the craft. "This is all that's left," the man said with that same smile.

The other men were also wearing those annoying smiles, so she asked why they seemed so pleased about having the craft stolen, and how did they know that their own men hadn't moved it? It was Captain Mendig who explained.

"A code number is required to start them: the same number for all of them. The code has to be keyed in within one minute

255

of the time the door is opened. There's an override, but it's well hidden. And you can make only one mistake with the code. After that, the craft self-destructs."

"Self-destructs?" she echoed, not familiar with the term, though she suspected what it meant. "You mean it explodes?"

"Actually," Captain Honek put in, "it *im*plodes, but the result is the same. Whoever was in that craft was vaporized along with it."

He glanced at Darian. "It seems to me that it would be a good idea to show you how to operate one of them."

Darian ignored him. "The fact that we haven't found any bodies suggests to me that they might have gotten away. But I tend to think they'd still stay in this general area in the hope that someone would have escaped to lead a rescue party to them."

Serena was thinking about the destroyed landing craft and what had happened to whoever was inside. She knew she would never be able to accept such violence, let alone relish it the way the men obviously did.

Then she recalled the world that was so much like her own, and Darian's explanation about the terrible weapon that might have killed those people without leaving a trace.

"What if they used that weapon you said they might have used on that other world—the one that leaves no trace of bodies?" She asked Darian.

"They wouldn't be likely to have used a neutro. They're big, heavy weapons, unsuited to being dragged about in a forest," he replied. "They'd have used stunners or lasers—as they did on me."

Serena said nothing. She hated all this. She had come on this mission to explore new worlds, not to listen to talk of death and destruction. As they began to talk about how to proceed, she walked away from them. Was the fault hers or theirs? She decided that perhaps it was both. She had been naive in her beliefs about this mission, even though she'd known there could be dangers. But neither Darian nor anyone else had tried to explain to her just what those dangers might be.

Captain Mendig called out to her, but as she walked back to the men, it was Darian whose steady, indecipherable gaze was on her. She ignored him and rejoined her crew. Captain Mendig told her they were going to use the anti-grav packs to return to their starting point, then spread out from there to search a wider area.

As she rose into the air, she was, for one brief moment, facing Darian. Their eyes met and she felt the warmth of memories flowing between them. She knew he was remembering—just as she herself was—that first time she'd flown, held securely in his arms. And she was recalling too that time on the world of the cliff-dwellers, when they'd ascended, hand-in-hand, up the colorful walls of a canyon. It all seemed a very long time ago—and a far simpler time.

Then they both turned and joined their respective crews, but for Serena, at least, the moment lingered. At this point, she needed to be reminded of what they'd shared, and of their love. She could only hope that Darian, too, was being reminded of that.

They covered in minutes the same ground that had taken them hours on foot, then landed and spread out once again, using the same crisscross pattern and regular communication. They didn't find anything for nearly an hour, until Serena spotted the first body.

She and Captain Mendig had moved apart a bit, though they were still within view of each other. So it was Serena who reached the hilltop first—and saw the lifeless body of a man, one of the crew members who'd been with Sevec when they'd come to tell her of their gift of the dance room.

She turned away from the sight to call to Captain Mendig, only to find that he had just reached the hilltop behind her.

"Stay here," he ordered as he started toward the body, some fifty feet away. She knew he was just trying to protect her from the ugly sight, but it was too late. She could already see the gaping wound and the charred uniform. He lay facedown, but she had recognized him by his very curly reddish-brown hair, unusual for Ulatans.

She was remembering that day—which also now seemed so very far in the innocent past—when there was a sudden brilliant flash of light that both blinded her and sent her flying backward into a clump of bushes.

She felt thorns pricking her skin, and when she tried to see what had happened, a black spot obliterated much of her vision. Nevertheless, she got to her feet and staggered back to the spot where she'd been standing.

Now there were two bodies instead of one. The Captain had been hurled against a tree and now lay crumpled at its base. Serena drew out her stunner and scanned the woods around them. The black spot before her eyes was already starting to dwindle.

There was no sign of anyone else. Only a few minutes had passed since they'd met up with one of the other crew members, so she knew it would be a while before they encountered any of them again. And there'd been no sound with the flash of light that could attract them.

Both horrified and terrified, and with her stunner at the ready, she tried to think what could have happened. An attack from above seemed unlikely. The body was in the middle of a fairly large open spot, where she certainly would have seen a craft or a flying man overhead.

As she thought about this, she ran over to Captain Mendig, but even before she reached him, she knew he was dead. His head lay at an impossible angle, the result of a broken neck, probably when he'd collided with the tree.

Fighting down her nausea, she rolled him over, after feeling for a pulse that she'd already known wouldn't be there. There were no marks on him, other than some scratches on his face that had probably come from the rough bark of the tree.

Think! she ordered herself. *Forget about what you've seen and think!* With her vision now largely restored, she scanned her surroundings once again. She couldn't believe that anyone could have sneaked up on them and then fired a weapon. Besides, if someone *had* managed that, why had they left her alive?

Perhaps she would never have thought about the motion-detecting spheres if she hadn't just been recalling the day that Darian had captured her while she was still holding her stolen prize. But as soon as that memory came to her, she began to wonder if something similar—but far more deadly—had been used here.

She left the dead captain and began to make a slow, wide circle around the other man's body, taking care to get no closer than she had been before. At first, she studied the ground around the body, searching for something that didn't belong. Then she forced herself to look at the body itself. And it was then that she saw something: a small gray cube, half hidden beneath his body. Although she could see it now that she was looking for something, Captain Mendig would not have noticed it—especially given the different angle at which he had approached the body.

A fresh wave of horror washed over her as she realized that this might not be the only body—or the only deadly device. She looked at her wrist-comm and saw that it was still more than ten minutes until their next scheduled communication. Darian had increased the intervals to a half hour, so they wouldn't have to stop so often. He'd reasoned that since they hadn't encountered any enemy, it was more and more likely that they'd gone.

But now she thought she understood what they had done. The enemy had guessed that they would return and that they would want to retrieve the bodies of their crew members. That meant that there could be more of the devices.

Serena was frantic. In ten minutes, who knew how many others could suffer Captain Mendig's fate. But did she have any hope of reaching Darian and Captain Honek when they weren't in a trance?

She turned her back on the two bodies and willed herself into a trance, then began to call both of them. She had told Honek that it was important to stay calm and avoid any strong emotions, but for her, that was now impossible. Yet she somehow remained in the trance and continued to call them.

Suddenly, she heard Darian's voice calling her name, followed a few seconds later by Captain Honek.

"Don't go near any bodies you find!" she warned them, then went on to explain what had happened.

Darian's voice overrode that of Honek. "Did you reach Honek?" he demanded, and when she confirmed that she had, he hurried on.

"Don't go near the body. It probably can't explode again, but I'm not sure. It could also be a signal to the enemy. Get out of there now, Serena! Don't use the anti-grav because that makes you too vulnerable. Can you find your way back to the starting point alone?"

"Yes, I think so."

"Start back, then—and tell Honek to do the same. I'm going to try to get to you sooner, using the anti-grav."

Honek was still talking, his voice a sort of static beneath Darian's voice. She told him what Darian had said, then left her trance and began to run through the woods, stunner in hand as she tried to keep an eye on the treetops and the surrounding forest.

But even in the midst of her own terror, she knew that Darian was taking a terrible risk by using the anti-grav and exposing himself.

* * *

She had reached the limits of her endurance and slowed down to a walk, satisfied that she was well away from the two bodies. But something in her had gone numb. She no longer felt the horror of what she'd seen. In its place was a terrible coldness that had drained her of all emotion. She kept walking, hoping she was retracing their earlier route, her entire body now aching, either from the blast that had knocked her off her feet or from her exertions.

By now, she had stopped scanning the woods so closely, but she was still watching the treetops, hoping to see Darian. And then she *did* see him, some distance ahead, moving at an angle that would take him away from her.

She stopped and tried to whistle, but her lips and mouth were parched and nothing came out but a rush of air. She tried again, desperate now as she saw him slowly moving away. Then, when she still couldn't manage it, she went into a trance and called out to him.

"Darian! I'm here—off to your right and back a bit!"

She saw him stop in midair, then turn to the right and start back. He might have called out to her in response, but she had let the trance go quickly, unable to maintain it any longer. And now that he was near, her legs simply gave way and she collapsed against a tree and sank to its needle-strewn base.

The forest was thick, and it took Darian some careful maneuvering to reach the ground. She sat there and watched him and ignored the tears that were streaming down her cheeks.

He landed and quickly stripped off his anti-grav pack, then knelt beside her and removed hers as well. Then he drew his thumbs across her cheeks to stanch the flow of tears.

"This isn't why I came on this mission!" she blurted out angrily. "I wanted to see new worlds—not dead bodies and cowardly enemies!"

Darian nodded as he knelt beside her. "I know. I should have stopped you from coming. But I was selfish. I wanted to be with you again."

"You couldn't have stopped me," she protested, though this was not the conversation she wanted to have. In fact, she didn't want *any* conversation. What she wanted was for him to hold her.

"Yes, I could have. When I was chosen, the Supreme Commander asked me if I thought your presence would be too disruptive. If I'd said yes, he would have stopped it."

He ran his gaze over her. "Were you hurt in the blast?"

"No, I don't think so. I was blinded for a moment and I ache all over, but that's all. Captain Mendig's neck was broken. That's how he died. And the Sergeant—the one with the curly reddish hair—was struck by a laser. Before I called you, I walked all around him. I guessed that it was some sort of device like those motion spheres. And I think I saw something nearly hidden under his body. That's when I realized that they might have done the same thing to other bodies."

"Serena," he said softly, "you don't have to prove anything to *me*. I already know how smart and brave you are. How could I *not* know it, when everyone else on board does?"

He leaned forward to bestow a fleeting kiss to her brow, then stood up before she could reach for him. "I know it," he said, his gaze sliding away from hers. "But I'm still having some trouble accepting it."

Over the next two hours, they found all the bodies—and all the exploding devices. The devices were safely detonated by the simple trick of tossing a rock or a log into the monitored space.

Darian had at first insisted that she wait at the landing craft rather than going out again, but their time was now very limited and her presence meant they could continue with three groups, so he gave in when she said she would go.

Captain Honek's crew found two of the bodies and Darian

found one, and she relayed the news as each man contacted her. Fortunately, her own group found none. Serena continued to feel numb and cold at the same time. She was barely able to manage the trances when it came time to communicate with Darian and Honek.

Then the three landing craft rose into the air and went back to the ship, bearing their sad burdens and silent, angry crews. Her own craft was the first to negotiate the airlocks and glide into the ship's cargo bay, and she stepped out of the craft to find the medical specialist waiting for her. Darian had broken radio silence on the return trip and had already informed the ship of their discoveries, and now she realized that he must have sent a message about her as well.

She waved off the man's suggestion that she come with him to the ship's infirmary, but because she couldn't bring herself to say that she was fine, she merely told him that nothing was broken and her vision was fully restored and all she wanted was to rest.

He acquiesced after she promised to contact him immediately if she discovered anything wrong, and Serena left the cargo bay hurriedly, not wanting to see the bodies that would soon be unloaded. On her way back to her cabin, she encountered a number of crewmen, who either murmured a few words or, in the case of one whom she knew well, gripped her shoulder briefly in a gesture of sympathy.

When she reached her cabin, she stripped off her old clothes, tossed them into the cleaner, then stood beneath the shower for far longer than the rules permitted. She wanted to feel something—anything—but it seemed that all her emotions had been deadened. And when she crawled naked into her bed and pulled the covers over herself, she fell headlong into a dream of home—her real home in a world where such things couldn't happen.

* * *

When Serena opened her eyes, the first thing she saw was the glitter of gold braid in the soft light of her cabin—not the colorful gardens of home that she'd been dreaming about.

Darian had pulled a chair close to her bed—as she had done when he was brought back—and like her, he'd fallen asleep. She lay there without moving, watching him and letting her mind replay all that had happened.

Now she felt the first faint stirrings of emotion, but it was not what she wanted to feel. Where before there'd been only a numbing cold, there was now a growing rage. She had been horrified by the Ulatans' device that had vaporized their landing craft when the enemy had tried to steal it—but she was well beyond horror at the enemy's behavior. They had turned the simple decency of men who wanted only to recover their dead into a way of slaughtering them.

On the return trip to the ship, she'd heard the men talking about pursuing their enemy to the limits of the universe, and she'd wanted then to beg Darian to turn back and go home. Now, as that rage gripped her, she too wanted to find them and destroy them.

She was horrified anew at this change in her. It was especially shocking given that she'd just been dreaming of her home world. And yet, it helped her understand the complex man who slept on next to her bed, his head tilted to one side in an awkward position.

She remembered his kiss and his rather halting statement about how he hadn't yet accepted her for who and what she was. Even then, she'd understood that it was meant to be an apology for his absence from her life for the past eight days.

Could we really have believed it would be so easy? she wondered as she watched him sleep. They came from such different worlds. She would never accept his dark world of violence and vengeance, even though she felt some of it in her now. And he could never truly imagine her world, even though he'd seen it himself.

The fact that he was a spaceman and she was a Trezhella and they had no future together was something they both knew, though they didn't talk of it. But now she knew that even the time they *did* have together was threatened.

She heard a faint buzzing sound and saw him jerk his arm at the same time. His wrist-comm had gone off. His eyes fluttered open—and immediately locked onto hers.

"Sorry," he said, straightening up in the chair and rolling his wide shoulders to get the knots out of the muscles. "I set it at the lowest setting, hoping it wouldn't disturb you."

"It didn't. I was already awake." She kept the covers around her, feeling unaccountably vulnerable in her nakedness.

"How are you feeling?" he asked, now standing up and moving away from her.

"I'm better," she replied in the same polite tone he'd used.

"We're on our way to the next world in this system. According to the experts, it's the only one left that could support life. So it must be their home world."

She didn't care where the ship was, or even where it was going. She wanted to hear him say that they could go back to where they'd been with each other.

"Tell me this, Darian. When do you think that you'll accept me for who I am?"

"Never," he said succinctly. "That is, if you mean I should consider you to be just another member of the crew."

"That isn't what I meant."

"Yes, it is. Except for making love with you, you want me to treat you like the rest of the crew—and I can't do that."

She opened her mouth to protest, then closed it again. She understood his dilemma, or at least she thought she did. He was telling her that he could either be the commander or the man—but not both.

"It's difficult enough to send my men into danger, but at least they're trained for it and they understood when they volunteered for this mission what they might be facing. But you're not male, you're not trained, and you didn't really understand the dangers.

"I convinced myself that I could keep you safe because I wanted you with me. It's the worst mistake I've ever made, and the most selfish thing I've ever done."

"I don't think it would have made any difference if I *had* known what I know now," she said quietly. "I *wanted* to come, and once I knew you'd be commanding the mission, nothing could have changed my mind."

She paused and smiled at her memories. "I didn't know then what I felt for you, Darian, but I knew that I wanted the chance to find out. And for us, that meant being together in space—the only place we *can* be together."

His wrist-comm chimed, and then Trollon's voice informed him they were making good time and would be in orbit around the next planet by day's end.

He hesitated. "I have to go. I've scheduled a senior officers' meeting for now, so Trollon can join us before he goes to sleep."

He turned and walked to the door, then stopped but didn't turn to face her. "I love you, Serena—more than I ever thought I could love any woman. But I can't be like the men of your world."

"Shenzi, so much has happened that I haven't told you about. How I wish I could talk to you now—to know that you're able to hear me. Please don't worry about me, though, because I am well and happy—or as happy as possible right now.

"It's just that my life has gotten to be so confusing. Maybe it wouldn't really seem that way to you, but I grew up in a simple place with simple people and simple, ordinary problems. You Ulatans live in such a complicated world that you must learn very early to deal with it.

"I also never thought much about the future, because in my world, you know that the future will be much like the present, which is much like the past. It's a strange irony that I have begun to think so much about the future now, here in space, where time often seems irrelevant.

"One thing that you can pass on to the others, including the High Priestess if you wish, is that the Sisterhood can and should change. I have earned both the respect and the affection of the crew, all of whom treat me like a sister—and they have earned *my* respect and affection as well. The Sisterhood *must* change its attitude.

"There are so many things I would like to tell you, but I cannot bring myself to burden you with my secrets now, even though I'd like very much to do so. This one thing I *will* tell you, but it is for your ears only, though that may change when we return. The reports I've sent you haven't always been accurate, but the lies contained in them are what I've come to call 'kind lies'—the sorts of lies you Ulatans tell in order to protect yourselves or others. Until now, I've never understood the reason for that.

"By the time I finish this report, we will probably be in orbit around the world where the enemy lives. Much as I like these spacemen, I have until now deplored what I thought of as their bloodthirstiness. But I feel differently now. This enemy must be destroyed! Nothing contained in the reports I've just sent you adequately describes how terrible they are. Darian's words fail to convey the pain he suffered at their hands, and they fail completely to convey the horror we all felt when they tried to use the goodness and decency of men who wanted only to bring home their dead comrades, to kill them for that goodness.

"I'm signing off now, before I give in to the temptation to tell you things you're better off not hearing. I will try to keep to our schedule in the days to come, but if I don't, please don't assume that something terrible has happened. My role here has changed, and whatever it may cost me now or in the future, I do not regret it."

Serena came out of her trance with a sigh. She'd said too much, though not nearly as much as she'd *wanted* to say. How very strange it was that she, who had always been comfortable alone, now desperately needed a confidant—even one like Shenzi, who might not be able to understand.

She left the communications room and went to the lounge, where more men than usual were gathered. Only an hour ago, when she'd gone to make her report, the world that now filled the window had been little more than a dim orb out there in the blackness. And even now, though it seemed close enough to touch, it was still hundreds of thousands of miles away.

She asked one of the men if the probe had been launched and was told that it had been, only moments before. He pointed, and then she saw the slender object falling toward the huge world. It was already so small as to be barely visible.

"It'll take longer to send back data," the man told her. "We're in a much higher orbit because we can't be sure what defenses they have."

"Won't they shoot down the probe?" she asked, recalling what she'd been told about the Ulatans' own defenses.

"They might, but probably not before it sends back some information. They're designed to evade any defenses—at least until they start to transmit."

"And if they shoot it down, that tells us something, too," another man added. "We'll know we've found them."

And then what? she asked silently. But she knew it was a question no one could answer. Even Darian could not answer it, though it would fall to him to make decisions.

Darian. She'd done her best to avoid thinking about him ever since he'd left her cabin that morning, leaving behind his parting words to both warm and torment her.

There would be no time now for them, and deep in her mind

where her darkest fears lurked, she knew there might *never* be a time for them. They could all die here.

Tired and beginning to feel that numbness taking hold of her once more, she left the lounge and went back to her cabin. As she pressed her hand to the doorplate, she foolishly allowed herself the dream that Darian would be there, waiting for her.

But when the door slid open and she saw him, she had to blink several times before she could convince herself that he was real.

Chapter Thirteen

Serena's breath caught in her throat. It was the man who stood there—not the commander. She could see the difference in his eyes, eyes that caught and held hers in thrall to their promise.

She stepped through the door and it slid closed silently behind her. Her lips were parted in surprise, the words not yet formed. He closed the small space between them and pressed one long finger to those lips.

"No words," he ordered huskily. "We don't need them. We never have."

Her gown joined his uniform in a dark heap on the floor. The rest of their clothing followed in short order. Darian reached out to take her hands, then brought one to his lips. His tongue touched the soft pads of her palm and she drew in a quavery breath, unable to believe that such a touch could be so erotic.

Still holding her hands, he turned toward her bed, then stopped and instead led her to the closet. His own bed was much larger, though she thought it hardly mattered when they were only moments away from two bodies becoming one.

But Darian surprised her. She ached to be joined to him, but despite the evidence of his own hunger, he wanted more. So they held each other, arms and legs entangled, her soft curves pressed against his hard planes as he kissed her slowly and deeply and very thoroughly.

Time seemed to stretch endlessly as they played with each other, fingers and lips and teeth nipping and gliding and roaming freely, all inhibitions cast aside. But it was an illusion. In reality, the waves of passion that were washing over them were becoming more and more insistent, urging them into the deeper waters, hurling them to the very brink of ecstasy, then easing off only to push still more.

Every part of her felt his touch—and yearned for still more. She laid claim to him as well—and also wanted more. And still they held back, even though every touch had become nearly unbearable.

And then, suddenly, the moment came when they could delay no longer, and they met greedily and flowed together and cried out as the spasms shook them both and her cries were interwoven with his groans. They held each other and held the moment, then slowly and reluctantly let it go.

Serena could feel his quiet contentment, which matched her own, the slowing of his heartbeat as it provided a counterpoint to hers, the pleasure that went beyond pleasure to something for which there was no word, in his language or in hers.

By the time his wrist-comm chimed, its sound muted by the distance to her cabin, they had fallen into a light doze. Darian left her to go get it, and she felt as though part of her own body had suddenly torn itself away from her. She wanted to scream in protest, but she knew this was the price. The man had been hers for a time—and now he was gone.

He returned with the wrist-comm, but not his clothes, and stood naked as Trollon's voice invaded their world. "Commander, the data is coming in now, and it looks like we were wrong."

"There's nothing down there?" Darian asked incredulously, his voice still carrying traces of their lovemaking in its slight huskiness.

"Nothing," came Trollon's voice in response. "And it's just completed its survey now. The air is breathable, there's water aplenty, and gravity is 1.2 of normal."

"I'll be there in a few minutes. Get the senior officers together."

He set the wrist-comm on a table and came over to sit on the edge of the bed. In the eyes that roamed slowly over her nakedness, she saw that she'd been wrong: the man was still there.

He trailed one hand lightly over her, tracing her curves. "How is it possible for one small, delicate body to possess such power?" he asked in a softly wondering tone. "How can you create a world where nothing else exists?"

She raised herself and kissed him slowly. "*I* don't create it, my love; *we* create it."

"We create it, and then it's lost," he said quietly.

"But we can find it again." She paused, thinking about Trollon's message. "If this isn't their planet, then where *are* they?"

"I don't know. Maybe we'll never know."

How could a world look wounded? she asked herself as she stared at the scene below them. And yet there was no other way to describe it. She couldn't even imagine what could have done such a thing, let alone why it had been done.

Like the world they'd visited last, this one had vast seas that covered most of its surface. And the oceans were the only thing left untouched. Huge gashes snaked through what remained of its forests and plains, edged by piles of raw earth and dead trees and rocks. And in other places, the earth had been left untouched, but the land was covered with the hideous stubble of trees sliced off to within a foot or so of the ground. As the landing craft dropped lower, she saw that the streams that flowed through the land to the sea were an ugly brown.

She had no doubt who was responsible for this—but why? Then that question was answered by the man across from her. "There's something down there they wanted," he said. "It looks like Taben after we finished with it."

Serena was horrified at his calm acceptance of the scene—not to mention his casual admission that the Ulatans themselves had done something similar to another world. She turned back to the window, and suddenly she understood. This is what would happen to her own beautiful world if the Ulatans ever found out what lay beneath its surface. She had not realized this before because her secret lay deeply buried beneath all that had happened over the past weeks.

Low-lying clouds temporarily obscured the surface as they continued their descent. The men were talking eagerly about the possibility that the enemy might have left things behind that would help assess their capabilities. And of course, the possibility remained that they might also have left men behind, though they had seen no indication of that.

Serena raised her eyes from the ugliness below and caught a glimpse of one of the other two landing craft as it leveled off and made a wide turn, heading for another part of this world. The third craft would be doing the same thing, though she couldn't see it.

She was still surprised that Darian had offered her the option of joining them. Fully dressed and once more the commander, he had said that the choice was hers. She had, of course, agreed immediately, knowing the difference her presence would make, since until they had seen it for themselves, they couldn't be certain that the enemy wasn't there somewhere and therefore didn't dare risk normal communications.

Did his invitation signal a change? Had he somehow decided that he could live with her duality as she had to live with his? She'd wanted to ask, but such was the fragile state of their relationship outside their private world that she decided to ask only herself.

Their craft landed on a grassy plain, near a river that ran brown with dirt from a nearby gouge in the soil. As the rest of the crew began to spread out, looking for anything the enemy might have left behind, Serena stayed close to the craft. She had no desire to see this world and, in any event, she had to go into a trance soon to hear what the others had to report.

As soon as it became clear that the enemy had left this place, they all strapped on their anti-grav packs and began to cover the territory quickly. Flying just above the denuded forests, dirty streams, and huge piles of reddish dirt was even worse than looking down from the landing craft. But the others seemed unaffected, speaking only of the types of equipment that must have been used and what had been extracted from this dead, ugly place.

Eventually, they all met at a predetermined spot in the center of the largest land mass. Serena didn't know why this place had been chosen, but when they arrived, she saw that it was the ugliest and most despoiled of all she'd yet seen. Once there had been forested mountains here, but she knew that only because a few trees had been left untouched, surrounding a blasted landscape that looked like a suppurating wound.

She landed awkwardly, having forgotten in her horror that the gravity of this world was slightly greater than that of Ulata and of the ship. It was merely another thing to weight her down, when she was already staggering under the knowledge of such destruction.

As she picked herself up, her gaze traveled to the untouched mountains beyond, and she saw that even they had not escaped unscathed. Now that she was closer, she could see a road cut through the thick forest, terminating at a spot about two-thirds of the way up.

Captain Trenman, the leader of their crew, already had his high-powered glasses trained on the spot. "Get the packs on," he said. "We're going up there. I think I've spotted a mine of some sort."

Serena had yet to unstrap her pack, so she started off ahead of them, rising until she was just above the fragrant firs that covered the slope. The smell reminded her of home, but it was a memory she would have preferred not to have just now. Connecting this place to her home in any way made her feel sick.

This time, she remembered to adjust her landing more carefully, and dropped down just a short distance away from the wide mouth of a cave. It appeared that the natural mouth had been much smaller; it had been widened and then reinforced with beams of some sort.

She heard the others arriving behind her, but instead of waiting for them, she walked toward the entrance. Though she was busy trying to deny it, something in her already knew what she would find.

"Serena, wait!"

Darian's sharp command cut through her mental fog, pulling her back from a childhood spent playing in caves like this. She hadn't known that he'd arrived. So she stopped obediently just outside the gaping entrance, then turned to see him already on the ground and unstrapping his pack.

"Don't wander off like that—and especially not into a mine. You can't possibly know what condition it's in."

His anger slid right through her. She *did* know what condition it would be in; she knew better than he could. But she said nothing and just stood there waiting as another man checked the beams around the entrance and then disappeared inside, carrying a light and another object whose purpose she didn't know.

"Commander! It's safe—but you're not going to believe this!"

Darian and the others hurried through the entrance. She waited, already knowing what they would find and belatedly wondering *how* she knew that. It could be anything—and yet she knew it was teldas.

Darian reappeared alone at the entrance. "What's wrong? You can come in now. It's safe."

She walked toward him, and when she started to pass him and enter the cave, he took her arm. "Are you angry with me? You should have known—"

She pulled her arm free and shook her head. And then she stared at the scene she knew she'd find, garishly lit by the bright lights some of the men held as they moved about.

The teldas were no longer there, of course. Only cleanly cut stumps remained on the roof and on the floor, creating barriers for the men as they made their way into the deeper recesses. She made her way among them, feeling suddenly light-headed.

And then she recalled another time in another cave many years ago, when she'd felt just this way. She stopped and stared up at the jagged roof of the cave and wondered why the light was getting dim. And then, almost before she could ask herself that question, the light went out completely.

Darian was still watching her, confused at her behavior, when he saw her look up at the roof, then begin to sway—and finally to fall to the floor. Cursing as he made his way through the rubble, he got to her just as several others noticed that she'd fainted.

He scooped her up into his arms and threaded his way back to the entrance, thinking about how she'd headed straight for

this cave of zhetlas without pausing to consider the dangers—
and then thinking about their past conversations. When the others asked what could have caused her to faint, he told them that it was probably the gravitational difference. But he didn't think that was it.

One of the men took off to get the emergency medical kit from the craft down below, but before he could bring it back, she was stirring. Darian waved the others back to their exploration, then knelt beside her and waited.

She apologized, then said she couldn't understand what had happened. He thought that she seemed genuinely surprised, which made him question his own explanation. He offered her the same reason he'd given the others for her fainting, and she accepted it, perhaps a bit too eagerly.

"Or maybe it was just being in a cave," she offered as she sat up and looked around.

"I thought you said that you'd played in caves when you were a child," he replied.

She refused to meet his gaze. "Oh. Yes, I did—but that was a long time ago."

She stood up, waving off his offer of assistance. "I'll wait out here while you explore the cave."

"I don't need to explore it," he told her. "They came and took all the zhetlas, but at least we know now that they use the same power source we do. And the fact that they're no longer here means they must have taken them all."

"Telonium," declared the geology expert on the crew. "That's what they were after."

He held up a small chunk of grayish rock with streaks of pale green running through it. Serena asked what it was used for, and the man waved toward the landing craft, parked some distance away, at the edge of this clearing where more digging had taken place.

"It's one of the elements of taseen, the composite used for landing craft and for the spaceships themselves."

"Is it rare?" she asked.

"Not as rare as zhetlas. Right now, we have a good source for it on a couple of worlds in our system. But the supplies are dwindling, so it's one thing we're looking for." He sighed. "Unfortunately, they beat us to it, too."

He tossed the rock aside and moved on. Serena picked it up again and studied it. There were places on her own world where this rock formed high walls around deep ravines in the forest. In fact, she'd thought about those places when they were on the world of the cliff-dwellers, because the striations on the walls of the canyons there had reminded her of this rock.

She stared out at the blasted landscape and in her mind saw her own world torn apart like this. The thought sickened her. If she and Trenek had gotten only a few miles farther along the trail before Darian and his men found them, Darian would have seen those gray walls with their thin green lines, and even now, Ulatans would be busy destroying the forests of her home.

Still, she thought, they *don't* know about it or about the teldas, and Darian himself had said that they weren't likely to return to her world because of the severe storms in that sector.

As the men moved around the heaps of rubble, bending now and then to examine something or put something in the big bags they carried, Serena raised her gaze to the hillside beyond the slag heap. They'd found more caves up there this morning, caves that had once been filled with teldas. This time, however, she'd stayed outside. But still, she'd known even before they did what they would find. And earlier, when they'd discovered more mine entrances some distance away, she'd known somehow that there weren't any teldas in there. Instead, they'd found traces of some precious metal.

But she didn't understand how she knew these things. She

was certain that it was the teldas, and not the gravity or the cave itself, that had caused her to black out—but why? She was totally unaffected by the teldas in the ship's power room.

She also suspected that, despite his words, Darian knew the truth as well, and she hated this barrier between them, this wall of secret knowledge.

Those secrets were especially painful to her now, because Darian seemed to be coming to terms with who she was. By day, she was only another crew member, and by night, she was his lover. But if he knew the truth . . .

"Serena! Come here!"

She turned to find Captain Trenman, her crew leader, beckoning to her, so she walked over to join him.

"This looks like as good a time as any to show you how to operate a landing craft. The others will be busy for a while."

She was tempted to ask if Darian had approved this, but she kept quiet. She wanted to learn, and if she brought up the subject of Darian's approval, that might not happen. Since Darian's crew was busy on the other side of this world at the moment, the timing was perfect.

"Is it difficult?" she asked as they both strapped on their antigrav packs for the short journey back to the landing craft. They would have walked if it weren't for the piles of rocks and dirt littering the space between them and the craft.

"Not much more difficult than a hovercraft," he replied as they ascended, then leveled off to return to the craft. "Have you flown one of them?"

"A few times. A friend showed me back on Ulata." Lania had let her take the controls twice, and it had been surprisingly easy.

The Captain's words proved to be correct. The landing craft was much bigger, but it operated in much the same manner. Everything was so automated that little skill was required. It was really no more than learning where all the various controls were.

"What is this?" She asked, pointing to a small lever between the pilot's and co-pilot's seats.

He chuckled. "You won't find *that* on a hovercraft, though I've wished I had one a few times when the traffic over Ul-tago gets bad. That's the control for the laser weapons, and it's simple, too. All you need to do is to aim the craft at the enemy and press the lever. The guidance system does the rest."

Then he pointed to another control she didn't recognize. "And this one erects a shield around the craft to ward off enemy lasers. It takes a tremendous amount of power and you won't be able to fly very far after you've used it—especially if you also switch on the super-charger there." He pointed to the lever next to it. "You use that to get out of the way in a hurry."

Serena practiced some landings and take-offs and he pronounced her ready to be a pilot. By this time, the rest of their crew had finished their work in this spot and were ready to move on. Captain Trenman remained in the co-pilot's seat and told her to ferry them to the next site.

Serena wondered if the men would accept that, so she watched their faces as they climbed aboard. Other than a few comments about the "new pilot," they settled in with no apparent misgivings. Of course, they could have been counting on Trenman to take over the dual controls if the need arose.

After she had taken them to the next site, she asked Captain Trenman if she could practice some more. He told her to go ahead, and then climbed out himself.

"Time to solo. You'll be fine. Just don't forget to come back for us."

Serena spent the next hour alone in the landing craft, taking care not to stray far from the crew, even though by now, no one had any concerns about the enemy. In fact, her presence down here this day wasn't even necessary because they were now using normal communications. But when she'd asked to come, Darian had agreed.

After assuring herself that she had the basics under control, she began to experiment with making tight turns, sending the craft into a series of spirals that made the ugly world below her tilt and spin. She was just beginning to enjoy herself when a familiar voice came over the craft's comm.

"LC-2, what in blazes is going on?"

Serena leveled out in a hurry and scanned the skies. Another craft was hovering nearby, not yet close enough for her craft's collision warning system to alert her to its presence. She thought about ignoring him, but decided that wouldn't be wise, so she picked up the mike and clicked it on.

"LC-1, this is LC-2. I'm practicing turns."

A brief silence greeted that, during which she began to suspect that Trenman might have overstepped his bounds by teaching her to fly.

"LC-1 to LC-2. All right. Just checking. Over and out."

Serena leapt and spun and arched and dipped, testing the limits of her body as she hadn't done before. Having an audience made a difference—especially when the audience was Darian.

They were in her dance room, and Darian had secured himself with a strap to the lowest handhold in one corner. Even so, he floated several inches above the padded floor. She'd been surprised when he suggested that she dance for him, since he'd shown no interest before.

He had as yet said nothing to confirm or deny it, but the rumor aboard the ship was that they were going home. There was no sign of the enemy, and today they would complete their survey of the last habitable world in this system. The two remaining worlds were deemed too dangerous to visit because they lay very close to the star that was the sun for this system.

But Serena thought neither about this nor about anything else as she surrendered to the music and let it guide her movements.

In fact, she was really in a light trance and just barely aware of Darian's presence.

The beautiful music swelled to a crescendo, and then stopped. She drew herself up straight and began a slow bow from the waist, with one hand tracing a spiral in the air: the traditional way that her people ended their dances. Then she floated over to the corner where Darian sat and gripped the uppermost handhold. The panel that controlled the gravity was just above his head.

He raised his head as she began to work her way down to him, then reached out to take her hand as she moved toward the control.

"Not yet," he said with a smile.

She shook her head. "I can't, Darian. If I dance any more, I'll pay for it later. It's hard work."

As she spoke, the music started again: a lovely, slow piece she'd danced to many times. Darian continued to hold her hand as he used the other one to free himself from the tether. "Dancing isn't exactly what I had in mind," he said dryly as he floated up to her.

"Oh?" she said as the heat of excitement surged within her. She too had thought about that—more than once. "So *that's* why you suddenly became interested in watching me dance."

"I enjoyed watching you," he replied huskily as he began to loosen the knotted tie around her waist. "And I'm going to enjoy watching *us* even more."

Serena smiled. She hadn't thought about *that*. All four walls were mirrored. The sensual heat spread even more.

"The mirrors were *my* idea," he said with a decidedly wicked grin. "And I have to confess that even at the time, I was thinking of a dual purpose for them."

"Even though seduction of a Trezhella is a crime punishable by death?" she teased.

"In this case, I can't think of a better cause to die for," he replied as he finally managed to pull off her blouse, then push it away from them.

It took them quite a while to rid themselves of their clothing, and then bundle it all up and tie it to the handholds. But that only allowed the eroticism to build.

And then they were floating free and naked, arms and legs entangled as they struggled to stay together. Darian had less experience than she did in this situation, but he learned quickly, and the extra dimension of freedom they had now was soon put to good use.

They floated around the room in a slow, erotic dance while the music swelled. She was lighter and more supple, while he had the advantage of much greater strength, and it all made for a perfect match.

The mirrored walls reflected back two entwined images: one big and muscular and bronzed, the other smaller and curvaceous and pale. She stood in place, her golden hair floating around her head, while Darian moved slowly down along the slender column of her body, his lips warm against her skin as he held her in place.

And finally, when their passion had become a roaring fire that could no longer be denied, she grasped one of the handholds and held on as he surged against her and into her, filling her with himself and driving them both over the edge into a sensual oblivion.

Exhausted, they sank to the floor and switched off the antigrav, then collapsed heavily against each other as their bodies reclaimed their normal weight.

"We're going to be late," she reminded him as her mind began to function again.

"I told Honek and Trenman to go on without us, and Sergeant Indo will take my crew. We'll join them later."

"What explanation did you give them?" she asked curiously.

"I didn't. I don't have to give explanations."

"But Darian, they—"

"I selected these men because they're the best and the brightest, and I'm sure there isn't a one of them who didn't figure it out long ago."

Serena stared at him. Was it true? She'd been trying so hard to conceal her feelings for him, and she'd assumed that he did the same. Certainly he did when she was around.

"The rumor among the men is that we're going home," she told him, even though she didn't want to think about it, let alone discuss it.

"We are." He got up and untied their clothing, then handed hers over and began to get dressed himself. "I haven't got it all sorted out yet, but I will by the time we get there."

She merely nodded. There was no need to ask him what he meant. But she wondered if even the power of the Vondrak name and the force of Darian's personality could move the mountains that would have to be moved to keep them together.

He took her hand and brought it to his lips. "Trust me, Serena. We will stay together."

"I *do* trust you," she replied. But still she doubted.

"Do you *really?*" he asked, his dark eyes boring into hers. "Sometimes, it seems to me that love and trust are two different things for you."

Then he spared her the difficulty of answering by opening the door and disappearing down the hallway to his cabin.

Serena piloted the craft up over the tallest mountains this world still boasted: mountains that had once been heavily forested, but were now reduced to ugly stubble. The forests of this world, she'd learned, were composed of very high quality hardwoods, and those who had come before them had apparently taken with them as much as they could. Darian had told her that it probably meant that they either didn't have such wood in abundance on their own world, or that they had badly managed what they did have. The Ulatans loved fine wood furniture as well, but they had long ago found a way to encourage rapid growth of trees, and to take down only those that were past their prime, leaving their own forests largely undisturbed.

Serena, however, was inclined to think that their enemy simply enjoyed destroying things, and this belief was given further credence by the remarks of the geologist yesterday about their methods of harvesting various ores.

Piloting the landing craft had by now become second nature to her, which unfortunately meant that she had too much time to think. Darian hadn't raised again the issue of trust between them, but it scarcely mattered. He had made his point—and he was right. No matter how much she loved him, she couldn't bring herself to tell him about the teldas and the telonium on her world.

And the reason for that, of course, was that no matter how much he loved her and how enchanted he'd been by her beautiful home, he would not hesitate to destroy it in order to get those precious items.

She was now over a large, placid ocean, the only place left untouched on this sad world. Below her, she saw a wide strip of white sand at the water's edge, behind which tall, rocky cliffs jutted out. A perfect spot to set down and go for a swim, she decided, so she maneuvered the tiny craft down onto the sand. The craft she was piloting today was much smaller than the others, with space only for the pilot and one passenger.

She left the craft in the shadow of the leaning cliffs and slipped off her boots, then walked to the water's edge. The foaming water that lapped about her bare feet was pleasantly warm, and it was so clear that she could easily see to the sandy bottom for some distance. It looked safe enough. They hadn't yet seen any animal life on this world, but that didn't mean there couldn't be dangerous creatures in its seas.

She was standing there uncertainly, trying to decide if she

should give in to the urge to go for a swim, when she heard a faint sound—a brief burst of very high-pitched sounds, to be exact. Then, just as she was trying to decide if she'd imagined it, it came again, exactly the same. And this time she decided it must be coming from the landing craft.

She ran barefoot back across the sand to the craft, just in time to hear the same brief series again, like tiny bells almost at the upper limits of her hearing. More curious than frightened, she opened the door and climbed into the pilot's seat to scan the various instruments. All the screens were blank, as they should be when the craft's power was shut down.

Then it came again, still the same series, emanating from the comm. She picked up the microphone, hoping that someone would be close enough to one of the other craft to hear her. She could reach the ship, of course, but because of the distance, minutes would pass before she could get a response from them.

But there was no response to her repeated calls. The terrain here was such that they often had to park the craft some distance away from the sites they wanted to check, and since they no longer worried about the enemy showing up, the pilots tended to wander about with the rest of the crew.

The tiny bells continued, faint but persistent. Serena began to wonder if it might signal some problem with the craft. But why would it be signaling that when everything was shut down?

After staring longingly back at the sea, she decided that she'd better return to the site where she'd left Darian. So she climbed out to retrieve her boots, which she'd left on the sand near the water's edge.

She had just picked them up when something above her caught her eye, and she lifted her head to see another craft approaching over the water. It was still some distance away, but something about its shape seemed wrong. Acting purely on instinct, she ran across the sand into the shadow of the cliff where she'd left her little craft. The same sounds were still being repeated, and even before she turned back toward the approaching craft, they had begun to take on the sound of a warning.

The craft didn't pass directly overhead as it flew inland, but it came close enough to confirm her earlier suspicions. It wasn't one of her crew's. It had a squat shape and was dark in color. All the ship's craft were gray-white and much slimmer in design. In fact, she realized now that the color of her own craft was probably the only reason the other one hadn't spotted her down here. In the shadow of the cliffs, it was virtually indistinguishable from the surrounding sand.

Serena didn't stop to put on her boots, but instead just threw them onto the other seat, then slid in and grabbed the mike again. Still none of the other craft responded. She switched on the craft's power and edged it slowly out onto the strip of beach, then took off. As soon as she was in the air, she called the ship, and after that, she followed the path of the other craft. The tiny bell sounds had stopped the moment she switched on the power.

"LC-4 to ship. Come in, *please!* I've just spotted an enemy ship."

And as she waited impatiently for a response, she scanned the skies ahead of her for the other craft. Then, just as she thought she had spotted a dark dot riding up over a mountain, the comm came to life.

"Ship to LC-4. The enemy is back! They launched two craft and we were able to get only one. Serena, this is Trollon. Where are you and where are the others?"

"I'm alone, heading back to the closest site. I tried to raise the others, but there was no answer."

287

"Get yourself hidden and wait until we can get down there with some help!"

"Right! Over and out."

But she had no intention of hiding. The dot she'd seen was the enemy craft—and it was headed straight for the site where she'd left Darian!

The site in question was a wide-open stretch, a formerly grassy plain where the enemy had tunneled into the earth and left great mounds of dirt and piles of rocks. It was the last site to be explored, in order to determine what they'd been after. And when Serena had dropped off Darian to rejoin his crew, she'd brought their little craft down next to the bigger craft—at least a mile or more from the site. There was no cover for them, and even the anti-grav packs, which could get them back to the craft quicker, would be risky. Darian and his crew would be perfect targets for the dark, ugly craft ahead of her.

She forced herself to stay well behind it, hoping that she wouldn't be spotted. And she continued to call urgently to them, even though by now she was certain that the bells she'd heard had been some sort of warning and were probably ringing there as well.

There was still no answer as she climbed up over the mountains and then down the other side, staying as close to the tree-line as she dared in the hope that would give her some protection. Her gaze strayed briefly from the other craft to the red lever between the seats—the lever that loosed the craft's laser weapons.

Sweat prickled her brow and icy shards pierced her spine. She knew what she would have to do, but she still couldn't quite believe it.

Now they were both flying low over the broad plain. The enemy craft made a wide turn to the left, and at the same time she swung her much smaller craft to the right to avoid being seen. Below her now was a field of grain, nearly the same color as her craft. She dropped lower—so low that the collision warning system began to blare at her. She reached over to switch it off without taking her eyes from the enemy craft. It must not have seen her, since it continued on its way—now headed in a straight line for the site.

As soon as she saw the beginnings of the former mining site, Serena increased her speed to the maximum without switching on the turbo-drive. It was time to stop worrying about being seen—and time to start worrying about whether or not she could stop the enemy.

She gained on the craft rapidly—but not rapidly enough. Its first target was the landing craft, and Serena watched in horror as a bright green beam of light shot from the enemy craft. The landing craft was engulfed for one instant in the same brilliant green, and in the next moment, she saw only a charred hulk.

But she had no time to wonder if anyone had been inside because the enemy craft was swinging around to aim at the crew on the ground, who were now scattering in all directions, desperately seeking cover.

She began to maneuver around to get behind it, but she was too late. Suddenly it swung its nose toward her, and at what was probably the last possible second, she remembered the shields and activated them. The whole world beyond the window turned green for a brief second and she felt the craft vibrate slightly. But she was alive and unharmed.

Both craft began a series of quick maneuvers, but Serena soon realized that she had the advantage. The other craft couldn't turn as quickly as she could. She sent her craft into a swift, steep climb, then turned sharply to aim at the lumbering enemy. She pulled the lever and twin beams shot out from the craft's stubby wings, ending in a vivid burst of green where the enemy craft had been.

But when the green was gone, the craft was still there. So it had shields as well. She had no time to consider what this meant as it turned and began to climb, aimed directly at her. Serena reacted instinctively, putting her own craft into a dizzying spiral, then leveling out just as the collision avoidance system warned her she was too close to the ground, which at the moment was tilting wildly beneath her.

She realized just how close she was to the rocky terrain when she saw the faces of the crew staring up at her, their mouths open in shock. With nowhere to hide from the enemy, they had stayed where they were.

And then, just before she saw the enemy in her rearview screen, she caught a glimpse of something that stayed with her even as she began climbing again, this time in a zigzag pattern. Under the bright sun, the heavy braid on Darian's shoulders reflected a dazzling light.

Darian Vondrak had seen numerous battles, and more than once he'd faced potentially disastrous breakdowns in space. But never in his life had he felt the fear he felt now, as he watched helplessly from the ground.

Even though he knew it had to be Serena up there, for a time he simply could not believe it. When he first saw the tiny craft heading at top speed for the enemy, he nearly convinced himself that someone else was piloting it. And now, as he watched her go through a series of breathtaking maneuvers, he was, quite simply, awed.

Twice the enemy fired at her, and twice his heart stopped beating. Would she remember the shields? Did she even know about them? The answer came quickly as the glow died away and she was still there.

The second time, she actually outmaneuvered the laser

beam, which struck only a glancing blow to the top tail fin. Spontaneous cheers erupted from the men around him, but Darian couldn't join in because his heart had surged up into his throat.

On and on it went, until he realized that she was deliberately drawing the enemy craft away from him and the others, trying to keep them safe. How had such daring and courage found its way into a woman from a world that had never known violence? And how had she learned to operate the craft as though it were no more than an extension of herself?

And then he realized that he knew the answer to the second question, at least. For one brief moment, he saw the dancer—and he understood. Only hours ago, he'd watched as she had performed the same loops and swirls and spirals, her slim figure reflected many times in the small dance room until it seemed that she had filled it with her many selves.

"She can't have much power left," one of the men said. "She's been using the turbo-drive and she's got the shields up."

Darian already knew that. Even as he watched her, some part of his mind was calculating just how long the tiny craft could continue. She'd have to fire soon, or there wouldn't be enough power left.

By now, the two craft were barely visible as she led the other farther and farther away, toward the distant hills. One of the crew had brought his binoculars with him, and without a word he passed them to Darian.

Serena glanced at the pulsing light just as a warning buzzer began to sound. The power supply was dwindling. She had very little time left. But she had succeeded in her first goal, which was to draw the enemy away from the men on the ground. She had feared that he might begin firing at them out of frustration at not being able to get her.

She feinted to the right, then hit the turbo-drive and shot to the left, at the same time putting the craft into a very tight turn. Suddenly, she was staring straight at the other craft. Her hand trembled as she reached for the lever. She knew there would be no other chance.

The twin beams shot out and intersected in a brilliant burst of green that blinded her for a crucial second. And then she was staring at empty sky, while the charred wreckage fell to the ground, trailing a thin line of smoke.

She had switched off the annoying buzzer, but the warning light had continued to flash—and now it stopped pulsing and remained on. She was over the mountain now, and she turned the craft, feeling it respond sluggishly. Belatedly realizing that she still had the shields in place, she switched them off, but it did little good. The craft was losing altitude steadily and the forest was rushing up at her.

She tried to steer a course for the plain, but she quickly realized that she couldn't make it. So she gripped the wheel firmly and tried to pretend that she was going to land on uneven ground instead of on treetops. And she did it.

For the first few seconds after the craft came to rest, Serena was convinced that it was still falling. Her hands gripped the wheel tightly as she stared at the greenery around her. Glossy leaves waved in the breeze, and the craft rocked gently as it settled more deeply onto thick branches. Some distance away, she saw smoke spiraling into the clear blue sky, either from the enemy craft or from a fire it had started when it fell.

Now that it was over, she could not believe it had happened. Everything from the moment she had swooped down from this mountain to aim herself at the enemy had become a blur— except for that brief moment when she'd seen Darian's gold braid flashing in the sunlight. That she remembered.

She forced herself to take her hands from the wheel and then slowly flexed her fingers, which had continued to curl even after she'd pulled them from the wheel. Then she pressed her face to the side window and looked down into the tree. She saw big, heavy limbs going all the way to the ground. All she had to do was to climb out and then climb down the tree. She could do that. She'd often climbed trees as a child.

A burst of hysterical laughter poured from her as she thought about that child, about the innocence of not knowing that one day she would be sitting in a flying machine after shooting down another flying machine on a world somewhere in the stars.

The laughter seemed to exhaust her reserves of strength. She gave up temporarily on her idea to climb down the tree. Instead, she tried to remember. But the only thing that she seemed to have stored in her memory of the battle was that sense that she had become one with this tiny craft, that she'd been dancing with it as she'd danced for Darian that morning.

That brought memories of their lovemaking, and she closed her eyes to see them better. Two bodies entwined, reflected in the mirrored walls. His hands, his lips, the feel of him inside her.

"Serena!"

Her eyes snapped open. Had she been dreaming? Then she jumped as the door she'd been half-leaning against began to move. Was the craft falling?

The answer was there almost as the question formed. She turned to see Darian's face only inches away as he opened the door with a manual crank. Of course. The anti-grav packs. How could she have forgotten that he could fly, when he'd been doing just that the first time she saw him?

He reached through the open door and undid her seatbelt, then gathered her into his arms, the movement made awkward by his pack. Behind him, she could see several other men

293

hovering. But hadn't Darian said that they'd already figured it out?

"I killed them," she said in a muffled voice that turned into a sob. "But I *had* to do it."

Chapter Fourteen

"I know," Darian said soothingly. "I know you had to do it. What I *don't* know is *how* you did it."

He extricated her from the seat carefully, then held her securely as he moved away from the craft. His expert gaze ran over it, and still he could not believe it. Somehow, she had shot down a far more powerful enemy and then landed on a *treetop*! Furthermore, except for a slightly singed tail fin, the craft appeared to be undamaged.

Darian Vondrak did not consider himself to be a religious man. His people worshiped an all-seeing and all-powerful god, and he had, of course, been raised in that faith. But secretly, in his youth and then more openly as an adult, he'd chosen to worship the god of science.

Furthermore, he knew by now that Serena's people worshiped no god at all. She believed only in what she could see and hear and touch: the return of life in the spring, the bountiful harvest in the fall, the miracles of birth and rebirth.

And yet, as he held her and stared at the craft, he felt the presence of an unseen hand in all this, answering the prayer that had come instinctively to his lips as he'd watched her lead the enemy away from him and his men to what had seemed at the time to be certain death.

But all of this passed through his mind in mere seconds—and then he turned his attention to their predicament. Even as he and several of his men were flying up here, he'd seen one of the other landing craft flying in from the west—probably Honek and his crew. His sudden appearance suggested that he knew something was wrong. Probably they'd heard what his own crew hadn't—the new warning system that had been devised to alert surface crews that danger had been spotted above on the ship. The pulses were ultra-high frequency that, it was hoped, would not be picked up by enemy ships monitoring normal communications ranges.

That meant they had at least one craft left. Trenman might be safe as well, but he wouldn't know that until they got back down there. And he also didn't know if there were any more of the enemy craft around.

But one thing he did know with cold certainty: those craft were not alone. They had come from the enemy ship that might even now be engaging in battle with his own ship.

Darian was tempted to contact the rest of his crew down at the site on his wrist-comm, but he knew he didn't dare do that. If there was another enemy landing craft around, he would be signing their death warrants.

Holding Serene securely in his arms, Darian signaled to the other men, and they all began to make their way along the top of the mountain and then down onto the plain, staying close to the treetops. She was quiet now, except for an occasional wracking sob, and he wished that he could just set down somewhere in the forest and try to soothe her. But there were lives at stake—including hers—and this was one of those times when he was torn between his role as commander and his love for her, a tug-of-war he was sure she didn't understand.

As they moved out onto the plain, he saw a landing craft coming toward them, and within seconds had identified it as being Honek's. He was still too far away to see if Trenman's craft had arrived at the site.

Honek veered off to the right to circle above the downed enemy craft briefly, then continued on up the mountainside. He would find Serena's craft and tow it back. Then they could recharge it from one of the others.

"Do you want us to go have a look at it, sir?" one of his men shouted, pointing to the plume of smoke that still rose above the downed craft.

"There probably isn't much left to see, but go ahead, then get back to the site," Darian shouted in reply. Serena stirred briefly at the sound of his voice, then became still again.

He flew on alone, carrying the woman he loved, hating himself for exposing her to this, while at the same time knowing that she had now saved his life twice.

He could see the site now and the tiny figures of the men, standing near the ruins of their landing craft. But Trenman was nowhere in sight. He slowed down and pivoted in midair to look back at the mountain. Honek was now hovering over Serena's craft, and then, just as he was about to turn back to the site, he saw the very welcome sight of Trenman's craft just clearing the mountaintop not far away.

Darian landed near the destroyed craft, and immediately several men rushed forward to help with Serena, the same question on all their faces. But she answered it even before he could, by trying to get to her feet.

Serena was dazed. The sight of the charred wreckage confused her until she remembered that it had been destroyed by the enemy craft before she could stop it. She struggled to her feet, then swayed a bit until she felt Darian's arm tighten again around her.

She gazed blearily at the men who surrounded her, their faces wreathed in smiles, and for some reason she thought of that time when she was on her first voyage as a Trezhella, when Shenzi had been so horrified at the group of men around her.

One of them brought her a cup of water, and she drank greedily as she tried to listen to the discussion. By now, she realized that Honek's crew was there as well, though the Captain himself was missing. She was about to break into the conversation to ask about him when she saw two—no, three—landing craft approaching. The second one was towing her craft with its scorched tail fin.

"Is everyone safe?" she asked as they all turned to watch the craft landing.

"Thanks to you, we are," one of Darian's crew said to the accompaniment of nods all around.

Serena had not as yet fully accepted what she'd done—or the near impossibility that she'd actually done it. But she began to understand as the men, including even Darian, crowded around the tiny craft with looks of wonder.

"I don't know what you're all staring at," Honek said as he climbed out of his craft and joined them. "It wasn't the craft; it was the *pilot*."

She saw Darian smile along with all the others, but his smile looked less genuine. She acknowledged the men's cheers and congratulations and laughed along with them at the suggestion that Darian nominate her for an award, but she wondered if, by saving his life again, she had driven a wedge between them once more.

The discussion turned to the ship far above them and what might be happening up there, and the men quickly grew sober again. From listening to them, Serena realized that she alone had spoken with the ship. So she told them about the brief contact, then learned about the new warning system for the landing craft.

Darian announced that he was going to take one of the craft and go up there to see what was happening. The others were to remain here for the time being, with Captain Honek in charge.

Serena wondered briefly if he had decided to go because of what had happened. Was this his way of reasserting himself after she'd saved his life? But then she remembered what someone had said about how he never sent men into danger that he would not take on himself.

Darian walked over to where she stood, slightly apart from the others. He did not touch her, except with his eyes, but from his firm stare she knew that this time he wasn't going to shut her out of his life because she'd saved it.

"I'll contact you in two hours. By that time, I should be there. But because I probably won't know the position of the enemy ship, I'd rather not use the comm."

She nodded, wanting to say so much that she could say nothing.

"I love you," he said softly, "for *everything* that you are."

Then he turned quickly and strode toward one of the craft, not even seeing the radiant smile that all the others saw.

As soon as Darian had vanished into the deep blue sky, Honek approached her and suggested that she rest inside his craft while they recharged the tiny craft she'd piloted. By the time that had been accomplished, she should be hearing from Darian.

"He had to be the one to go for two reasons," Honek told her as they walked to the craft. "First of all, if anyone is going to take a risk by going up there now, it has to be him. That's the way he is. And secondly, it's bothering him a lot that he's left Trollon up there to fight the enemy."

"Yes. I understand," she said as she climbed into the craft.

Honek stood in the open doorway, smiling. "You are one

very brave woman, Serena—and when we get home, everyone should know that."

"But they won't," she replied. "They can't—unless you mean that the crew will talk."

"The crew will do what Darian tells them to do, even after we return home. But a lot of us think it's time to shake things up a bit." He shrugged. "It's up to Darian, though, and telling the world about your heroism isn't the only thing on his mind."

Serena wondered what he meant—their present situation or the situation that would confront them when they returned to Ulata? Darian had said that he would "work it out," but she still didn't believe that was possible.

"Were you in a trance when you fought that enemy craft?" Honek asked.

"I don't know," she answered honestly. "I might have been. I can't remember much about it, except it seems to me now that it felt like the craft was an extension of my body."

"Several of the men who had seen you dance that one time said that what you were doing reminded them of that."

"It felt that way," she agreed.

"Hmmm," he said thoughtfully. "That has interesting possibilities for future training, just as kra-toza does. We're learning a lot from you.

"This will be my last long voyage," he went on. "I'm going to be teaching at the Academy."

Serena was surprised, and it apparently showed.

"I've never really had stars in my blood the way Darian and most of the others do. Besides, there is a lady back home whom I intend to marry, and she's made it very clear that she's not going to marry a spaceman." He paused and shrugged.

"Of course she may not marry me anyway. By the time I get home, she'll be finishing up her medical training—one of the first graduates of the new Women's Institute."

"Why should she change her mind because of that?" Serena asked.

Honek laughed. "It does me good to hear you say that. I hope you can meet her. I think the two of you would get along just fine."

The brief interlude with Honek had the beneficial effect of calming her, but as soon as he was gone, she found herself confronting her fears for Darian and her horror at what she'd done.

Still, what Honek had said stayed with her, hinting at the possibility of a happy future back on Ulata. It felt like a small treasure to be tucked away in her mind for now—rather like finding the first violets of spring and knowing that more were to come.

She had set her wrist-comm to alert her when it was time to make contact with Darian, but when she found herself unable to fall asleep, she climbed out of the craft. She didn't want to be alone with her fears and the presence of the men going about their business was reassuring.

But then she discovered that one of their tasks wasn't reassuring at all. With both of the remaining craft temporarily unusable as they recharged, the men had donned their anti-grav packs and were now carrying back various charred remnants of the enemy craft to be taken back to the ship for study. The sight of them made her feel the horror all over again. She had killed men she'd never even seen, and somehow that made it even worse.

But she'd seen what they'd done, she reminded herself. They'd carved a path of destruction through space and they would have killed her and everyone else.

She thought again about her home, about its simplicity and peace, and she decided that people paid a very heavy price for progress. Perhaps, somehow, her own people knew that instinctively.

Her wrist-comm chimed as she was sharing some food with

the men, and immediately all conversation halted. Now, in their expressions, she saw the fear they'd been hiding, and shards of ice pricked her spine as she got up to leave them.

Having studied the Ulatans' religion, Serena knew that this was a time when they would have offered a prayer to their god. She wished that she too had that comfort of believing that some unseen being could keep Darian from harm, and just before she slipped into her trance, she too prayed.

His voice was strong and clear, and Serena very nearly slipped from the trance as waves of relief washed over her. But the news was not good. The ship was there and undamaged, but the enemy was close by, staying just beyond the range of the ship's heavy weaponry as a Force Five storm—perhaps the same one they'd fled earlier—was once again bearing down on them.

"There's no time for me to come back," he told her. "Tell Honek to get everyone onto the craft you have and leave behind whatever he has to."

He signed off before she could protest that there couldn't possibly be enough space for them all. So she hurried to Honek, hoping that he could prove her wrong.

Honek took the news of the approaching storm with a grim nod, then ordered the men to start clearing out the cargo bays of both craft.

"You're going to carry *men* in the cargo bays?" she asked in disbelief.

"It won't be the first time," he replied. "It's not very comfortable, but it's pressurized. Do you want to pilot your craft?"

When she looked doubtful, he told her that pilots who had engaged in combat were always urged to fly again as soon as possible. It was the same thing her people always said of those who'd been thrown off a horse, and though that had never happened to her, she understood the wisdom behind it. She agreed and Honek said he would fly co-pilot with her.

In the end, they actually left very little behind. The men crammed themselves into the two cargo holds with some good-natured joking, and they left behind the ugly, scarred world that Serena knew would live on forever in her memories.

As they rose through the clouds, Honek explained to her the intricacies of docking with the ship, then pointed to two panels above their heads that she'd never noticed before.

"If the craft is hit and the shields are breached, the oxygen masks in there will come down automatically. Just fasten the strap around your head and breathe through it."

"Are you expecting that to happen?" she asked as renewed fear slid through her.

"No, but it pays to be prepared. You're just learning piecemeal what every cadet learns. Even this little craft can withstand a break in its skin for a brief period of time, but we can't live without air."

"What about the men in the cargo bay?"

"They have masks with them," he assured her.

She breathed an audible sigh of relief when she saw the great ship above them, glowing softly in the reflected light of the world they'd just left, which itself was reflecting the light of its sun.

But her relief was short-lived because a moment later she heard those tiny bells ringing in their familiar sequence. Honek swore and craned his neck, looking all around.

"The enemy ship?" she asked.

"Yes. I don't see them. They aren't likely to get very close, but they could launch something at us."

The next moments were tense as they got closer and closer to the ship, with still no sight of the enemy. Then suddenly, she saw the tiny object coming at them just as Honek shouted. Once again, her reaction was purely instinctive, but this time, she had far less maneuvering space because the ship was just above them.

She hit the turbo-drive and at the same time turned the craft nose down and dived beneath the ship. When she looked back, she saw the object strike the bottom of the ship with a flash of bright light.

"It hit the ship!"

"It can't do it any harm. Go up over the top and try again to reach the bay door. I'll watch for more."

She climbed over the ship and put the craft into a narrow arc aimed again at the cargo bay. "Forty-five degrees to starboard!" Honek called, then pointed because she didn't know what he meant.

This time, the object was much closer and coming straight at them. Caught in the middle of her turn, she tried to reverse it, then cried out as there was a crunching sound and a bright flash on Honek's side of the craft.

"Honek!" she screamed as he slumped forward, now hanging by his restraining strap.

There was a popping sound above her and the masks tumbled out. She began to gasp for breath and pushed her face into it, then strapped it on and reached over to do the same for Honek. It was then that she saw the gaping wound in his upper arm.

She turned her attention back to the front window—and saw yet another of the small, cylindrical objects hurtling at her. This time, though, she managed to get out of the way and dive once more beneath the ship. As she turned, she saw the other landing craft also trying to get away.

The tiny missiles continued to come and she continued to evade them, all the while trying to stay close to the bay door. Lights were flashing on the control panel and several alarms were blaring. She didn't have to look to know what it meant. If she didn't get the craft inside the ship quickly, it would be too late.

Now farther from the ship than she had been before, she made one last, desperate run for it, zigging and zagging wildly and not slowing down as Honek had instructed her as she approached the bay door, which was now open.

When she felt the blow to the craft, she was sure that they'd taken another deadly hit. The craft rocked wildly, and then, incredibly, settled down. Beyond the window was a sight that brought tears to her eyes. They were in the first lock.

The bumping around brought some indecipherable sounds from Honek, and as the craft glided along through the locks, she released her restraining strap and bent over him.

"We're safe, Captain. We made it."

His eyelids flickered briefly, but he said nothing. Then she became aware of faint cries from the cargo bay. She was startled for a moment, having almost forgotten about the men in there. But as she listened now, she could tell that they were cries of joy, not alarm. They must know from the sounds around them that they were now safe inside the ship.

The craft slid through the final lock into the huge cargo bay. Serena didn't even wait for it to roll to a stop at the end of its track. Instead, she opened the door and leapt out.

"Honek's been wounded!" she cried as soon as she saw the medical specialist heading toward her.

By the time he crawled into the craft to tend to Honek, the men had gotten the cargo bay door open and were tumbling out, looking shaken but unhurt.

"Will he be all right?" she asked the medical specialist when he moved out of the craft so that Honek could be taken out and put onto a stretcher.

"He'll live, but he might not regain full use of his arm." When he saw the look on her face, he hurried on. "I meant, until we get home. There's only so much I can do here, but they'll be able to fix him up fine."

Serena had just begun to worry about the other craft, and was about to ask, when the airlock slid open and it rumbled into the bay, apparently unscathed. Captain Trenman leapt out as she had done, then stood there staring at her craft. She walked over, since she hadn't yet seen the damage from outside.

She told him about Honek. He stared at the crumpled, charred skin of the craft and shook his head. "He was doing some damned fancy maneuvering," he said, then turned to stare at her. "Or was that *you* at the controls?"

"It was me," she acknowledged.

He shook his head again. "They told me about your run-in down there, but I thought they were exaggerating. Now I know they weren't."

The men had begun pouring out of Trenman's craft and the cargo bay turned into noisy greetings and questions. Serena chose that moment to slip away. She wanted badly to see Darian, but she knew he would be in the control room, and he would know that she was safe. So she started wearily to her cabin.

But when she got there, she knew she had to see Darian, even if only for a moment. It wasn't exactly proper protocol, she knew, but then neither was it protocol for a Trezhella to be piloting a landing craft, and certainly not in battle. Besides, she didn't think the Commander would object—or if the Commander did, he would be overridden by the man.

In contrast to the chaos in the cargo bay, all was quiet in the control room when the elevator doors slid open. Darian's back was to her as he sat in his chair, talking to one of the men. But several others spotted her, and by the time she stepped off the elevator, the control room was quiet no more. Every man in the room was cheering loudly and clapping.

For someone who had paid scant attention to her appearance before, Serena somehow chose this moment to be reminded of her tangled hair and her dirty old clothes.

Darian was by now getting up from his chair and coming toward her as the other men turned back to their display screens. He reached out to take her arm, then stopped when he saw blood on her sleeve.

"It's Honek's blood," she told him. "He—"

"I just spoke to the infirmary," he said, interrupting her as he ushered her toward the door that led into the stairwell. "He'll be fine."

"I know I shouldn't have come up here," she said, assuming that was why he was pushing her into the stairwell.

But she had barely gotten the words out before Darian hauled her into his arms. "Ahh, love," he said softly. "Do you know how hard it is for a man to be so helpless, while the woman he loves turns into a warrior with skills even *he* doesn't have?"

She smiled up at him, understanding for the first time the grim humor she'd heard from the men in such situations. Before, she'd thought them rather peculiar when they'd made jokes at times like this.

"I understand." She grinned. "But if you should decide that you need my help running the ship . . . "

Darian cut her off by covering her mouth with his in a soft kiss that promised much more to come.

The next day and a half were tense. The enemy ship continued to test their defenses, always staying beyond the range of the ship's most devastating weapons. Several times, Serena listened as the crew talked about the enemy's capabilities, but she understood very little, except that enormous firepower was being unleashed against them. And yet, not once did she ever feel or see anything. In the blackness of space, two enemies were circling each other, with neither yet the clear winner.

But at the same time, a force greater than both of them combined was bearing down on them—the great cosmic storm, now deemed by the experts on board to be beyond the Force Five designation, in a category all its own.

She saw nothing of Darian during this time. He sent Sevec to tell her that he would be napping as needed in the control room, and it was through Sevec and Captain Honek, whom she visited regularly in the infirmary, that she learned more than was broadcast over the ship's comm.

Darian was playing a waiting game. He assumed that the enemy knew about the approaching storm and would, at some point, turn and head for home. Then they could follow. But as the storm drew ever closer, that game became ever more dangerous.

"They're moving!"

Darian leapt up from his chair and rushed to the display. There was no doubt about it, the enemy was on the move—headed directly into the path of the storm!

A tense silence fell over the control room as they watched the small dot on the display screen move closer and closer to the huge green blob that represented the storm.

Serena heard the details from Sevec, who was kept busy providing food and drink for the exhausted crew in the control room.

"He thinks they've decided to commit mass suicide in order to drag us to our deaths with them," Sevec said in an awed tone.

Serena could not imagine such a thing. "Maybe they don't know about the storm," she suggested.

"They *have* to know about it. Their ship is powered by zhet-las just as ours is."

They stared at each other, unable to believe that any commander would deliberately sacrifice his men like this.

"The only other possibility," Sevec went on, "is that they know something we don't know. That's what's worrying Commander Vondrak most."

"I don't understand."

"Well, we know that they're far more familiar with this system than we are, even if it isn't their home. We haven't had a lot of opportunity to study the big storms close up—but they have."

"Time of contact for them," Darian demanded.

The man who sat before the display began to punch some keys. "One hour at present speed, sir."

"Stay put!" Darian ordered the Chief Pilot. Then he turned to the cadet who hovered at his elbow, ready to do his bidding.

"Call Lieutenant Commander Trollon and tell him to meet me right away in the infirmary."

Then he turned over command of the control room to the other Lieutenant Commander and hurried to the elevator. He'd spoken to Honek just a short time ago and knew that his condition had improved sufficiently for him to be part of this decision.

Honek had been Darian's first selection for the crew—even before Trollon. The decision had surprised the Supreme Commander, since it was well known that Honek didn't have stars in his blood as all true spacemen did. But Honek had something that Darian considered to be even more important—a fine analytical mind and a willingness to speak up without regard to furthering his career. Furthermore, because of their mutual passion for kra-toza, the two men had become good friends.

When he entered the infirmary, he was glad to see that Honek looked as good as he'd sounded over the comm. And he was even happier to see Serena there at his bedside. How he'd missed her! Just seeing her welcoming smile drove away, for a few seconds at least, all the tension and exhaustion of the past few days.

Their eyes met and held and Darian knew, with more gratitude than he could ever hope to convey to her, that she understood his neglect of her, and understood as well all the things he hadn't had time to tell her.

"Would you like me to leave?" Honek said dryly from his bed.

309

Darian chuckled. "It sounds to me that you're ready for duty again."

"Something tells me that if you're down here, I must be on duty again, whether or not I'm ready."

"I have a decision to make," Darian replied, nodding. "Trollon will be joining us."

"Then *I'm* the one who should leave," Serena said.

"No!" Darian replied, more forcefully than he'd intended, drawing a chuckle from Honek. "I mean, you can stay if you like."

"What the Commander is *really* saying, Serena," Honek drawled, "is that he's capable of thinking and staring at you at the same time."

At that point, Trollon walked in, unshaven but bright-eyed. Darian lost no time bringing the two men up to date on the situation.

Serena listened as they talked. The enemy craft appeared to be headed directly into the storm. They knew they could overtake him because they'd learned enough over the past few days to know that their own ship was both faster and more maneuverable. And Darian thought the enemy knew that as well, which was why they hadn't made an attempt to flee. By staying in place just beyond the range of the ship's biggest weapons, they were relatively safe.

"They don't have any way of knowing that we use zhetlas just as they do, so they may not realize that we've been tracking that storm, too. They could be thinking that they can lure us into it."

"But how can they hope to escape it themselves?" Honek asked.

"That's the toughest part to figure," Darian said, nodding. "Either they're willing to commit suicide to kill us off, or they know something we don't know."

"Meglid's theory," Trollon said, nodding. Serena wondered who Meglid was.

"Right. So our choices are to follow them and destroy them before the storm gets us both, or to leave—and we have to decide *now*."

"How are the zhetlas holding up?" Honek asked. "Because we're going to lose some if we get any closer to that storm."

"We're in good shape—better than expected at this point," Darian told him.

"Then I vote that we go after the bastards," Honek said with grim determination. "They've already killed six of our crew, not to mention the inhabitants of two whole worlds."

"I agree," said Trollon. "But we'll have to blast them instead of using the neutro, because we won't have time to tow their ship away, with the storm so close."

Darian nodded. "You're right. That would be cutting it too fine."

The discussion continued for several more minutes, but Serena could see that the decision had been made. And she could also see, in the glances that Darian sent her way, why he'd felt the need to talk it over. She could feel his urge to protect her and the crew waging a battle against his desire to destroy a vicious enemy.

They left the infirmary, and Trollon returned to his cabin. Darian waited until two crew members passed by in the corridor, then drew her into his arms. "I don't want you in danger like this," he muttered against the top of her head.

She tilted her face up to his. "I don't want to see *anyone* in danger—but you've made the right decision."

There was a desperate eagerness to their kiss, a hunger for what they couldn't have now, and beneath that, a knowledge that they might never have it again. Darian's hands roamed over her, molding her to him, imprinting her on his body. She could feel the leash on his self-control becoming taut, then stretching toward the breaking point.

She throbbed with wanting him, ached for the feel of him inside her, yearned to feel the driving force of him. But she knew—and he knew—that there was no time now. Both of them trembled as they slowly let go of each other. And then he was gone.

They followed the enemy, hoping to catch him and destroy him before the storm could destroy them both. The zhetlas were their chief concern at the moment, because the closer they came to the storm, the more likely it was that many of them could be destroyed. Darian divided his time between watching the enemy ship move ever closer to the edge of the storm, and watching the monitor that watched over the zhetlas.

It was a delicate balancing act and one that required making instantaneous decisions. Although Serena was not on his mind consciously, she was still there, deep in his very soul. Darian was a risk-taker, but now there were greater limits to his willingness to take risks—and that too, in a subtle but powerful way, affected the complicated equation.

Then, suddenly, when they were within moments of being able to loose their weapons against the enemy, he began to change direction, veering away from the storm on a track that would cut through only its outer edge.

Darian ordered an adjustment in their own course, still following the enemy. Anxious minutes went past—and then they were within range.

The ship fired its weapons just as the enemy suddenly picked up speed. But it was too late for them to get away. With grim satisfaction, Darian watched as the dot that represented the enemy disappeared from the display screen. Others, watching the ship itself through the window, saw the brilliant flash that signaled victory.

But there was no time to celebrate. They were now caught in the leading edge of a storm far more powerful than any they'd ever encountered before.

The ship began to turn away from the storm, and for a few moments, they were certain they would make it. But then Darian watched in horror as the storm suddenly spun off two miniature versions of itself—one of which headed straight at them at enormous velocity!

Chapter Fifteen

Serena awoke from another dream of home as Darian joined her in the bed, dropping heavily beside her and then gathering her to himself. She had many questions, but now was not the time to ask them. Instead, she held him and kissed him and soothed him and tried to be grateful that at least they were together. He was asleep within moments, but she could not find that peace again for herself.

The tiny but powerful storm spawned by the great storm had badly damaged the ship. The navigational system was in disarray and nearly all the zhetlas were showing cracks, with some of them having been totally destroyed.

Before she'd gone to bed a few hours ago, a probe sent out to gain information about a nearby world had reported back that it was habitable, but apparently without intelligent life, unless its residents were too backward to have any form of electronic communication.

They had quite literally stumbled upon this world, having no idea at all where they were. But they needed a place to set down, so that they could try to repair the navigational system while at the same time using old-fashioned methods of figuring out just where they were.

Although no one was saying it outright, Serena knew that their situation was desperate. They would never see Ulata again. The damaged zhetlas could not carry them that far—unless, by some miracle, the storm had deposited them much closer to their own star system than they knew.

Darian seemed to have aged ten years in the two days since their encounter with the storm. She knew that he was blaming himself for their predicament, though no one else was. Honek had told her that Darian's timing had been perfect, and that if it hadn't been for that small storm that had spun off from the large one, they would have made it. It was a phenomenon they couldn't have anticipated, because it had never been seen before.

Everyone on board was focusing on their individual tasks and trying to blot out the reality—herself included. She had continued to make her reports, each time hoping that she might hear Shenzi's voice. But she didn't, and that fact only diminished still more the possibility that the storm had brought them closer to home.

She burrowed closer to Darian and finally fell asleep again, finding peace in his arms as he had found it in hers.

Serena landed on a bare hilltop and squinted into the distance, where the great ship lay in the midst of a vast plain of tall grasses. Above her, the clouds were beginning to thin out, revealing a deep blue sky. Everyone was hoping that tonight would be clear, as the past two nights had not been.

The navigational system had been repaired, and other less essential repairs had been made as well—but they still did not know where they were. That information had been lost as they were tossed about in space by the storm. They knew only that they were not in the system they'd been in when the storm snatched them up and flung them through space, and they were not on a world they had previously explored. As Honek had remarked dryly, that left only a "few billion possibilities."

The crew, even those not engaged in making repairs, had stayed close to the ship after making a few over-flights to determine that this world was uninhabited. Serena had at first found this behavior to be strange. On other worlds, the Ulatans had always explored as much as they could.

But now she thought she understood. They were clinging to their ship, trying to hold on to one last piece of something that was familiar. Back home on Ulata, they might claim that space was their true home—and many would probably *still* say that—but the simple truth was that they were homesick.

And neither were they ready to consider the possibility that they might have to live out their lives on this world, despite the fact that all of them had known that might happen. Some of them had even helped to load onto the great ship the supplies that would enable them to survive on another world.

Serena, therefore, had undertaken to explore this world herself, at first with the tiny landing craft and now with the anti-grav pack. She found it to be a pleasant enough place, with a great, placid sea, many lakes and swift-running streams, broad plains and low, thickly forested hills.

But if she had learned something about the men, she had also discovered something about herself. Slowly, over the past days and weeks, she had begun to look forward to their return to Ulata, and then, after a period of rest, to more space voyages with Darian. And if Darian was busy thinking of a way to keep them together, so too was she. It was their destiny to live and love among the stars.

Suddenly a shadow spread over her. She looked up, thinking that the clouds were returning, and saw the small landing craft hovering just above her. The pilot circled, tilting his wings, then settled to the ground behind her. A moment later, Darian stepped out.

He said nothing as he walked to her, then drew her into his arms. There was too much silence between them now, though she was as loathe to break it as he apparently was. All their lives were on hold until they could study the stars.

"Come with me," he said. "I've found a spot—a mossy bank beside a little stream. Does that sound familiar?"

She smiled. "Yes, I think it does."

So she gathered up her anti-grav pack and stowed it in the craft and they flew off into the lowering sun until Darian found the place again. And very much like that first time, there were no words.

They cast aside their clothing quickly, then made love slowly, savoring every nuance, lingering in each moment. They knew each other so well by now, and yet each time still felt new and wondrous.

And afterward they lingered, watching as twilight crept through the land and the heavens darkened and the stars began to come out. But with the stars came a chill wind, and so they dressed and returned to the hovercraft. She climbed inside, but Darian continued to stand there, staring up at the stars. And when he finally climbed into the craft, he said nothing and she asked nothing.

There was total silence among the crew as the Chief Navigator and his assistant took their readings, then disappeared into the ship. Serena, for once, did not look at the heavens. Instead, she too went into the ship to make her scheduled transmission.

The reports were lengthy because she'd made no transmissions for three days. When she had tried to transmit while they were being carried by the storm, she had entered into a trance only to be driven out of it immediately by a terrible roaring in

317

her ears. At that point, she'd remembered hearing about a similar occurrence when a ship carrying another Trezhella had unexpectedly encountered a cosmic storm—many years ago, before the Space Agency had become adept at tracking them.

So she described, in Darian's calm, clear words, all that had happened to them, then went on to give all the incomprehensible data that always made up most of the reports. And she wondered, as she always did, if anyone were hearing her.

When she had finished, she took the elevator down to the cargo bay, then stepped through the wide door. A bright moon silvered the plain, and on the ground, glowing globes provided a soft light near the ship. Darian started toward her, then stopped. She heard sounds behind her and turned to see the Chief Navigator and his assistant. They all three walked down the ramp to join Darian.

"We're in the Bennari Quadrant," the Chief Navigator said.

The name meant nothing to Serena, though she knew that the Ulatans had long since divided the known universe into four huge sections. But she knew all she had to know from the man's voice and from Darian's face. It was too far.

Darian merely nodded, then walked back to the tense, waiting men. He repeated the Chief Navigator's words in a loud, clear voice that carried easily in the crisp night air, and Serena watched as thirty-two faces lost all hope.

Serena awoke in Darian's dimly lighted cabin, surprised to discover that she'd slept at all. She sat up, pushed the hair from her eyes, and glanced at the clock, wondering where Darian was. He had come to bed with her, and they'd held each other in silence, neither of them able to find words, and in the end knowing that no words were necessary. She remembered wondering at one point if all couples were like them, or if it was different for them because they had once been unable to use words.

Then she recalled the dream that had probably awakened her. As she re-created it in her mind, she realized that it was a very strange dream indeed. Most of her dreams lately had been of her old home or of her life on Ulata. But this one had been different.

In the dream, she'd been in the control room of the ship, staring out the window into the blackness of space. Except that it hadn't been black. She shook her head, as though to jar loose some meaning for what she recalled.

Beyond the big window, millions of tiny, bright lights had glittered in the eternal darkness. She had a sudden memory of traveling at great speed, which was strange, because unless they were in the vicinity of a planet, there was never any sense of movement at all on the ship.

Then another memory surfaced—this time, not from the dream, but rather from something that had actually happened. On one of the hovercraft trips she'd made with Lania to see her new home, her friend had taken her to a remote region of Ulata where winter lasted nearly the entire year. Ulatans went there for winter sports. Serena had been interested because snow fell very rarely on her home world, and never in the vast quantities that she saw in that place.

It had begun to snow as they were circling the tall peaks—slowly at first, and then much more heavily. She'd found herself entranced as she watched the snowflakes through the windows of the hovercraft, rushing at them and creating the same strange illusion as in her dream. But of course it couldn't be snowing in space—or at least she didn't think such a thing was possible.

And that wasn't the only impossibility from the strange dream. She also recalled a huge, glowing green blob out there in the darkness of space: a pale, luminescent green around the edges, shading to a more vivid green and then to a shade so dark it was almost black at the center. And with that came another memory of great speeds, of the ship hurtling through space directly at that blob.

She thought there might have been more to the dream, and she wasn't at all certain about the sequence. Had she seen the snowflakes first, or the eerie green blob? She didn't know, but for all the strangeness, what stayed with her most vividly was that impression of great speed, of being flung off into space after striking something.

The dream disturbed her because it was so incomprehensible. She didn't know if others dreamed such outlandish things, but her own dreams had always made sense—or at least they had after she had discovered the Ulatans' psychology. Even her childhood dreams of floating among the stars had come to make sense years later.

The door to the cabin slid open, and Darian's tall, dark form was briefly illuminated by the light from the corridor before the door closed again. She looked up at him questioningly as he began to shed his uniform.

"I couldn't sleep," he said as he slid naked into the bed and drew her to him.

She thought about telling him of her dream, but before she could, it slipped away again, buried beneath a rising tide of sensations as his mouth covered hers and his hands began to lay claim to a body that already belonged to him.

Over the next few days, Darian kept the crew busy. Everyone, except for a few men assigned to the control room, gradually shifted to the same schedule, adjusting to time on this world.

They began to explore the planet more carefully, creating detailed maps of each sector. They sampled the soil and air and water and checked wind speeds and directions. A tiny vehicle Serena had never seen before was carried aloft beneath one of the hovercraft, then dropped into the ocean with a two-man crew aboard, to study the invisible world down there.

Fascinated by the prospect of seeing such a place, Serena asked if she might go on one of the undersea explorations. But the Sergeant in charge explained that the two men making the voyage were experts in sea life, and she would have to wait until they had finished their survey.

She continued to be surprised at the knowledge that each man on the crew possessed, in addition to the long, difficult training that had prepared them for space travel. The Sergeant explained to her that every cadet who entered the Space Academy had to select a specialty to pursue in addition to his regular studies.

"That way," he told her, "we're prepared for anything."

And then he lapsed into a grim silence that she saw all too often lately. What was left unspoken was that nothing had really prepared them for the situation they now found themselves in. They all knew it was possible that they might be marooned on a distant world, but being Ulatans, they'd never accepted that fate completely.

Serena did her best to hide her own anguish, knowing that however terrible their situation was for her, it was far worse for the others. She and Darian had each other, but these men would never see their loved ones again. Worst of all was seeing Sergeant Roslev, whose wife had given birth to a son he would never see.

And yet, when she saw the grim faces and the occasional moisture in the eyes of the men, she was certain that none of them had truly accepted their fate. In all of them remained the hope that they would somehow find a way to go home.

That hope surged one day when a surveying crew that Serena had joined discovered a series of caves high on a mountainside. She knew, even as they approached the entrance to the first one, that they wouldn't find teldas there, but she kept silent, letting the men discover that for themselves.

And while they engaged in a fruitless search of the other

caves, Serena thought about all the caves of her old home—and about the secret that no longer mattered. It would be cruel, she thought, to tell Darian about it now.

Darian continued to produce his reports and she continued to transmit them, adding long reports of her own about the men and their quiet courage. She no longer believed that anyone heard her, but like the rest of the crew, she followed Darian's orders.

She now made her transmissions only once a day, usually at night. On the evening after the discovery of the caves, she finished her transmission and sat there staring at the telda and thinking.

Darian had told her that there weren't enough zhetlas, or teldas, left to make another long space voyage. But she wondered if there might be enough to make the voyage to her home world. If so, the Ulatans would have enough to last them for years, perhaps centuries. And that meant a ship could come here, to rescue them.

That thought sent a thrill of excitement through her—but only for a moment. If there *weren't* enough teldas to get a ship to her world, she would be causing him more pain for nothing. And despite the fact that the zhetlas looked to her like teldas, they might, in fact, not be the same thing.

And then, of course, there were her own people to consider. Their world would be destroyed and their lives would be changed forever.

In the end, she decided to say nothing—at least for the time being.

Like the others, she still clung to the hope that a way would be found to get them home.

While Serena kept herself busy working with the surveying crews and learning to help make the maps, Darian was spending his days, and sometimes his evenings as well, with Trollon and Honek and a few of the other senior officers, onboard the ship. He never told her what he was doing, and she didn't ask, but among the crew, rumors were rife—the desperate rumors of desperate men.

Serena paid these rumors no attention, tuning the men out when they began to speculate in words she couldn't understand anyway. But she thought it wrong of Darian and his officers to allow false hope to live among the crew—if indeed that was what it was.

Most of the men were now spending their nights sleeping beneath the stars, but Serena and Darian slept in his cabin. And although she was only subconsciously aware of it, that decision wasn't made just to afford them privacy. The fact was that she no longer wanted to see the stars. The girl who had once spent untold hours staring up at them and creating fanciful objects from their configurations had become a woman who avoided them completely. And she assumed that Darian felt the same way.

She was, therefore, surprised when one evening he suggested they take the smallest landing craft and get away from the ship for a time. When they flew off in the direction of the spot in the woods by the little stream where he'd taken her before, she assumed that he had nothing but lovemaking on his mind—a welcome change, as far as she was concerned, because he'd seemed distant and distracted when he'd first come to her.

But to her surprise, he set the craft down on the top of what she now knew was the highest peak on this world, and when she stepped out, she saw him lift his eyes to the heavens. She followed his gaze, but only briefly. Every instinct she possessed told her that he had brought her here for a reason.

"I wanted to talk to you before I talk to the crew," he said in his commander's voice—a voice she hadn't heard in a while.

"Some years ago, a physicist named Meglid came up with a theory about the storms and the zhetlas. As you probably know,

323

we avoid the storms even as we harness their power, because the closer we get to them, the more stress is put on the zhetlas, and they break. That's why we're here now.

"But Meglid had this theory that a ship could approach a storm at a high rate of speed, then veer off sharply and gain even more speed—*much* more speed—without damaging the zhetlas. It was his belief that a single, powerful encounter with them wouldn't damage them.

"That theory was never put to the test because we couldn't afford to lose so many zhetlas, but I think that's just what our enemy was doing when we blasted them."

She frowned, not quite understanding what he was saying.

"They headed straight for the storm at what had to have been their greatest speed, then began to veer off right at its edge— just before we blasted them. We've gone over and over the data from those few seconds, and from what we can tell, they had just begun to accelerate at a speed they couldn't possibly have managed on their own.

"We've reached a decision to put it to the crew for a vote. We can try to do the same thing—and it might give us enough power to get back to our own system." He paused and stared at her.

"Or it might destroy every zhetla on board and leave us stranded in space. We have an auxiliary power source, but it wouldn't last more than a few days."

"And then we'd die in space," she said quietly.

He nodded, still not taking his eyes from her. "I think it is a risk the men will want to take."

"Is it a risk *you* want to take?" she asked.

"Before you came into my life, I would have said yes without hesitation. Now, it's . . . more difficult. We have each other, and we could live out our lives on this world, but . . . "

"But here we could only be content," she finished, then raised her own eyes to the stars. "And out there, we could be happy."

"Yes," he said simply.

"Then I cast my vote in favor of going," she stated, still staring at the heavens and thinking about the times she'd imagined herself in that darkness for all eternity.

Darian came up behind her and slid his arms around her, drawing her back against him as she continued to stare at the heavens. Tears were welling up in her eyes, but just before her vision began to blur, she spotted something familiar. She rubbed at her eyes and stared again, and there it was: the group of stars that she'd long ago named "the lamp" because it was shaped like the elongated lamps with a curved handle at one end that her people carried with them sometimes, rather than torches.

She turned in the circle of his arms. "Darian, there is something I must tell you—a secret that no longer matters. Or rather, one that will matter only if we reach Ulata. I don't know if my reports are reaching Shenzi, but perhaps you'll want to report it to the Space Command. But if you do, you must promise me—"

She stopped, aware that she was babbling incoherently—and then aware of the stunned look that suddenly replaced his frown of incomprehension.

"I'd forgotten," he said in a tone of disbelief. "I didn't want to think . . . "

"You forgot what?" This conversation was growing more confused by the moment.

"You were about to tell me that there are zhetlas on your world," he said, and now his tone had changed to one of barely controlled excitement.

"Yes. I thought you might have guessed, but—"

Darian swept her into his arms, lifting her off her feet and then swinging her around in a circle. She was half convinced that he'd gone mad. Then, when he set her down again, she followed his gaze to the heavens and saw again the star group she'd named the lamp.

"Darian," she said. "Will you please explain yourself? What possible difference can it make now that there are teldas in the caves at home?"

"Teldas?" he echoed, lowering his gaze to frown at her. "What does that mean?"

"That's what we call them."

"But they're the same thing as zhetlas?"

His gaze was so intent that she had to look away. "I think so. At least they *look* the same. I had my first vision—my first trance—when I was playing in one of those caves. And it happened every time after that, though I somehow learned to control it. And then, after I got older and stopped playing in the caves, I began to go into trances anywhere."

"But they look the same?" he persisted. "How many are there?"

She faced him squarely, determined to make him understand why she had kept it secret.

"There are probably more than you could ever use. Most of my people think there are caves beneath our entire world, and there are teldas in all of them. We've never been able to tell how deep they go because no one—or at least, no adults—can get through the teldas and we have no way of cutting them. That's why—"

"And they're all the same?" he asked, interrupting her excitedly. "They're all like the ones in the ship's power room?"

"Yes. I'd never seen the kind that is in my communications room. Darian, stop interrupting me! I want you to understand why I couldn't tell you before, and—"

"I know why you wouldn't tell me, but you're wrong, love! We can get them out of there without destroying your world. It will be more difficult and take much longer, but we can do it without disturbing anything."

"You could?" she asked, having now given up trying to

speak more than a word or two. She would have loved to share his excitement, but she didn't understand it.

"Of course. We wouldn't destroy a world that's inhabited. And we'll pay your people for them, whatever they want."

"I don't think they'll want anything—except to be left alone."

"Then we'll do that—to the extent that we can. But think about this, Serena. That ship we destroyed was powered by zhetlas, too, and if they don't already have others like it, they will at some point."

Cold horror slid through her. "You mean that they might find my world someday?"

"That's certainly possible—even likely, because wherever they come from, they're probably closer to your world than Ulata is."

He smiled at her. "Perhaps the best payment we could make to your people would be to guarantee their safety."

"You could do that?"

"We could surround your world with a series of space-based weapons that would prevent anyone else from getting anywhere near your people. They can easily be programmed to let us through, but repel anyone else."

She said nothing, because her head was spinning with all that he'd told her. It just didn't seem possible that the Ulatans could have what they wanted most, and yet her people could continue to live as they chose—and in total safety from whatever evil lived among the stars.

"But that's all in the future," Darian said, the excitement still in his voice. "And now we've got a future—or at least a much better chance at one."

"Oh." Her mind spun some more, bringing her back to their present situation.

"Your world is much closer than the Ulatan system," he explained. "And what that means is that we won't have to take

327

as great a risk to get there. It's still a risk, but our chances are much improved. And if you're right about the things you call teldas, then we can get home again. And if you're wrong, at least *you'll* be home, and the crew won't have to live out their lives in isolation—assuming, that is, that your people would accept us."

"Of course they would. It would never occur to them *not* to welcome you. Darian, just how much does this improve our chances?"

"I don't know yet, but we'll figure it out as soon as we get back to the ship." He grabbed her hand and all but dragged her back to the landing craft.

"You see, I was totally focused on trying to get us back to our own system. I never gave a thought to your world, even though I already suspected you might have zhetlas there. At least, I knew there was something you were lying about, but I tried to forget it—and I succeeded."

He turned to her as the craft rose into the night. "Did you really think we would do to your world what those people did to that other world?"

"Yes. I knew how valuable the teldas were to you, and when we were on that world, I heard one of the men talking about how it reminded him of another world that your people had destroyed."

"Ahh, I see. But what he *didn't* say was that that world was not only uninhabited, but also had no water and a poisonous atmosphere. So there was no reason to be careful—and plenty of reason to get in and out as fast as we could."

He reached out to take her hand. "I wish you had trusted me—and trusted my people. But you will learn to trust us."

When they reached the ship, all the men were outside, gathered in small groups. Serena saw expectant looks on some faces as

Darian rushed her past them. It was obvious that some sort of rumor had been spreading.

But he ignored them as he led her up into the ship, through the cargo bay and into a stairwell she hadn't known existed. "Where are we going?" she asked as she hurried to keep up with him.

"To the power room," he replied. "When you were there before, you were probably too busy hiding your interest in the zhetlas to examine them that closely. Now I want you to take a good look at them."

By this time, they had emerged from the stairwell into the corridor in front of the power room. Serena didn't really think it was necessary for her to see them again, but she understood that he wanted to be as sure as possible before he told the crew.

They went through the first door, quickly put on the protective suits, and stepped into the decontamination chamber. When the door then opened into the power room itself, Serena could not prevent a cry of surprise.

More than a third of the zhetlas that had been there before were gone completely, apparently crumbled to dust and swept away. And as she approached those that remained, she could easily see the cracks on many of them. In order to satisfy Darian, she inspected them closely, but she knew she was as certain as she could be that they were identical to the ones in the caves—or nearly identical.

"There *is* a difference, I think," she said carefully. "Some of the ones here are different from others—less translucent." She stopped, realizing that wasn't really true any longer. Had she been mistaken before?

"I *thought* there were some here that were a bit different," she said, walking along the rows.

"There were," he confirmed. "Are the ones in your caves all alike?"

329

"I think so. At least, it seems to me that they're more like these." She pointed to the row nearest her.

"More translucent, you mean?"

"Yes. But Darian, it's been years since I was in one of those caves."

"Still, you said that you played among them?"

She nodded. "It was fun to play games there—even more fun because the adults couldn't go in. The teldas are so close together, you see. Some hang from the roof and others come up from the floor. In places, they even meet."

She frowned, now caught in her memories. "There was one cave—a cave I found long after I'd grown too old to be playing among them—where some of the teldas seemed to be clear. I'm not sure, because they weren't near the entrance, and the light was dim—but that's the way I remember them."

"Clear," he echoed in a reverent tone. "Could you find that cave again?"

"I think so, though it may take some time. I found it once when I was out in the mountains."

They left the power room, removed their bulky suits, and stepped out into the corridor again. "Darian," she said, taking his arm and bringing him to a halt. "You must understand that I can't be completely sure."

"I *do* understand that," he said, but the gleam in his eyes told her that he had already dismissed her reservations. "Come up to the control room with me. It won't take long to redo the calculations."

While Darian and the men he'd summoned huddled around one of the work areas in the control room, Serena looked out the window at the men who were gathered outside. What if she was wrong? How could she trust a memory years old—and a memory of something that had seemed unimportant at the time? And even if the teldas *did* look exactly the same, couldn't they still be different?

330

She didn't want to build false hopes for these men—or for herself, either. Her only source of comfort was in knowing that if they did reach her world, but could go no farther, at least the men could live out their lives in a better place than this.

Then she realized that she would certainly be able to contact Shenzi from her home world. After all, she'd contacted the Sisterhood inadvertently when she'd lived there. And maybe the Ulatans would find a way to reach them there. After all, Darian had said that they were working hard to find a substitute for the zhetlas.

Her hopes began to soar—at least until she turned away from the window and saw the men still busy at their computers. Darian had said that going to her world would be less risky— but getting there at all still depended on the truth of that theory he'd talked about.

Still, when she saw them all nodding and smiling, she let hope blossom again.

"There's still some risk," Darian told her. "But not nearly as much as there was before—that is, if Meglid was right."

"I still don't understand, Darian. Either you fly into a storm or you don't. I understand that my world is closer, but I don't see how that makes any difference if you're going to fly into a storm."

"Come over here, Serena," Honek said. "Let us show you."

She walked over to him as he began to punch some keys, and when she saw what came up on the screen, she stopped and gasped. It was that strange green blob she'd seen in her dream.

"This is the storm that got us," Honek said. "Or rather, this is the main storm. It spawned a smaller one that got us. But see how it's not all one color? That's because it's most powerful at the center."

He hit some more keys and the screen split, now showing two of the storms. "See those little black dots? They represent the ship. The one on the right is our estimate of how far into the

331

storm we'd have to go to get the energy we'd need to get home. The one on the left is our new estimate—to get to your world."

She could see that there was quite a difference. "I saw that before," she said, frowning. "I saw it in a dream, but I didn't know what it was."

The men were all staring at her now, and she rather wished she hadn't mentioned it. "I also saw something else—tiny, bright lights out there." She gestured toward the window.

"Sharry's lights," Darian said. "We've all seen them. It happens only when the ship is traveling faster than the speed of light, and no one knows why they're there. When did you dream this?"

She told him, and Darian smiled. "You were probably picking up on my thoughts, because that's when I first started to think about Meglid's theory and how the enemy ship might have been attempting that."

They went outside, where the crew sat in small groups among the scattered glow-lamps. All faces turned toward Darian as he walked into their midst. The night was so silent that Serena could hear his footsteps on the soft grass.

In his usual clear and precise manner, Darian told them everything, then paused briefly before going on. "The decision must be yours. You all know that we can stay here indefinitely, and that there's even a chance that we might be rescued someday. And you know now the risk we'd be taking if we try to reach Serena's world. And even if we *do* manage to get there, we could be marooned there. She could be wrong about these things she calls teldas.

"I want you all to think it over, and we'll take a vote in the morning."

As soon as Darian had finished, one of the men stood up—a Lieutenant Serena knew was quite popular with the crew.

"Sir, we already guessed most of what you told us—except for the part about Serena's world, that is. And we're already in agreement. We want to try it. We were ready to try it even when the odds weren't as good as they are now."

Darian was silent as his gaze roamed over the whole group, all of whom nodded. "In that case, we'll see if we can find ourselves a storm."

Chapter Sixteen

Two days later, they found their storm. Using one of the landing craft, they had launched several small satellites that could "look" into space and spot the great cosmic storms. Darian declared it to be perfect for their purposes—a Force Four, which meant it was less powerful than the one that had resulted in their being here. And within a few hours of receiving the report, they were lifting off in their crippled ship.

It took them another day and a half to reach the storm, a time that saw the crew divided between stoicism in the face of possible death, and hope that they might yet make it home. Serena continued her daily transmission, adding at the end of Darian's dry reports her own observations of the crew and their bravery.

Darian had asked her permission to send a report on the telda caves and she agreed. She understood without asking that he wanted to make sure the Space Program could continue if the Ulatans could somehow get to her world, which he believed might be possible. His report included a special request that they not disturb her world any more than absolutely necessary, and that they protect it from invaders.

Serena was so overcome with anguish as she transmitted this report that she slipped out of her trance twice and had to repeat herself. Nothing that had yet happened had made her so aware of the very real danger that they could all die soon.

She made what could be her final transmission only hours before they were to fly into the storm. Darian's report was thankfully brief, and when she had sent it, she added what could well be her own last words.

"We are now less than an hour away from the storm. If we make it, I hope to hear your voice again, Shenzi—at least after we reach my home. But if we don't make it, my last request is that the Sisterhood not use my death as an excuse to refuse any long missions in the future. Darian says that it might be possible for you to get to my world, and I hope there will be a Trezhella on board who can find a way to explain to my family what happened to me—and how happy I've been."

She had planned to say more, but once again found herself in tears and slipping out of the trance. So she ended it there, then prayed to the god of the Ulatans that it would reach Shenzi.

She left the communications room and started back to her cabin, but before she'd gotten there, her wrist-comm chimed and Darian's voice was speaking to her.

"We'll be making contact in about thirty minutes, and I want you here with me."

Serena didn't bother answering him; instead, she rushed to the elevator. She had so wanted to be in the control room with him, but she'd been reluctant to ask, knowing how busy he would be.

When she stepped off the elevator, she found the control room far more crowded than usual. All the senior officers were there, although they generally worked in shifts. Darian's chair was empty, but she quickly spotted him standing before the big, curved window.

She walked over to him and slipped her hand into his, and they both stared into the darkness of space. She knew now that the storm was invisible, but she still imagined it as it would look on the display screen—a frightening green mass waiting to devour them.

One of the men began a verbal countdown while others hunched tensely at their screens and keyboards. Darian turned to her only once, but said nothing. They had fallen in love without words, and they didn't need them now.

"We're in!" came the cry from the man nearest them, and still holding her hand, Darian positioned himself between two of the displays. One of them showed the storm and their present position, and the other showed a series of numbers that she guessed probably showed the strength of the zhetlas.

Suddenly, an alarm sounded and the ship veered to the right so sharply that she was nearly thrown off balance. Darian's hand tightened around hers as he continue to watch the two screens. And then they saw the sight they were waiting for— thousands of tiny, bright lights rushing at them.

For a long moment, the silence in the room continued as they all watched the lights. And then suddenly they were all cheering. They had made it! The ship was now hurtling at incredible speed toward her home star system!

Darian wrapped his arms around her. Even in the midst of her happiness, Serena remembered the rest of the crew. "Shouldn't you tell them?" she asked.

He reached over and pressed a button and she heard more cheers boom out from the comms. "They're all in the lounge and they saw Sharry's lights, too. They know."

A grinning Sevec appeared with a tray of glasses containing the pale golden wine that was always served at Ulatan celebrations. Normally, it would have been forbidden to men on duty, but obviously Darian had made an exception this time.

But there were three men who were not yet celebrating, and

after a few moments, Darian slipped away to join them. Serena asked Honek what the three men were doing.

"The last work they'll be doing for a while," Honek replied with a chuckle. "They're calculating how long it will be until you can welcome all of us to your old home."

Darian left them and picked up a microphone. After the chime that signaled an important announcement, he spoke to everyone on board. "We will arrive at our destination in seventy-two hours, plus or minus two."

They stared at each other from across the crowded room, and Serena easily caught his thoughts: they were going back to where it had all started for them.

Her people had a saying: "At every ending, there is a new beginning." The Ulatans believed the same thing, but said it differently: "The wheel has come full circle."

The euphoria following their close encounter with death wore off quickly, however. The zhetlas had suffered more damage from their brush with the storm, and each new crack was cause for great concern. Normally, the only men to enter the power room were those whose job it was to monitor the ship's power supply—and even they went there rarely, since the zhetlas were closely monitored electronically.

But Darian told her that nearly every man onboard had requested to see them, and after some hesitation, he had approved the requests. He confessed to Serena that even he himself had given in to the urge to see them. Serena was secretly amused at this. It seemed that no matter how much the Ulatans justifiably boasted of their science, they still didn't quite trust it.

Still, hour by hour, they moved closer to her home world, still traveling at the incredible speed made possible by the storm. At one point, she walked into the dining area to find Darian and Honek deep in a discussion of what the proof of Meglid's theory meant for the future of space travel.

"And if Serena really did see clear zhetlas, we might have a power source that could withstand *any* storm," Honek said excitedly.

"Why is that?" she asked, hoping that she could find that cave again. She was rather less certain of its location than she'd admitted, because she hadn't wanted to tell Darian that something he regarded as being a great treasure had meant so little to her.

"It's the impurities in them that cause them to break down," Darian explained. "Or so we believe, at any rate. That's why the ones in the power room—the clearer ones—are better than the one in your communications room. And speaking of your communications . . . ?" He arched a brow questioningly.

She shook her head. "Nothing yet. I wonder if the zhetlas really *do* have something to do with it—for long distances, at any rate. Remember that when I first transmitted, I was in a whole cave filled with them. And later, when I wasn't in a cave, I might still have been close to them, if my people's belief that the caves are everywhere beneath our world is correct."

"So what you're saying is that you have to have the talent, but if you have it, it can be enhanced by the presence of zhetlas."

"It's possible," she said, nodding.

"And maybe it isn't really a talent, but instead something that can be learned," Honek suggested. "After all, Darian and I both managed it because of our kra-toza training."

"Yes," she said, hiding her discomfort. "But remember that you couldn't communicate with each other—only with me."

"No one is suggesting that the Sisterhood should be eliminated," Darian said quickly, proving that she couldn't hide anything from him. "But it might just serve as a way of convincing them to change. After all, the only reason the High Priestess agreed to let you come with us is that she knew we would go anyway, and she fears that the Sisterhood could slowly become irrelevant."

And they could, she thought. Despite Darian's soothing words, she had no doubt that Space Command would be glad to be rid of their dependence on the Sisterhood. In fact, she was quite certain that Darian himself would feel the same way, if it weren't for her.

When they were less than a day away from the outer rim of Serena's home star system, they encountered another storm. Darian had told her that this was his greatest fear. The prevalence of powerful and unpredictable storms in this sector was the reason the Ulatans had stayed away from it in the past. The ship changed course to avoid it, but one by one, the remaining zhetlas began to crumble. Serena was once again in the dining area when Darian announced over the ship's comm that they had been forced to switch to the backup power system.

She could see the mental calculations on the faces of all the men present. They would just barely make it—if no more storms appeared. The storms could no longer affect the zhetlas, but they were still dangerous.

"Well," said Captain Trenman to the assembled group, "there's always the old boomerang trick."

The others nodded grimly and he explained it to Serena, who had never heard the word. "Back when we were still trying our best to depopulate our own world, it was a favorite weapon." He described it to her. "In this case, what we do is aim ourselves at the gravitational field of one world, then bounce off it to reach another world. It's a last-ditch measure because it can damage the ship. But our Commander is the only one who's ever done it successfully—and on his very first command at that."

And in the end, that was just what they did. Serena was once more in the control room as they approached Traneed, one of the three planets around her home world that her people called "day stars" but which the Ulatans referred to as "gas giants," meaning that they had little solid mass.

Despite the desperate nature of their situation, Serena felt confident as she stared at the brightly banded world that filled the window. They could not have come this far for it to end here. Darian's tactic would succeed; she was sure of it.

As it had done once before with the storm, the ship flung itself toward Traneed with its last reserves of power, then shot off at an angle that rocked the ship violently. Strapped into a vacant seat in the control room, Serena watched Darian's face as he swiveled his own chair, studying all the screens.

For a few precious moments, the ship seemed to level out—and then it began to vibrate. Alarms went off, only to be silenced quickly. Men hunched over their keyboards, their bodies tense. The lights flickered briefly. More alarms sounded. Serena saw that Darian's gaze was fixed on one display, and as she watched him, his expression grew grimmer and grimmer.

No! she cried to herself. *It can't end here!*

Darian's gaze flicked briefly to her, and she was soothed by the warmth of his love, a warmth that lingered even as he turned his attention back to the screen. The vibrations continued until it seemed certain that the great ship would shake itself to pieces.

Serena had no idea how much time passed as she sat there, her eyes on Darian as he calmly issued orders. Then suddenly she saw the grimness leave his face and his wide mouth begin to curve into a smile. She was so totally focused on him that it took several seconds for her to realize that the vibrations had lessened.

Darian unstrapped himself from his chair, and she did the same. They met in the center of the control room, and he slid an arm around her and turned her toward the window.

There before them lay her home—a beautiful pale blue world thinly banded by gossamer clouds. Arm in arm, they stood and watched as it became steadily larger until it filled the entire window.

"It needs a name," he told her. "We didn't give it one because we didn't expect to return here. The honor of naming a world goes to the Commander who first sets foot on it. I've decided to name it Serena: a beautiful world named for a beautiful woman."

She laughed, startled. "I recall thinking, when Lania took me to Vondrak, how incredible it was to have a great city named after you—but an entire *world?*"

"Without you, we wouldn't be here," he reminded her gently.

But it quickly became obvious that the crew felt the same way about Darian, because the cheers that erupted were for both of them.

"We're going to have to set down," Darian said. "The ship's been damaged. I had planned to leave it in orbit and use only the landing craft so we wouldn't frighten your people too much. But no one lives on or near that desert, do they?"

"No. My people don't ever go there. A small group of explorers went to the desert many years ago, but no one has ever gone back."

"Then that's where we'll land."

The crippled ship descended slowly to the world now named Serena. And so Serena saw the great desert with its blazing white sands for the first time, and she saw it from a ship that had traveled through the stars. She had always longed to see the desert, but the journey was too far and no one else had been interested.

Hand in hand, she and Darian stepped through the door of the cargo hold into the brilliant sun and a hot, dry breeze. Far off at the horizon, she saw a dark smudge that marked the beginning of the forests she had once roamed—forests that might be hiding the greatest treasure the Ulatans could hope to find.

"Well," said Darian, "are you ready to take me to meet your family?"

341

Serena nodded, already thinking about their reaction. Trenek would have described the men who had taken her away, so perhaps the shock wouldn't be quite so great as it had been for her when she'd first laid eyes on the Ulatans. But despite Darian's assurances, she knew that the lives of her people were about to change forever.

So, while the rest of the crew, under the command of Lieutenant Commander Trollon, began to assess the damage to the ship, Darian and Serena set off in the smallest of the landing craft. And just after dawn, they reached Serena's town.

"It looks like no one's about yet," Darian remarked. "Do you think we should set down somewhere in the hills and walk into town?"

"No. Set it down in the town square. They will have to get used to landing craft sooner or later." And a lot more besides, she thought.

Darian set the craft down gently on a grassy area near the town hall. Serena stared at the familiar houses as she climbed out of the craft, wondering if anyone had seen them yet. Most people would be awakening about now. She had decided to wear her old clothes rather than her uniform so that she would be more easily recognizable.

Darian joined her and looked around warily. She saw the stunner on his belt and asked him to put it back in the craft. "Trenek must have told them about it, and it will frighten them."

He hesitated only briefly, then did as she requested. She took his hand and stood there, waiting to see if anyone would come to greet them.

Slowly at first, and then in a great rush, they did. But they kept their distance even as they spoke her name in wondering tones. Then, just as Serena was about to address them, the gathering crowd parted and her parents were there, summoned, no doubt, by the others.

Overcome with joy at seeing her family, Serena ran across the grass and flung herself into their arms. Minutes passed in a joyous reunion as all her relatives and friends crowded around. Then she turned, and through a haze of tears, saw Darian still standing near the craft, towering over everyone else. She drew her parents with her as she walked back to him.

"Serena, is this the man who stole you away and hurt Trenek?" her mother asked nervously. Serena answered in her own language.

"Yes—but he is also the man I love. I know he must seem frightening to you and you must hate him for taking me away. But he's a good man and I think you will understand why he did what he did when I have a chance to explain."

She introduced them and Darian bowed solemnly to each of them, drawing bemused looks from both her parents and the others who now moved closer to this giant stranger.

"Have you explained yet why I took you away?" Darian asked, and Serena saw some people recoil from the harsh sounds of his language as well as his much deeper voice.

"Not yet—but I told them that I love you."

Darian smiled at her, and she saw her people's fear change to puzzlement. Raising her voice to be heard by the ever-growing crowd, Serena told them all what she had told her parents. It would have to do for now.

Then she saw Darian's gaze fix on someone behind her, and she turned to see Trenek pushing his way through the crowd. Although she had known she would be seeing him again, she was still startled. How could she ever have thought she would be happy with him? And then she realized, with a flush of shame, that she was now seeing him as Darian and other Ulatans saw the men of her world—small and pale and weak.

Trenek stopped before her and stared from her to Darian. "This is the man who took you away!" he said accusingly.

"Yes, Trenek, he is. But I love him."

"Tell him that I'm very sorry I had to hurt him," Darian said, drawing Trenek's attention away from her.

She translated. "He's not a man of violence, Trenek. And besides, the weapon he used on you could easily have killed you if he'd wanted that to happen."

"But he took you away," Trenek persisted. "How can you love him?"

Serena sighed. It was going to be a very long day, and in the end, neither Trenek nor anyone else was likely to understand. She was both happy and sad—happy to see her family and friends again, but saddened by the realization that a chasm as vast as space itself had opened up between them. She had once told herself that this could never be her home again, but it was now apparent to her that her heart hadn't listened to her mind.

"Serena," Darian said, reaching out to take her hand and drawing her out of her self-pity, "I think it would be best if I go and leave you here for a while."

"Yes," she said, "I think that would be best." He certainly couldn't be enjoying the unabashed stares of hundreds of people, and besides, she knew that he was concerned about the damage to the ship.

"Will I shock them if I kiss you before I leave?" he asked with a smile.

"Probably," she replied, then stretched up on tiptoe and kissed him instead, ignoring the startled, gasps of those around them.

She watched as Darian returned to the hovercraft, then rose slowly into the air. The others watched, too, their mouths open in wonder, as her own had once been—in a different lifetime.

Serena's mother hugged her again. "You've come back to us. He must be a good man, to have brought you home."

Serena returned her hug and decided then and there that she would make a few adjustments to her story, using some of the "kind lies" of the Ulatans.

* * *

She was waiting on the green, staring into the lowering sun, when she saw at last the tiny craft as it began a slow descent from the wooded hilltop. It had been a bittersweet eight hours, an emotionally wrenching day. And for one brief moment, as she stood there waiting for Darian, the past year and a half—nearly four years for her family—seemed no more than a dream, even though she'd spent this day trying to explain that dream.

Darian stepped out of the craft and smiled at her, then took both her hands. "I was half afraid they might try to hide you somewhere—and you weren't even wearing your wrist-comm."

"They would never do such a thing," she told him. "I didn't wear the wrist-comm because it would have been only one more thing to have to explain. How badly damaged is the ship?" she asked, not yet ready to try to explain her people to him.

"Worse than I'd hoped, but not as bad as I'd feared. We can make it spaceworthy again—if we have zhetlas."

Serena shuddered inwardly. She still feared that the teldas would turn out to be different. But she took a deep breath, then told him that she could take him now to the cave closest to town, the one she had played in as a child.

So they climbed into the craft and she directed him to land it again on the far side of the hill. "It's just up there. If you look carefully, you can see the entrance, just to the right of that tree with the double trunk."

"I see it. Let's go." He reached into the back of the craft and took out what appeared to be a very small piece of luggage.

"What's that?" She asked.

"A device that will tell us if your teldas are our zhetlas—or if they just look the same."

They left the craft and walked down into the ravine, then onto a narrow, worn path that led up to the cave. As they started up the path, a group of children came toward them from the cave, laughing and shouting—at least until they saw Darian.

"It's all right," she told them. "I am going to show our guest the cave."

The look they gave her suggested that they thought it was pretty silly for two grownups to be interested in caves. Caves were for children. When they had gone on, Darian chuckled.

"I think we had better leave this one untouched. It looks to me as though they think we're invading their playground."

"That's it exactly," she said, grateful for his understanding.

By the time they reached the cave's mouth, Serena's heart was in her throat. She hesitated, but Darian had no such qualms and switched on his light as he stepped through the entrance, bending over nearly double in the process.

A moment later, Serena followed him, even more worried now because she hadn't felt that awareness she'd felt when they'd found the ruined caves on that other world. She could only hope that it was because she *knew* what was in the cave.

At least, she thought as she looked around, seeing it better now because of Darian's light, she hadn't wrong in thinking that they *looked* the same. But still, she held her breath as Darian opened the tiny suitcase and pulled a sort of wand from it, then held the wand against the nearest telda as he studied something in the suitcase.

Then he turned to her with a smile that answered her question. He set down the case and swept her into his arms, and their laughter rang out, echoing crazily in the cavern.

"Even if the other caves are different, there are enough here to get us home—and still leave the playground intact," he said happily.

"They're all the same," she assured him. "Except for that one I told you about. And I have no idea how deep this cave is."

Darian aimed the light at the rear of the cavern, where a high archway led deeper into the hill. "This is incredible. It would take only a few caves filled with as many as we can now see to provide enough fuel for a century's worth of exploration. And if you're right about the clear ones . . . " He shook his head, smiling.

"There are far more than a few," she told him. "In fact, I asked several people how many there are. No one really knows, but they all say there are hundreds, just around the towns and villages. And there are probably far more in the forests."

He picked up his little case and they walked back outside. "So you told them that we need the teldas?"

She nodded. "They said you are welcome to them. They didn't even ask if you would destroy anything to get them. That surprised me at first, but then I realized that they simply have no concept of machinery that could do the kind of damage we saw on that other world. It's just beyond their understanding."

"Did you tell them we would pay whatever they ask?"

"Yes, but they couldn't understand why you would pay them for something so useless." She grinned at him. "That, Darian Vondrak, is intended to be a lesson in humility."

He laughed. "The lesson is noted. But what about the satellite defense system?"

"Umm—well, I didn't bring that up. In fact, there were quite a few things I didn't tell them. Do you think it could be put into place without their knowing about it?"

"I'm sure it could, though if anyone tries to get through, they would certainly see the flash."

"Probably not," she said. "The only person who ever stared at the heavens doesn't live here anymore."

They were walking back to the landing craft and Darian stopped, then hooked a finger beneath her chin and raised her face to study it intently. "Today was difficult for you," he said.

"Yes. They don't understand why I intend to leave again, and they really weren't all that interested in my life now—other than to know that I'm happy.

"It *hurts*, Darian, and yet I know it shouldn't. I wanted them to be interested, to be curious. And yet I worry that having your people here will change them. It doesn't make sense."

He kissed away her tears. "The chances are that they *will* change, love—but it will be very slowly. Maybe they would like a hovercraft, because it would mean that they can visit friends and family in other towns more easily. And then perhaps they will decide that it would be nice to be able to talk to their friends and families without having to go there at all.

"I think you should tell them that they can have these things—and more—and then just let them think about it. Let them pick and choose how they will move across several centuries. I think you need to trust them to make good decisions."

She smiled. "What you're saying is that I have the same problem with *them* that I had with *you*."

The voices filled her head, weaving around each other and over each other. After silence for so long, Serena was unprepared for the deluge of sound—and her trance slipped.

"What is it?" Darian asked anxiously.

"Voices! I can hear them again!" She clasped her head as though to hold them there.

Darian smiled and bent to kiss her. "Then they will surely hear *you*."

With the imprint of his lips still on hers, she returned to the trance—and the voices. "Serena calling Shenzi. Are you there?"

What followed was utter silence. Dozens of voices simply halted in mid-sentence. And then her head rang with the same voices calling her name joyously. Only when Shenzi's voice called out did the others stop. And across the galaxy, reports and messages were delayed as Trezhellas listened in.

"Oh, Serena, I can't believe it! I've been crying for days—ever since your last transmission. We all thought . . . "

"You've been *receiving* my transmissions?" Serena asked, astounded.

"Yes, every one of them. It was so frustrating, not being able to reach you. Where are you?"

"On my home world."

"And the caves? Are they really filled with zhetlas?"

"Yes, they are. Darian says there are more in the one cave he's seen than can be used in a century—and there are hundreds of caves."

"When will you be home?"

"I'm not sure. It must be in Darian's report. He would like to speak to the Supreme Commander."

"You *are* coming back, aren't you?"

"Of course."

"I can't wait. We'll have so much to talk about."

Serena smiled at her friend's dry tone even as she tried to remember what she'd said all that time when she'd been certain no one could hear her. "I'll sign off now. When can you get the Supreme Commander there?"

"He told Her Excellency that he could be here within the half-hour, any time we heard from you."

She slipped out of her trance and told Darian. "I know you have much to tell him, but . . . "

Darian stopped her with a kiss. "I'll keep it brief."

"I can't possibly find it this way," Serena said with a sigh. "The only way I can hope to find it is to follow those trails down on the ground, where everything will be familiar."

"All right. Let's return to the ship and we'll take a landing craft to town and see about borrowing some horses."

"I'm sorry," she said as they began flying back over the forest to the desert.

Darian reached out to take her hand. "I'm not. It will be a sort of vacation for us."

When they reached the ship, one of the scouting crews was just returning, and the men who had stayed behind to work on the ship were gathered around them, listening in awe to their descriptions of the caves that had been found. Darian had ordered the crews to explore the forests closest to the desert—and farthest from her people's homes. That way, they could take the teldas without disturbing anyone.

But what she and Darian were seeking was the ultimate prize—the clear teldas she'd seen long ago on a solitary journey into the forest.

It was midday by the time they reached the town, and the green was filled with people. When they looked up and saw the craft, they immediately began to scatter, but Darian flew off and landed on a nearby hillside, saying that he didn't want to "inconvenience" her people by parking the craft in their midst for several days. Serena was both amused and touched by his obvious concern for her people—a concern that, to her amazement, appeared to be shared by the Supreme Commander, who had inquired, during his conversation with Darian, if the zhetlas could be taken without "unduly disturbing" her people.

They walked hand-in-hand to the village, then stopped briefly at Serena's home to tell her parents of their intentions. Then, after having more food pressed upon them than they could possibly consume, they went to the stable. Someone had obviously informed the stable-keeper that they would require horses, because when they arrived, Serena's mare and a chestnut stallion were already saddled and waiting for them.

Serena hugged her pretty mare, then turned to Darian and asked, rather belatedly, if he knew how to ride.

"I've been riding since I was three," he told her as he swung easily into the saddle, drawing appreciative stares from the small group assembled there.

They rode out of town, past still more staring people, and Serena felt compelled to apologize for their behavior. "It's just that they've had no experience with anyone so different from them."

Darian waved off her apology. "I find their honesty refreshing," he said. "And it makes me realize how strange we must have seemed to you. There is an innocence to them that my people must have lost centuries ago. After we return, I hope to spend some more time with them, and the men are asking to meet them as well."

"Yes, I know," she replied. "Several of them have mentioned it to me. As it happens, we celebrate a midsummer festival next week, and I thought that might be a good time to introduce them all. But of course we'll have to visit the other towns as well. If you like, I'll arrange for that."

Darian chuckled. "If the food is anything like what we've just had, we may not be able to get the ship off the ground after that. I was thinking that we might offer them rides in the landing craft. That might set them to thinking about whether or not they'd like any for themselves."

Serena wondered if anyone would accept the invitation. *She* certainly would have.

Soon, they were deep in the forest, riding side-by-side, with the well-trained packhorse trailing along behind them. Serena was grateful for this time they would have, because after living day-to-day in space, she now felt the future rushing at them—a very uncertain future.

Darian had said once that he would find a way to keep them together, but he'd said nothing more about it. She'd found it easy enough to believe at the time, but now all she could see were the problems.

Thanks to the teldas, there would be many more space missions, but would they be permitted to make them together? And what would Darian's family have to say about them? She knew enough about the old Ulatan nobility to know that they married

351

among themselves. And what about the Sisterhood? Even if Darian's family accepted her, could she remain a Trezhella and not live in the compound?

She slanted a glance at the silent man beside her, wanting to talk about all this, and yet not wanting to disturb the peace of this precious time together.

They came to the first of many intersecting trails and Serena turned without thought onto the trail that led upward into the higher hills. Then she decided that she'd better stop thinking about the more distant future and start trying to remember where that cave was.

"I'm not really sure that I can find it again," she told him. "It was years ago. I think I must have been fifteen or sixteen at the time. No one in my town had ever seen teldas like that, but if we can't find them, I can always ask in the other towns. Still, I think I would have heard about them at some point if they had. They were unusual enough to have been talked about."

"Even if they're worthless," he replied with a chuckle.

She laughed. Darian had told the Supreme Commander— through her, of course—about her people's attitude toward the teldas, which had, according to an aside from Shenzi, stunned the man into temporary silence.

She tried to recapture her memories of that day. It seemed to her that she should have felt their importance, that somehow she should have known that they would one day become a great prize to the man she loved. But all she could remember was that she'd found them to be a minor curiosity, of no more importance than discovering a new type of flower—less important, actually.

During the rest of the day, they made several more turns onto new trails, and each time it felt right to her, though that could have been nothing more than hope on her part. Darian, at one point, expressed concern about finding their way back again and said that he'd brought along the markers. She decided to let him use them, even though it wasn't necessary.

As the day turned toward evening, they found a pretty spot near a stream to settle down for the night. After tending to the horses and then eating the food that her mother had insisted they bring along, despite their having provisions from the ship, they settled down to watch the last of the daylight vanish from the sky. Darian had propped himself against the thick trunk of an ancient tree, and she leaned back against his chest, happy despite the dark clouds on their personal horizon.

"Since your people don't have a religion, do they still have wedding ceremonies?" Darian asked.

The question startled her at first, but he'd been asking questions about her people earlier. "Of course," she said. "They gather together all their relatives and friends for a big celebration. The ceremony itself is quite brief. The couple simply announces their eternal love for each other and declares their wish to become one—and that's it."

"Would your family agree to that?"

She twisted around to stare at him. "Agree to what?"

"To our having that ceremony before we leave. You could teach me the proper words."

She scooted out of his arms and stared at him, stunned. "When did you decide you wanted to do this?"

"As soon as I knew we were going to make it here. I got to thinking about how Ulatan marriage ceremonies would seem to you, and I guessed that you might want to be married here as well."

"As well?" She echoed. "Are you saying that you intend for us to be married on Ulata, too?"

He looked surprised. "Of course. But it's a long and formal process there, and—"

"Darian, I know that we can sometimes read each other's

thoughts, but it doesn't work that way all the time. You never said anything about marriage."

"I said we were going to stay together," he protested. "What did you think I meant?"

"I don't know what I thought. Mostly, I've tried to avoid thinking about the future."

He smiled. "Well, you'd better start thinking about it. As I see it, our only real problem is convincing the High Priestess that you should be allowed to remain a Trezhella after we're married.

"But it seems to me that when she finds out that spacemen can be trained through kra-toza to communicate with each other, she might be desperate enough to agree to *anything*."

"But you couldn't communicate without *me*, so the Sisterhood is still needed."

"*We* know that—but *she* won't."

Serena stared at him and suddenly her wicked grin matched his. "So we let her think that the Sisterhood could really become irrelevant. I think that might work."

"Especially since the top Commander in the entire fleet will naturally want his Trezhella wife to accompany him on all future missions."

"But your whole crew knows the truth," she pointed out.

"It's a secret they'll be happy to keep. I'll tell them that it can be their wedding gift to us."

She sighed happily. "So you intend to tell the whole truth when we get back—even though you lied in the reports?"

He nodded. "Old Valens will chew me up a bit, but he'll understand. After all, between the two of us, we've saved the future of the whole space program."

"But will your family understand—about us, I mean?"

He reached out and drew her into his arms. "They'll accept you. They were quite taken with you. And my sister will welcome you to her heart immediately."

"It all sounds so simple," she said doubtfully.

Darian kissed her. "We could use a bit of simplicity right now."

"You mean you climbed up there all by yourself?" Darian asked, staring up at the steep, rocky slope.

"Yes. It's the highest hill around. I camped up there so I could be closer to the stars." She grinned at him. "And I even managed to get up there without an anti-grav pack."

They strapped on the packs and rose slowly up the rocky face of the mountain. Only for the past few hours had she been sure she'd found the way to the cave. Now she hoped it would yield all that Darian believed it would.

They landed on a wide rock ledge in front of the low entrance to the cave and removed their packs. Darian grabbed his light and crawled through the mouth of the cave, while she waited outside. A moment later, he backed out again with a frustrated look.

"I can see them, but I can't get to them and I didn't bring along a cutter."

"Show me how to operate that thing and then hold the light," she said, indicating the small case he'd used before.

He showed her, then knelt behind her as she crawled into the cave and began to make her way through the broken teldas at the entrance. When she could see beyond them, she was surprised to realize that the cave was much deeper than she'd thought—and the strange, clear teldas reflected the light back at her from a very great distance.

"Darian, there are hundreds of them back there," she called as she stood up and began to weave around the translucent ones in the front. "Maybe more than hundreds. They go back as far as I can see."

She finally reached the first of them and held the wand to it, then pressed the button as he'd told her. After she had made her way back to the entrance, she handed the case to him, then laughed happily when she saw his expression.

"They're off the scale," he said in an astonished tone.

He took out a small cube that would transmit the location of the cave to landing craft, then crouched before the cave as though to reassure himself that the teldas inside were real. And after that, they stood hand-in-hand and stared up at the sky, both of them thinking of worlds as yet undiscovered—and of a love already found.

Epilogue

Seven years, Serena thought. Seven years of floating among the stars, of finding new worlds and new people, of conquering old enemies and forging new alliances. And now they were memories that would have to last a lifetime. The long voyages into the unknown were over.

But it has been enough, she thought—and she knew that Darian felt the same. She knew because they could read each other's thoughts so well now that speech was almost unnecessary between them.

And it was right, too, that this final journey should be back to the place where it had all begun. Beyond the window, the world called Serena floated in eternal darkness, growing larger by the minute.

In six months, she would become the new High Priestess of the Sisterhood: a very different Sisterhood, though there were still many challenges ahead. But at least she knew there would be no problems with the new Supreme Commander—or at least none that she couldn't handle.

A pair of arms slid around her from behind, gently caressing her swollen belly. "I guess he's decided to wait and be born down there," Darian said as he kissed the top of her head.

"I told you he would," she replied. "But he'll still have stars in his blood."

THE MAGIC OF TWO
SARANNE DAWSON

Quinn knows he seems mad, deserting everything familiar to sail across the sea to search for a land that probably only existed in his grandfather's imagination. But a chance encounter with a pale-haired beauty erases any doubts he may have had. Jasmine is like no other woman he has known: She is the one he has been searching for, the one who can help him find their lost home. She, too, has heard the tales of a peaceful valley surrounded by tall snow-capped mountains and the two peoples who lived there until they were scattered across the globe. And when she looks into Quinn's soft eyes and feels his strong arms encircle her, she knows that together they can chase away the demons that plague them to find happiness in the valley, if only they can surrender to the magic of two.

___52308-6 $5.50 US/$6.50 CAN

Dorchester Publishing Co., Inc.
P.O. Box 6640
Wayne, PA 19087-8640

Please add $1.75 for shipping and handling for the first book and $.50 for each book thereafter. NY, NYC, and PA residents, please add appropriate sales tax. No cash, stamps, or C.O.D.s. All orders shipped within 6 weeks via postal service book rate. Canadian orders require $2.00 extra postage and must be paid in U.S. dollars through a U.S. banking facility.

Name_____
Address_____
City_____State_____Zip_____
I have enclosed $_____ in payment for the checked book(s).
Payment <u>must</u> accompany all orders. ☐ Please send a free catalog.
    CHECK OUT OUR WEBSITE! www.dorchesterpub.com

★ *Futuristic Romance* ★

Star-Crossed

Saranne Dawson

Bestselling Author Of *Crystal Enchantment*

Rowena is a master artisan, a weaver of enchanted tapestries that whisper of past glories. Yet not even magic can help her foresee that she will be sent to assassinate an enemy leader. Her duty is clear—until the seductive beauty falls under the spell of the man she must kill.

His reputation says that he is a warmongering barbarian. But Zachary MacTavesh prefers conquering damsels' hearts over pillaging fallen cities. One look at Rowena tells him to gird his loins and prepare for the battle of his life. And if he has his way, his stunningly passionate rival will reign victorious as the mistress of his heart.

_51982-8 $4.99 US/$5.99 CAN

Dorchester Publishing Co., Inc.
P.O. Box 6640
Wayne, PA 19087-8640

Please add $1.75 for shipping and handling for the first book and $.50 for each book thereafter. NY, NYC, and PA residents, please add appropriate sales tax. No cash, stamps, or C.O.D.s. All orders shipped within 6 weeks via postal service book rate. Canadian orders require $2.00 extra postage and must be paid in U.S. dollars through a U.S. banking facility.

Name_____
Address_____
City_____ State_____ Zip_____
I have enclosed $_____ in payment for the checked book(s).
Payment <u>must</u> accompany all orders. ❑ Please send a free catalog.

Destiny's Lovers

FLORA SPEER

She is utterly forbidden, a maiden whose golden purity must remain untouched. Shunned by the villagers because she is different, Janina lives with loneliness until she has the vision—a vision of the man who will come to change everything. His life spared so that he can improve the blood lines of the village, the stranger is expected to mate with any woman who wants him. But Reid desires only one—the virginal beauty who heralds his mysterious appearance among them. Irresistibly drawn to one another, Reid and Janina break every taboo as they lie tangled together by the sacred pool.

___52281-0 $5.50 US/$6.50 CAN

Dorchester Publishing Co., Inc.
P.O. Box 6640
Wayne, PA 19087-8640

Please add $1.75 for shipping and handling for the first book and $.50 for each book thereafter. NY, NYC, and PA residents, please add appropriate sales tax. No cash, stamps, or C.O.D.s. All orders shipped within 6 weeks via postal service book rate. Canadian orders require $2.00 extra postage and must be paid in U.S. dollars through a U.S. banking facility.

Name_____
Address_____
City_____State_____Zip_____
I have enclosed $_____ in payment for the checked book(s).
Payment <u>must</u> accompany all orders. ❏ Please send a free catalog.
     CHECK OUT OUR WEBSITE! www.dorchesterpub.com

To Touch The Stars

Tess Mallory

Eagle is enjoying the quiet serenity of Station One when suddenly it is attacked by a rebel spacecraft. Before he can defend himself, he is pinned by a beautiful droid who demands to know the whereabouts of a child. Skyra will let nothing—and no one—stand in the way of finding her little sister, for Mayla is the only hope of freedom for the rebels. But the more time she spends with Eagle, the more she feels something stronger than compassion for her prisoner, something that makes her burn with delicious turmoil when she envisions his sleek muscular form. And only in his arms does she find an ecstasy like none she's ever known, one that lifts her high enough to touch the stars.

___52253-5 $4.99 US/$5.99 CAN

Dorchester Publishing Co., Inc.
P.O. Box 6640
Wayne, PA 19087-8640

Please add $1.75 for shipping and handling for the first book and $.50 for each book thereafter. NY, NYC, and PA residents, please add appropriate sales tax. No cash, stamps, or C.O.D.s. All orders shipped within 6 weeks via postal service book rate. Canadian orders require $2.00 extra postage and must be paid in U.S. dollars through a U.S. banking facility.

Name_____
Address_____
City_____State_____Zip_____
I have enclosed $_____ in payment for the checked book(s).
Payment <u>must</u> accompany all orders. ❑ Please send a free catalog.

HEART'S *Prey* JAN ZIMLICH

She is a wild woman with flowing coppery tresses and luminous emerald eyes. Yet Rayna Syn is so much more to Dax Vahnti: She is his assassin. The savage beauty's attempt on his life fails, but the Warlord cannot let his guard down for a moment, not even when the lovely creature with wild russet hair enchants his very being. His need to possess the wondrous beauty is overpowering, yet the danger she presents cannot be denied.

___52277-2 $4.99 US/$5.99 CAN

Dorchester Publishing Co., Inc.
P.O. Box 6640
Wayne, PA 19087-8640

Please add $1.75 for shipping and handling for the first book and $.50 for each book thereafter. NY, NYC, and PA residents, please add appropriate sales tax. No cash, stamps, or C.O.D.s. All orders shipped within 6 weeks via postal service book rate. Canadian orders require $2.00 extra postage and must be paid in U.S. dollars through a U.S. banking facility.

Name_____
Address_____
City_____State_____Zip_____
I have enclosed $_____ in payment for the checked book(s).
Payment <u>must</u> accompany all orders. ❏ Please send a free catalog.
            CHECK OUT OUR WEBSITE! www.dorchesterpub.com

Shielder

CATHERINE SPANGLER

Unjustly shunned by her people, Nessa dan Ranul knows she is unlovable—so when an opportunity arises for her to save her world, she leaps at the chance. Setting out for the farthest reaches of the galaxy, she has one goal: to elude capture and deliver her race from destruction. But then she finds herself at the questionable mercy of Chase McKnight, a handsome bounty hunter. Suddenly, Nessa finds that escape is the last thing she wants. In Chase's passionate embrace she finds a nirvana of which she never dared dream—with a man she never dared trust. But as her identity remains a secret and her mission incomplete, each passing day brings her nearer to oblivion.

___52304-3 $5.50 US/$6.50 CAN

Dorchester Publishing Co., Inc.
P.O. Box 6640
Wayne, PA 19087-8640

Please add $1.75 for shipping and handling for the first book and $.50 for each book thereafter. NY, NYC, and PA residents, please add appropriate sales tax. No cash, stamps, or C.O.D.s. All orders shipped within 6 weeks via postal service book rate. Canadian orders require $2.00 extra postage and must be paid in U.S. dollars through a U.S. banking facility.

Name_____
Address_____
City_____State_____Zip_____
I have enclosed $_____ in payment for the checked book(s).
Payment <u>must</u> accompany all orders. ❑ Please send a free catalog.
     CHECK OUT OUR WEBSITE! www.dorchesterpub.com

The Midnight Moon

Stobie Piel

Dane Calydon knows there is more to the mysterious Aiyana than meets the eye, but when he removes her protective wrappings, he is unprepared for what he uncovers: a woman beautiful beyond his wildest imaginings. Though she claimed to be an amphibious creature, he was seduced by her sweet voice, and now, with her standing before him, he is powerless to resist her perfect form. Yet he knows she is more than a mere enchantress, for he has glimpsed her healing, caring side. But as secrets from her past overshadow their happiness, Dane realizes he must lift the veil of darkness surrounding her before she can surrender both body and soul to his tender kisses.

___52268-3 $5.50 US/$6.50 CAN

Dorchester Publishing Co., Inc.
P.O. Box 6640
Wayne, PA 19087-8640

Please add $1.75 for shipping and handling for the first book and $.50 for each book thereafter. NY, NYC, and PA residents, please add appropriate sales tax. No cash, stamps, or C.O.D.s. All orders shipped within 6 weeks via postal service book rate. Canadian orders require $2.00 extra postage and must be paid in U.S. dollars through a U.S. banking facility.

Name_____
Address_____
City_____State_____Zip_____
I have enclosed $_____ in payment for the checked book(s).
Payment <u>must</u> accompany all orders. ❑ Please send a free catalog.
        CHECK OUT OUR WEBSITE! www.dorchesterpub.com

THE WHITE SUN
STOBIE PIEL

Sierra of Nirvahda has never known love. But with her long dark tresses and shining eyes she has inspired plenty of it, only to turn away with a tuneless heart. Yet when she finds herself hiding deep within a cavern on the red planet of Tseir, her heart begins to do strange things. For with her in the cave is Arnoth of Valenwood, the sound of his lyre reaching out to her through the dark and winding passageways. His song speaks to her of yearnings, an ache she will come to know when he holds her body close to his, with the rhythm of their hearts beating for the memory and melody of their souls.

___52292-6 $5.50 US/$6.50 CAN

Dorchester Publishing Co., Inc.
P.O. Box 6640
Wayne, PA 19087-8640

Please add $1.75 for shipping and handling for the first book and $.50 for each book thereafter. NY, NYC, and PA residents, please add appropriate sales tax. No cash, stamps, or C.O.D.s. All orders shipped within 6 weeks via postal service book rate. Canadian orders require $2.00 extra postage and must be paid in U.S. dollars through a U.S. banking facility.

Name_____
Address_____
City_____State_____Zip_____
I have enclosed $_____ in payment for the checked book(s).
Payment <u>must</u> accompany all orders. ❑ Please send a free catalog.
   CHECK OUT OUR WEBSITE! www.dorchesterpub.com

Ariel's Dance
Chloe Hall

On the recreational world of Mariposa, every form of exotic pleasure is available—along with every vice abhorred by Dekkan's people. But the interstellar diplomat has no need to fear such tawdry temptations—until the night his special hormone-inhibiting patch begins to fail and he meets a sexy butterfly dancer named Ariel. Barging into her dressing chamber seeking a stolen family heirloom, he seems so deliciously naive to Ariel that the firebrand decides to have some fun. But giving Dekkan his first taste of desire has unexpected results: Suddenly her own heart is at risk.

___52285-3 $4.99 US/$5.99 CAN

Dorchester Publishing Co., Inc.
P.O. Box 6640
Wayne, PA 19087-8640

Please add $1.75 for shipping and handling for the first book and $.50 for each book thereafter. NY, NYC, and PA residents, please add appropriate sales tax. No cash, stamps, or C.O.D.s. All orders shipped within 6 weeks via postal service book rate. Canadian orders require $2.00 extra postage and must be paid in U.S. dollars through a U.S. banking facility.

Name_____
Address_____
City_____ State_____ Zip_____
I have enclosed $_____ in payment for the checked book(s).
Payment <u>must</u> accompany all orders. ❏ Please send a free catalog.

ATTENTION
BOOK LOVERS!

Can't get enough of your favorite **ROMANCE**?

Call **1-800-481-9191** to:

✳ order books,

✳ receive a **FREE** catalog,

✳ join our book clubs to **SAVE 20%**!

Open Mon.-Fri. 10 AM-9 PM EST

Visit **<u>www.dorchesterpub.com</u>**
for special offers and inside
information on the authors you love.

We accept Visa, MasterCard or Discover®.
LEISURE BOOKS ♥ LOVE SPELL